THE JUDAS DECEPTION

Betrayal has never been so deadly

MIKE SCOTT

Copyright © 2017 Mike Scott.

The right of Mike Scott to be identified as the author of this work has been asserted in accordance with sections 77 and 78 of the Copyright Designs and Patents Act 1988.

In this work of fiction, the characters, places and events are either the product of the author's imagination or they are used entirely fictitiously.

PROLOGUE

Spencer Harris looked up at the cathedral dome, a succulent breast offered to a neglectful deity. Sunlight poked nervously through the mosaic glass, settling on the plaque in front of him.

"Love is patient, love is kind," he read. "Hear that, my sweet, you have to be kind to me. Breakfast in bed, scrub my back, all that."

"Spence, sssssh!"

He leaned closer, notwithstanding his paunch, and continued to read aloud. "It does not envy, it does not boast, love is not proud, blah, blah. Utter bollocks. To think that you used to believe all that self-serving twaddle! I'll tell you what love is, it's waking up next to you, my sweet, giving you a good..."

"Will you be quiet, you fool?"

"Quiet? How can I be quiet when my heart is soaring? When my lips are singing! When my eyes are dancing with love and joy and sinful lust." He waggled his eyebrows.

"Keep your voice down, you big buffoon, people are looking. Everything you say vibrates off the walls."

"Let them hear, my sweet. Let each indulgent word reverberate off the walls of this great citadel until they crumble from the vibrations and their parting echoes ring out with the cry that I lov..." Spencer stopped abruptly, his eyes fever wild.

His companion looked at him. "Spence? What is it? Are you alright?"

"By Christ, my sweet, you are a genius. A fucking genius. Miraculous. Nothing short."

The genius in question blushed profusely, head bowed as he shied away from the glances of those around. Quite what he had done to merit the accolade was beyond him but in the time he had known Spencer Harris he'd learned not to try and fathom the thoughts that spilled from the man.

"To think that I brought you to this great bastion of farce, this vast amphitheatre of absurdity to mock and ridicule the life that you once thought so precious and fulfilling. And, instead, you inspire me. Direct me. Open my eyes. Paul on the road to Damascus, John tripping on Patmos, all that. Oh, you beautiful man, I could kiss you if we weren't likely to get stoned!"

"Stop it, Spence. Please! Come on, let's get you out of here."

"Indeed, my dear, it has served its purpose. Last piece of the puzzle, so to speak."

"Really? You think you've solved it?"

"Me? You were the one that solved it, my sweet, you and that brilliant grey matter that hides under those wonderful fiery locks. I have merely recognised your revelation for what it is."

"But what is it?"

"Let's go and see, shall we?"

CHAPTER 1

It's strange the things you think of when you're dying. Even now as he lay bleeding he could still feel his bow-tie irritating his beard. He hated the damn things, liquorice coloured off-cuts like Beelzebub's used tissues. Maybe if he'd taken a little longer trying to get the perfect knot tonight he wouldn't be lying here now. But it was too late for all that.

The day had started with such promise, a fragrance in the air like God was cooking bacon for a morning after sandwich with Cambridge as his frying pan. For Dr Stephen Simms, there was little to suggest that today was different to any other and certainly nothing to indicate that it would be his last.

Had he known would he have preened his waxed moustache with such fastidiousness in the heated mirror of his male only domain? The laundry basket, a fickle mistress at the best of times, had proven to be a kind benefactor to his exaggerated lob, swallowing whole the pair of silk shorts. Maybe his celebrations would have been more fervent had he suspected that he would never get the chance to try again. Or perhaps his morning run could have been postponed or prolonged depending on his motivation for such a masochistic act. But how could he know that fate had received a telegram from the devil himself instructing that a malevolent surprise be concocted for Simms on this very day?

For now, however, he contented himself with his usual trawl for assassins as he meandered his way across town, paying particular attention to the long shadows that could easily conceal a killer. He pushed his steel rimmed glasses onto the bridge of his nose to give him optimum vision as he surveyed the throng for would-be attackers. This had been his habit for the last three months, ever since signing on to the University's Assassins' Guild, a game played mostly by undergrads but in which Simms couldn't resist indulging his love of role play. It had started as a harmless prank with three names emailed to him from the games organiser shortly after signing up. He had to track down the three and organise their untimely deaths each by a different method. His first kill had proven to be surprisingly straight forward. A simple letter was all it took.

"Dr Simms?"

"That's what it says on the door," he responded without looking up.

"Ammm, well my name is Susan Wallace and I got a letter…"

"Susan, of course, come in. Have a seat."

"I don't really understand why you would want to see me. Have I done something wrong?"

"You have nothing to worry about, Susan. I'm afraid it was just me abusing my position to get the opportunity to meet you."

"But why?"

"So that I can kill you."

"You really said that to her?" This from his good friend Ant Bradley when he had told him all about popping his homicidal cherry.

"Oh yeah. And then I pulled out a cap gun from my desk drawer and fired three rounds straight through her heart. Bam, bam bam. The look on her face was priceless. Honestly, I don't know if she was more relieved or angry. Part of her wanted to thank me for not kicking her off her course while the bigger part of her wanted to rip my head off for conning her."

"You really do have too much time on your hands," Ant responded, shaking his head mockingly.

Kill number two had followed the template of his first success but met with a much more wary adversary who had no connection to the language faculty.

"Is this to discuss some library work?" he asked upon arrival.

"Actually, that isn't why I asked you here but I may just have something for you in the MML library. First, I just need to do this." The plastic knife had broken as he pulled it across the poor boy's throat but they had both agreed that it was a righteous kill although Simms suspected that his victim's enthusiasm to die had more to do with the prospect of paid work.

That just left him with number three, an elusive foe and four year veteran of the game for whom a little more thought would have to be given to entice him into the open.

Such were the simple contemplations of the man as he ambled towards his office. Even at this early hour, the city was alive. Returning rowers, wet with the mist of river water and sweat. Yummy mummies on city bikes with child-friendly appendages transporting their offspring to this year's favoured prep. Students, a bloom of ethnicity, deliberating lecture theatre or latte maker. Even some tuxedo wearing stragglers from the previous evening's ball, their legacy framed forever in the survivors' photo.

Simms followed their progress as he considered his own plans to attend the final ball of the year later that evening at the invite of a very attractive visiting lecturer, a date he would not keep.

The Sedgwick site, which housed the language faculty,

was a strange construct from the seventies. Propped uneasily on a series of columns, the resultant wind tunnel beneath provided ideal test conditions should a formula one vehicle ever venture into the car park. Even a calm morning such as this still captured whatever breeze lingered, giving Simms a little ventilation before entering the stuffy building.

"Good morning, Dr Simms."

"Good morning, Veronica. Any messages?"

"Just a call from Dr Bradley. He asked if you could ring him when you got in."

"I'll lose half my morning talking to that reprobate. Nothing else?"

"That's it. Just another day in paradise. Oh, and I've opened your post and left it on your desk. Except..." As a plump fifteen year old, Veronica Garner had held on for a long time to her mother's mantra that her puppy fat would disappear as she grew. Twenty years on she had doubled in size with a fortitude to match and she managed to inject a sizeable portion of this into that one word.

"Yes?"

"Well, one of them was just a piece of card in an envelope with your name on it that had been dropped through the door. When I opened it the card was covered in something sticky. I think it was strawberry jam. I had to wash my hands afterwards. Anyway, I've put it on your desk but away from everything else."

"Who was it from?"

"It didn't say. All that was written on it was 'Gotcha'."

Simms would later chuckle to himself as he recalled his secretary's face when told that she had been the victim of a poisonous substance sent by a deadly assassin. An innocent slain down in the midst of the brutal battle that befalls us as he reported on the Guild's forum, jam being one of the recognised substances that inflicted death upon contact. But not the deadliest. No, this was reserved for Marmite, considered the most potent of contagions exacting instantaneous death upon contact, even if the recipient was wearing protective clothing (read gloves) so the description on the forum read.

Buoyed by his miraculous escape and armed with a tactic which had passed him by until now, he prepared another letter, this time coating the bottom of the page with a thin layer of Marmite, placing it on a fold which the reader would have to open to see the text. This he hand delivered to the Porters' Lodge at nearby Selwyn College where his last adversary resided. He later got confirmation via the forum that his attempt had been successful and that he was now in the second phase of the game. This meant, as well as being given a fresh set of targets, that his name was now released to more players and his vigilance had to be greater than ever.

Given the carefree manner with which his final Friday was unfolding, it's surprising to think that a man in his position would concern himself with such trivialities. But still there was nothing to alert Simms to the lot which awaited him. Even an argument with a student could not derail his good humour.

"I honestly believe that there's more to it than that, Dr Simms."

"I appreciate your enthusiasm, Alan, but you're missing the whole point of the exercise. I arranged for you to go and study the text so that you could see just what a mess it's in. Thousands of pieces, trying to link them all together. Like some priceless jigsaw puzzle."

"Exactly! And why is it in such a state? Why haven't they put it all together properly? Why is so much of the text missing?"

"These are not new questions, Alan. There are hundreds of articles written by any number of authorities in the field answering those very issues. I honestly thought that your research was going to be so much more enlightening, that you were going to dazzle us with your brilliance. Instead you sit there and tell me about conspiracy theories. I can tell you right here, if you want to be regarded with any respect in this field, you had better come up with something a bit more original than the document has been tampered with."

He always prided himself at having a good relationship with the students he supervised. He was no pushover but was always there for them when they needed a helping hand. Losing his temper like that had been a first for him and he couldn't help but wonder if it was because the student in question had raised the same questions that Simms himself had asked ten years earlier when doing his own PhD. Questions that he never really had found a satisfactory answer to.

After the student left, he had called on some old colleagues and suggested that they take another look at the text they were considered such experts on. As Simms sat wondering if someone really was trying to hide something his thoughts were interrupted.

"I've got the Master for you," chimed Veronica.

"Okay, put him through."

"Ah, Simms, dear fellow, how are you?" then, before he could reply, "Just checking on tonight. Don't want you forgetting. This article of yours is going to bring us a lot of favour, a lot of favour indeed."

Simms pondered for a moment how the Master would react if he suggested that the article in question, due to be published soon in a prominent journal, may all be based on a giant lie if his student had anything to say about it but decided against it for now.

"Thank you, Master, very kind of you to say. Perhaps a word with you and some of the senior fellows after dinner

The Judas Deception

wouldn't be amiss just to discuss potential challenges to the position I've adopted."

"Concerned you may have got it wrong?" the Master laughed.

"Just want to be sure that we've considered everything."

"I'm sure you're worries are for naught, dear chap, for naught. But if it puts your mind at rest, we'll talk later." Then adding, "Oh, and for once in your life, my good fellow, please don't be late. Don't want to keep the money men waiting, cheque books might get lost otherwise."

And it was this admonishment that was now foremost in the mind of both Veronica and the faculty head, Dr Samantha Davison.

"Why is he still here?" Sam Davison emerged from her office, her sharp movements matching her suit.

"I've told him he's going to be late." Veronica's face was stone.

"Would you two stop fussing," replied Simms from his office.

Sam walked to the open door of Simms's office and leaned against the frame peering at her deputy. If he hadn't have been so preoccupied with the book he was studying, Simms would have seen a look of concern in the doleful green eyes as she considered him.

"Stephen, don't you have better things to do with your time rather than get involved in this wild goose chase?"

Simms turned towards her, a rueful look on his face. "The boy may have something, Sam."

"You've been here before, Stephen. How did that work out for you?"

"I know, I know. But I just want to check out something he said. It may be nonsense…no, strike that, it probably is nonsense but I've made a few discreet enquiries and I'm just waiting to hear back." He wondered if he should mention the mysterious and intriguing text he'd received but decided against it until he'd checked out the details.

"Well, in the meantime, can I assure poor Veronica that whatever you have her doing will wait until after the weekend and that you are going to get changed and head off to dinner?"

"Alright, I'm going. Christ, you two could nag for England."

"I'm from Jamaica," Veronica shouted.

Simms fought valiantly for another ten minutes but he was outnumbered and his foe artful in the ways of manipulation. Conceding, he donned the tuxedo that Veronica had picked up for him, using his office as a makeshift changing room. Trying desperately to get his bow tie to hold some sort of shape, he muttered obscenities to a number of deities, none of whom he believed real, before he finally got something semi-respectable. He turned towards the window, soaking in the sights and sounds of the city he loved.

There is no place like Cambridge when the sun shines. Heaven itself with all its eternal spasms of joy could not compete with the delight that Simms felt when this citadel lit up. Lovers sitting hand in hand on the bank of the river, their feet dangling just above the water, oblivious to whatever petty disputes they had dwelled on yesterday. Families enjoying the warmth of the evening as they ate ice cream or queued for a punting tour of The Backs, the children exhausting themselves with their running and mischief. The sound of evensong could just be heard above their screams and the smell of barbeque and lavender and contentment filled the air.

He had lived in Cambridge for over fifteen years and still marvelled at how fresh it felt as he walked through. He checked his watch before heading towards the door, fearful that he was running late thanks to the blasted bow tie.

The Judas Deception

He paused as he exited the building, a tingling on the back of his neck giving rise to a sixth sense urging him to beware. But even now, this late in the day he was no wiser to what awaited him so, heedless to such feelings, he continued walking. Even assassins had better things to do on a beautiful June Friday.

He thought back to his earlier argument, perhaps that's what had him on edge. And then there was the strange text telling him to check out a book in one of the stores in town. He looked at his watch. If he hurried he could probably just catch them before they closed. And it was only two minutes away from College so he wouldn't be that late.

He turned down Market Street towards the square, his attire drawing the odd glance but nothing more as black ties were commonplace in Cambridge. Indeed, as it was May week, there would be lots of people dressed in their finery.

May week was the traditional celebration of the end of exams at Cambridge when the Colleges held their balls and Simms thought it typical of the place that it actually lasted for ten days and was held in June thereby meriting neither word in its title. He began to think of his date later with the luxuriant brunette who promised to make a delightful dance partner whatever the tune. A glance at his watch told him that he should get a move on.

The shop was just closing up when he reached the door, one of the owners doing his best to shepherd people out whilst stopping anyone else coming in.

"Hi Brian."

"Stephen! How lovely. You're not going to try and get me to let you in just as I've managed to clear this place, are you?" It was all Simms could do to stop himself from smirking at Brian's attempt to be strong and masterful, in stark contrast to his voice and mannerisms.

"Two minutes, Brian, that's all I need. I know exactly what I want."

"Go on then, you devil. But hurry up, Jeremy is trying to total up the till and he doesn't like to be kept waiting. Two minutes. I'll be counting."

Simms headed straight for the Language section to find the book he had been directed towards. He scanned the shelves, searching for the tome until he spotted it misfiled on the top shelf. Reaching for it, he stretched his tall frame and slid the volume from its hiding place. A fluorescent pink sticky tag protruded from one of the pages, marking it for easy access. Captivated by the cryptic manner in which a clue had been randomly left for him, he began to open the book at the marked point.

He was so absorbed in his thoughts that he never heard the creak of floorboard nor sensed the presence of someone standing behind him. He did, however, feel the sharp burning sensation as a knife plunged deep into his left side and was pulled upwards with some force. So unexpected was it that he had no time to admire the precision with which the knife had penetrated, avoiding the obtrusive ribcage and carving effortlessly through tissue and muscle to pierce his heart with such delicacy that it continued to pump for minutes before realising that it had been decommissioned. His lack of experience in such scenarios was belied by the manner in which Simms played his role, pausing artfully before collapsing, his breath already raspy, hand reaching for the hole in his side.

And there he lay, thinking about bow ties and how anxious he had been to be on time. Just a couple of minutes longer and he'd have been too late for the shop and gone straight to College. He could be eating lobster and drinking champagne now.

He found himself thinking how strange it was that the

stronger the flow of blood leaking from his body the weaker his hold on life became, like they were on drawstrings. Then, perversely, on the mess that he was making on the carpet, wanting to apologise to Brian and Jeremy for any damage and insisting that he pay for it to be cleaned.

His final thought as he drew his last breath was that someone really had taken the rules of Assassin much too literally.

CHAPTER 2

The starched white tablecloth hid the imperfections of the room, a distraction from the banal small-talk and uneasy fidgeting. Professor Daniel Huxley glanced at his watch. Where the hell was Simms?

"There's a man who missed his calling. He's so bloody late for everything that hindsight is normal vision for him," the man next to him murmured.

Huxley smiled. "I could do with some food soon to counter this," he responded, holding up his champagne flute, the crystal from his hometown of Waterford, casting a spectrum of light onto the wall. He felt his phone vibrate in his pocket. Normally he'd let it go to voicemail but now it offered him an escape as he fished it out and made his way into the garden.

"Hello?" More question than greeting as he didn't know the number.

"Danny, thank Christ I got you."

The accent was heavy with Bostonian drawl. It had been a few months since Huxley had last heard it, "Oh, hi Paul, how nice to hear from you although to be honest now's not…."

"Sorry, Danny, but can we skip the pleasantries. I need help and I didn't know who else to call."

"Sounds serious. What's up?"

"It's Alan. He's in trouble. He needs help. Big time."

"What's happened? Is he alright?"

"Well, he's not hurt if that's what you mean but…"

Huxley waited, then "What's happened, Paul?"

"Christ, Danny, I just don't know. He called me. Told me he's with the police being questioned about a murder."

"A murder!" Conscious of being overheard, Huxley moved further into the garden. "A murder?" he repeated, quieter this time.

"Seems he was at the scene of a murder earlier."

"Jesus! So, did he see what happened? Is he there as a witness?"

"Not exactly."

"What's that supposed to mean, Paul?"

"He was seen sneaking out the back door of a book shop where a man had just been murdered. And not just any man, it was his own tutor."

"You mean Simms?"

"That's him."

"Simms is dead?" Huxley actually took a step backwards, reeling from the news. "My god, that's terrible." He felt bile rising in his throat and thought that he was going to be sick. "Are you sure?"

"That's about the only thing I am sure of. I didn't get much out of the kid but he knew it was definitely his tutor. Thinks he's going to be accused of it because they had an argument earlier. He needs help, Danny. He needs someone with him who's going to look out for him until I can get there."

"If it's a police matter, Paul, then I'm not sure what I can do."

"Come on, Danny-boy, keep the false modesty for others, we both know that you're the best person to go to." There was anger that the Bostonian accent did nothing to soften.

Huxley sighed. "Where is he now?"

"He's at the bookshop on Crescent. Prestige, the one with all the alcoves."

"Okay, I'm just in College so I can be there shortly. Where are you?

"I'm in the States but I'm going to get a flight this evening."

"But this is a UK number you're on?" queried Huxley, confused.

"Christ, Danny, the call's being re-routed through the London office. What is this, a fucking interrogation? I just need you to help me out, alright?"

Huxley was taken aback by the ferocity in his friend's voice and thought that the answer seemed contrived but knew that this wasn't the time to question it. Instead he continued, "Alright, Paul, I'll do what I can." And then, "There's no way Alan could have got himself mixed up in something, is there?"

"Christ, no! Not a chance in hell. The boy's a genius with his whole life in front of him. He'd never do anything to jeopardise that. And I know I'm his dad, so of course I'm going to say that but, believe me, I know my son and if he says he didn't do it then he didn't do it."

"And did he say he didn't do it?"

"He didn't have to."

CHAPTER 3

Huxley returned to what had now become a wake, the news spreading quickly.

"Oh, Daniel, what a terrible business. Terrible." The Master, a brilliant mathematician, was often mocked out of earshot as doing his two times tables such was his habit of repeating himself.

"Terrible indeed," agreed Huxley. "I'm afraid I have to go, Master."

"Of course, dear boy, go, go. Who could have done such a thing? Who?" This latter to the still silent crowd now all feeling foolishly overdressed.

Huxley exited through the Porter's Lodge, a portal to another world as he passed from the tranquil to the absurd, the busy street full of Friday evening revellers. He walked the short distance to Rose Crescent but found his way blocked by a blue and white police cordon and a shoe-in for the constabulary first fifteen. Huxley produced his ID. Confused the young constable radioed ahead. Even from where he stood, Huxley could hear the invective crackling through the receiver but he was waved in regardless. He entered the shop and immediately spotted a longer-haired version of Alan Donovan than he remembered but undoubtedly the same boy, though looking drained and distraught.

A couple of constables sat nearby with bored expressions, their attention directed towards the large canvas draped from the ceiling further along. Behind which, thought Huxley, was Simms's body.

He was wondering if he should go through when the canvas was pulled to one side and a tall, thin man in a crumpled suit came through before letting the drape fall back into place. But not before Huxley glimpsed a pool of red on the carpet.

"Vice-Chancellor," said the thin man, "To what do we owe the honour?"

Huxley now knew who the constable had been conversing with on his radio. "I'm here to offer any assistance that I can, Inspector Blackburn."

"Well, I appreciate your very kind offer, Professor, but I think we have everything under control."

"I don't doubt it for a second, Inspector, so I'm sure you won't mind my taking a look around. And having a chat with my student," nodding towards the boy who sat head in hands.

"Let you look around?" Blackburn's voice rose in incredulity. "What do you think this is, a travelling circus for all and sundry to come wandering through and watch the clowns?"

"I'm not here to pull rank on you, Inspector, I just want to see things for myself and make sure that my student's best interests are being looked after."

"Pull rank? What the fuck is that supposed to mean? He looked at Huxley, waiting a second before continuing. "You're not on about the Cambridge Constables? You have got to be shitting me. That's nothing more than a tin pot organization here to wipe the backsides of local dignitaries and conduct the odd disciplinary hearing for a student who's farted during formal hall. This is a fucking murder, Huxley, so don't be giving me any bullshit about jurisdiction."

"Regardless of what you believe our functions to be,

The Judas Deception

Inspector, the fact remains that this is squarely in my jurisdiction and you are only here by my decree. Now, I don't want to stop you from conducting your investigation but I expect full cooperation from everyone." He stared intently at Blackburn, waiting until the Inspector broke eye contact. "You can start by filling me in on the facts so far."

"Fine." Meaning that it was anything but. However, Blackburn knew it was pointless getting into a pissing competition with a man like Daniel Huxley.

"I have to warn you, it's pretty gruesome, a lot of blood Professor so careful not to get any on that nice tuxedo. You'd better put these on." Blackburn handed him a pair of white shoe coverings.

"I'll be just fine, Inspector," Huxley answered, putting the coveralls over his shoes.

As they walked through the partition, Huxley was hit by the smell. He glanced down at the body which was being fussed over by SOCOs dressed in full white coveralls. The little he could see turned his stomach and the pool of blood surrounding the body caused the bile to rise to his throat once again. Swallowing hard, he followed Blackburn further into the body of the shop, grateful to get away from the corpse.

Blackburn stopped in one of the many alcoves that gave the shop such character. "At the moment, we don't have a lot to go on. We got a call from one of the owners. Apparently he and his partner, and I mean that in every sense of the word," raising his eyebrows in Huxley's direction to emphasise his meaning, "if you get my drift."

"In glorious nineteen seventies Technicolor."

"Yes, well they were cashing up for the evening when Simms arrived. They were just about to close up but Simms was a regular and said that he knew exactly what he wanted so they let him in. He went around the corner and they continued with their counting waiting for him."

"And?" queried Huxley.

"The pair own the rooms above the shop and Jeremy, he's the older of the two – trust me, it's obvious, a real May and November if ever I saw one," rolling his eyes as he said it. Huxley rolled his eyes too but for another reason entirely. "He needed a piss….sorry, I mean, and I quote, 'to use the gentlemen's room' so went upstairs leaving…" here he consulted a notepad, "Brian to go and hurry the good Dr Simms along. He came down here and found…" Blackburn indicated the body with a sweeping flourish.

"So what did he do?" replied Huxley, keeping his eyes fixed on the Inspector.

"You mean apart from the wailing and gnashing of teeth? Well, he ran straight to the phone on the counter and called us, shouting upstairs to Jeremy to come down because 'something terrible has happened'." His voice went up into a high pitched whine as he mimicked the shopkeeper's words.

"So where does Alan fit into all this?"

"Oh, I'm coming to that, don't you worry, Vice-Chancellor."

Huxley ignored the use of his title knowing that it was just Blackburn's way of trying to wrestle back some authority.

"While Brian was on the phone to the emergency operator, Jeremy went to check the body. When he turned the corner he saw someone disappearing behind the last bookshelf down there," pointing to the far end of the shop, "and so he called out. When they didn't stop he went chasing after them."

"That was a bit foolhardy."

"He's a piece of work, believe me. 'I'm not letting any scrawny wee fucker get the better of me!'" This time he dropped his voice into a deep baritone and affected a Geordie accent as he imitated the older of the two owners. "Anyway, he reaches the back and finds the emergency door wide open. Your student was trying to scramble over the wall outside. He grabs the boy's foot and pulls him down before putting him in an arm lock and frog marching him back to the counter. He then, you'll like this, shoves him onto one of the chairs behind the counter and winds the telephone cable around him to hold him in place until we got here."

"Nice."

"Isn't it? As I said, a real piece of work. Ex forces I believe."

"Certainly inventive."

"Yeah, well, then they held him there until the first unit arrived and secured the area."

"So where are they now?"

"Upstairs. I have a couple of men taking their statements."

"And they never left the counter the whole time Simms was in the shop?"

"Do you honestly think I don't know how to do my fucking job, Vice-Chancellor?"

Huxley noticed the aggression in Blackburn's tone and decided to say nothing, allowing the inspector to carry on in his own time. "It appears that they may have stepped into the back alcove behind the counter for a little 'comforting'," he actually made the inverted comma sign with his hands much to Huxley's private amusement, "as Brian had given himself a paper cut on the ledger." Again, he rolled his eyes.

"So the shop was unattended for a bit?"

"No more than a minute so they say. And there's a bell on the door that they would have heard if anyone had come in or gone out during that time."

"So the thinking is that whoever did this came in through the back door?"

"Emergency exit only, doesn't open from the outside. Chances are the killer had to already be in the shop."

"But how did they know that Simms was going to be here?"

"I don't know yet. Perhaps they arranged to meet him here. Or perhaps it was a spare of the moment act and it didn't matter who the victim was. All I know is that I've got one dead body, one silent suspect and two faggots who were too busy pleasuring each other that they didn't notice a murder being committed less than twenty feet in front of them! No wonder he needed to use the 'gentlemen's room'!" Again with the quote marks.

"Sorry, did you just say 'suspect'?"

"Of course he's a fucking suspect. He was found fleeing the scene of a murder, what would you call him?"

"Me? I would say he's a possible witness. And I would also think it was in your best interests to treat him as such rather than going all heavy handed and getting him to clam up."

"You sound just like Pepper."

"George is here?"

"Upstairs with the two fagg…owners."

"Maybe I should have a word with him." Huxley and Pepper were long standing friends and Huxley knew he could get a better feel for things from him than he ever would with Blackburn.

"Yeah, well I've been thinking, if you're going to stick your nose in where it doesn't belong, maybe you and old Lonely Hearts could liaise with each other thereby keeping you out of my fucking way."

"I think that might be best for us all, Inspector. Now, perhaps I could have a word with my student?"

"Be my guest. He's not saying anything to us."

CHAPTER 4

From his vantage point behind the counter, Alan Donovan listened to the exchange between the two men before they disappeared behind the awning. Forced to endure the torture of having to look at the dead body while waiting on the police, he was glad when they put it in place. Now he watched as it was drawn back and Professor Huxley reappeared, striding purposefully towards him. He hoped that his dad knew what he was doing. The policeman followed and Alan put his head down on the counter and sighed.

As Huxley approached, the two constables standing guard moved away at a nod from Blackburn.

"Hello Alan." Huxley sat next to him.

"Hi Professor Huxley, how are you?" He looked up as he said it, his eyes peering through thick rimmed black glasses, and Huxley couldn't help but think there was a casual air to the greeting that belied the situation. It was like they had just bumped into each other whilst out for a bit of a browse in a book store.

Huxley examined the lad, the customary student uniform of jeans and t-shirt looking remarkably well pressed. Neat freak he thought. The designer trainers and Maurice Lacroix timepiece completed the ensemble and, but for the dead body lying twenty feet away, he could have been just another Cambridge grad out on a Friday night haul.

"Your dad called. He's very worried. Are you alright?"

"I've been better to be honest, sir. I'm sorry you had to get involved. I'm sure you've better things to do. I'm just so scared." The accent wasn't as strong as his fathers but he still did that strange inflexion that Bostonians do with their 'r's so it came out 'skeeed'.

"That's why I'm here. Do you want to tell me what happened?"

"I'm not sure. I don't want to say anything that will incriminate me. I heard what you said to the policeman earlier. You know, about taking charge of the investigation. Something about the university police. So that would make you a policeman too and dad says you should never talk to the cops. Not without a lawyer."

"It's not quite like that, Alan. It's all to do with the Cambridge Constables. Have you heard of them?"

The young man shook his head, his hair falling over the front of his face as he did so.

"Well, essentially they are the university's police force. They were formed under the Universities Act of 1825 when the University was given the authority to form a police force to look after its students. As Vice-Chancellor, I'm Head Marshall so I'm in charge of the force and can appoint selective people to serve as constables. We're here to make sure that the rules are adhered to, discipline unruly students, make sure that the university's reputation is upheld, that sort of thing. But under the Act every constable was given full police powers within a four and a half mile radius of Great St Mary's Church. And that still applies today as much as in 1825. So I have the authority to take charge of any police investigation within that jurisdiction if I want. But I think it would be a bit foolish of me to try and

The Judas Deception

take over a murder investigation, don't you? Probably best to just let the police get on with their job while I do mine. And, right now, that's to make sure that you're protected."

"Wow, that's kinda weird, right? I mean, why four and a half miles? Pretty specific, huh?"

"I guess at the time that encompassed the whole of the university site. Not any more, mind, but the legislation is still in place." Huxley paused before getting the conversation back on track. "So, do you want to tell me what happened?"

"Sure. That is, I'll tell you as the Vice-Chancellor of the University and my dad's friend, not you as a policeman and Head Honcho or whatever."

"Head Marshall. And no, I'm here as your protector and your guardian until your dad is able to get here. Think of me as your legal counsel for now, okay?"

"Okay. Not that I know much. I mean, I was just browsing around in here when I saw Dr Simms come in. I really didn't want him to see me as we'd had a bit of an argument earlier and…"

"Tell me about the argument," interrupted Huxley.

"Well, not an argument as such, that makes it sound like more than it was. Honestly, it was nothing, just a silly disagreement. Nothing heavy. I mean we're not talking anything that would…"

"Make you want to kill him," Huxley finished.

"Oh god, no. It wasn't anything like that. I mean a petty disagreement about my work, that's all. Just something really stupid."

Huxley looked at the boy, his face flushed, hands fidgeting with a pen on the desk.

"That's fine, Alan. I believe you. . So you had a bit of a fall out, these things happen. Then what?"

"Yeah, well, it was enough for me to just want to be by

myself for a while. Lose myself in something, not have to interact with anyone. So I came here to sit and brood."

"All afternoon?" questioned Huxley.

"As it turns it, yeah. I didn't really mean to stay that long but I just got lost in what I was reading, tucked away in one of the alcoves, no-one bothering me. It was lovely. And then I saw him."

"Simms?"

"Yeah, Dr Simms, standing right there, his back to me. I'd decided to pack up but when I stood up he was right there. I just couldn't handle the thought of him him sneering at me again so I ducked back into the alcove. When I heard the bell on the door ring, I thought he must have gone but I when I looked he was still there, browsing through a book."

"Hold on. You heard the bell go?" Huxley asked.

"Yeah. I mean he hadn't been there for long, maybe just a minute or two, but I thought it must be him leaving as the place was pretty empty. I know they were chucking people out."

"Did you see anyone else?"

"No. Just Dr Simms still standing there. So I hid again."

"And then what happened?"

"Well, I heard a noise like something falling. Maybe a book or something. I peeked round to check and saw Dr Simms lying on the floor. He looked kinda strange, just lying there twitching. I thought he was having a fit or something so I started to walk towards him. Then I saw the blood. I just froze. I didn't know what to do. When I heard footsteps coming towards me I panicked. What if it was the killer? What if he'd seen me? I jumped behind a pile of books, trying to hide."

"And who was it?" Huxley queried, anxious to draw the facts out from the boy before he became too traumatised.

"It was just the owner. The younger one. I saw him looking at the body. Then he screamed and ran."

Huxley could see the boy's distress but waited for him to continue.

"I was scared rigid. I didn't know what to do. So I ran too. I made for the front door but then I heard someone coming so I turned and ran the other way. I was so frightened and I just wanted to get the hell out of there. The emergency door was in front of me so I pushed it open and tried to jump the wall outside but it was too high. I managed to scramble to the top but then I felt someone grab hold of me and pull me back. I thought it was the killer and he was going to kill me as well."

"Did you see someone? Another man? Is that why you keep saying 'he'?"

"No. Honestly I didn't. I just sorta presumed."

"Okay. But it was actually one of the owners who grabbed you."

"Yeah. Then he put me in an arm-lock and marched me through the store. He was shouting at me the whole time. And then we had to go past the body. I just felt sick. I kept telling him it wasn't me."

"And then the police arrived."

"Eventually. It was, like, ages. I was tied to this chair and couldn't move. I could see Dr Simms lying there. Even when I closed my eyes the image was still there. Then the police came and untied me but started asking all these questions like they thought I might have something to do with it."

"What did you tell them?"

"Nothing. I didn't say a word except to tell them I wanted to call my dad. He's always saying about how dumb people are talking to the police, that their words can get twisted. So I said I wanted to call him then just clammed up. Eventually they let me use my phone. He told me to say nothing and sit tight, that he was on his way and he'd send help." The boy gave a rueful smile.

Huxley sat back in his chair and looked at the boy. He was trying to get a measure of how much he was holding back. He knew there was more but couldn't be sure how much more. There were footsteps on the stairs behind him and he turned to see Sergeant George Pepper descending towards him. Pepper extended his hand in greeting.

"Dan, what the fuck are you doing here?" His frame bore testament to a fondness of Sunday roasts but he was more stocky than fat, carrying it well. He had a scar above his right eye, courtesy of a drunk in his native Glasgow who had glassed him when he tried to break up a bar fight. In stark contrast to his ruddy complexion, the white scar tissue appeared to shine like it had been polished, a badge of honour worn with pride, the receding hairline offering him no protective cover.

"Nice to see you too, George," responded Huxley, taking the proffered hand.

"You here to look after the laddie?" indicating Alan. "Aye, that makes sense," he continued as Huxley nodded his confirmation. "Listen, I'm afraid I need to get him up to the station, take a statement and that, you know, Dan?"

"I appreciate that, George, but can't it wait? The boy's just been through it a bit tonight. Anything he has will keep until tomorrow."

"No can do, I'm afraid. Blackballs will do his nut if I don't get him into HQ now. It's all I can do to stop him from charging the laddie."

"Well can I at least come with him?"

"Aye, I don't see why not. Although you're not exactly dressed for it, Dan," pointing towards the tuxedo.

"At least I can still get into mine," playfully patting his friend's stomach.

The Judas Deception

"Aye, fuck you too. Right, come on if you're coming."

Once outside they made for a patrol car, a uniformed constable behind the wheel. Pepper ushered the pair into the back seat.

"I'll see you over at the station, Dan. I've got my own car parked further down." With that he closed the door, trapping the two inside, the locks automatically engaging.

They drove onto King's Parade before joining the busy traffic on Trumpington Street. Donovan had remained silent throughout the whole exchange with Pepper and was now looking anxiously around him.

"Don't be panicking," soothed Huxley. "It's just all part of the procedure. Tell them what you told me, they'll draft a statement and then we can be on our way."

Huxley doubted this would be the case but he wanted to try and calm the boy who was becoming quite agitated the closer to the station they got, the car now passing by Parkers Piece in the heart of the city.

Suddenly a cyclist shot out from the parkland right in front of them, causing the constable to slam on his brakes.

"Bloody idiot!" he shouted. "Honestly, some of the morons who ride bikes in this city deserve to be run over."

He was about to move off again when a car came tearing out of a side street opposite heading straight towards their car.

"What the hell is this prick up to?" The constable watched, expecting the car to right itself and turn away from them but it kept coming, moving faster all the time.

Huxley looked in astonishment as the driver, face masked with a balaclava, made directly towards them. He knew the car wasn't going to turn.

"Get down," he commanded Donovan, grabbing the boy and forcing him to duck into the foot-well.

The crash was deafening, metal upon metal, shards of glass

spewing across the back seat, covering the pair hunched there. The impact came on the driver's door, sending the patrol car into a spin and they braced themselves as they headed for the trees on Parkers Piece, momentum bumping them over the kerb and onto the green. There was a terrifying explosion as an out-hanging branch from a mature oak shattered the rear window and pierced the seat beside Huxley, the tip catching the hem of his jacket. As the car finally came to a thumping halt against the trunk of the tree, Huxley checked to see if everyone was alright. The driver was dazed but otherwise seemed unharmed, the reinforced doors doing a good job of protecting him. Alan Donovan sat upright, fear written across his face.

"We've got to get out," he screamed. "We've got to. The car's going to explode. I've seen it in the movies."

"Calm down, Alan. I don't think there's any imminent danger of that," replied Huxley although he wasn't convinced.

Donovan began kicking at his door but there was no way it was opening so he looked around to the shattered rear window.

"This way, Professor," he called as he began to climb through.

Huxley watched as his charge disappeared over the boot of the car, wondering what the hell was happening. Could this all be linked with Simms's death? Confused he followed Donovan out of the car just as the constable forced his door open and climbed out, a gash on his right leg causing him to wince with pain as he tried to support his weight. Huxley could see other motorists getting out of their vehicles to look at the carnage, some wondering if they should help while others just wanted a better view. He saw Pepper running from his car towards the crash site and was about to head towards his friend when Donovan grabbed him.

"We've got to get out of here, Professor. Something's

happening and I don't like it one bit. I can't go into that police station. I don't think I'll come out alive."

Huxley looked at the young man, alerted by the urgency of his tone as much as by what he said.

"What are you not telling me, Alan?"

"I'll tell you everything I know but not here. We have to leave. Now!"

CHAPTER 5

ROME – 1970

Father James O'Connell knew that he had reached a crossroads in his life. The Church was big on crossroads, preaching that everyone had key moments when crucial decisions had to be made. Thousands of priests like him assisted with these decisions every day, guiding people towards the best choice. But as he sat alone in his room, O'Connell knew that this was a decision he had to make on his own.

At thirty he was still as fresh faced and youthful looking as he had been when he had decided to join the priesthood and his shock of unkempt red hair was as fiery as it had ever been. But the innocence that had shone from his eyes all those years ago was gone.

As a lad, he had been born and raised in Kilmorac, a small village in the west of Ireland, untouched by post war profligacy. It was the sort of place where the beauty of the countryside compensated for the lack of anything else to do and where young boys had to make their own fun. Micky Byrne was the self-appointed chief who had led O'Connell and his contemporaries on a wave of petty mischievousness before graduating to matters of more consequence. When, on a rare sunny day in the region, he came across Micky cutting the ears off a rabbit, O'Connell knew even then that there was a different moral compass within him. It was the only time in his life that he had ever raised his hands in anger and he had gotten a bloody nose and thick lip for his trouble, not to mention a knife held against his throat for a few seconds before Micky Byrne had been wrestled from him by a passing priest who had heard the cries.

It was obvious to everyone who knew him he was a gifted child, if not to O'Connell himself. But, when encouraged to embrace the teachings of the church and involve himself in the rituals of being an altar boy, even he recognised his talents. He was happy to have something into which he could channel his energy and which challenged his abilities and it came as no surprise to anyone in Kilmorac when he was accepted into St Patrick's College in Naymooth, Ireland's main seminary.

It wasn't unusual for boys from his village to go into the priesthood and he certainly hadn't been the first. Indeed, the incumbent priest for his village had been a local lad who was a few years older than O'Connell and had encouraged him to apply with the belief that he would make a fine role model in any community.

But rather than take up a role in a parish, his talents were much more specialised and when he began a research post at the College after his training, focusing on holy literature and ancient texts, this was a break from normal tradition.

It was an arena in which the young priest excelled and his expertise did not go unnoticed. He was recommended by the Head Priest of the College for a place on the Council of the National Senate at the tender age of twenty three and then, three years later, in 1965, he had received an invitation from the Primate of All Ireland. Entering the sombre and hallowed sanctuary of a man who he revered, O'Connell was filled with trepidation not knowing why he had been summoned to the office of the highest holy authority in the land.

"An archivist, sir?"

"Your good work hasn't gone unnoticed, James. It's a very privileged position."

"I feel very honoured, sir, thank you. I'm just a little taken aback. I don't really know what I was expecting but it certainly wasn't this. I don't know what to say."

"Say yes. It's as simple as that, James."

"Of course. Yes. An archivist. Oh my. Will I still be based at St Pat's, sir?"

"James, this is a central appointment."

"Yes sir."

"You do understand what a central appointment is, don't you?"

"Yes sir." He paused. "Actually, no sir."

"James, you're going to work in the Vatican."

"The Va…the, ah, the Vati…sorry, what?"

It took several days for him to realise the significance of the position and that he was going to live in the heart of the Catholic Church. His mother was so proud when he returned home to prepare for his move and the news was soon all around the village that one of their own was off to live in the Vatican. The local newspaper ran an article and for days prior to his leaving, Father James O'Connell was a bit of a celebrity in the village and surrounding area.

He remembered how exhilarating it had been but this was nothing to the excitement that he felt when he arrived in Rome. Even the drive from the airport had been awe inspiring as he passed buildings and monuments that he had only ever seen in pictures.

He craned his head as they passed the Coliseum, his mind unable to grasp that this was the real thing. Wanting to stop he had asked if that would be possible but the Monsignor accompanying him had witnessed this reaction too many times before to allow their journey to be delayed. O'Connell looked crestfallen only to perk up immediately as they crossed the Tiber and he could see St Peter's Basilica in front of him. But rather than drive towards it the car veered to the right and the huge golden dome of the palace disappeared from sight.

His head still spinning from the enormity of it all, O'Connell watched as they drove through a guarded gate into a rather dull looking courtyard surrounded by drab red brick buildings. Somewhat disappointed that they had seemingly reached their destination, he emerged from the car and was ushered through a nearby door. It was only once inside that he found himself immersed in splendour beyond his wildest imaginations. Splendour that he often took for granted these days but that he wondered now could he live without it. Because that was the choice he was faced with.

CHAPTER 6

Huxley was caught in two minds. He looked towards Pepper then at Donovan. The boy was already moving quickly away and he knew he risked Donovan running off by himself if he didn't follow. He could see that the boy was scared but there was more to it than that, almost as though this had been rehearsed. But then again, how could it have been? There was only one way he was going to find out the truth so he followed after Donovan, the two hurrying across the parkland and onto the busy streets beyond.

They continued through the Friday night crowds, Huxley deciding that it was best to lose themselves amongst the throng. Throughout the walk the pair conspired to remain silent. Reaching the Maypole pub, they went inside and ordered drinks. Under the wall of noise Huxley felt compelled to speak.

"Do you want to tell me exactly what the hell is going on?"

"I'm really not sure." Donovan looked down at the table.

"Come on, Alan, what is it that you're not telling me?"

"It's stupid, really. Just a feeling that I'm being watched."

"What's that supposed to mean? Watched by who?"

"I honestly don't know. It's ever since I returned from my research trip. That's what Dr Simms and I were arguing about earlier. I tried to tell him but he started shouting about wasted

The Judas Deception

opportunities and I never really got the chance to say how worried I was about it all."

Huxley eyed him, looking for any sign that he was being played, but the boy's fear seemed genuine.

"I think you'd better tell me everything from the start," he said.

"Okay. Well, it's to do with what I'm studying."

"Which is?" asked Huxley.

"The language used in Coptic texts, especially in the Gnostic gospels, and how it relates to the Egyptian texts of the time."

"The Gnostics?"

"Yeah. More specifically one Gnostic in particular."

"Go on," prompted Huxley although he had a good idea where this was going.

"The Judas Gospel."

"I had a feeling you were going to say that."

"I know it's your field of expertise, Professor, that's why you're probably the one person that can make sense of what's going on."

Not for the first time that evening, Huxley felt a certain unease.

"Well, I'm not so sure about that. My expertise lies in a very specific aspect of the Gnostics. Languages have never been my thing."

This wasn't exactly a lie. Languages didn't come as easily to Huxley as most other things which meant he viewed them as an area in which he lacked expertise. But he spoke several fluently, was proficient in many more and could stumble his way around most written texts to a capacity that would embarrass the most brilliant scholars the world over.

His fascination, however, had always been the historical provenance of such texts so his linguistic abilities had proved to be of only secondary importance in the field he was considered the primary expert within. Principally with the Gnostic gospels and, in particular, the Gospel of Judas Iscariot. He felt his best tact was to act dumb and let Donovan play the role of specialist.

"My interest in such texts was always elsewhere," he added.

"Yes, I know. I've been trying to factor in some of your research to weave into my findings." There was an element of hero-worship in Donovan's tone.

"Perhaps we can worry about that at another time. Why don't you tell me about your work up to now?"

"Ok, so I met with Dr Simms today to discuss the findings from my latest research trip. I went to The National Geographical Society in Washington to study the original document. I mean, Dr Simms really put a lot of effort into getting me the permission needed to not only see the text but actually be allowed to examine it. It was fantastic."

There was excitement in Donovan's whole demeanour as he described his trip and the chance to see one of the most fascinating ancient texts up close. Huxley found his enthusiasm infectious and almost forgot their predicament.

"So you met with Simms to discuss this trip then?"

"Yes, I got back a few days ago and we'd arranged the review for today. So it was the first opportunity I'd had to tell him about my findings."

Donovan looked up, waiting for the prompt, his eyes darting excitedly.

"Which were?" asked Huxley, playing his role as interviewer.

"Well, you've seen the text, right?" Huxley nodded. "So, it's in such a poor state and kinda all over the place. Like a priceless jigsaw puzzle as Dr Simms likes to describe it." He stopped suddenly, his face clouded. "I guess that should be liked."

Huxley could see that the boy was still looking very pale. He decided that another drink might help.

Huxley went to the bar of the iconic old pub and managed to make it through the Friday night crowd just before Downing College's first fifteen came tumbling into the place on what was obviously a celebratory end of season night out.

As he waited for the drinks he looked around the place. It was still the same now as it had been some twenty years ago when Huxley and Alan's father had come here with the college football team for much the same reason.

He looked up at the walls which were adorned with shirts and scarves and other such paraphernalia from the University's various sporting teams. It was one of those institutions in Cambridge that passed from generation to generation and if there was a pub crawl arranged in the city you could be sure the Maypole would be on it.

Huxley thought about those days when Paul and he would sit with a drink in hand and wonder what life had in store for them. He was certain that neither of them could have come up with anything like this.

Returning to the table he put a drink in front of Alan and indicated for him to continue.

"I guess I was really lucky to be so up close and personal with this amazing document. It was a joy to be able to study it every day. But then I began to wonder just why certain bits of text were linked with others. I mean, who decided that they fit together?"

"You know that these aren't new questions, Alan?"

"That's exactly what Dr Simms said. He basically just laughed it off asking me if I thought I was the first person to come up with this theory and hadn't it been studied to death already. I felt really foolish."

"But you weren't convinced he was right?"

"No. I mean, he didn't even ask me for any evidence, just said that I had gone off on completely the wrong track and that it was a pity that I had wasted my time with such an historic and important document. It was like he was saying 'I spent all that time arranging your visit and look what you did with it'."

"So, why are you so convinced that you spotted something no-one else has?"

"To be honest, I'm not sure that I have but I thought I found an inconsistency with the translation. I thought it could be the centrepiece of my PhD."

"But Simms didn't agree."

"And then some!"

"And you think all this might be linked with his murder?"

"I really don't know, Professor. It's just so weird. I mean, it's not as though I started shouting 'Eureka' at the top of my lungs when I spotted the inconsistency but I had the feeling that I was being watched a lot more carefully after making the discovery."

"So you didn't share it with anybody?"

"No way. This was mine. I thought it would be a great way to get my work noticed."

"But maybe you found it hard to hide your excitement, drew a bit of attention to yourself without realising. Enough to have someone check on what you were doing."

"I guess it's possible. But I don't really understand what it would have to do with all this." He motioned with his hands as if the interior of the pub was to blame for everything that had happened that evening.

"You said that you got the feeling someone was following you," said Huxley.

"Yeah. Or maybe not following, just watching. I don't know. It's just a feeling. Kinda stupid, eh?"

"I don't think we can afford to overlook anything at this stage, Alan. What else did you tell Simms at your meeting?"

"That was pretty much it. He said that I should go away and think about the direction that I wanted to go with my PhD. Suggested a meeting in two weeks' time and that I should come with a proposal for my written work."

"And that was it? You left?"

"Yes, I couldn't get out of there fast enough. I had spent all last week thinking about what it was I had to tell him and considering how I could incorporate it into my studies and within ten minutes of sitting with him he had dismissed the whole thing. I just wanted to go somewhere and be alone to think."

"So that's when you headed to Prestige?"

"Pretty much. I stopped for a coffee and something to eat on the way and wandered around town for a bit but I've always found Prestige a great place just to lose yourself with your thoughts so that's where I ended up."

"And you were there all that time until Dr Simms came in?"

"Yeah. I must have been there a couple of hours maybe. It was fairly quiet. Maybe a few students like me sitting in the alcoves and thumbing through books, some people browsing but I was pretty much just left to myself which is exactly what I wanted. It was only when they started to clear people out that I looked at my watch and I realised the time. So I got up to leave."

"And that's when you saw Simms."

"I couldn't believe he was right in front of me. Either I walked right by him or hid until he left. I chose to hide."

"And now you're worried that if they did that to him then perhaps you're next."

"I'm really frightened. It's not as though I know anything

but someone might think otherwise. I mean, you've got to admit, that was no accident with the police car. I think someone wanted to stop me talking to the police."

"You know you're going to have to though, don't you?"

"I know." Donovan looked up, tears in his eyes. "So what do we do now?" he asked.

"I think the best thing to do is for me to call George Pepper. He's a good man. He'll understand why we left the crash site. I'll tell him that I will take responsibility for your well-being for tonight and that, tomorrow morning, we'll be happy to meet with him and Inspector Blackburn to give a full statement. In the meantime, I mean it, you will stay with me so I know that you are both safe and well and to make sure that Blackburn doesn't try and call on you in the middle of the night when you're tired and confused."

"I ought to phone dad and tell him that I'm with you."

"That's a good idea. It might also be worthwhile if we call into College and advise the Master of the situation. I know he'll be worried. Although probably more about the reputation of the college than anything else," he added sotto voce.

"Was he married, Professor?"

"Who, Simms? No. I get the impression he fancied himself as a bit of a playboy. I had to warn him off the female staff on more than one occasion."

"You don't think he could have been killed because of..." Donovan left the sentence unfinished.

"It's always possible. But then most of those who would have had reason to want to were gathered in the Master's Lodge for a dinner in his honour. Indeed, apart from the few fellows currently researching elsewhere, Simms was the only member of staff who wasn't present."

"I keep thinking about why there. I mean, if someone wanted to kill him why do it in a book shop while it's still light and there are people around? Why not wait until night time and get him after the dinner when he's walking home?"

"Yes, I've been thinking about that too. It does seem strange that it happened in that exact place and time, almost as though it couldn't wait. One thing is for sure though, Alan, there's a lot more to this than first meets the eye. Hopefully a good night's rest will help put things in a new light."

The pair finished their drinks and made their way out into the still warm evening, the tables outside full of people enjoying their Friday night, unaffected by the events of earlier that evening.

As they made their way back along the street heading towards Trinity College the two were completely oblivious to the figure in the shadows watching them.

CHAPTER 7

Huxley took his phone from the inside pocket of his now slightly dishevelled dinner jacket and, while Alan made the call to his father to update him, Huxley rang Detective Sergeant George Pepper.

"George? It's Daniel."

"Dan, where the fuck are you?"

Huxley smiled at both the immediate shortening of his name, a trait of the English that Pepper had picked up in his years living there, and his friend's blunt manner.

"Nowhere of any consequence, George. I just wanted to let you know that we are fine and see if you had any news?"

"Oh, I've got news for you alright. The news is that Blackballs is going to shove a rocket so far up your arse when he sees you that you'll think it's Chinese new year and Mardi Gras rolled into one! What the fuck were you thinking running off with the only person who might be able to shed some light on this whole fucked up business?"

Huxley paused, allowing his friend a moment to gather himself having vented his agitation. The two had known each other for years. Pepper had been born in Glasgow but moved to Cambridge as a young man, the result of promotion and a transfer to CID. Having joined the police force when he was nineteen and walked the beat for a few years in his native city,

The Judas Deception

he used the experience gained to his advantage and a move south of the border. He was a solid, dependable type, words that were frequently used on his appraisal forms and ones he knew meant that he was never destined for the hierarchy of the service.

There had been much deliberation on his part before taking his sergeant's exam some ten years ago, at the age of thirty five, knowing, if he got it, the ribbing that would result from the combination of his rank and name. But with five kids and a wife who only worked part time, he had no option but to go for the extra money. Having got the promotion he knew even then that he had gone as far as he was likely to, not having the grace and refinement to cut it with the top brass. In other words, he spoke his mind a little too frequently for his superiors and exposed the folly of their thinking all too often.

But what made him an awkward figure within the police was exactly what Huxley found so appealing about him, the two having met some years earlier. Huxley had just been appointed the youngest ever Head Tutor of Trinity College and found himself in a difficult situation as he became aware that one of his students was distributing drugs. So he had been put in touch by a mutual friend with Pepper. The manner in which Pepper dealt with the situation had impressed Huxley and the two had developed a friendship since then.

Over the years it had proved mutually beneficial and, with Huxley's appointment three years previously to Vice-Chancellor of the university and the power that such a position instilled, the pair had worked closely together on a number of matters. This had resulted in Pepper taking on the role of University Liaison Officer meaning that he worked alongside the Chancellor and Vice-Chancellor and the university's own constables. But neither of them had dealt with anything quite as serious as this and the tension in his friend's voice was evident to Huxley.

"It was a spur of the moment reaction, George. I mean, what the hell happened there? Did you get the guy driving the car?"

"Nah, he got away. I was focussing on making sure you were alright and, by the time anyone thought of checking the other car, our friend was long gone. Witnesses came up with the usual shite, masked man, average height and build, went in four different directions all at once. Utter bollocks. Are you both okay?"

"I'm touched by your concern, George."

"Aye, well, you can swivel on my concern, I was really only interested in the laddie."

"We're fine, although the boy is obviously very shaken. He's not going to be much use to anyone tonight."

"Look, Dan, I honestly don't see the kid in the frame for murder. I couldn't get much out of him but from what I saw this was a young lad in shock. I'm not picking up killer from any of that. Of course, he could just be a brilliant actor and old Lonely Hearts here falls hook, line and sinker for the act, but I've been around long enough now to know the difference between genuine shock and general indifference. Inspector Blackburn on the other hand is a prick of the highest order, as both you and I know, and he thinks you've done a runner with a murderer to protect the precious university."

"For what it's worth, George, I can't see him as a killer."

"That's all very well, Dan, but he still probably has valuable information for us, even if he doesn't know it."

"Which is why I want to arrange for him to come and talk to you. But not tonight. Let the lad have some time to get over what happened and try to get some rest. I'll bring him to the station tomorrow morning."

"Blackballs is not going to be happy. In fact he'll do his nut as soon as I tell him. Don't be surprised if the lad gets a knock on his door at two o'clock in the morning."

"That's why he's staying with me tonight. And, before you say it, I won't be staying in my house, I'm going elsewhere. Best if I don't tell you, that way you don't have to lie when asked."

"Fair enough, Dan, but I hope for your sake you know what you're doing. This was a nasty killing in broad daylight in a pretty busy part of town. Someone wanted Simms dead and they wanted it done in a hurry. If they think that Alan Donovan has anything that might result in them being caught they might come looking for him."

"You think Simms was targeted?" Huxley was surprised his friend seemed so certain.

"Can't see it any other way, my friend. Blackburn has us chasing our tails over some random killing which allows him to put your boy right in the middle of things. But this was too precise. Too efficient. Random would be about power, making a statement, wanting everyone to marvel. There are a million and one better places than a bookshop at closing time to do random. No, someone wanted Simms dead."

"That's what I was afraid of. It puts some things into perspective."

"Yeah? How so?"

"For starters, Alan was Stephen's student. That is to say that Simms was his tutor."

"And?"

"It's nothing really, George, I just get the feeling that there is something not being said. I don't know if he's deliberately hiding anything or whether there's anything actually to hide but…" Huxley tailed off, not sure himself what it was he was trying to say.

"Well, like I say, if the killer thinks that he has something that might help us then it could put him in danger."

"Yeah, which is another good reason for him not to stay in his room tonight. What else have you got so far, George?"

"Not much really to go on. This was someone who knew what they were doing, another reason why I don't think your boy's got anything to do with it. The knife went in below the ribcage and was then forced up and twisted before being pulled out. Death wasn't instantaneous but it wouldn't have taken too long. Forensics are still there taking carpet and cloth samples but this looks like a quick job so I'm not expecting much transfer. An autopsy will be done tomorrow but what's to find? We know how he died, when he died and where he died, what we don't know is who did it and why"

"I'm not sure that Alan's going to be much help in that department. From what he's said he didn't see anything."

"Yeah, but maybe when we question him we can get him to focus. Target what he heard or caught out of the corner of his eye or even sensed. Something he doesn't realise the significance of but might be useful to us when we put it together with what we know."

"I know, George, but I'm just saying, don't be expecting him to come in and gift wrap this for you. He's mister deaf, dumb and blind when it comes to the murder. Maybe that's just in the hope that everybody leaves him alone, but I doubt that there's much there."

"Apart from your funny feeling." Pepper smiled as he said it, hoping that the warmth he felt for Daniel Huxley came across in his voice.

"Yeah, apart from that."

"We'll see. Just make sure you have him in nice and early in the morning. It's going to be all I can do to keep Blackballs from tearing the city apart tonight to try and hunt you down."

"If anyone can do it, I'm sure you can, George."

"Yeah, thanks for nothing, mate. Listen, you be careful out there, ok?"

CHAPTER 8

Huxley found Alan leaning against the wall of the Round Church.

"Did you get through?"

"To Dad? Yeah. He's ok. Worried still, I guess. He says he's going to fly in tomorrow to come see me. I told him that it was fine and that he didn't need to but, well, you know dad."

Huxley did indeed know Paul Donovan very well and he wasn't surprised in the least that he was planning on coming. Paul had always been single-minded, even as an eighteen year old undergraduate when the two first met.

They shared a set as it was referred to in Cambridge parlance. This was a set of rooms provided by the College consisting of separate bedrooms and a shared social area, bathroom and kitchen. These were much sought after because of the extra space they afforded. And because of the famous former tenants who had roomed before. It's pot luck who gets them and so it had been when the pair had been allocated their set.

History tells us that firm friendships have been made by such chance and certainly in their case the two had enjoyed their time together. But it would be hard to call them inseparable and, once Paul had returned to the US to pursue his law career, the two had seen little of each other. Donovan senior had a lack of faith in others and, although he considered Daniel

Huxley a brilliant and able man, he would, nevertheless, time and again redo something that his friend had already done just to check that it was right. This had been a constant throughout their relationship and, whilst not bothering Huxley in the least, he had no doubt in his mind that Paul Donovan would want to be here as no-one, not even Daniel Huxley, could do a better job than him.

"What did you tell him?"

"I gave him most of the facts. I didn't mention the car crash, it would only worry him. I just told him that you'd taken charge of things and got me away from the police so he's pretty happy about that. He said to thank you. And I'd like to thank you too. Really. Without you I don't know where I'd be."

"You're still going to have to go and face a police interrogation so don't be thanking me just yet. And there's still the small matter of someone trying to find you because they think you know something. Let's get through tonight and if we're both still in one piece then you can thank me." He winked at Donovan who smiled awkwardly back.

A quick stroll brought them to the main gate of Trinity College, dominated by the statue of King Henry VIII. Huxley looked up at the imposing figure of the College's founder knowing that the image hung there deliberately as a reminder to all who passed through the gates of the standards expected of a Trinity man. Or woman since as late as the nineteen seventies, thought Huxley, only too aware of how difficult some people in the College found moving into modern times. The statue had a sombre, regal air although the original sceptre once held in his right hand had long since been replaced by the leg of a stool, the swap made in the dead of night by a foolhardy undergraduate many years ago and never corrected by the authorities who recognised the benefit of such legends to the publicity of the College.

They passed through the Porter's Lodge, Huxley greeting the bowler hatted residents of the lodge who had just come on for the night shift and who would oversee the comings and goings of college life throughout the night.

"Good evening, Bill."

"Good evening, Professor. Terrible business about poor Dr Simms." It didn't surprise Huxley that the porters were already familiar with Simms's death. Indeed, he thought that they would probably know more than most, at least with regard to the facts. The porters were the lifeblood of any college and knew everything going on within college life. Huxley remembered the many times when he had been bailed out by such custodians whilst a student here and wondered where the eminent and illustrious of our society who had passed through the great gate throughout the years would have ended up but for the assistance and discretion of the Porters.

As a rule, College accommodation is for students. The exception to this for most Colleges is the Master's accommodation which is normally a large house within the main College grounds. Trinity's is situated off the great courtyard towards the Backs, affording a wonderful view of the river. The house was still well-lit suggesting that not all the invitees had abandoned ship.

Huxley knocked on the front door and it was answered by the College Butler. They were ushered into the dining room where there was still a small gathering.

"Good evening, again, Master," Huxley began.

"Ah, Daniel, come, come. Good of you to return, old boy. How are you?"

Huxley glanced around the table. He found it hard to disguise the distaste he felt at those who evidently felt that the death of a colleague was a poor excuse to let a good meal go to waste.

The Judas Deception

Along with the Master, he wasn't that surprised to find Professor Fredrick Hansel, a German born historian who had been at the College for as long as Huxley could remember. He looked remarkably youthful but Huxley reckoned twenty years could be added to the oft guessed mid-fifties. The smattering of salt and pepper around the temples simply served to enhance his handsome face and add to the ambiguity of his age. Unlike the others sitting with him, Hansel had a firm frame that the rich food and ample wine of College life hadn't softened. He obviously looked after himself and Huxley wouldn't be surprised to see him in the gym tomorrow morning working off his dinner, the vestiges of which lay in front of him. Huxley thought he looked vaguely embarrassed as he covered the plate with his napkin.

Which is more than could be said for the man sitting beside him. Dr John Connelly, the College Dean, seemed beyond any discomfiture whatever the situation. Huxley remembered him joining the faculty during his days as an undergrad. Connelly had quickly succumbed to the lifestyle on offer, paying little heed to the biblical admonishment of excess, his bulbous nose a map of intemperance. A doctor of divinity and theological tutor to the students of the university, Connelly was a figure of ridicule. Known as the Vicar of Dribbly amongst the student body, he was mocked for his bumbling mannerisms, his strange accent but, above all, for the thick, black hairpiece which he sported. He had a faraway look in his eye and appeared oblivious to Huxley's presence. It was as though he was expecting dessert rather than news of the death of a colleague.

Sitting opposite the pair, Huxley looked now to see the indomitable figure of the College Bursar. Responsible for the finances of one of the richest institutions in the whole of the UK, Charles Worth had an arrogance about him that went with the role. This was matched by his size, which had topped six feet when he was just fifteen and had gained another six inches since. Time and his many years feasting on the diet on offer at Trinity had ensured that his girth was in keeping with his height. Another veteran, he had recently caused a stir by marrying someone half his age.

But it wasn't she sitting to his left now. It was, to Huxley's immense surprise, Dr Samantha Davison. Huxley found her presence more perturbing than the four pompous men with whom she sat, although the plate in front of her appeared to be unused. As the Head of Department for Modern and Medieval Languages, she was Simms's immediate boss and Huxley hoped that this might explain her presence at the table.

Huxley fixed his attention on the Master. "I would be lying if I said that I was fine, Master, but I thought it only proper to update you." His tone had a harsh edge as he tried to keep his anger in check.

"I appreciate it, old boy, appreciate it. Damn police won't tell me a thing. Other than you've absconded with their prime suspect. That's what they said. Absconded. Had to call Samantha, ask her to join us, see if she could shed any light. Turns out she didn't even know that poor Simms was dead, did you dear? Can you believe that?" If the Master had picked up on Huxley's displeasure he was doing a good job of masking it as he responded in his usual distracted tenor.

Huxley glanced towards the ashen faced Samantha Davison, relieved that she hadn't partaken in the macabre feast.

"I have no doubt the police would have got to Dr Davison soon enough. Obviously now, when they do, it will be less of a shock to her."

There was a note of exasperation in his voice now as his annoyance at the lack of respect on show became evident.

Progressive as it was, there was still enough of the old guard around to keep the College rooted in tradition. He had no doubt the meal had served as a counsel of war as they discussed how best to deflect any bad press.

"Be that as it may, Daniel, I thought it would be prudent to check with Samantha in case there was anything that Simms was working on that could potentially embarrass his good name and reputation. It would be a shame to have the police misinterpret something in their ignorance. A terrible shame."

"Yes, well I have no doubt that it was his reputation that you were considering." He turned to Samantha and asked, "Is there anything relevant that you can add to the investigation, Doctor?"

"I really can't think of anything," she said, her voice barely a whisper.

"But you still haven't told us what is actually happening with the investigation, man." Huxley looked directly at Charles Worth who had voiced this dissent.

"That's because there is very little to tell, Charles. You probably know more than I do at this stage."

"I doubt that. You have been at the heart of the investigation. You have seen the body. Spoken to the person in charge. So you must tell us what you know." The didactic delivery of Hansel betrayed a man who was obviously used to being obeyed. Huxley turned towards him, matching the man's intensive gaze.

"I am happy to tell you everything I know, Fredrick, but I fear that it won't match your expectations."

"Well, perhaps we are the best judges of that," countered Hansel.

Huxley gave a brief summation of his findings and his subsequent disappearance with Alan Donovan who had stood quietly in the background throughout all the posturing. He skimmed over their discussion in the pub saying only that Donovan knew nothing of substance and that he would give a full statement to the police the following morning.

Having concluded, he was about to take his leave when Samantha Davison excused herself and asked if she could walk with them.

"Yes, of course, my dear, go, go. Daniel will ensure you get home safely, won't you Daniel?"

"It would be my pleasure."

As she collected her coat, the Master pulled him to one side and said, "Daniel, please don't think me callous, it really wasn't my idea to continue with the meal after, well,... you know. Bad form if you ask me. But the lobster was cooked and it would have been an awful waste. Believe me it was a solemn affair. Very solemn indeed."

"You have no need to explain yourself to me, Master."

"Oh, but I feel I do, Daniel, I do. While you are out there protecting the good name of the University and the College, I don't want you thinking that perhaps we are conspiring behind your back in the event of your failure. Nothing could be further from the truth, nothing, dear boy."

"That's good to know," Huxley responded, all the while thinking that was exactly what they were doing.

He walked to the door, held open by the butler, and joined Donovan and his new ward, the beautiful Dr Samantha Davison.

CHAPTER 9

ROME – 1970

O'Connell pondered the sheer majesty of his surroundings, the proximity of the hierarchy of the Church, the atmosphere of learning and reverence and, best of all, a library full of texts and documents the like of which he had never seen. There was room after room of manuscripts and books detailing everything that anyone could ever want to know about the Catholic faith, even texts he thought long since destroyed. Yet here they were preserved and it was his job to study them.

He couldn't imagine a more perfect setting and he was good at it too. Soon he was given specific projects to work on, reviewing specialised documents, sometimes even restricted texts. He recognised that his trustworthiness was being tested given the subject of the material but he was a zealot and he recognised the need to subjugate an enemy in order to teach them about faith. So, as shocking and terrible as some of the accounts were, O'Connell knew that they were for the greater good. The spread of Catholicism was the most important thing. It was without question that he accepted what he found with a tolerance that would later embarrass him.

After sometime he believed himself immune to whatever horrors the texts would unveil. He focused on the document itself and the history that lay behind it and soon became expert at authenticating texts, tracing their historical provenance.

The archives were set deep in the heart of the city, underground in vast chambers that had been dug centuries before. It was here that the air was actually a preserving rather than destructive element offering protection to texts and papyrus that were hundreds or sometimes thousands of years old.

O'Connell was one of thirty three such employees, each working alone in a designated area, privacy and confidentiality of paramount importance. Although friendly with many of his colleagues they would never discuss work and his day would often pass without any contact from those around him as each busied themselves with their respective tasks.

It was his practise to often work late into the evening as he found himself absorbed by the exercise he was undertaking, this being his passion as well as his job. On one such evening he heard his name whispered. Raising his head from his desk, he turned to see an old priest, his creased face and clouded eyes betraying a lifetime of work within the underground chambers. O'Connell knew the priest to be a native of Mexico named Sanchez but in all his years working alongside him O'Connell had rarely heard him speak. The surprise obviously showed on the younger man's face.

"Don't be alarmed," Sanchez said in English. The voice was like gravel and O'Connell moved closer to the priest and greeted him in Spanish thinking that this might help.

"No, English, speak only English. It is more difficult for someone to understand if they are listening."

"Who are you talking about?" asked O'Connell. "Who would be listening?"

"Ah, so young, so naïve. You remind me of what I was like when I first came here."

O'Connell studied the older man with some concern,

wondering if he was rambling because he was ill. "Are you okay, sir? Do you want me to get help?"

Sanchez grabbed his arm and held him in what, to O'Connell, was a frighteningly tight grip. "Please," he said, "indulge an old man. Come, sit with me. We are alone, I have already checked. Everyone has finished for today. They will not be back. I know their habits. I have watched them all very carefully."

By now O'Connell was fearful but the man had relaxed his grip so he felt that perhaps he just craved some company and that maybe a few minutes conversation would satisfy him. O'Connell retrieved his chair and sat next to the old man's desk.

"I have watched you for some time now," Sanchez began. "The work that you do, your demeanour, your mannerisms. They tell me a lot about you. Before, you would look with wonder upon a fresh document or text. Now, you are filled with dread." He held up a hand anticipating protest from O'Connell. "I know. I can tell. I see it in your eyes. You fear that you might read something else portraying this great institution in a less than favourable way."

O'Connell hesitated before replying, mainly because the old man was right. But this was something that he hadn't even admitted to himself let alone told anyone else. "It's not fear of what I will find, rather of how it would be misinterpreted by others outside of the church if it ever fell into the wrong hands."

The older priest smiled. "You think I am testing you and perhaps you are right. In a way I am testing you. But you should not be afraid. I know already what is in your heart. I know what you think and how you feel. I know because I, too, once felt it."

"What has happened to stop you feeling?"

"Oh, years of being institutionalised. Wasting my life away authenticating and translating documents, each one more horrific than the last until I became immune. But I always regretted allowing myself to become desensitised."

"I think you are being a little hard on yourself, sir," O'Connell responded.

"Please, don't patronise me," Sanchez responded angrily. "I am not here for me. I am here for you. It is too late for me but you," he paused, lowering his voice again, "you have a chance to stop this. To release your conscience. To live your life. Not to be condemned to what these bastards want you to become. Look at me." Raising his voice he stared straight into O'Connell's eyes, the stare seeming to pierce right into the young priest's soul. "Look at me. Do you want to become this." Sanchez stood and held his arms out to his side as if on a crucifix which, O'Connell realised later, he was, at least within himself.

"What is it that you want from me? I don't understand," stammered O'Connell who was transfixed by the old man's performance.

"I want you to listen. I have a story to tell you which might just save your life."

CHAPTER 10

They made their way back out onto the street in silence. As they left the College behind, Samantha Davison turned to Huxley.

"Thanks for walking with me, Professor, but I can assure you that I am perfectly fine to make my journey alone. However, I did want to escape my gaolers and you provided an excuse. I also wanted the chance to speak with you alone."

"Dr Davison, I must admit I don't know whether to be flattered or offended."

"Firstly, it's Sam or, if you can't manage such familiarity on a first date, Samantha will suffice. And I doubt your ego needs the constant massaging of me referring to you as Professor."

"No, Daniel will do just fine. Or Dan if you have the irrepressible English infection to shorten everything to its lowest denominator. I take it you two already know each other from the faculty," he added, indicating Alan.

Sam nodded. "Good to see you looking so well, Alan. I can only imagine what an ordeal this has been for you."

Donovan gave a shrug before replying, "I've had better days, Dr Davison."

"Sam, please," then, "good, now that the formalities are taken care of perhaps I can speak to you about something which I think may be important."

The vibrancy in her voice and the colour in her cheeks made Huxley realise the whole damsel in distress thing back in the Master's Lodge had been an act and made a mental note to never underestimate this woman.

As they passed Great St Mary's Church, the clock struck nine and they had to negotiate their way through the bar-hoppers, their Friday frivolities untouched by the events close by. Only later when they found their path blocked by a police cordon on their way to Gardis would they notice something amiss. Barred from their usual kebab stop, many would turn to the food vans in the square, the Trailer of Life and Uncle Franks or, as they were known, the Van of Life and the Van of Death, the need to satisfy some ying and yang. Perhaps the rumours of murder nearby would see the sales at the Van of Death somewhat down that particular night.

The three continued along King's Parade, the evening sun reflecting off the stained glass in the chapel, a kaleidoscopic profusion of colour. Even with the streets less crowded here they huddled close, keeping their conversation private.

"I got the impression that my summons to the Lodge tonight wasn't merely to ask me about Stephen's work. It was more of an interrogation, like they were looking for something specific. I was so shocked at the news of Stephen's death that I just couldn't focus. Then, when I recovered, I felt so angry at the callous manner they were treating the whole thing that I couldn't share what I know with them."

Both Donovan and Huxley looked at her, their curiosity piqued.

"Which is what?" asked Huxley.

"I'm not sure but he was definitely excited about something. Shortly after his meeting with you today, Alan, he came to see me. He didn't go into details but I know he felt annoyed. He admitted that it was probably just his own frustrations

The Judas Deception

at never having found satisfactory answers to all the objections you raised, the same ones he raised many years ago. He mentioned that there was something that you said that had intrigued him. Enough that he spent the rest of the afternoon examining dust covered books and surfing the internet. Next thing I know he's running around practically shouting eureka. I was looking for the bathtub that he had just jumped out of such was his excitement."

"So you think that he believed me after all?" asked Alan.

"He certainly believed something. I could hear him on the phone making a few calls. Then he started running back and forth to the library, bringing back text after text like he was looking for something specific."

"So did he tell you what he found?" asked Huxley.

"Alas, no. Which is part of the reason I never said anything to the wise men back there. I couldn't face their condescension at my unfounded theories."

She turned towards Alan who was looking a lot brighter than he had all evening and even had a glimmer of excitement about him.

"Maybe you could tell us what it was that you discussed?"

"It would be a lot easier if I could show you rather than tell you. I've got a copy of the text in my room," responded Donovan.

"I don't want you going back there tonight. I think Blackballs…I mean Inspector Blackburn will be watching for you. I would rather not bump into him tonight."

"There's always the Faculty," suggested Samantha.

"Can we get in at this time of night?" Huxley queried.

"I've got keys, I've got codes, I've even got my tag," said Sam, holding up her electronic ID. "What else do we need?"

"Sounds good to me. And perhaps the sort of place that detectives are likely to ignore in the search for us." Huxley was getting the scent of something and he too was becoming excited by doing something positive that might point towards whoever had killed his colleague.

They turned onto Silver Street passing first Queen's and then Darwin College. Both were lit up as their respective Balls got into full swing and plenty of people spilled out from their grounds. The trio continued towards the Sedgwick Site reaching the MML Faculty where Sam worked.

The building was in darkness and there was an eerie quality about visiting such a foreboding place at this time. The sky was still light and the temperature remained high as the evening delivered on its earlier promise of fine weather but it still did little to take the edge of such a large, deserted structure.

There were screams and the sound of running footsteps as a group of girls, late starters to the evening's festivities, made their way out of Newnham College opposite, one armed with a water pistol. The noise was amplified as it echoed off the building and all three gave a shiver of apprehension.

The three shared a giggle together as the realised how tense they had become and it seemed to relax the mood a little as Sam got her keys and made for the door. Once in, she cleared the alarm then led them upstairs.

The building was a result of an architectural competition in the sixties and had reflected the contemporary designs of the time that had favoured raised buildings. So, save for an entrance at either end of the E-shaped construction, the ground floor of the building consisted of only a stairwell to lead to the floors above. Students could then use the open space below to sit and study, weather permitting.

Sam negotiated a series of locked doors before they reached the office of the late Dr Stephen Simms.

"So, what is it we're looking for?" asked Huxley as they crowded round the desk.

The Judas Deception

"Well, for starters, we need a copy of the Judas Gospel in its original language," said Alan and Sam pointed to one lying open on the desk. "And there's a document by Irenaeus of Lyons that references the gospel."

"Ah, good old Irenaeus," said Huxley.

"Sorry, I don't mean to give you the idiot's guide but it just helps put in context what it is I've found."

"Carry on, Alan. In this scenario I am happy to be the idiot." Huxley gave him a smile of encouragement, thinking that the more ignorant he acted the greater the role Donovan would assume.

"Well, I suppose the whole premise of my PhD is that the original translation of the text doesn't seem right to me when looked at alongside the reference in Irenaeus. The Gospel confirms that Jesus asked Judas to betray him. But Irenaeus suggests that there's more to it than that."

"Okay, nothing new there but I'm guessing there's a bit more to it than that," Huxley commented.

"Yes, of course," continued Alan. "My main focus has always been on a specific part of the text from which there are quite a few bits missing. The translation is based on guesswork."

"I think you'll find that it's extremely well educated guesswork."

"Yeah, sure, I'm not dissing the translation, merely pointing out that there is always room for misinterpretation."

"Good luck with that," chimed in Sam. "Many have tried to challenge the original translation but it has been accepted as being a superb rendition. The accuracy of the interpretation is exceptional and it is very highly regarded. I can see why Stephen was concerned if that was the tact you were trying to take."

"Ah, but what if there was a way of proving that some of the linked pages didn't actually fit together?"

"The only way that you could possibly do that would be to see more of the text."

"Yes and no. Because I was focusing on one particular piece that allowed me to speculate a little on the missing text and how it then links with the pages that follow. This is why I needed to see the original papyrus."

"So Stephen arranged your visit to National Geo so you could study it."

"Exactly."

"And what did you find?"

The young man looked up at his audience, a glint in his eye that betrayed his excitement. "More than I could ever have expected," he said.

CHAPTER 11

The pair stood waiting for Donovan to expand on his rather cryptic revelation, their collective silence reminiscent of a music teacher waiting for their pupil to stop playing Chopsticks and break into Rachmaninoff.

"I think you'd better tell us what it is you think you know," said Huxley in a controlled manner. He got the impression that it was all a bit of a game to Alan and he was fighting the urge to shake the boy to his senses.

"Okay, the section I was interested in was…," Donovan leafed through pages, "here," he concluded, pointing towards the replica of the manuscript. The others leaned in to read the part he was indicating. "The papyrus is actually quite disintegrated on this bit," he continued, "and towards the bottom the translation has been based on partial words and context. I really wanted to study the original to see if there was another acceptable translation that may work."

"And?" This from Sam, sounding a little exasperated.

"It was all a bit inconclusive."

"Alan, I think you'd better stop wasting our time beating around the bush and get to where you're going. A man is dead, your tutor no less. So anything you might know that could help us find out how and why would be good to hear."

"Sorry, Professor, I was only trying to give you all the details."

"Relevance, Alan, is probably the most important piece of advice that I can impart to you if you plan to carry on with your studies."

"Sorry," he repeated sheepishly.

"So?" prompted Sam.

"Okay, what if I was to say that I saw something that I shouldn't have?"

"Something as in more of the original?" Sam was open-mouthed with amazement.

"Yes."

"How? Where? Who?" stammered Sam.

"Well, I found someone who had."

It was Huxley's turn to voice his disbelief. "People have been searching for years for any fragments of the document that may still exist without any success. But it just falls into your hands?"

"Like most things, it was pure chance. It's astounding the difference looking at the actual papyrus makes. My trip was the first time I had ever seen the real thing. Everything is kept in special conditions and you have to wear protective clothing all the time and use special gloves to handle the parchment. It's amazing. Some of it is so delicate that it's kept locked in a safe room that requires a special pass to access."

"And you saw something in there?" queried Huxley, anxious to move things along again.

"No, nothing like that. I didn't even have access. Not many people do. They told me at my first briefing that only three people in the world have authority. They call them the holy trinity." Donovan smirked but then read the impatience on Huxley's face. "Anyway, it's really all thanks to my girlfriend that anything happened."

"Your girlfriend?"

"Yes, Debbie. She works at National Geo as an assistant to the Director of Artefacts. I met her when she was doing a Masters here in Cambridge. She was on sabbatical and went back to her job a few months ago. Her boss loves her, was completely lost without her and is so glad that she's back."

"And he happens to be one of the holy trinity," added Huxley, seeing where this was leading to.

"You guessed it, Professor. So when she told him that I was there to study the Judas gospel he was really helpful. He took quite an interest in my work and I ended up spending a lot of time with him. So much so that I guess he felt he could trust me."

"With what?" asked Huxley.

"Well Max, that's his name, Dr Max Redding, he told me that he had recently been contacted by a private collector who had been offered a fragment of the original Judas Gospel and wanted it authenticated before he made the purchase. So he invited me to come with him."

"Just like that, you got to go along and visit a collector and see this parchment?" The incredulity in Sam's voice was clear.

"As I said, it was all by chance. Right place at the right time. I just got lucky. He invited me along, passed me off as an expert on Coptic scripts and someone who could help with the authentication."

"And was it authentic?"

"There was no doubt in my mind as soon as I saw it."

"Wow. This is huge." Sam Davison was so overcome she had to sit.

"Indeed," added Huxley who was also mulling over the significance of the revelation. In his years studying the provenance of the Gospel of Judas Iscariot he had chased so many rainbows when it came to original text findings. There was plenty of evidence to suggest that many of the pages were missing but it was generally accepted that these had disintegrated after the initial discovery of the parchment some forty years earlier, when it had been kept in poor conditions. But there were some who believed that parts of the manuscript might have been secreted away as collectors' items. Could it really be that Alan Donovan had chanced across one such find? "What happened then?" he asked.

"Ummm, well, nothing."

"Nothing! You mean neither of you thought to tell anyone? An original missing piece of possibly the most significant manuscript of our time and you just kept it to yourselves?" Huxley stopped to take a deep breath, wondering if his anger was a result of jealousy.

"We couldn't," Donovan shouted back, "we'd signed confidentiality clauses. And I promised Max. I'm only telling you now because Dr Simms is dead and I want to try and help find his killer."

"Alright, calm down you two, arguing about the whys and wherefores isn't going to help us solve anything right now." Davison turned to Alan, her soft eyes holding his. "So this is what you told Stephen earlier?"

"Not exactly."

"What's that supposed to mean," chimed in Huxley, his temper still bubbling close to the surface.

"I didn't want to break my promise to Max. So instead I told Dr Simms a tale about seeing a different photo which seemed to show an anomaly in the text. But he wasn't having any of it and seemed more concerned about my going off at a tangent. Said I'd completely wasted my time and had probably besmirched his reputation."

"Well whatever you said was obviously enough to have

got him thinking. And as a result he may have dug a little too deeply into something he shouldn't."

"What was in the text you saw, Alan," asked Huxley offering a conciliatory olive branch.

The young man seemed grateful at the change of tone and smiled as he responded. "It was most of a single page with text on either side and I recognised it as being part of the narrative referred to in the Irenaeus commentary. And from it I was able to see that two of the linked pages from the original text didn't belong together."

"How can you be so sure?" Sam Davison moved effortlessly into professional mode.

"Well, for starters, the tense was wrong."

"Seems an unlikely mistake for the translators to make," queried Huxley.

"Yes, but they only had a partial bit of the final word on the page to work with so had to use best judgement. Using the rest of the text they decided that the continuity existed with another passage at the start of a different page so linked the two together and used that to direct the tense."

"But you think that those passages shouldn't have been linked and that the page you saw is actually the next in sequence."

"That's right. I'm convinced of it."

"So show me what it was that you saw," Sam continued, indicating the copy still open on the desk.

Alan ran his finger down the page until he reached the last line.

"Here," he said. "See, this," pointing to the final word on the page, "is translated as 'has ever comprehended' but I believe the original actually says something slightly different."

He started writing the text beside that listed on the document before revealing it to the others.

"I suppose you two would string me up if I said that it all looks Greek to me?"

Alan laughed nervously while Sam groaned and rolled her eyes at Huxley's attempt at humour.

"Coptic text is actually an ancient language that uses a modified Greek alphabet to write ancient Egyptian," she countered. "That's what we're looking at here. And the subtle change in the text that Alan has written changes the meaning completely. I would translate that as.....'will ever accept'?" This last a question to Alan who nodded his agreement with Sam.

"That's how I translated it too."

"Which means that the pages can't fit and there are pages missing from that part," said Huxley. "The question is where are the rest of those pages and what do they contain?" he concluded.

"The million dollar question," added Donovan.

Something in the young man's tone raised an alarm in Huxley's head and he absorbed this comment and stored it alongside everything else that he'd encountered that night. It was all still quite hazy but he thought he was beginning to see a picture emerging and how some of the pieces of the puzzle fit together. And he wasn't sure that he liked the look of what he saw.

CHAPTER 12

"You know we're going to have to tell the police this, don't you, Alan?" declared Huxley.

"We can't. No! I promised. I only told you because of…"

Huxley cut him off. "Alright, alright." He motioned with his hands for the young man to calm down and said "I promise you that we won't share that part of the story with anyone else." He looked at his charge to ensure that he had his full attention. Donovan stared back hard waiting for some caveat to this atonement but nodded an acknowledgement to Huxley who continued, "Providing there is no need to. And when I say that," he added quickly, seeing Donovan's agitation, "I mean that only if it becomes a matter of life or death. Okay?"

Donovan was about to raise an objection but the steely stare that he was faced with, Huxley's eyes seemingly casting a tractor beam, held the young man transfixed.

"I said, okay?" repeated Huxley.

"I guess," came the surly response.

Huxley was conscious of his promise to Pepper of presenting Donovan in a fit and proper state the next morning. Whilst it would be nice to have a direction to point the police towards, Huxley was more concerned with ensuring that he actually had a co-operative ward who was relaxed and obliging rather than agitated and provocative. "So where do we go from here?"

"I wonder if this was what Stephen was getting so excited about earlier. If he made the connection himself," said Sam. "What bit of Irenaeus did your fragment refer to?"

"The bit I saw gave an account of Jesus and his relationship with each of his disciples, suggesting that he regarded Judas as the most trustworthy of them all."

"And you think that it leads on to Judas giving his real reasons behind betraying his friend?"

"I'm saying that it makes sense given what is stated in Irenaeus. I think that someone is deliberately hiding the missing pages as they don't want people to know what those reasons are."

"That's quite a leap, Alan. What makes you think that someone is hiding them? Isn't it more likely that some of the pages were stolen to sell on the black market, such as the one you saw?" Huxley wanted to see exactly what it was that Alan was implying.

"I don't think so. There has been a lot of speculation over the years about how the pages fit together and the best consolidation of the missing text. But no-one has ever mentioned that this part of the text might be short of a few pages as the translation seemed to fit and the flow of the text and continuity of the story all pieced nicely together. I think someone was happy for people to believe that what was there was correct."

"What do you think, Sam?" Huxley was perturbed by the picture forming in his mind and was hoping that Sam Davison may help point him in a better direction.

"I can see the sense in what Alan is saying. Although I always understood that the best thinking on the missing text was that it had been lost or destroyed. I've never really considered that someone was deliberately hiding it away."

"Okay, before we start seeing conspiracies under every rock, let's just take a step back," countered Huxley. "There are

The Judas Deception

a number of schools of thought about the Judas gospel, especially seeing how it was first discovered. While it was found in the mid-seventies, it wasn't until the late nineties that it was made available for study. This gives rise to the usual conspiracy theories that we are only being allowed to see the bits of it that the powers that be want us to." He put on a deep, ghoulish tone when voicing this last that caused Sam to giggle. "But was the manuscript deliberately tampered with or did the papyrus simply disintegrate over the years through poor preservation? Well, now we know there is at least one other page that has survived that then begs the question, are there any more?"

"And where?" added Sam.

"When I was doing my original research of its provenance, everyone I spoke to in connection with the text said that there had always been rumours that the Church tampered with it," Huxley said.

"That's right," chipped in Alan, "you said when they were discovered they were simply held in place by a bit of string. Once untied the pages were loose from one another. And, if I remember correctly, you wrote that they couldn't have been in Egypt for all that time as where they were discovered would have offered no respite from the heat and they would have disintegrated long before now."

Huxley was about to comment when there was a loud clanging from the alarm. "I thought you switched the alarm off," he shouted to Sam who was moving towards the door.

"I did," she responded, having to turn her head in Huxley's direction, "but that's not the intruder alarm, that's the fire alarm."

"Fire!" Both Huxley and Donovan shouted it almost in unison as they ran into the corridor. Sam was running towards the exit but there was already a large amount of smoke. She reached the door they had entered through, her hand already over her mouth to try and act as some sort of filter as the smoke got denser. As she pushed against it she found that the door wouldn't open. Huxley and Donovan reached her as she tried to force it open but, failing once again, she turned to them.

"It's blocked," she shouted.

"Blocked? What do you mean, blocked? It can't be blocked, we came in this way." Huxley was ducking low to try and breathe cleaner air as the smoke began to fill the corridor. He realised the futility of his question but he was trying to get to grips in his own head with exactly what was going on. He and Donovan joined Sam in putting their combined weight against the door but they couldn't get it to move at all. Whatever was blocking it was going to take more than their collective force to shift and they didn't have the time to try anything else as the fumes were becoming overpowering.

Sam shouted, "Keep low and follow me," as she made her way back along the corridor. The air was clearer back this way and she thought they must be heading away from the main source of the fire. But, as she reached the corner that led to the fire door, she found herself faced with an inferno. She turned back, the horror written all over her face, stopping the two men short as they tried to follow her. She shook her head and ran back towards the office they had just vacated. She closed the door once they were all back inside.

"There's a fire at either end of the corridor, the only exits are at each end so there's no way of reaching them now and, I suspect, we would only find that the other door is blocked in a similar way. It appears that someone doesn't want us to get out of here."

"How long will that door act as a barrier?" asked Huxley.

"I don't know for sure. They're proper fire doors, all the offices have them, but that can mean anything between ten and thirty minutes from memory."

"Let's call it ten. We've already had two so we only have about eight minutes left before that door is breached. Then," he continued grimly, "at a guess, I would say about thirty seconds before this entire room is engulfed in flame and everything within it consumed, including us."

"It has to be the window then," said Donovan.

"Security windows. Break proof glass and they only open a few inches to stop anyone from jumping out."

"Great, just what we need. They have security windows but no sprinkler system. Okay, there has to be another way." This from Huxley as he tried to think through the options. "We could try breaking the glass but that might take too long and we still have a fifty foot drop to contend with. Or we could wait for the fire brigade."

The look from the others told him that wasn't a preference.

"Alright, then the only other way is up." He pointed to the ceiling.

Jumping onto the desk, he pushed the ceiling tile above him which came away easily creating a gap large enough to fit through. He then hauled himself up beyond the suspended ceiling using the support grid which the tiles rested on. The heat hit him full in the face but the smoke was minimal. Above him he could see the roof beams and he reached for the nearest one and used it to pull himself all the way up into the eaves. He pressed his hand hard against the sloping surface above but there was no give.

"Give me something heavy that I can hit against the roof," he called below.

Donovan reached for a bronze statuette which sat on the edge of a bookcase. As he did, the smoke began to seep beneath the door. Grabbing the heavy statue, he climbed onto the desk and reached up as far as he could, stretching his arm with the statuette until it felt like it would come out of the socket.

Huxley bent down to try and take the figurine from Donovan but, as he did so, his foot slipped off the ceiling grid and he lost his balance. As he fell the arm of his dinner jacket caught on a protruding nail from the roof beam and brought him up short, his feet suspended in the air, his full weight hanging on his jacket. For the briefest of moments he registered how fortunate he was to use top quality tailoring which probably saved his life before he felt someone push his legs back towards the grid. He looked down to see Samantha Davison reaching up and shoving with all her strength and he used that momentum together with his own upper body strength to haul himself back up.

Grabbing the statuette from Donovan, he swung it against the insulation and roof tiles above. He felt something give and swung again and again until a hole appeared in the roof and fresh air flooded in. He called to the others to climb up, reaching down with one hand, this time making sure he had a firm hold on the roof beam, and hauling first Sam and then Alan up alongside him. Sam put her head through the hole and then forced her shoulders and arms through, using them to squeeze the rest of her body onto the roof. Donovan tried to follow but found it tougher as he was too big. Sam began tearing at the slates around her to widen the gap. With his own effort, and that of Sam pulling and Huxley pushing, he made it through to join Sam, nearly slipping down the steep slope of the roof before Sam managed to grab him and help him balance.

Unfortunately, with air now pouring into the building from the hole, the fire below was being fed with oxygen and there was an explosion as the office door was blown off its hinges and the room was engulfed in flame. Huxley jumped for the hole and squeezed his upper half through but struggled as his legs had nothing to propel themselves off and they hung helplessly below him.

Sam and Alan grabbed his arms and pulled but it wasn't enough and Huxley feared that his plans to run the Great North Run later in the year might be hampered by a lack of lower limbs. Then, as his feet scrabbled below him, he found some purchase as they hit upon a roof beam now swallowed up in flame. He pushed with all his weight hoping that the beam wouldn't collapse from underneath him and take him down to his certain death. Clawing with his upper torso, he forced his way onto the roof with the others.

"Quickly," he said, "we can't hang around here, the whole thing is on fire below us and this roof will collapse before long.

They began to scramble over the roof, balancing precariously, mindful of the slope leading to a drop that would probably kill them. Sam took the lead, instinct guiding her towards safety. She spotted the fire escape over in the far corner of the building where the fire door would have led them to. It was external and so free from flames and she knew that was where they had to get to. She started to head in that direction, the others following.

The sound of sirens and the reflection of blue flashing lights against the night sky told them that the fire brigade had arrived but, as they were on the far side of the building with the peak of the roof in between them, they couldn't see nor be seen themselves. They moved gingerly as they neared the edge and Sam manoeuvred herself so she could reach down with her legs. They touched something hard below and she tested it before putting her weight on it. She dropped down and realised that she was standing on top of a chair that had been jammed up against the door handle to prevent it from being opened. It now served as a platform to allow her to reach the fire escape and she was able to guide the others.

They ran quickly down the steps of the fire escape, the adrenaline that comes from near death fuelling them. As they descended Huxley looked back to see flames emerging from the roof that they had just been standing on. He realised that they had been just moments from being swallowed by fire and that whoever was responsible had meant for them to die.

If he didn't know it already he now recognised that this was a very dangerous game that they were caught up in and, for the first time that night, he was genuinely worried.

CHAPTER 13

The fire escape led onto a courtyard garden at the rear of the building. They continued running, putting distance between themselves and the heat of the flames. Unconsciously they were also moving away from any help that may be on offer.

"Is everyone okay?" asked Huxley. As the oldest and most senior, he felt that it was down to him to take charge, even if events were spiralling out of control. This had clearly been a deliberate attempt on their lives. With that in mind, he knew they had to be very careful how they proceeded from here.

Alan held up his left arm and said, "I cut myself when I was climbing out through the hole in the roof but it's nothing serious."

"Let me see." Sam moved towards him to examine the wound. "Hmmm, it looks like quite a deep cut, you need to get a dressing on that. Come on, let's get round to the front and we can get that seen to."

"No," cried Huxley. The others turned to look at him, such was the vehemence in his voice. "We can't take the chance. Somebody followed us here and deliberately trapped us in a burning building. That wasn't someone playing a prank or even giving us a warning, it was someone trying to kill us. Now, I have no way of knowing for certain if it's linked to what we're doing but it's a hell of a coincidence. And I would think that there is every chance that whoever is out to get us will be watching to see if we come out of that building, alive or dead. I'd rather not give them the opportunity to finish the job."

"You think they'll be watching, even with the police here?" Sam could see what Huxley was driving at but thought that going to the authorities was the best course of action. Although that would probably consist of them sitting around for hours answering the same questions over and over and trying to convince various people of the import of their find. She was too tired for any of that as the adrenaline rush began to wear off and the extent of the ordeal hit home.

"Fires attract crowds. Our would-be killers could very easily join them and check to see if they bring any bodies out. It is pure chance that we came out of the far side of the building. I think we should take advantage of that bit of good fortune."

"So what do you suggest we do?" asked Sam.

"Well, we've already ruled out College and my house. Now, with this, I'm guessing it won't be too long before the police are knocking on your door too."

"Well, whatever we do, we need to do it quickly and get Alan's arm looked at soon as I'm not happy with the amount of blood that he's losing.

"There's a house in Grantchester that I know about, we could use that. I'm sure no-one would find us there." Huxley had thought about their options earlier and had considered the Grantchester house as a possibility but favoured something closer to the city. Now he was inclined to put a bit of distance between them and the city even if it was only the four miles that would take them to Grantchester.

"Whose house is it? I mean, can it be traced back to you? The police are going to get pretty annoyed when they can't get hold of any of us and starting calling on family,

The Judas Deception

friends and known acquaintances. Perhaps even to a house in Grantchester?" This last was posed as a question as Sam queried Huxley's idea.

"It's an empty house that can't be traced to me. In fact, I'm pretty sure they could ask anyone that knows me and they wouldn't learn about this place. That's why I think it's the best place for us to go. Besides, where else is there?"

"Fair enough. How are we going to get there? It's quite a walk and Alan needs medical attention soon. Have you got a car that we can use? And isn't there a chance that the police might be watching it?"

Huxley had been thinking about this. He had already discounted using his own car but had an idea.

"Probably," he replied. "But I do have access to the University Centre and there are vans stored there. We could head there and take stock."

"What are we waiting for," said Sam.

There was movement at the back of the burning building as the fire brigade made their way around to tackle the blaze from both sides. The three were now far enough away to remain hidden but they were restricted in where they could go. They began to make towards the boundary of the site and, once there, climbed over the gate that led into the grounds of the University Library.

The sky was beginning to darken but was still light enough for them to be able to see well ahead of them and they looked over at the tall central column of the library that rose into the fading sky in front of them, the building looking like a large inverted T. Huxley had always thought it odd that somewhere which, by decree, got a copy of every book published, would limit the available space to display that wealth of knowledge and wisdom.

Like so many things about the university, it didn't make

sense to him but, because it was such an institution, it was simply accepted that this was how things were done. It frustrated and amused him in equal measure but it was his job, his home, his life and he loved the place with all its foibles and couldn't imagine being anywhere else. Although, right now, he would love to be elsewhere if it meant being out of the clutches of the police and any psychotic killers who might want him dead. He just needed some time to think.

They passed through the library car park and onto the path at the side that led down towards the river Cam. From there they could follow the course of the Cam towards The Anchor pub besides which was the University Centre.

With the sun setting Huxley was grateful for the lighting all along the path which ensured that they could see both well in front and behind. The proximity of the path to the river and the surrounding parkland made it a popular place for joggers, dog walkers and courting couples so there was plenty of activity but nothing which appeared sinister. Nevertheless, Huxley stayed on high alert, knowing that someone had obviously followed them before without any of them realising it and he intended to be more watchful this time.

The Anchor was another iconic pub that had a prized position right on the river and overlooking the mill pond, a great spot to watch people punting. Upon reaching the pub, they made for the alley that ran along the back towards the University Centre.

Turning into the alley they saw the shape of a man at the far end, his back to them. He was peering along the road straight ahead as though looking for someone. The man turned side on to them to follow the path of the road with his gaze and the three could see him all the better now. He had a young face, early twenties maybe, with a long nose that gave it an angular look, almost Picassoesque in the light, his straw hair absorbing the last of the sun's rays as the summer sky turned bright peach around them. His limp shoulders were accentuated by the dinner jacket hanging from them like he had left it too late to hire his tux and had to settle for one two sizes too big, the sleeves almost covering his hands. But not the gun that he held in his left hand, clearly visible to the trio and that stopped them dead in their tracks.

The man must have noticed the movement out of the corner of his eye and turned his head to look at them, the gap between them seeming to shrink to almost nothing as they peered at the weapon. The gunman didn't make any immediate move but there was enough in his body language to convince Huxley that his gun was not for show. He grabbed the other two as he turned to run back out of the alley, half expecting to find his way blocked by another henchman waiting behind but finding no such obstruction.

The gateway into Queens' College was directly opposite the alleyway and Huxley ran straight over, Sam and Alan following behind. As it was the night of the Queens' College Ball there was security on the front gate in the form of hired bouncers to ensure that no-one gate-crashed the £150.00 ticket only affair.

Huxley headed straight for one of the burley men fitted out in full DJ regalia but yet so obviously hired help than paying guest, such was the uncomfortable manner in which he wore the monkey suit. His muscles tensed as if expecting trouble and the extra-large jacket struggled to contain his vast frame as he eyed Huxley with suspicion.

"There is a man with a gun across the street," began Huxley, turning to look over his shoulder to see if the guy was following.

"Yes, sir, and what would you like me to do? Kill him with my bowler hat perhaps?"

Huxley was taken aback by the insolence of the bouncer but more surprised by the casual, almost bored manner in which he absorbed the news. He was about to assert his authority when he saw a group of tuxedoed fresh-faced youths approaching the ticket collectors, each of them with guns in their hands. It was only then that he noticed the back drop behind the main gate guiding guests into the world of Bond…. James Bond. The theme of the Ball was 007 and the guns were all part of the get up for the evening.

Huxley realised that the bouncer had been standing at his station for over three hours now and must have had numerous comedians coming up to him already asking him if he had seen Pussy Galore or could he make them a Martini, shaken not stirred.

Even as Huxley stood there reappraising the situation one of the boys awaiting entry turned to the doorman and asked "Hey, Mac, what's it like in there? Good, eh?"

His mate standing behind answered "He'd like to tell us but then he would have to kill us," before leading the guffaws from the group.

Huxley looked towards the bouncer, a wry smile on his face and said, "Sorry, I really didn't mean to…" He tailed off, the look on the bouncers face telling him all he needed to know. Seven more hours of this, it said, and this was supposed to be easy money.

Feeling rather foolish, Huxley turned back to his companions who had followed the whole exchange.

"I guess we're all a little jumpy," consoled Sam. "It's only natural after what we've just been through."

"Yes, well, if we keep on like that then we'll end up seeing spooks round every corner."

Just then, Donovan let out a cry of pain. Both Huxley and Sam looked round at him to see what had provoked it and found him holding his still bleeding arm, a sudden pain having shot through as he was jostled by a crowd of passing revellers. He looked back at the pair with an apologetic grin on his face.

"I think we need to get that seen to sooner rather than later," commented Sam.

"Well, they are bound to have a first aid room in here," said Huxley. He walked over to the table where a number of the organisers were gathered, checking tickets. As Vice-Chancellor he was a well-known face and he used this to his advantage as he explained the situation to help gain them entry into the hallowed ground of the ball, being ushered by a young history student who recognised him instantly and was only too happy to help. She led them to a room beside the Porter's Lodge where a couple of St John's Ambulance medics were sitting looking a little bored.

"Thank you, Sandy," said Huxley to their usher, bringing a flush of red to the young girl's face as she hadn't introduced herself and she realised that the rather dishy, brilliant and, most importantly, eligible Professor Daniel Huxley knew who she was. She gave him a dazzling smile revealing her braces and practically skipped back to her post.

"Do you have that effect on all the girls?" smiled Sam, taking a seat by the door as the medics set about patching up Alan's cut.

"I can't say I've ever noticed," replied Huxley, joining her.

"Oh, come on now, Daniel, are you honestly trying to tell me that you don't know how the women of this university swoon every time the handsome Professor Huxley flashes them a smile?"

"As long as that's all that I'm flashing!" He gave a disarming smile before continuing, "You see, that's part of the problem, Sam. There are many who think I shouldn't have such a responsible position. Perhaps I'm too young or too outspoken or too radical for their liking. So everything I do gets scrutinised. Hell, you know that fraternising with students is frowned upon in most circles. Within mine it is down-right forbidden and god help me if I give the wrong impression to some poor besotted undergrad who thinks that just because I remember her name and compliment her on the essay that I must fancy her."

"Oh, I don't mean just the students, Daniel. I'll bet that every woman in your building falls over themselves when you ask for something to be done."

"If only that were true," he laughed, "they're more likely to tell me to get stuffed and do it myself."

"Ahhh, the famous Irish charm, playing down your influence and the esteem which every right-minded person within this university holds you in."

"Why, Miss Moneypenny, you're making me blush," he replied in a poor imitation of Sean Connery.

She laughed, showing off a row of perfect teeth and Huxley found himself wondering if Samantha Davison had worn braces when she was an undergrad. They looked at each other and, for a moment, forgot about the predicament that they found themselves in. Then the spell was broken as Alan Donovan came walking over to them, his arm patched up and a bit more colour in his face.

"So what now?" asked Alan.

"Well, much as I like the idea of a party I still think the best thing for us to do is to get to somewhere a bit more quiet and discreet. Grantchester fits the bill nicely, I think."

"So, back to the University Centre?"

"Let's do it."

As they stood to leave the room they were approached by a middle-aged man with more hair under his chin than on his head that it made him look like he had his face on upside down. His glasses magnified his eyes making the intense stare that he give seem all the more threatening and his drab grey suit made him stand out in the sea of tuxedo clad bodies that enveloped the ball.

"Ah, Professor Huxley, I'm so glad I caught you. One of the students said that they had seen you coming this way." He rubbed his hands together nervously as he walked towards the group before putting them into his jacket pockets rather than offer them in introduction.

"I'm afraid you have the advantage of me," replied Huxley, waiting for an explanation of some sort.

The man drew alongside him and whispered harshly, "Indeed I do," as he jammed something hard into Huxley's side. Huxley looked down but saw only the man's hand consumed by a jacket pocket but he could guess that his hand was firmly holding a pistol which he was pressing hard into Huxley's side. "I suggest you and your cohorts come with me," he continued in his stage whisper, indicating that Sam and Alan should go in front. Seeing that they could do very little without endangering their companion, they complied and the man directed them outside to the party.

Huxley was annoyed at the simplicity with which they had been trapped and knew that their captor wasn't inviting them along for a quiet chat. His mind raced through the options available to him and their potential outcomes and he didn't like any of them at all. Not for the first time that evening he wondered just what the hell had they gotten themselves into?

CHAPTER 14

Rome – 1970

The two priests talked long into the night, the older telling O'Connell about his early life in Mexico before coming to the Vatican. He spoke about his family with great affection and O'Connell found himself captivated by the easy manner and wistful way in which Sanchez told his story. Then, without warning, Sanchez said that they must go but, if O'Connell wanted to learn more, that he should work late again the following evening. Before they left the catacombs for the evening, the old priest admonished O'Connell not to speak about their conversation with anyone.

"And when you enter the chamber tomorrow you should not acknowledge me in any way. Behave as you always have before, with courtesy but not familiarity. This is very important."

Bemused, O'Connell did as the old man instructed, finding it quite easy as Sanchez didn't even acknowledge O'Connell's existence whilst others were present, spending his day hunched over his desk and ignoring everyone around him. It was only when they were on their own that he shook himself from his reverie and began speaking. T

his became their habit, both remaining until the rest had finished for the day before they would begin to talk. Their conversations progressed from Sanchez's life story to discussions

The Judas Deception

on faith and the role of the Church in society past, present and, even, in the future. Sanchez would test the young man's faith, his questions both provoking and insightful. He was a wise old man and had learnt a lot in his years and he enjoyed sharing his experiences with the younger version of himself, testing the young priest's boundaries with questions and revelations.

This continued for a couple of weeks, a pattern developing. One night, in the midst of their discussion, Sanchez looked earnestly at the young man before him.

"Do you think that the documents that you work with should be made available to other scholars?" he asked, a smirk already on his face as he anticipated the stock answer he would receive.

"I think that some of the texts we hold would be used against us by those who are not sympathetic to the Church. And even practising Catholics may find it difficult to understand the context in which the document was written. Without knowing the circumstances then the content might be a little confusing."

"Confusing? Hmmm, interesting choice of word. Do you mean that, in the wrong hands, there are those who would try and use the contents to destroy the Church and all it stands for?"

"I suppose if you want to be crude about it then, yes, that's exactly what I mean," replied O'Connell, amused at the dramatic intonation that his friend had used for the latter part of his question.

"And would that really be such a terrible thing?" Sanchez looked at the young man to gauge his reaction to such a direct query.

The Irishman considered this, wondering where the old man was trying to lead him. Rather than respond with the usual rhetoric that had been drilled into him from a very young age about the all-powerful Church of Rome and its place in the world, O'Connell simply shrugged.

"Maybe it wouldn't at that." He couldn't explain why he answered in that way, perhaps it was the first time in years that he had actually allowed his brain to engage on its own rather than robotically conform to the ideals and beliefs that had been fed to him throughout his life. Whatever the reason, it was like a switch had been flicked inside of him and his demeanour must have shown this as the old priest smiled in a way that O'Connell had never seen him do before.

"Now that I have your full attention", he said, "I think there is something that you need to know, something that I wish someone had told me when I was your age. Perhaps I would have considered my future a little more rather than wake up one morning and realise that my life is over and it has been totally wasted."

"Why do you say that? You know that it's not true. You have given invaluable serv…"

Sanchez cut the young man off with a wave of his hand. "Please, my friend, we have come too far to content ourselves with platitudes. Let me finish and then you can decide for yourself."

"I am at your service, holy father." O'Connell was rather taken aback by what he had just said, but he meant every word. There was, without doubt, a stirring within him that had been resurrected since these late night discussions with Father Sanchez and he found himself trusting the old man implicitly.

Ever since their initial conversation, O'Connell had come to recognise that he really was filled with dread each time he reviewed a new piece of material. The manner in which, in the past, the Church had controlled those under its mandate had been appalling and O'Connell often found it difficult to stomach. Now he was beginning to face up to the truth

The Judas Deception

of exactly what it was he felt and he was keen to explore this further under the tutelage of his new found mentor.

"What would you say if I told you that the documents that you have worked on were only the surface of the corruption that the Church has been involved in?"

"What do you mean?"

"What if I said that there is another archive, so secret and so restricted that only the holiest of holies know anything about them?"

"I assume by 'holiest of holies' you are referring to the hierarchy of the Church?"

"Indeed," replied Sanchez.

"Well, I imagine, like any institution or society of a certain size and stature, there are skeletons best left firmly in whatever closet they are hiding," O'Connell said. "And why would those in charge of the wellbeing of the Church bother us minions with the minutiae of any such charges. But I can't imagine that they can be any worse than what I have seen already and I would think that, if what you say is true, there is good reason for these documents to be hidden away. Perhaps because they relate to more recent events and it would harm the reputation of some still active within the church or their immediate family. And anyway, how do you know that there is such an archive if it is only available to those much higher than you or I?"

"I do so enjoy your flowery language at times, my friend. And you are right that there are some more recent affairs which we are not privy to all the information. But there is much more to it than that. I am talking about documents and manuscripts which would challenge the credence of the church as a whole if ever they were discovered."

O'Connell looked at him in wide eyed fascination.

Sanchez continued, "A few years ago, before you came to work here, I was involved in a project which took me outside my usual scope. It had been a long, long time since anything had piqued my interest enough for me to explore the history of the text which I was reviewing but this suddenly grabbed my attention. The actual document itself wasn't particularly fascinating but I was intrigued enough by its contents to want to learn more. The cardinal in charge of our section at the time began to take a very keen interest in what I was doing. Evidently it had been brought to his attention the books and texts which I had been checking out of the archive. He advised me that perhaps it wasn't a topic that was fit for study and that I should leave it alone. Obviously I felt obliged to obey his instruction but something nagged at me and so I began to do a little bit more research later in the evening when I was alone." He indicated the chamber around them. "Some things don't change, eh?"

O'Connell laughed. Sanchez allowed himself a little chuckle but then his face became stony.

"It happened in the dead of night," Sanchez said. "I was asleep in my room when the door suddenly burst open and I was dragged from my bed in only my sleeping gown. There were four of them, Swiss guards but not in their usual uniform. Two held me, one on either side while the others marched behind as they dragged me protesting along the corridors of the building. I was taken down staircases and along tunnels and through locked doors I had never seen before and, indeed, have not seen since. Eventually I was brought to a room in a part of the Vatican where, even now, I couldn't tell you where it is."

O'Connell sat opened mouthed as he listened and couldn't quite believe what it was he was hearing but he realised that the old man was speaking the truth because he could see the fear in his eyes.

"Here," continued Sanchez, "I was put into a chair, not asked to sit, I mean forcefully put into it like I was a criminal.

They strapped my arms and legs to the chair and told me that it was for my benefit although no-one told me why. Still to this day I cannot explain to you why I was strapped there except that someone didn't want me to be able to get up from that chair until they were finished with me."

"My God, what did they do to you?"

"Nothing terrible, don't worry. This isn't another of your horror stories that you have to hear about. They simply questioned me. In front of the chair there were two large spotlights making it very difficult to see anything beyond. The men who questioned me remained behind the lights, hidden in the shadows, their voices difficult to focus on as they would take it in turns to ask me what they wanted to know."

"What did they ask you about?" O'Connell could see how emotional the older priest had become whilst telling his tale and he wanted to help him, to comfort him in some way. But he could only sit in fascinated horror and listen.

"They asked about the research I was doing and why I had taken so many documents out of the archive recently. When I explained what I was trying to do they told me in no uncertain terms that I was not to pursue my interest in the area I had strayed into. They said that some things are best left to those in positions of authority within the Church who knew what was best for the organisation as a whole. I was not harmed in any way physically, you understand, apart from the straps but there was definitely an underlying threat throughout the whole time. I felt intimidated."

"How long did they keep you for?"

"Oh, I don't know. Perhaps an hour, maybe more. It was hard to say."

"And your questioners never showed themselves during that time?" asked O'Connell. Sanchez shook his head by way of reply. "So you have no idea who it was that ordered this…," he struggled for the right word, "this inquisition?"

"Well, it's strange you should ask that. When the questioning came to an end the guards who had been standing against the wall all that time were ordered to release me from the chair and take me back to my quarters. As they did so, my inquisitors made the mistake of beginning to file out of the room. As they passed out of the door into the lighted corridor beyond, I was able to see some of their faces. Perhaps, in all, there were a dozen men. Some I only got the merest glimpse of while others wore hoods which were raised to cover their faces. But there were a few that I saw quite clearly. I didn't know or recognise them for the most part, not surprising when you consider the amount of people who live and work in this place. But there was one face that I did know immediately."

O'Connell looked at the old man expectantly. He knew that everything up until now had been to bring him to this point and he felt ready. However, he was wrong.

Sanchez watched closely as he said, "It was that of Monsignor Domineco Di Natele."

O'Connell wasn't sure what he had expected but it certainly wasn't to hear the name of the Chaplin of His Holiness, the Pope's right hand man. Sanchez concluded, "I knew then that I must either accept the instruction given to me or face the wrath of the Holy See, a wrath which you and I know only too well from the documents we read every day. I was too old to begin a fight like that. But I have lived in hope of finding someone who isn't." He looked up to try and read the expression on O'Connell's face. The young priest sat bewildered.

Sanchez said, "I hope in you, my friend, I may have found just such a voice."

CHAPTER 15

Huxley moved gingerly through the crowd of young men and women who were enjoying the various recreations on offer at the James Bond themed ball. Some of the revellers greeted him fondly or smiled in his direction but Huxley ignored them, the gun in his side focusing his attention and guaranteeing his compliance. Ahead of him, Sam and Alan provided a makeshift shield as they threaded their way towards the river bank as indicated by their captor who seemed perfectly at ease with the mechanics of the situation.

All around them the beautiful gardens of Queens' College had been overtaken by marquees and stalls providing entertainment for the hundreds of guests. On their right they passed a tent where a ceilidh band were striking up and the caller was busily giving instructions to the hapless dancers trying to follow her lead. To their left, some James Bond wannabes were taking aim on the shooting range that had been set up, the metallic targets appearing in a random sequence and presenting themselves seemingly frozen in a death or glory style charge for a few seconds before ducking back behind an obstacle. White jacketed waiters moved among the throng with trays of canapés and cocktails, dodging the increasingly boisterous carousers as the blend of gin, Benedictine and cherry brandy started to take effect.

Through it all their captor moved easily, indicating to his foe that they follow the pathway as it branched left towards the river and the famous Mathematical Bridge that spans the banks of the Cam and allows access to the far side and further land and buildings owned by the College.

The Mathematical Bridge was one of the most famous sights in Cambridge as Alan Donovan was all too aware. The barrage of questions he was asked while conducting punting tours bore testament to that. He had researched the basics about the bridge in order to answer these so he knew it was built in 1749 and is a wooden construction designed using tangent and radial trussing, hence the name. It was said to have been designed by Sir Isaac Newton while he was at the University and that his original design was completely self-supporting and required no nuts and bolts. Years later the fellows of the College took it apart and couldn't put it back together again so resorted to the use of nuts and bolts thus giving the bridge its current structure.

None of this, of course, was true, as he knew only too well, but it was a good story for the tourists who would take a punting tour along the river, the job helping to subsidise his meagre student grant and, although from a wealthy family, his father was of the opinion that Alan should experience Cambridge in much the same way as he himself had as a hard-up undergrad.

Alan would tell the story to those sitting in his punt as he propelled them towards the bridge, he standing on the flat platform at the end of the boat much like a gondolier, while they clicked and whirred with their cameras. Then, as he gave one last shove before ducking down himself to pass under the bridge, he would explain that this was just a myth as the bridge had been designed by William Etheridge and built by James Essex using driven iron spikes to hold it all together. And, he would add, with a pause for effect, Sir Isaac Newton had died in 1722, some twenty seven years before the bridge had been built. This always raised a laugh amongst those tourists who understood him well enough.

But he wasn't laughing now as the bridge came into view, he and Sam leading the way towards it. He turned to see the line of punts that were set along the bank beside the bridge, offering guests the opportunity of a romantic punt along the river, chauffeurs bedecked in candy striped jackets and boaters waiting to smoothly guide them down the gently flowing waters. As one of the candy stripers turned in expectation of his services being required he recognised Alan, the pair working for the same punting operator, and approached to greet him. He walked up the bank onto the path just in front of them and the man with the gun hesitated slightly as he considered what to do.

Huxley took the opportunity of the distraction to push the man off balance and then watched as he stumbled and fell face first onto the ground. The candy stripers standing by their punts a few yards away ran towards the prone figure to help him up and, as they did so, Huxley and Donovan shared a look as the same idea jumped into their head.

Alan headed straight for the nearest punt, leaping onto the platform and grabbing the pole that had been jammed into the river bed at an angle to hold the boat in place against the bank. As he did so, Huxley grabbed Sam's arm and guided her into the seats in the middle of the punt before joining her and sitting alongside. Alan pushed off and started punting them down the river and away from the commotion behind. From their seat Sam and Huxley could see the form of their captor standing on the river bank and looking at the fast disappearing boat as Donovan propelled them with the skill of an experienced punter, the gap between them growing all the time.

Had it not been for the theme of the party, the young man

in candy striped jacket and boater hat may have thought it unusual that his punt had been hijacked and would have been even more perplexed by the command from the bespectacled man in the drab grey suit. But, as it was a James Bond themed party, he simply chuckled to himself when the man shouted for him to 'follow that punt'. When the man produced a gun and pointed it at him and repeated the command, the candy striper, having seen plenty of guns throughout the evening, simply shrugged and guessed this was all part of the entertainment on offer. So he stepped onto the platform of the next punt and waited for the man to climb in before starting off in pursuit his friend.

By the time the pursuers had pushed off, Alan and his passengers were well ahead with a lead of a hundred yards and growing as he used the momentum built from his strokes to move them at an increasing pace. His fellow Scudamores compatriot, however, had a reputation to uphold, being considered the fastest punter on the river and began to close the gap, thinking himself part of a spectacle organised by the Ball committee and happy to fulfil his role within it. He thrust the pole down onto the river bed and pushed with as much strength as his rippling biceps would allow before twisting the pole and pulling it out of the water and plunging it into the river again beside him, allowing the pole to slide easily through his fingers in the practised manner that had earned him his reputation.

Huxley and Sam, sitting in the seat that allowed them to watch what was happening behind, could see the punt gaining, the fading light notwithstanding. They could, also, make out the figure of the man with the upside down face leaning as far forward as he could in his boat, kneeling down so that he was facing the way they were moving.

They both saw the man's right arm rising from his side and pointing towards them, his left being used to hold it steady,

The Judas Deception

and could just make out the shape of the pistol that he was now pointing at them. With their lead down to seventy yards now and the chasing punt gaining on them, they realised that they were sitting targets out here in the middle of the empty river. Huxley shouted a warning to Alan who, using the punting pole as a rudder, began to manoeuvre the boat closer to the bank on the near side of the river where the shadow was heavier.

They heard the shot long after the bullet had hit them at some nine hundred miles per hour and so it was with comic after-timing that all three of them jumped at the sound before seeing the bullet hole that had appeared in the seat just two inches from where Huxley was sitting. Huxley couldn't help but think afterwards how easy it would have been for Alan Donovan to have frozen at that point and thereby make them easy prey for their pursuer but, somewhat heroically, it actually prompted the young man into even more fervent action and he propelled them forward to a turn in the river that lay ahead. Huxley felt helpless as he watched the man behind level his gun at them once again knowing that his aim was only going to get better as he got used to the movement of the punt. But, before any further shot was made, the punt disappeared from sight as they made the turn. This put them out of the line of sight of the boat behind and gave them some respite from any further immediate attack but they knew that it was going to be short-lived as the enthusiastic chauffeur behind did his utmost to close the gap.

Huxley recognised that they probably had at best twenty seconds of a lead before the second punt would traverse the turn and, once again, they would be within range of their attacker.

He surveyed the scene around him, Alan continuing to move them along, hugging the near side bank which ran along the back of some of the most famous Colleges in the world.

They were passing King's College, the Chapel looking spectacular from the river, the spotlights used to illuminate it at night showing it off in all its magnificence as darkness began to take hold, but Huxley didn't have time to take in the splendour. Rather he was assessing their best option before the chasing boat brought the gunman within sight of them once again.

Ten seconds became fifteen and he knew that at any moment they would once again be exposed to the clutches of a man who had made it clear that he wanted to stop them any way he could. Huxley's heart started beating faster than ever before. There was a clear stretch of river ahead of them, at least another thirty seconds before they would be at the next turn, and until then they would be sitting ducks.

As the seconds counted down, Huxley desperately looked for a solution. He turned and saw the front of the boat behind come into view, its lone passenger hunched over the end, lookout and head gunner rolled into one. The only thing in their favour was the angle taken by the candy striper had the punt pointing towards the far bank and it would take him a couple of strokes to right it and bring them into line.

As Huxley was looking at the trajectory of the chasing boat he noticed the greenery on the far bank of the river. He turned to once again look ahead and saw the trees lining the far side, their branches overhanging the river. Huxley remembered that it was a fun practise of those normally punting to guide the boat towards the trees and thereby force the passengers to have to duck down below the branches. But now they would provide cover from their attacker if they could get under them. It also had the added advantage of taking them onto the tightest part of the next turn in the river thereby removing them from any sight lines all the quicker.

He spun round to face Alan, looking beyond him to see the progress of the boat behind, and instructed him to make for the far side. The river not being very wide, Donovan made it in two strokes, immediately taking them under the overhang of a tree just as the boat behind righted itself towards them.

Although a little hindered by the foliage, Donovan still kept up a pretty fast pace and his compatriot who, truth be told, was feeling the effects of a heavy May week, was beginning to slow, thereby widening the gap between the two. But still not far enough for Huxley's liking.

The gunman was sitting poised once again, trying to get a fix on his moving target. With the overhanging branches providing some natural shelter, he was finding it difficult to get a clear shot but he knew that they couldn't stay hidden forever. Huxley realised that the protective shrubbery was running out and they would soon be exposed. He looked at Sam and could see her mind racing through their limited options. With the next turn near, Donovan began to steer their boat at an angle which took it away from their pursuer and here he pressed home his advantage and accelerated, adrenaline fuelling his progress. Huxley knew that their lead was fleeting and now was their best hope of escape.

"Have any of you tried bridge hopping in your time?"

It seemed an odd question to ask given that they weren't out for a pleasant night time cruise down the river but Sam could see the wheels in motion in Huxley's head so guessed there was a purpose to the question.

"Once or twice in my younger days," she replied.

"Of course," said Alan, "all the time."

They were referring to the practice of approaching a bridge whilst punting down the river and giving the punt a huge shove to propel it under the bridge whilst jumping from it onto the bank, scrambling up the bank, climbing onto the bridge, running across and then back down the other side to join the still moving boat. Huxley looked ahead and saw Garret Hostel

Bridge in front. They would be upon it within seconds and he was hoping that they could launch their punt to sail beyond it while they themselves would be on the bridge with no intention of re-joining it. If they could move out of sight before the other boat made it around the turn then it may be a minute or more before their hunter realised what they had done.

"Ok then, I think it's time to practice our bridge hopping skills and get into the shelter of Garret Hostel Lane before our friend even knows what is happening."

Donovan got them as close to the edge as he could, the bridge only a few feet away now and Sam made the leap onto the bank without any problem, Huxley following behind. Just as the front of the boat started under the bridge, Alan gave it one final almighty push and jumped for the bank but, as he pushed on the pole, a surge of pain pulsed through his arm from his earlier injury.

Up to now, adrenaline had masked his discomfort but now the agony hit him as he tried to make the jump and he missed his footing, landing short of the bank. He was still clutching the pole and used this to prevent him from hitting the water immediately, hugging himself around the slender frame as he tried to negotiate the final couple of feet to get him to the bank.

Huxley stretched across from the bank to try and reach his hand but Alan's injury prevented him from stretching to grasp the helping hand and he slid down into the water.

Sam and Huxley crouched over the edge of the bank to help the boy ashore, both aware that their time was running out. His clothes were soaked through and he was shivering violently.

With no time to waste, Huxley ushered them ahead to scramble up the embankment towards the bridge above while he grabbed the pole before pulling it out of the river towards

The Judas Deception

him and discarding it amongst the undergrowth by the side. He followed the others and joined them as they climbed over the edge of the bridge, Sam thankful, not for the first time that evening, at her decision to wear trousers. Huxley looked down at the river just as the chasing punt came into view. They were at the far side of the bridge and visible to anyone on the river, the ornate decoration of the bridge offering limited protection, the gaps in the stonework big enough for a hand to pass through. Or a bullet.

The hunched figure on the boat below saw them as they ran across the bridge to the shelter of the Jerwood Library on the far side. He instinctively fired, the bullets screaming off the stone spheres which adorn the top of the bridge. The three ducked low as they climbed up the steep hump-back slope that made the bridge such a difficult passage for cyclists crossing over.

As they reached the apex they were dangerously exposed, their only advantage being the ever darkening sky, and Huxley urged them to stay low and head for the safety of the alleyway in front. He stopped and ushered the other two ahead of him, Donovan looking a sorry figure in his drenched clothing with Sam guiding him by his good arm.

Huxley looked back into the gloom and, as he did so, saw the gunman shift his weight forward to take aim, Huxley right in his sights and caught in no man's land. Having missed with five shots already he was down to his last bullet and intended to make it count. He fired.

CHAPTER 15

Rome – 1970

O'Connell returned to his quarters after his latest twilight discussion with the priest from Mexico, his head spinning. Everything they had spoken about previously had been leading to this point. Could the Church really be hiding secrets so inflammatory that they would even threaten their own priests? Thinking about all that he had read, he knew only too well that they could. But what was he prepared to do about it? What could he do?

Sanchez had told him to think about everything they had discussed and, if he decided that he needed to know more, to meet again the following evening. He knew that sleep was pointless. Sitting on the edge of his bed he did the only thing he had ever known to do when faced with difficult decisions. He prayed.

The following day passed so slowly. Sitting at his desk he stole surreptitious glances at Father Sanchez but the old priest sat, as ever, hunched over his work, seemingly oblivious to all around him. Steadily, one by one, his co-workers began to leave their posts for the day and O'Connell considered for the briefest of moments of going with them. After all, wouldn't that be the easiest thing to do? This was his whole life, the only life he knew. He had never lived in the real world. His whole adult life had been a sheltered affair from home to seminary to here in the Vatican and yet now he was questioning the values that had been instilled in him by all those he had trusted. Was he really prepared to leave this behind and go it on his own? But in his heart he knew that he couldn't carry on living a lie and that there was only one choice to make. He had to do it.

Eventually, once they were alone, his friend turned to him and said, "So, you decided to stay?" The intonation made it a question, almost as though offering O'Connell one last chance of escape. For Sanchez knew that this was the point of no return.

"I've come this far. I guess it would be foolish not to hear what you have to tell me."

"This, my friend, is where it gets exciting."

"I'm not sure that your definition of excitement is the same as mine."

O'Connell was trying to adopt a relaxed manner but inside his stomach was churning. What was he doing? His world was about to be turned upside down. Was he really prepared to give this up because some foolish old priest had whispered a few sweet-nothings to him? But he knew that Sanchez had never cajoled him into anything and that he was there because he wanted to discover the truth.

Sanchez watched his student. "I trust you, James. I trust you with everything that is in my heart. Because I know that your heart is pure and that you long for your soul to be cleansed. What I will tell you tonight will put you in grave danger but I know that you are ready for this."

It was the first time that the old man had used O'Connell's name and he found it rather comforting. It made him feel that Sanchez had personally selected him for this task, this crusade even.

"The document I was working on when I received my

warning related to one of the Gnostic gospels," Sanchez continued. "It was a simple text which stated that the betrayal of Jesus was an act of revenge by Judas, a malicious deed borne out of jealousy."

"Well, I suppose that is one interpretation that could be applied," O'Connell responded.

"Indeed. It is not the first time that I have read such a commentary. But this particular text was not one of the great historians from the fifteenth or sixteenth century who we know capable of such wild accusations. Rather the document in question dated back to the time that the gospel in question had been written."

"That is interesting," commented O'Connell. He knew from experience that such documents were normally much more factual rather than speculative. "Which gospel did it refer to?"

"This is where it gets difficult. It is that of Judas himself."

"Ah, well, that does present quite a problem. How can you reference a gospel that doesn't exist?"

"Exactly. But I had to try, you understand. I focused my search on those trusted writers who have spent their time analysing the Gnostics and determining why they were excluded from the bible. Although the Gospel of Judas has never been found, there are some references to it which have been used to determine its content over the years."

"And what did you find?"

"Nothing. That was the problem. I came to a dead end."

"Oh." O'Connell felt a bit deflated. Was that it? This endless build up and a story about a midnight abduction all because he had looked up a reference to a long forgotten gospel.

"Until, that is, I discovered a book that I had never seen before. It was quite a recent publication, well recent by our standards at least," he laughed. "Perhaps sometime in the last twenty years or so."

"That is positively brand new for us," chuckled O'Connell. "What did it say?"

"The author claimed that the Gospel of Judas Iscariot was not lost. He said that it was, in fact, hidden." Sanchez looked up to see what effect his words were having on the young priest beside him.

"I don't understand," said O'Connell bemused. "What's the difference?"

"Well, you see, he says that the original document was discovered by the Church quite some time ago and deliberately hidden away because the material within it was so inflammatory."

"That's just the sort of nonsense that those who oppose us make up all the time. Really, Father, I can't believe that we are having this conversation."

"Do you trust me, James? Do you trust me as I trust you?"

"Of course I do but you know..." He didn't finish his sentence as Sanchez lifted his hand in appeal for him to stop.

"I thought exactly the same thing at first. In fact, I wasn't even going to bother reading any further. But I wanted to see how he had arrived at this conclusion so I signed the book out of the archive. That was my first mistake. It would appear that it was this action that brought me to the attention of my cardinal."

"You mean when you were told to stop your line of research?"

"Yes, but not immediately. However, when I began to look for documents that were mentioned in this book, that's when I was told to stop. But I was fascinated by what had been written and I wanted to find out more."

"So you continued trying to find these other documents?"

"Indeed I did and that's when I had my little visit in the middle of the night. After that I was too afraid to search anymore. At least, I was too afraid to look inside the Vatican. But outside, that was a different matter."

"What do you mean?"

"I took a long overdue vacation. A trip away from here to refresh myself so I told my superiors. Oh, I didn't do it immediately afterwards, nothing so foolish. I went back to my work and my routine and allowed myself to drop off their radar. But after almost a year I decided to go and visit this author myself."

"You did? How on earth did you manage that?"

"It really wasn't that difficult. There was a note about the author in his book saying that he was a lecturer at Cambridge. So I took a trip to England in order to find him."

Sanchez described his visit, first going to London and registering at a hotel just in case anyone took an interest in his movements. Then spending his days visiting the many museums and galleries the city had to offer. Only once he felt that he had established a cover for himself did he feel brave enough to jump on a train to Cambridge. It was here that he met Spencer Harris.

"Spencer contends that there is a cache of documents that are so dangerous to the Church that they keep them hidden away. Only those with the highest authority can ever see them."

"What documents? Where? In here?" O'Connell gestured at the chambers around him, his enthusiasm for the tale growing.

"Alas, these are questions I cannot answer, my friend. At least not adequately enough. For that you need to speak to the man himself."

Sanchez explained that since their initial meeting he had been in secret correspondence with Spencer Harris. "There is a hotel in Rome, the concierge is a friend of my brother, a man who can be trusted. I visit every week for coffee and he tells me tales of home. I pass him an envelope addressed to my family. He then puts it in a different envelope and sends it to Spencer. It is a neat arrangement and one that necessarily bypasses the Vatican's own postal service."

"This sounds like a lot of subterfuge for something so negligible. I mean, this is just pure speculation."

"Perhaps so, but I already ruffled feathers just by looking for a few documents. Can you imagine what would happen if anyone found out that I was questioning the exactitude of the Church?"

O'Connell considered this and wondered where it was all leading to. "So, what do we do now?"

"We, my friend, do not do anything. I am too old and weak to be of any more use to Spencer. But I promised him that I would watch for someone of good character, someone fed up with the corruption he saw unfold in the name of Christ, someone with the zeal and passion and strength of character to change. That is why I have told him about you. The question is, are you ready to meet with him?"

CHAPTER 16

In moving his weight forward to set himself for the shot, the grey suited gunman had upset the balance of the punt and the boater clad figure at the back was caught off balance mid-stroke. He tried to recover his stance but, in reaching for the pole, completely lost his footing and fell into the water, knocking the punt towards the bank as he did so. The gun, which had been pointed directly at Huxley, was thrown off course just as the bullet was fired and, as Huxley made a dive down the steep descent of the humpback bridge, he heard it whistle above him and strike the perimeter wall of Trinity College beyond.

Huxley shook off the fear that had caused him to stand like a deer in the headlights and, instead, used the surge of adrenaline that coursed through him to take charge of the situation. He would later shiver when he considered just how close he had come to being shot but for now he realised they had to move quickly before their marooned attacker managed to get to the bank and follow them.

The three ran as fast as they could down the lane between the two old Colleges and headed for what they hoped would be the relative safety of the hustle and bustle of King's Parade where their collaboration had begun earlier that evening.

Huxley still thought their best course of action was to

get out of the city altogether and the safe haven of a quiet, anonymous house in Grantchester appealed to him even more now. The drenched figure of Alan Donovan made this all the more urgent and Huxley led them back towards the University Centre, the thought of commandeering a university van the only course of action he could see open to them.

They hurried along the street which was busy with revellers as the city's nightlife began to take hold. As their progress became hampered by the crowds, Sam leaned in close beside him, taking his arm as though they were lovers out for a stroll, and whispered in his ear.

"I'm worried about, Alan. We need to get him out of those clothes as quickly as possible and get that arm checked out."

"My thoughts exactly. But we can't let him go back to his room, not with the police looking for him and now these deranged killers seemingly chasing after him."

"You think he's the target?"

"I think that we're all targets but have no idea why. So I can't say if the two of us are simply collateral damage or whether it's all of us that are in danger because they think we know something. Either way I don't want us to be hanging around here for any longer than we have to and that means not going back to his rooms to allow him to change."

"I think the best thing that we can do now is go straight to the police, don't you?" she asked.

"Normally I would agree with you but, while we're target practice for persons unknown, I'm inclined to keep a low profile. And I don't think he'd go meekly if we tried to bring him in." He offered a thumb over his shoulder to indicate the slouching figure behind.

"So you're still hell bent on going to your safe house in Grantchester?"

"Until we have a better idea what's happening, I think it would be sensible for us to rest up somewhere quiet, so yes."

"And you really don't think anyone will know to look for us there?"

"My main concern is getting us there in one piece. Once we're there I'll tell you all about it. For now I'm just asking you to trust me. Okay?"

"Okay. But will there at least be clothes that boy wonder can change into?"

"Clothes, blankets, towels, a nice hot shower. There's even a first-aid kit if you fancy having a look at his wound. And brandy."

"Well why didn't you say so sooner, what are we waiting for?" She grinned as she delivered this.

Donovan followed the pair, unable to hear their whispered exchange but knowing that they were talking about him. He was freezing from where he had fallen in the river and wanted to get changed out of his wet clothes as soon as he could. But he was also relieved that his practice of keeping his valuables in a waterproof plastic bag in his pocket had proved to be worthwhile.

It was a trick he had learnt when he had started doing punting tours, the old hands telling him that, no matter how good he was, he would end up in the water sooner or later and that he should always protect his valuables. It had just become second nature to him, after that, to keep his phone, wallet and keys in a waterproof plastic bag no matter where he was going because, in Cambridge, you never knew when you would end up on the river.

He checked his phone as he plodded along behind and found it intact. Glancing up to see the two still arm in arm and engaged in their conversation, he took the phone out of the bag and typed a short text message which he then sent

The Judas Deception

before placing the phone back in the bag and returning it to his pocket.

As they neared the University Centre, down the same alleyway where the silhouetted gunman had spooked them earlier, Huxley fished for his keys to open up the depot. But as he bent to grab the padlock he found that it had been smashed open by someone already. Fearing another trap, Huxley backed away from the gates, motioning for the others to follow.

They ducked back into the shelter of the alleyway. Huxley explained what he'd seen.

"It could be student high jinx but…." He let that hang.

"So what do we do now?" asked Sam.

"My vote is not to walk into what could be a trap given what has just happened to us."

"Agreed."

"So, with Grantchester being our best option, I think we need to find another way there."

"We could always punt," suggested Alan, his teeth chattering with cold as his clothing stuck to him.

"Except for one small problem. We don't have a punt."

"But I can get one," replied Alan.

"Where from?"

"Over there," he said, pointing in the direction of the large boathouse that was the headquarters of Scudamores, the main punt operators on the river. "I work there and have the key to the locks they use to tie up the punts."

The river Cam runs right through the city but by the Anchor the river splits, part of it running into a mill pond that carries on round the back of Darwin College before coming to an end by The Granta, another riverside pub. The other part then carries on towards Grantchester but can only be reached via a lock as the river is raised above the level of the mill pond.

It is here that students, determined to head away from the

city for an afternoon of peace and quiet, can be seen hauling the heavy wooden, flat bottomed boats up the rolling tumblers of the lock to get to the next part of the river. Scudamores had very sensibly sited their boat house so that it covered both the upper and lower reaches, allowing those less energetic or in a hurry to simply hire a punt from the upper reaches.

Knowing this, Alan Donovan headed straight for the upper level of the boat house and used his master key to unlock the end punt which was chained to those alongside. Huxley helped Sam climb into the punt and take a seat before turning to do likewise for Donovan.

"What are you doing?" asked Donovan as he reached for the long wooden punting pole that he had already demonstrated his expertise with in using it as both propeller and rudder.

"You're cold, wet and injured and punting us is only going to cause more damage to the wound."

"I'll be fine and anyway, I do this as a job so I'll be much quicker than you."

"Don't be so sure. I did my share of summer jobs in my student days, including the whole punting thing, so climb aboard, sit back and enjoy the ride."

Donovan could tell this was an argument that he wasn't going to win so climbed in and took a seat opposite Sam as Huxley mounted the flat wooden panel at the back of the punt from which the boat was piloted.

Huxley expertly gripped the pole and used it to push them off from the wooden walkway to which the punts were chained, then smoothly and effortlessly allowed it to the slip through his fingers and down into the river where it touched the bottom before grasping it and pushing against it to drive them off. As he did so, he twisted the pole and pulled it back towards him, repeating the action a couple of times before angling the pole into the water and using it to steer towards the middle of the river.

"Nicely done, Daniel," said Sam appreciatively.

Huxley was glad that the darkening sky did not afford enough light to show the blush of pride he was now displaying. He hadn't realised until now just how much her good opinion meant to him.

A man of achievement and accomplishment, Daniel Huxley had been naturally good at almost everything he had ever set his mind to throughout his life. A gifted scholar, he had been offered a place at Cambridge when he was just sixteen but chose to defer for another year fearing he would be too young to appreciate college life.

Once there, in the hallowed environs of Trinity College, the richest if not the oldest of the Colleges, his natural abilities were nurtured and his brilliance started to shine for all to see. And it was archeology that captured his heart as he began to learn the secrets of ancient cultures and civilisations through the texts, documents, dwellings and artefacts that they left behind.

By the time he had completed his thesis on the Gnostic gospels he was already regarded as one of the foremost experts in his field and his doctorate on the Gospel of Judas Iscariot propelled him into the upper echelons of academia.

Offers from all over the world flooded his inbox but his heart belonged to Cambridge and his home was Trinity College. It was here that he had left behind the awkward, cautious young boy from Waterford and developed into the man who would become the youngest Vice-Chancellor in the eight hundred year history of the University.

And it wasn't only his academic achievements that brought him pre-eminence as it turned out he was no slouch in the sporting arena as well, representing the college at football, cricket and rugby as well as being part of their most successful men's eight for years which saw them crowned Head of the River for the first time in their history.

This honour befell the winner of the famous Cambridge bumps which took place in early June each year. The River Cam is mostly narrow as it runs through the city, and there is not enough room for rowing boats to race side by side. So the authorities came up with a different style of racing to allow for serious competition between the colleges. This involves the boats lining up one behind the other over a certain stretch of the river, the objective being to catch the boat in front and 'bump' it. In reality this means the boat in front conceding that they have been caught with either the cox in the boat or the coach by the side acknowledging that they have been bumped. However, there are times when a particularly obstreperous coach or cox might refuse to concede so the chasing party have no choice but to ram into the boat to let them know that they have, indeed, been bumped. Crowds of people line the river banks throughout the week of the races and Pimms is drunk by the jug full throughout as they cheer the passing boats, the adorning of greenery from the bushes and shrubs along the river bank indicating the victorious rowers.

Huxley had been part of the crew that had started the week in seventh position in the men's' first division but who, by the end of the week had successfully made their way up to the rankings as they dramatically rowed down the last boat in front of them on the final day to become the Head of the River.

It was a different stretch of the river to where they were now, but Huxley's love affair with all things Cambridge had grown that day and he loved being on the river any time he could. The success of the rowers had seen three of them, Huxley included, called up to the university crew for the annual battle with Oxford that took place on the Thames each

The Judas Deception

year in early spring. It had meant five o'clock starts and hours of training every day for eight months but to be selected was an honour. And those early mornings paid off when he was chosen to represent Cambridge in the most famous boat race in the world and was part of the winning crew in the 1995 race.

Here on the punt they were going at a much more sedate pace, given the mode of transport, but Huxley was conscious that they still had a lot to think about and discuss and wanted to get under cover as soon as possible, so he was propelling them along as fast as he could. It was as they passed under the bridge at Coe Fen that they heard something from up ahead and sensed rather than saw movement. Huxley slowed the punt to listen more carefully and soon made out the familiar sounds of drunken revellers.

"I think there's a boat load of Champagne Charlies heading towards us," he said, referring to the richer students who liked to go on midnight picnic punts with some fine food and champagne.

On guard after the fire and aware that someone was now taking more of an interest in them than he would like, Huxley was wary about being seen so he decided to steer the punt over towards the bank.

"What are you doing?" Although Sam's senses were also on high alert, her main thought was to get to a safe place as soon as possible and being on the river on the outskirts of Cambridge in the middle of the night with god knows who chasing them didn't strike her as the safest of places to be stopping to take in the scenery.

"I just want to let the others pass. I think it would be better, for the time being, if no-one saw us."

"So, what are we going to do? Get out and hide in the bushes until they pass?" There was an element of sarcasm in her comment and Huxley, once again, noted the feistiness of the woman coming to the fore. She clearly didn't think that stopping on the river and playing hide and seek with a boat full of drunk students was the right thing to do and she was letting him know by her tone.

"Well, when you put it like that, then, no. But I would suggest that..."

Alan suddenly sprang up from his seat and leapt up onto the bank. He had started to feel extremely nauseous during the ride up the river and now that the punt was alongside the river bank, he took advantage of the proximity of the bushes to be sick.

Sam quickly followed him while Huxley, secured the boat in place before he too made his way up onto the river bank.

He found Donovan hunched over, retching as his body reacted to the confusion in his mind. Sam was standing over him, a hand on his back to reassure him.

"I think shock may have set in," she said to Huxley, her voice low.

"What should we do?"

"I don't know. Perhaps we're making a mistake trying to get away from everyone. Maybe we need to go to the police now and tell them what has happened to us and get Alan some medical attention."

"But the police have him pegged for murder and me as an accomplice and the first thing they'll do is put him in a room for questioning. I don't think he's in any fit state to do that now. Besides which, we have someone trying to kill us, so they patently don't like the fact that there is a possible witness to the murder or, in fact, that there are people snooping around in their business."

Just then there was a noise from the river and the three froze in terror as the events of the last couple of hours hit them and they wondered what new threat had now found them.

CHAPTER 17

ROME – 1970

Sanchez had it all worked out. O'Connell would go for coffee on Saturday to the hotel where his friend worked. There he would be given a note with instructions on where to go and how to get there. He was to follow them exactly.

And so here he was sitting on the Spanish Steps surrounded by hundreds of tourists having just spent the best part of an hour seemingly walking in circles as he followed the directions given. Unsure of what to do now, he looked around him, aimlessly watching visitors to the famous monument bedecked in the standard uniform of shorts and t-shirt to combat the beating sun. He, of course, was dressed in his full black vestment and was slowly melting away in spite of sitting in what little shade was on offer. So distracted by the view, he was startled when someone approached him from behind and spoke.

"Sorry for all the cloak and dagger stuff, old boy. Force of habit I'm afraid. Too many enemies if you know what I mean. English alright for you? I only ask as I know some of you Irishmen are quite particular about your Gaelic. Less colonial. Happy to use it if it helps although I do find it a somewhat limited language. Harris is the name, dear boy, but you should call me Spencer. All my friends do and I do so hope that we will be friends." He grasped the young priest by the hand.

O'Connell wasn't sure what he had been expecting, the image in his mind somewhat blurred based only on Sanchez's ambiguous and dated description. Later he would find it difficult to recall because the reality was so overpowering but he had a vague recollection of expecting someone old and wizened and, for some reason, slight.

The truth was the man who stood beside him was the most larger than life character that he had ever met, although he recognised that his exposure to people had been somewhat limited throughout his life. Tall, much more so than O'Connell who himself stood five foot ten inches in stockinged feet, and with a girth to match, the man should have looked clumsy and ungainly but O'Connell felt that he moved like a ballet dancer as he reached out a chubby hand in greeting.

Dressed in a bright blue suit that was obviously made to measure, such was the precise cut of the jacket and the sharp crease in the trousers, he cut quite a dashing and youthful figure for a man who had been chasing manuscripts for as long as he had. The freshly shaven face bore traces of talcum powder, the scent of which permeated the young priest's nostrils and hinted at spring flowers that mingled delightfully with the oil he wore on his huge dark Buffon-styled hair that added another couple of inches to his tremendous height.

But it was the shine in the eyes that most captivated O'Connell, an intense knowledge of all that life had to offer escaping from them and drawing any onlooker in like a tractor beam.

"Let's get a proper look at you then, there's a good chap. My, my, aren't you a fine example of the species. Come, walk with me. I know this delightful little bistro does a fantastic asparagi alla Parmigiana." He started down the steps before O'Connell had the chance to say anything leaving the young Irishman with little option but to follow.

O'Connell had learned from Sanchez that this man had been part of the team that had uncovered the Dead Sea scrolls and that he had never stopped believing that there was something strange about their discovery. He alleged that it was a cover up to hide something potentially even more damaging and spent a large portion of his time telling anybody who would listen.

Viewing O'Connell as a fresh audience, he launched straight into his theory over antipasto of Prosciutto e melone leaving the young priest slightly bemused. But the food was divine, the wine crisp and chilled and the restaurant sufficiently cool for O'Connell to feel comfortable.

"Got a bit of a task for you, old boy, if you feel up to it. An initiation, let's call it." His throw away manner removed any insult from the word. "Have to wonder at a priest from the Vatican wanting to meet me, makes me wary, puts me on guard, no matter what that old bugger Sanchez has to say about you. What do you think?"

Up until that point, O'Connell had only been required to give monosyllabic answers and so was somewhat taken aback that he was now being asked to say something. He wasn't even sure what the question was. "Ammm, I guess that might be okay. I mean, I'm sure that you will find me up to any task you have in mind."

"Jolly good. Rather simple actually. I want you to steal something."

"You want me to what?"

"Steal something. From the Vatican."

"But I'm a priest, for pity's sake. I can't go around stealing things."

To say that the young Irishman thought him to be the craziest person that he had ever met was an understatement but it was obvious from the casual air and tone of the request that this was, to Spencer Harris, a perfectly normal thing to ask a near total stranger to do, priest or not. Rules were for other people and Spencer believed in doing what he wanted when he wanted.

"Why ever not? Considering the lies that your sort peddle every day all in the name of profit. That's profit with an 'f'. Fish on Friday? What a racket. Bloody fish and chip shops springing up from Harrow to the Hebrides and back again all thanks to that nonsense."

"But it's a sin."

"My good man, if we all stopped doing things because they are a sin then we might as well go off and live in a fucking monastery."

"Well, I already do."

"Yes, but you want out of the game from what I hear."

For the first time in their conversation O'Connell felt himself scrutinized and he realised that behind all that bluster lay a very shrewd mind. "Yes, well, perhaps I do. But I haven't made a firm decision about that yet. And stealing?"

"It's nothing sacred, don't worry. You won't go to hell for it. Simple thing really. See if you're actually up for the fight. Show of faith, if you will. Don't want to be standing here with my pants down round my ankles only for you to go running of to report me to the head boy."

"What is it you want me to steal?" O'Connell said, surprising himself with how easily he had caved. He was fascinated by this character in front of him and felt elated to be part of the whirlwind that being in his presence entailed.

The reply when it came was wrapped in a smile and O'Connell was enveloped within its warmth as he heard the words that hung upon it. "Nothing of any significance. Just an official Vatican seal, nothing more. A simple and, dare I say, mediocre act of treachery for one as capable as you. You can do that, can't you? Have access, all that? Not a problem for you, is it?"

O'Connell shook his head in response. He wanted to express reticence, to stand his ground and say that it was one thing to be interested and intrigued by what lay on the other side of this door but it was quite another to betray his principles and the commandments by which he lived his life. In reality he could but smile at the cheek of the request and the manner in which it had been delivered. But, even in spite of the charm of the man and the promise of unknown riches of information that might be gained from befriending him, he still managed to maintain some dignity and asked for time to consider Spencer's proposal.

"Expect nothing less of you, dear boy. Would be disappointed if you didn't need time to consider. Three days, then. I'll give you three days. Follow the same pattern with the hotel and the directions and I'll come and meet you again. If you don't show then I'll take it that you are out. No hard feelings and all that. Hell, even if you decide it's a no, turn up anyway and I'll show you the bits of Rome that the Church don't want you to know about." He finished with a raucous laugh that reverberated in the small restaurant, a twinkle in his eye that was full of mischief but in a most loveable way.

All too soon the meal was over and O'Connell was on his way back to the Vatican already wondering just how he was going to undertake the task set for him. For he knew even then that he would do just about anything to please Spencer Harris within whose presence he felt alive. Perhaps for the first time in his life.

Spencer had advised that, if he did want to be involved, then he had better book some leave as the next part of the plan would take them on their travels. Excited by the prospect, O'Connell arranged to take a sabbatical from his duties, begging fatigue and a need to recharge his batteries. He said he wanted to travel for a while and perhaps write a book. His cardinal was only too happy to agree, the young priest never having missed a day of work in the whole five years he had been at the Vatican. He would miss the hard work and application that the young man put into his duties and wished that some of the others would show a similar commitment, but he was delighted that Father O'Connell was going to take some time for himself. Burn out was always a problem with priests and it served them well to take some time off occasionally.

For his part, O'Connell was blessed with a generous salary which he rarely had any need to spend, everything he required provided for him within the sanctuary of the holy city. So money wasn't a concern and, with his cover story in place, he felt ready to execute the next part of his plan.

The night before he was due to meet Spencer again, he found sleep impossible to come by. He spent most of the night tossing and turning before rising early in the morning, excitement mixed with nervous energy making any thought of breakfast a definite no. He went for a walk through the streets of Rome just to occupy his mind before returning mid-morning to the Vatican. Having counted the minutes he was no longer able to contain himself and made his way down to his normal area of work for one last time.

As part of his job, from time to time, he needed to write official letters to request information or documents from institutions so he had used an official seal before and knew where there was one kept in the area that he worked. The problem was that it was with the cardinal in charge of the section and he would have to gain access to the drawers of his desk to get it.

O'Connell entered the section to find most of his colleagues already in place and announced to them that he had come to say his goodbyes before he set off on his voyage. Most

The Judas Deception

of the priests approached him to wish him well, chattering excitedly about the adventures he would have. Their elation seemed disproportionate to O'Connell and he realised what a lonely existence it all is, so easy to remain blind to this until someone or something breaks the routine. He happened to be the one that was going off into the big, bad world and everyone wanted to be a part of his journey if only in spirit. O'Connell found it amusing that his good friend Father Sanchez remained crouched at his desk the whole time, not showing any interest in the commotion, playing his part right to the end. Finally, the head of the section came over to wish his young charge well.

"Actually, sir, before I go, there is maybe something you can help me with." O'Connell spoke in his near perfect Italian, the native tongue of his cardinal.

"I will do whatever I can within my powers to help you, Father. All you have to do is ask."

"I intend to start my journey following in the footsteps of St Francis of Assisi and I know that you are quite the expert in this area. I was wondering if you could point me in the direction of a book I could use as a guide." He was counting on the cardinal's vanity, the man having produced a book of his own specifically about the life of St Francis.

Excitedly, the cardinal told him he had just the thing. "Wait here, I'll go and get it right now. Don't go away."

This was much easier than expected, he thought, having anticipated that he might have to cajole the cardinal into fetching a copy for him. But instead, with his boss doing his bidding unprompted, O'Connell simply walked over to the workstation and, under the guise of tying his shoelace, grabbed the keys from the desk and opened the drawer below. His heart was beating out of his chest and he was finding it difficult to breathe but he somehow managed to act casually while he reached inside the drawer, rising to a standing position as he did so. Spying the seal, he pocketed it together with a strip of wax which is mixed specially for the Vatican.

By the time the Cardinal returned with the book the Irishman was standing idly by the entrance to the section waiting for him, thanking him profusely as he took the book and walked out the door. When his bos noticed it was missing and whether he ever suspected O'Connell, was not something that the young priest ever worried about as he walked out of the Vatican that day feeling free for the first time in his life.

He turned to look at the ancient stone walls that marked the boundary of the smallest recognised country on earth thinking that this might be that last time he ever saw it. But he was wrong and the next time he wouldn't find it so easy to leave.

CHAPTER 18

As they huddled behind an insubstantial bush listening to the hushed whispers carried to them on the clear night air from the river beyond, Huxley realised what was happening and ran out from cover and back towards the river bank.

He arrived in time to see three tuxedo clad young men preparing to jump from the punt they had been travelling on into Huxley's boat, much to the amusement of their remaining passengers. Huxley's immediate reaction was that this was another attempt to attack them but then, seeing that those left in the other boat were three scantily clad females, he realised that his was just some high jinx as the boys showed off to their respective partners, probably with the intention of letting the punt loose from its tenuous mooring to float free in the river.

"What the hell do you think you're doing," demanded Huxley in his most authoritative tone, startling the three just as they made the jump towards the moored punt. Two of the would-be pirates made it but the third slipped as he hesitated in his jump and fell into the river. In the commotion that followed his two compatriots, caught red handed, were torn between helping their friend out of the water and getting back into their own boat to try and flee the angry figure shouting at them from above.

Their misery was compounded as one of the girls looked

up and, seeing who it was that had confronted them, whispered a little too loudly, "Oh shit, it's Huxley," then, realising that she could be heard added rather sheepishly, "Hi, Professor Huxley."

Huxley was used to being recognised throughout the city given his position so it came as no surprise that someone had identified him here, the moon providing ample light on such a clear night. Famed for his memory and ability to recall names and faces with ease, it was no real feat for Huxley to distinguish from the voice just who was guilty of the expletive, especially as he was responsible for teaching her.

"Good evening, Sally. Are you having fun?"

"Sorry Professor, we were only having a laugh," her Liverpudlian accent bouncing off every syllable.

"It wouldn't have been so funny for me to arrive back here to find my punt gone, now would it?"

"No, sir." This came as a series of mumbles from all of the interlopers who, realising that they had just try to steal the punt of the Vice-Chancellor of the university, were feeling a bit sorry for themselves. What they didn't realise was that Huxley was in no mood to engage them in any sort of conversation so thoughts of taking their details for further disciplinary action was the furthest thing from his mind.

"Right, I suggest you help your friend out of the river before he either freezes to death or catches something nasty and then get yourselves home for the night. I'm sure the porter of whatever college you've taken the punt from will rest easier when he knows it's back in one piece."

"Yes, Professor. We'll go now and take it straight back, I promise."

"I'm holding you to that, Sally, and I'll be checking with you on Monday, do you hear?"

"Yes, sir." This again came not only from Sally but from

The Judas Deception

the rest of the gathering who, by now, were all back in their own punt including one very sodden young man.

Huxley watched as one of the girls got up on the platform and took over the punting duties and thought about how the age of chivalry was very much gone. He stood watching as they negotiated their away back towards town and then, once they were out of sight, he returned to see what was happening with Alan and Sam.

He found them both waiting for him out of sight of the river, Donovan looking a little better.

"How are you feeling?" asked Huxley.

"I'm fine, thanks, Professor, don't be worrying about me. I think it was just all a bit much and it got to me."

"I'd be surprised if it didn't." He glanced at Sam who was standing behind Alan and she gave a slight shake of her head indicating that she was still worried about the young man's health and state of mind.

"I think it might be best for us all if we get to Grantchester and get indoors as soon as possible," she said. "Nice and balmy as it is on this lovely summer night, I think it's going to get a lot colder very quickly and it's not going to do any of us any good to be out in the open, especially in wet clothes."

"Yes, and maybe a shot of brandy to help steady our nerves," added Huxley.

"Good idea. Let's get back on our way."

They made their way back into the boat and Huxley, once again, took on the punting duties, this time giving it all he had and propelling the boat along at quite a good pace. The trip to Grantchester was one that was normally done over a leisurely hour but Huxley was there within half that and found a suitable place to moor.

"Okay, where to?" asked Sam as they stepped up onto the bank and began to walk towards the centre of the village.

It is said that Grantchester has the highest concentration of Nobel Prize winners living within it. As a small village some four miles south of Cambridge, it serves as home to many of the academics working at the university along with the odd rock star and pulp fiction novelist. The houses are large and scarce, the residents wealthy and private, and the community small and close-guarded. The sort of place, thought Sam, where people wandering the streets at night stand out and strangers entering houses would be noticed.

She was wondering if this was, after all, the best place to hide out when Huxley stopped outside a large, two storey country house set back from the road, its driveway looping around to the front of the house where a battered Land Rover sat parked out of view until it was upon them.

It was certainly a house of substance and Sam was pondering just how much a house like this would cost when Huxley produced a key from his pocket and opened the front door.

They entered a dated hallway with rooms off either side of it, the doors open to reveal threadbare carpets and tired furniture that weren't quite antique but give it a few years. As old and fusty as it was, the house was surprisingly clean and had the air of being maintained if not exactly lived in. But the overwhelming feature about the house that could not be ignored was the sheer number of books. They were everywhere. In bookcases, on shelves, stacked one on top of the other from floor to ceiling, all shapes and sizes and genres.

Huxley pointed towards the stairs, which too were more book repositories than steps, and gave Donovan directions to the bathroom where he could shower and change.

"I'll leave some clothes outside," he added as the young man began to climb the stairway.

The remaining pair meandered their way through a

chicane of books to arrive in the kitchen where Huxley expertly retrieved glasses and a bottle of brandy with evident practice.

"So, what is this place?" asked Sam as she took the proffered glass from Huxley. "Surely not yours?"

"Is that your way of telling me that you think I'm too much of a neat freak to have a place as haphazard as this?"

"Actually, I suppose it is. I just can't picture you living like this." She indicated the hallway full of piles of books. "But more that you wouldn't be so dumb as to bring us somewhere that could be so easily traced by…well, whoever." This last was delivered rather ominously.

"I think you might be surprised by the number of dumb things that I am capable of doing. But, on this occasion, you're right. This little treasure trove is a property that is owned by a Trust managed by a society that I'm a member of. It belonged to an old don who bequeathed it with quite strict instructions as to how it could be used. The Trust never really found a proper use for it because of the restrictions and it just sat for years gathering dust. Until I discovered it, that is. Now it's become a bit of a refuge for me. I sometimes hide out here when I want some thinking time."

"And nobody knows that you come here," added Sam.

"That's the beauty of it. It's my secret sanctuary."

"So no-one would think of coming here if they were searching for you."

"No-one," confirmed Huxley.

They heard the shower overhead stop so Huxley led the way upstairs to one of the bedrooms where he began to fish in a closet which Sam hadn't even realised was there, so well hidden as it was behind yet more books. He threw a pair of jeans onto the bed before adding a t-shirt that said 'I do whatever my rice crispies tell me to!'.

She laughed as she read it and, pointing towards it, asked, "Is this yours?"

"Mmmm, one of my collection. I like to wear something a little frivolous underneath my formal shirts at work. Even though no-one can see it, at least I know it's there and it reminds me to never take things too seriously."

Adding some socks and underwear to the other items, Huxley handed them to Sam and said, "Give Alan a shout and tell him that there are some clothes for him outside the door when he is ready and give me a minute to change out of this tux and I'll meet you downstairs."

Having done as instructed, Sam made her way downstairs. She found herself drawn to the room beside the kitchen which looked as though it was used more often than the others. It appeared to be a library yet, bizarrely, it was the only room in the whole house that didn't have books strewn everywhere other than the shelves which lined the walls. The only relief from this was the strangely shaped picture window which looked out onto a rose garden shining in the moonlight which now lit the sky.

The window was like a large rectangle with the corners cut off giving it an almost ovoid shape with an unusual flourish at the top which reminded Sam of an old German soldier's helmet with the spike on top that was common during the First World War. It was unusual and she was trying to think if she'd ever seen any other windows shaped like that when Huxley came into the room now dressed in jeans and another of his t-shirts. This one read 'Atheism – A Non-Prophet Organisation'.

"Quite appropriate given your well documented views on the bible," she said, nodding towards his t-shirt.

"Just something to keep me sane in a world which is so steeped in tradition that getting anything done can be quite the chore." He smiled at her as he said it.

The Judas Deception

"So do the books come with the house or are they your contribution?"

"Most definitely with the house. One of the restrictions."

"What, not to get rid of them?"

"Not to move them."

"Really?"

"They can be used but the piles must remain where they are."

"How bizarre."

"Tell me about it. You can see why nobody has been able to do anything with the house over the years."

"Apart from you."

"Lucky break for us, though, eh?"

"Hold on, you said that it was in the hands of a society that you're a member of. What about the other members? Don't they know that you use this place? I mean, didn't you have to get their permission or put it to a vote or whatever?"

"Nope, it's not really that sort of organisation."

"So who is it?"

"The Rosicrucians."

"Aren't they a religious organisation? I wouldn't have placed you in something like that."

"Quite the opposite, in fact. We are an altruistic society dedicated to exposing the hypocrisy at the heart of the church and the lies perpetrated by people in the name of religion."

"But I thought they were regarded as the forerunner for Protestantism? Didn't I read that somewhere?"

"Probably in some inaccurate historical tome which claims that the Rosicrucians sided with Luther during the reformation. But, in fact, the only reason that this was seen as true was because the society was challenging the Catholic Church at the time, so were tarred with the same brush. But we had nothing to do with the Protestantism movement as we made our stance clear that there is no god but only the goodness of man which is what we promote."

"Sounds very philanthropic."

"Rosicrucianism is all about promoting the harmonious development of mind and heart and an all-embracing altruism. It's ….." Huxley watched as the smirk on Sam's face broke into a giggle that she couldn't supress.

Seeing the look on his face she stumbled out an apology. "I'm sorry, I didn't mean…"

"No, it's alright. This is why I don't go around shouting about my involvement with them. As soon as you mention an organisation like the Rosicrucians everyone immediately looks at you funny and judges you based on their preconceptions. There are some things about the association that I try not to take too seriously."

"So how did you end up joining them?"

"Well, because I was invited to join."

"That's it? They invite you so you say yes?"

"It's invitation only so I couldn't have joined any other way."

"I see. You're just trying to get me back for laughing at you and your precious society."

"You did ask how I joined." He gave her a grin and raised his eyebrows at her comically.

"Okay then, why did you join them if you don't really believe in all they stand for?"

"Well, just because I don't take the whole philosophy of the organisation too seriously doesn't mean that I don't appreciate what they are trying to achieve. Anyway, the most important aspect of their work is what attracted me towards them in the first place."

Taking her cue, Sam asked, "And what would that be?"

"Their belief that the religion and religious orders cherry pick what they think people should and shouldn't know and that they hide precious artefacts and documents from public view if they don't correspond with the image that they try to portray."

"Quite fortunate for you that that just happens to be your field of speciality."

"Hence my invitation to join. It's an area that I became very fascinated in when I was about Alan's age and I recognised that the great authorities on the subject were all closely linked. As I got deeper and deeper into my research I came into contact with them quite frequently and I could tell that they liked the direction that I was taking. Some of them made their work and libraries available to me. The man who lived here was one of them."

"Anyone that I should know? I only ask as I know that there have been many famous Rosicrucians over the years if rumours are to be believed."

"There have been and still are. It's not exactly a secret society as such but it tends to be something that is perceived quite negatively at times and overshadows the person or work that one is trying to promote. So it perhaps isn't something that members shout about hence its membership is clouded in rumour and inference. I can tell you that some of the great and good from the seventeenth century onwards have been members but I doubt that Spencer Harris would feature much on your radar unless you had a particular interest in the Dead Sea scrolls."

"That's who lived here?"

"Yes, this was his house. He was a fellow at Trinity and quite the authority on the Gnostics."

"Until you came along and usurped him."

"If I thought for a moment that my work was half as good as anything that he produced I would be a proud man."

"High praise indeed," replied Sam.

"He was a brilliant scholar. And quite the character, so they say."

Just then the pair heard Alan come back downstairs and Huxley called out to him. Alan followed the sound of the voice and entered the room moments later looking quite natty in the designer jeans and flippant t-shirt that Huxley had left for him. They were of a similar build but the t-shirt did look a little tight on him.

"Let me see now," began Huxley, looking him over, "not a bad fit at all. Comfortable enough?"

"The shoes are bit tight," Alan replied, looking down at the white trainers that Huxley had put with the clothes, "but nothing I can't put up with. Thanks ever so much for letting me use them. Whose are they?"

"They're mine and I'm just glad that they do fit you otherwise you would only have those wet things of yours to dress back into and that would not be pleasant."

"Well thank you, Professor. So this is your place? Isn't that, like, asking for trouble? Surely the police will be able to track us to here?"

"I've just been over this with Sam. You don't have to worry, it's not my place and no-one is going to be able to trace it back to me or even think that I would come here. It belonged to a friend of a friend who left it to him and a few others when he died. It is registered to the National Trust as an asset on their books but is not open to the public. It's just a way of keeping nosy people from finding out who uses it. Which suits our purposes perfectly tonight."

"Right, let's get that wet bandage off you and see how the arm is."

Sam reached over and gently undid the knot that held the tourniquet that was still in place on Alan's arm and lifted it up

The Judas Deception

to have a look. Turning to Huxley, she said, "You mentioned something about there being a first aid kit in the house."

"You'll find one in the bathroom."

She disappeared out of the room and they could hear her go upstairs before returning a minute later with a first aid kit in her hand.

"I need to clean that wound out and it's going to sting a bit so be prepared," she said, before applying a medicated wipe to Alan's cut which ran from just below his shoulder down to his elbow. He winced as the alcohol from the wipe burned at the open wound but held onto the drink that Huxley had poured for him, periodically sipping it to distract him from what Sam was doing. She got some gauze and covered the length of the wound with it before applying a tight bandage. Once finished, she said, "That should do for now although I really think that, the first opportunity you get, you ought to have it looked at by someone at the hospital and get yourself a tetanus jab."

"Thank you, Doct...., I mean, Sam. I feel much better, thanks, honestly I do. I think it's, well, everything that happened, I mean, it's just really hard to take in. Even now I can't quite get my head around the fact that someone tried to kill us. Twice in fact. That's what happened, isn't it? Someone deliberately set that building on fire knowing we were inside and trapped us in there and then tried to abduct us and shot at us."

"That's what it looks like, yes."

"But who? Why?"

"I wish I knew, Alan," replied Huxley, then, " think that's what we need to find out so maybe now is as good a time as any for you to start telling us the truth about exactly what is going on."

CHAPTER 19

ROME – 1970

When he arrived at the hotel to receive his instructions, O'Connell was rather taken aback when he read the note he was given.

> *Take a room here for a few nights. I will be in touch with you soon. Sorry for the delay but it can't be helped. Try the Cipolline all'agrodolce here, the best in Rome in my humble opinion.*

There was no signature but it was unmistakeably from Spencer. So O'Connell did as he was instructed, waiting patiently in his hotel room for a message, wax and seal kept in the breast pocket of his cassock which he still felt most comfortable in, it having been his normal mode of dress for the past ten years.

He was distracted, finding it hard to settle on anything and wished fretfully that he had some way to contact the enigmatic Englishman who had whet his appetite for adventure.

Three days passed, seemingly endless to the young priest, for he still thought of himself as such, as he wandered the streets of a city he had never truly seen before, his excursions outside of the sanctity of the Vatican limited to special

The Judas Deception

functions and the occasional stroll. He had never allowed himself to walk aimlessly round the spectacle that was Rome and tried desperately to enjoy the pace and buzz of the eternal city but found, instead, that he hoped only to chance upon the burly, well-dressed figure of Spencer Harris and find out more about their quest.

Counting down the minutes each night he would eventually fall into a fitful sleep and wake with a rush of excitement that perhaps there was a message waiting for him at that very moment at Reception. It was only on the third afternoon as he returned from a blurred walk, after a light lunch that he couldn't even recall, that the Concierge called him over and handed him an envelope which had arrived by courier an hour before.

O'Connell chastised himself for wasting a precious hour that could have been spent with Spencer but then opened the note to read a message telling him to be at La Buca di Ripetta at eight that evening. It was simply signed 'S'. He asked the Concierge for directions and was pointed towards Via di Ripetta in the heart of the city.

Like an anxious schoolgirl going to the prom, O'Connell found himself sitting on the edge of the bed in his hotel room at four o'clock already groomed and waiting for the clock to move inexorably round, minute by minute. By six he left his hotel and walked to the restaurant, arriving before it was even open such was his excitement, eventually consoling himself with a walk around the nearby Piazza del Popolo to pass the time.

Finally he returned to the restaurant where he found Spencer already waiting for him. He stood to greet the flame-haired Irish priest with such enthusiasm that O'Connell found himself a little embarrassed by the effusiveness of the welcome but flattered too. Spencer waved him to a chair opposite, the table set for two in what was an intimate setting, the tables packed closely together in the fast filling room.

"Best restaurant this side of the Tiber," declared Spencer. "Hell, this side of the fucking Med. Marvellous, truly, truly marvellous. I've taken the liberty of ordering the pear ravioli for your starter, you won't find anything better for a thousand miles and, believe me, I know what I'm talking about," he finished, patting his portly frame. His voice both filled the room yet was gentle in tenor, his baritone bringing goose-bumps to the back of O'Connell's neck.

O'Connell wondered whether he should mention he had stolen the seal to get the formalities out of the way but Spencer didn't appear particularly concerned about the task he had assigned. The younger man had thought it would be the first thing that was asked and had prepared the story in his head, making it sound more dramatic than it had been. But now he was just happy to bask in the company of this character that had occupied his thoughts for the past few days.

By way of introduction, Spencer began by telling him about his journey of discovery ever since he had been part of the team who had uncovered the Dead Sea scrolls. Working as a United Nations observer, he had been in the region when the scrolls had started surfacing around Bethlehem and had been on site when the first cave where they were concealed was uncovered. In all there were nine hundred documents uncovered over a period of six years in eleven different caves he said, flourishing his story with gestures and movements that simultaneously captivated and alarmed the young priest such were their intensity.

Each new discovery was subjected to authentication tests and all were found to be from biblical times. Spencer oversaw the excavation and authentication of the documents and then was involved in arranging for them to be auctioned. What he couldn't understand was why, throughout the whole process and with every religious organisation it appeared wanting to be involved or claiming rightful ownership, no such claim was made by the Catholic Church.

"Didn't ring true, old chap. Bloody anomaly." He sipped his wine liberally, relishing the evening and his captive audience. "No interest whatsoever. Not a sniff. Seem strange to you?"

O'Connell was about to say that it did but didn't have time before his host continued, "Course it bloody does. That's because it was. Greatest discovery of historical and religious texts ever and not a shred of interest. From the largest church in the world? Fucking ridiculous."

It was almost as though the Church knew they were there, he surmised, and were of no particular significance. Small fry compared to what they held in their own vast archive.

"Made me wonder what they were up to. Planted the bloody things there themselves perhaps? A sanitised set of texts for everyone to salivate over, keep the juicy stuff hidden away."

Captivated, he began to investigate further, taking some of the scrolls and testing them.

"Wanted to ensure that they'd been there for hundreds of years and not scattered there Tuesday week ago," he declared to anyone who cared to listen.

But the tests were inconclusive and could only confirm that there was evidence of a build-up of residue consistent with sea salt that could have been gained from the scrolls being there two years or two thousand years.

He paused for more wine, the pear ravioli having been replaced by a rack of lamb. O'Connell devoured his with relish as he had never tasted anything quite so sublime and he was overwrought with the sensation of pleasure that drowned him as he considered the evening.

"Not boring you, old chap? Wearing you down with my insidious waffle?" Again he didn't wait for any firm answer from his guest, merely accepting the smiling eyes and half nod that he received as an invitation to continue.

Spencer explained that the provenance of the scrolls was a matter of great debate and dispute but the most widely held belief was that they were written by a Jewish tribe whose settlement was close to the caves. But there are many, to this day if he was to be believed, and O'Connell was in no doubt that this great man was someone to be trusted so he believed most fervently, who discount this and think that the scrolls were written by different groups, especially given the diversity of subjects covered within.

"Do you know that only forty per cent of the scrolls were actually biblical manuscripts? Almost two thirds of them were apocryphal or sectarian manuscripts. Written to lay down the law, subjugate the hoard, keep them in their place." Then, looking up to see his charge nodding, he said, "Of course you fucking do. Look who I'm talking to. I'm sorry, my dear chap, most terribly, terribly sorry. You must think me a pompous and patronising old fart. Forgive me."

"Nothing to forgive, ehmmm, Spencer." His voice came out scratchy as it was the first thing he had said for almost an hour so he took a sip of his wine before continuing. "I appreciate that I am a very naive and sheltered priest who has been taught a specific doctrine and, even though I know the facts of the history you are recounting, I must, alas, confess that I have never really considered the significance of it all. Nor have I ever questioned what it was I have been told."

As he looked at the beaming smile in front of him, he found his audience waiting patiently for him to continue, the look on Spencer's face filled with glee as his new toy came to life.

The Judas Deception

Glad to oblige, he said, "In my time as an archivist within the Vatican, I had access to hundreds of documents, thousands even. Texts and manuscripts from throughout the history of the Church and the growth of the Catholic faith," then, dropping his voice to a whisper for fear that, even in the din of the now packed restaurant, someone would hear him other than his intended target, "documents which describe in great detail the brutality of some of those who enforced the will of the Church. Even then I still accepted that it was a different time and that these methods were probably the only effective way to make people realise that they had to do as the Church directed for the good of their soul and their community. It never occurred to me that there could be anything other than the best of intentions when I read these documents. But I see now that I have just been fooling myself all this time and that there are things that I simply must question, things I must know."

Spencer nodded enthusiastically and, seeing his new friend had come to the end of his soul searching for now, continued his narrative.

"No doubt in my mind that the scrolls came from a number of different sources. Too eclectic, too diverse, too fucking unbelievable that one tribe had gathered all these together. Some say that the tribe acquired writings and teachings from other sects over the years. That's why there are such a variety of views represented in the documents. Bloody nonsense."

No, he believed the texts had a number of sources. So, the big question was then, how did they all come to be gathered in one place? In fact, it was more than that. Not only were they all neatly packed together in caves beside each other, less than a kilometre apart, but how was it that they had never been discovered before.

"Not exactly isolated, these caves. Nor hard to get too. Hell, half the fucking UN team were the size of baby hippos with gammy legs and one eye missing and they were able to get in and out without any difficulty. You telling me that no-one had ventured into them for two thousand years? Whole thing's fucking preposterous."

As a student at Cambridge, Spencer's main discipline was as an Egyptologist specialising in cryptology and he had been on archaeological digs over the years that had taught him plenty about tracing the provenance of artefacts. This had developed over time into an interest in particular with anything relating to the history of the Jewish faith and gathering evidence of their migration from Egypt to modern day Palestine and Israel. So, when the scrolls began to surface around Bethlehem in the late nineteen forties, he used his position as a United Nations Observer to get on the team who went to investigate.

"Bunch of bloody clowns, the lot of them. Wouldn't know an ancient biblical text from a rhino's arsehole."

So, as he was experienced both in the methodology of tracing the history of such documents and familiar with the region and the history of the people, he chose a specific codex, that of the book of Isaiah, and began tracing its history. He found that it was referenced in a number of texts of the time and it was easy to follow the progress of the book, set down in writing for the first time in around the year five hundred BC.

The Isaiah scroll that was part of the discovery in the Dead Sea caves was dated as around one hundred and fifty BC and was placed with the Essenes tribe, the sect who many believe are responsible for the entire collection. However, Spencer was able to trace the movements of the tribe pretty accurately up to around one hundred and twenty CE and knew that their final settlement had been in Jerusalem some one hundred and fifty kilometres away.

During their travels they had been based, for a brief period, close to the region of the caves, but it made no sense to say that they had been responsible for the entire collection and that they had placed them all in these caves only to abandon them when they moved on.

"They weren't displaced nor did they suffer any terrible calamity which resulted in them fleeing the region in a hurry. Weren't wiped out by famine or pestilence or any of the other four horsemen thereby leaving the collection unattended. They weren't attacked by snakes or eaten by wolves or overcome with the desire to fornicate with their own family, although most of them probably did anyway. No, when they moved it was premeditated and with deliberation. So, what, they just forgot to take all their precious teachings with them? Left them to gather dust in caves. Wandering towards Jerusalem with the feeling that they'd left something behind but couldn't quite put their finger on what! Why would they just abandon all these important documents?"

He looked expectantly at O'Connell who realised that he was expected to answer. "Ahmm, they wouldn't," he stammered.

"Course they fucking wouldn't!" He practically shouted this and O'Connell felt pleased that he had so obviously given the right answer that the smile on his face couldn't get any larger.

It made no sense, Spencer went on, so he started to take more and more of the documents and trace their origins. He became convinced that they came from a number of different sources, tribes who lived in assorted regions, some of whom had passed by the Dead Sea on their travels and many who hadn't been anywhere near that area. He also found that they had existed at different times and that the history of some dated back further than others while there were those whose movements could still be traced to five hundred years CE and beyond. It didn't make sense to say that these groups would abandon large collections of teachings and writings. So Spencer came to the conclusion that they hadn't.

"Just not possible, dear chap. Ridiculous to think otherwise. So where did they come from I hear you ask? Where indeed? Can only have been put there by someone else. Someone who gathered all these diverse documents from numerous sources and put them all together as a single collection. Someone who planted them there deliberately."

O'Connell he sat rapt with the story that his new guardian was telling. He was so wrapped up in everything that Spencer was saying that he had forgotten all about the task he'd been set. So he was somewhat disarmed when the burly figure looked at him then and asked if he had stolen the seal. Stumbling on his words O'Connell told him that he had, knowing at that moment that if he hadn't he would have left that very minute and stolen the Pope's washbowl if Spencer had wanted it instead.

"Excellent, my dear chap, knew you would. Never doubted you. Man for the job and all that. Now, let's get out of here, go somewhere a bit more private so I can tell you what I intend to use it for. Think you'll get quite a kick out of it."

CHAPTER 20

Huxley carefully watched the young man's reaction. He knew that Alan was holding out on them but couldn't decide just how much or how significant it might be.

For Donovan's part he was so taken aback that he actually stumbled backwards, falling into a seat.

"I…I don't understand…are you saying that I…I have something to do…" Donovan stammered out the words and Huxley could only admire his skills as an actor but he decided there was nothing to be gained by pressing the issue for now.

"Alright, Alan, calm down. I'm just trying to figure out what is happening. I thought I might jar something out of your subconscious with a bit of a push." Then quickly, before Donovan got a chance to interrupt, "Right, let's recap to see if there is anything that jumps out at us. First, we have a dead college tutor, killed in the cold light of day in a public place albeit by someone who was careful not to be seen or caught. Alan here is caught up in the middle of it all because he happened to be in the wrong place at the wrong time so it would seem. Not only are you found beside a dead body but it's that of your tutor with whom you had rowed earlier. All in all, not a good scenario so you ring your dad, he says sit tight, he's coming to get you and you sit in silence until I arrive. Everyone with me so far? Have I missed anything?"

"Sounds about right to me," replied Donovan.

"So you're with the police, I turn up and you fill me in on events so far." Huxley paused and gave the young man an appraising look. "Just as a matter of interest, what would you have done if I hadn't come along when I did?"

Alan looked a bit taken aback at the question having settled into a reverie as Huxley had started his analysis. "Emmm, I don't really know," he stumbled, "I hadn't thought about it. Events just kinda unfolded around me. I guess I'd have sat it out and waited for dad. I'm sure he would have found someone to help me until he got here. Given what has happened since then I'm thinking that might not have been such a bad thing."

Huxley saw a fire in the young man's eyes that had not been there before, almost as though he had decided that attack was the best form of defence. It was almost accusatory, as though Huxley was responsible for everything that had happened to them. Huxley wasn't a great believer in coincidence and thought there was more to Donovan's presence in the shop than he was letting on but he didn't think that the boy could have been responsible for a cold blooded murder. So he was willing to give the young man the benefit of the doubt for the moment and proceed with his narrative.

"Well, for better or worse, I did turn up. I took advantage of my status and gained entry to the crime scene. I then somewhat abused my position by spiriting you away from the scene of the crime."

"Only because we were attacked while in the police car," added Alan.

"Yes, very true, but the police don't quite see it that way and are not happy about this and set about trying to find us, accusing Alan of being a potential murderer and me an accomplice. They ran, m'lud, ergo guilty as charged. Still on track, am I?"

Nods from both. Sam Davison eyed the open bottle of brandy but thought better of it.

"Any coffee around here?" she asked.

Huxley headed to the kitchen to oblige and found himself joined by Sam.

"You're being a bit hard on the lad, aren't you?"

"Sorry, I'm just trying to focus his mind, get him thinking about things that will help solve the problem rather than the problem itself. I'll go a bit easier.

The pair returned with three mugs of black coffee. If there were any complaints about the lack of milk, it didn't stop any of them from sipping their drink.

"Okay," continued Huxley, grateful for the short break to ease tensions a little, "so then we head back to Trinity to update the Master and meet up with you, Sam. From there we come up with the idea that we should maybe take a peek at whatever Simms was working on today to see if it provided any clues as to why he was killed. In spite of it being a spur of the moment decision and us not telling anyone of our whereabouts, we end up trapped in a building that has been deliberately set on fire and our exits are blocked to prevent us from escaping. Does that about sum it up?"

"It still hasn't sunk in properly," voiced Sam. "Even now, when you're talking about it, it's like it happened to someone else."

"Yeah, I know what you mean, that's it exactly," piped in Alan. "I mean, I know that it was us but it's like I was watching it all on a screen in my head."

"Well I can't wait for the big screen release because that's going to be one hell of a movie," Huxley joked, then seeing the looks he was getting he added, "What? Too soon?" Anyway, let's get back to our summation. The burning building tells me a couple of things. Firstly, someone knew where we were so they must have been following us."

"Or tracking us," said Donovan.

"Tracking us? How?" queried Sam.

"Like on our phones or some shit like that." He took his mobile out of his pocket and examined it.

"Possible," responded Huxley, "but unlikely. Although I'm certainly not dismissing it. The other thing that it tells us is…"

"We're doing something that somebody really doesn't like," finished Sam.

"Precisely. And they either think there's a potential witness to the murder that they want to eliminate."

"Or they believe that we could stumble across something that they don't want us to find." Sam looked at the two men. "So which do you think?"

"I don't much like either of them. And it was worrying that they found us so quickly. I mean, look at how they trapped us at Queens' right in the middle of the ball. That was barely fifteen minutes after we escaped the fire," added Alan.

"Don't worry, Alan, I hadn't forgotten about that. I was just coming to it. Anyone want to voice their thoughts on how they managed to find us so quickly?" Huxley looked at each of them in turn.

"Maybe Alan's right and they are tracking us somehow. Following our phones or monitoring our…" Sam tailed off. "I don't know, the whole thing is just so absurd."

"And yet very real," said Huxley, the voice of reason. "Perhaps they are tracking us. I personally think that they followed us from the Faculty. They were probably watching the building from all angles."

"If that is the case then there must be dozens of them," said a worried Alan Donovan.

"Certainly a few of them anyway, yes," Huxley agreed.

"Do you really think that our phones could be bugged or something?"

"And does that mean that they can find us again?" There was definitely a touch of fear in Donovan's voice and Sam turned to him and smiled her reassurance, but inside she was very apprehensive.

"We've been here for almost an hour already and no-one has come knocking on the door yet. I really think that we could end up totally paranoid if we go down that path," said Huxley. "Let's all just keep calm and look at the whole thing rationally. They have probably been following our movements all evening right from the book store. They tried to get us when we were in the police car. Then there was the Faculty. And then finally at Queens'. I think if they were tracking they'd have found us by now given how easily they got to us before."

This seemed to have the calming effect that he had hoped for and Huxley checked to see if they were both ready to analyse the events some more. Sensing that they had settled a little he continued.

"That brings us to the abduction. I take it neither of you recognised the guy who had us at gunpoint?" They both shook their head. "I thought not. It was the speed at which it all happened and his assurance throughout it all, that's the scary thing."

"What do you think he'd have done with us if he'd got us away from everybody?" This time the fear was very real in Alan's voice.

"I don't think that's worth dwelling on at all, Alan. Best to focus on the fact that we managed to escape him thanks to your wonderful punting skills."

"You two should have a race sometime," chirped Sam, anxious to steer the conversation away from Alan's question.

The laughter broke the tension and they all visibly relaxed.

"So where do we go from here?" asked Huxley.

"Do you really think that Stephen could have been killed because of what he was working on?"

"I think it's a real possibility. By burning down the Faculty they almost eliminated us and they made certain that they got rid of any clues he could have left in his office", said Huxley.

"Yeah, but they can't destroy what's on the internet," responded Donovan. "We can get all the documents and texts that they destroyed on there."

"Well, there's a laptop over on the desk if you want to have a look. Just because the house is old and the decor dated, it doesn't mean that it doesn't have modern facilities like wi-fi connections and superfast broadband. Be my guest," he finished, gesturing Donovan towards the desk.

"But what are we looking for?" queried Sam. "We've already established that there's probably an anomaly in the original text and that there are additional pages. But without knowing what they contain we can't really make any progress."

"We could check the commentaries of the time to see if they suggest anything about why Judas betrayed Jesus," offered Donovan.

Huxley nodded to Sam to go to the boy and she picked up on his desire to keep Alan occupied no matter how flimsy the premise.

As they settled at the desk, Huxley rose and began to roam around the room, stopping to browse the books all around. Books had been a large part of his life and he loved their touch, smell, feel, the knowledge that they contained. He was never happier than when in a library and, despite the mustiness of this old, rarely used house, he found himself very comfortable within this temple of knowledge.

He often came here just to sit and read and he admired the former owner's fascination with the Gnostic gospels evident

The Judas Deception

by the number of books that referred to these particular texts. They detailed the discovery, translation, significance and impact of the gospels and Huxley enjoyed immersing himself in the subject that he loved so much. He perused works that he had referenced many times together with some more obscure texts, then paused as he noticed something interesting out of the corner of his eye.

He reached for a book entitled 'The Lost Gospel of Judas' which was one of Spencer Harris's own works and one that Huxley had referenced many times before. However, what he noticed about this particular copy was the small label on the base of the spine indicating that it was a library book. He had never spotted this before, not surprising really given the number of tomes throughout. There were multiple copies of this particular one scattered all round the house. So why would he have a library copy as well, wondered Huxley, surely he hadn't wanted to just make sure there was a recent stamp in his own book.

He had never known Spencer Harris but had heard that he was as crazy and wild as he was brilliant. Huxley opened up the cover to see when the last stamp had been made but as he did so he sensed more than saw the corner of a piece of paper that had been stuffed into the spine of the book. He worked the edge of the paper and eased it out slowly. A piece of paper, as it happened, hidden by Spencer Harris the night before he died.

CHAPTER 21

Rome – 1970

Upon leaving the restaurant, Spencer and O'Connell walked towards the nearby river, enjoying the mild spring evening. Spencer led the way, silver walking cane striking out in front of him as he fulfilled the role of the archetypal Englishman right down to the suspenders on his Argyle socks. Everything that he had said in the restaurant, he told the young priest, was well documented. He had written books on the provenance of the Dead Sea scrolls and had discussed in great detail his belief that the documents had been gathered together by a particular group, tribe or organisation.

"Don't give a stuff who might have overheard us. Nothing new there. Just the fat Englishman on his hobby horse, all that."

But the interesting bit, the bit that he had been working on now for some years but hadn't documented in any way for fear that it would fall into the wrong hands, that's what he wanted to discuss in more private surroundings. Summoning a taxi he invited O'Connell to get in ahead of him before directing the driver in perfect Italian.

By more private he meant his hotel room, a comfortable but in no way grandiose space in a secluded hotel close to the Spanish Steps. The doors to the balcony were closed and a broom shaft had been stuffed into the handle to prevent anyone from opening it from the outside. It meant that the room was rather stuffy but it was obvious that Spencer considered security more important than comfort.

Having taken off his jacket and draped it over the back of a chair, he offered O'Connell a drink before indicating for the young man to sit down. Fetching a bottle of whiskey and a couple of glasses he sat next to O'Connell and asked him for the seal as he poured a measure out for each of them. When the priest produced both seal and wax he applauded him on his initiative.

"It's just such details that will prove to be the success of the plan," he bellowed.

"What plan is that?" enquired O'Connell, intoxicated from the evening as a whole and the alcohol in particular.

"All in good time, my boy, all in good time."

The room was littered with books and documents, every surface seemingly covered. In fact, he'd taken the adjoining room too just so he didn't have to clear a space when he needed to sleep. As well as books and documents he had lots of maps, dozens of them spread out on the floor and he pointed to some as he fell back into his narrative of before, only this time with a fervency in his eyes that suggested that he was speaking about his true calling.

There were maps of countries, regions and even one of the world with annotations all over. He explained that when he read something that he didn't think was accurate, he would make a note to research the answer or write down the correction right there and then if he knew it already. Or if he discovered something that he found interesting or, perhaps, relevant to what he was doing at the time he would highlight this. It was just his way and the map was one such example of a work of Spencer as he called it.

He returned to his theme that the scrolls had been gathered together by person or persons unknown and deliberately placed in the caves.

"You see what I'm getting at, don't you, my boy. Obvious when you see the whole picture. Absolute garbage to think otherwise. Pure fantasy. Yet they would have us believe that these documents just happened to turn up one day. Utter shite."

He set about trying to find out who could have and would have done this but drew a blank every time he tried to trace the timeline of any individual document. It was only as he researched later texts that he found some references to biblical manuscripts in writings from the Church in the twelfth and thirteenth centuries. He was sure that these references related to some texts supposedly only discovered with the Dead Sea scrolls.

Of course, when he asked about the discrepancy he was simply told that the bible was put together from a great many texts and accounts of the same events but by different commentators. That the references used could be attributed to any number of these which had been quoted throughout literature. Spencer wasn't convinced.

He set about checking the Church's history when it came to documents and texts and how they would treat such material. He found that the history of any given text seemed to come to an abrupt end when the society that had held it fell under the influence of the growing Church of Rome.

"Whether through choice or force or because the creatures of the black lagoon told them to, who knows? I found it odd that, whatever the circumstances, as soon as the fucking Pope and his band of merry men came calling suddenly all reference to these texts ceases. Poofhh, just like that." He blew on his hand.

"You think the Vatican owned the Dead Sea scrolls? But

why...." O'Connell didn't get any further than that as Spencer raised a hand and indicated for him to stop.

"I know what you are going to ask and it is an all too natural reaction, my beautiful James." If O'Connell was embarrassed by the overly familiar soliloquy he didn't show it, secretly filled with joy at the description. "Why would they have these documents and then put them into caves? Having done that, why then show no interest in their discovery nor shout that they actually belonged to you? And why not try and retrieve them again? It all makes so little sense."

"Well, yes, it does. I mean, I can understand why you think someone gathered all these texts together and planted them in the caves and I'm as intrigued as you to find out who could have done this and when they put them there. But, even if what you say about the Church taking control of the documents is true, and I'm not conceding that point to you just yet, why would they then leave them in caves in the middle of a hostile region?"

So Spencer took him through books and maps and documents that all pointed towards the Church and its influence overwhelming regions and societies at various times in history. Then he would link these with the last references to manuscripts found in the Dead Sea scroll collection. And O'Connell had to admit that there was a discernible pattern that suggested the documents in question did seem to disappear from history whenever the Church came into a region and became the predominant force in that culture. Whilst it may not have convinced the young priest of everything that Spencer was proclaiming, he did have to accept that there might be something to the Catholic Church having had the opportunity to take ownership of these documents.

"Couldn't they have been driven underground as the Church began to assert its influence on the region and made the beliefs held by the community outlawed? So therefore they hid the documents and they end up going elsewhere?"

There was joy in Spencer's face as he found in his charge an inquisitive mind who wasn't simply prepared to roll over and agree with whatever he might spout and he gave O'Connell a beaming smile as he listened to the question.

"My dear, sweet boy, that is a very valid theory," conceded the larger man, "but the reason that the Church was so easily assimilated into these communities is because the beliefs were those of followers of Christ. So why would they hide Christ centred doctrine and teachings?" He raised his eyebrows towards his guest both in question and supplication as he looked to win his audience over. "And there's also the question of how all the documents from countless regions get conveniently lumped together as one jackpot prize?"

"Well, perhaps it became known as a safe haven for any documents or manuscripts that people didn't want the Church to get hold off?"

"And then was forgotten about for centuries before being discovered by chance?" There was a certain facetious tinge to Spencer's voice and O'Connell simply smiled sheepishly as he realised how daft the notion was and sat back waiting for Spencer to continue his narrative.

He went on to state that, by James's own admission, these documents had been in the hands of the Vatican at one point or another and so it was hypothetically possible for them to have been the custodians of these for a time. He then began to show the young priest references made by scholars from the Church throughout the centuries to documents and manuscripts that coincided with those found in the Dead Sea scroll collection.

It certainly appeared to O'Connell that they had access to these documents at a time when they were supposed to be hidden away in a cave that no-one knew about. And he recognised that he wasn't just some layman being influenced by a very persuasive enthusiast but this was, in fact, his very own chosen profession so there had to be something to it.

Spencer said that he had continued with his research which then led him to ask why these documents had then been placed in such an area as the Dead Sea and left to be found by chance.

"I mean, forget about the who, although it can really only have been the Catholic Church. But forget about that for now, let's look at the why. Hell would anyone take these documents, these priceless artefacts, and dump them in the middle of a fucking desert? Just doesn't make any sense. Fucking Bedouins found them. Didn't know their worth. Started selling them in nearby markets. Most important documents of our time being sold alongside camel meat and fucking flying carpets! Can you imagine?"

O'Connell gave a laugh as the great man before him delivered his lines like an actor on stage.

"Question is, while they distract us with all these trinkets what jewels are they keeping hidden away? First rule of magic, dear boy, give the audience something to focus on while you perform your vanishing trick. Something didn't ring true for me. So while everyone else was salivating over the scrolls, I was busy trying to see under the Church's skirt."

He found that he wasn't the first to try this. Prior to the Second World War there were others who had done the same research as himself and were questioning the whereabouts of the manuscripts which had been referenced in books and writings from Church scholars. Quite a few had approached the Church to ask if they knew anything about these and the Vatican found itself under increasing pressure from a number of sources to open its archives.

"Whole thing was a bloody stage show. Throw some

sanitised crumbs to the beggars to distract them from the meat. Or stop anyone else getting their hands on anything that would expose the sheer hypocrisy of it all. Found themselves being harried to open up their vaults, have to come up with a plan. Use the war as cover, plant a pile of safe texts somewhere where they'd be found, plead ignorance to their provenance when they are. Everybody looking one way, they slip out the back with the juicy stuff.

"But why not just destroy any offending documents?" asked O'Connell, already knowing the answer.

"My dear James, these are historic documents of great import that might furnish us with answers to questions that have yet to be asked. And they may also be useful to use against people in future circumstances. Whilst they may not have information which is conducive to Catholic doctrine, to destroy them would be tantamount to sacrilege."

"But it would be a lot easier than keeping them for fear of discovery."

"That, perhaps, is true but then they have such dedicated personnel who see to it that these things are never discovered."

"You mean the Church has enforcers to prevent certain things from being discovered?"

"Well of course they bloody do. You know it, I know it, the Pope himself knows it but does nothing to dissuade them. Think of the thousands of documents that you have seen yourself, sweet James, and tell me that you can honestly say, hand on heart, that the Catholic Church would not stoop to such depths to protect its way of life."

O'Connell looked at this wonder of a man in front of him and knew then and there that everything he had said was true.

CHAPTER 22

Huxley carefully began to unfold the slip of paper that he had found, gingerly picking at the edges which had obviously been pressed together for quite some time.

Looking up from the computer screen where he and Sam were searching for what they needed, Alan asked, "What have you got there, Professor?"

"I'm not entirely sure, Alan. I can't get it open. Probably just an old love note that a student left in the spine of the book. Any joy with what you are looking for?"

It was Sam who answered. "It's hard to say, really. We've got a copy of the Judas Gospel up on the screen and have checked it again with regard to what Alan remembers seeing on the additional original page and it's definitely different. There are also some sites claiming that the document is a fake and that the real gospel is hidden in the vaults of the Vatican but they seem to be written and populated by the crazies of this world."

"But there is this one site," added Alan, who was keen to point towards anything that would validate his testimony that the translation was incorrect. "It says that there have always been rumours that there is a missing section from the Judas gospel detailing the real reasons for his betrayal and that these pages have never been found."

"But the counter argument to that," said Sam "is that the document was incomplete when found so of course there are bits missing and this shouldn't be viewed as a conspiracy. After all, before Alan's revelation earlier this evening, I had no reason to believe that there might be a problem with that particular part of the text. I mean, it does lead nicely into the betrayal and then concludes with Judas's death so it suggests that everything from that section was there already. But you're the expert in this field so what do you think?"

"Well, as I said before, I've always known about the rumours, of course, and that's what got me so interested in the Gnostics in the first place, that and their great historical import. Some very great people have dedicated their lives to finding out the truth about documents just like the Judas Gospel, a truth that has been concealed by the Church over the centuries."

"Why, what are they so afraid off?"

"That's the question, Sam? I believe that the Church have a number of documents hidden away that will never see the light of day because they prove that the bible is a farce and that the whole principle that their faith is built on is a lie. You only have to look at the books that they rejected when constructing the new testament to realise just what nonsense it all is. Why is it that Paul's first two letters to the Corinthians were accepted but the third one wasn't? Or the Gospel of Luke chosen ahead of that of Peter or Thomas? Because all of them and the rest of the books and manuscripts that were rejected have something which is against the doctrine of the Church. But the most surprising omission of all is the Judas Gospel. It's the earliest work and was written by his own brother who he was very close to. So what's in it that makes it so controversial?"

"From what I have read of it there is nothing revelatory about it. It seems like a very ordinary account of the life of

The Judas Deception

Jesus and, in fact, is written with a lot of tenderness and love," said Sam.

"It is. Actually it's probably one of the most caring accounts of the life of Jesus and his relationship with his disciples and the people that he came into contact with. I've spent a long time studying the document and I know it from back to front. There is nothing derogatory in it at all and nothing that would upset the Church. So why discard it when it is the closest thing to a first-hand account of the life of Jesus?" Huxley looked at his audience to see if they were interested in him continuing. They were both listening intently so he carried on.

"The Gospel is the most generous portrayal of Jesus, it is written with a lot of love and affection. Even before it was discovered, the works that referenced it all suggested that there was a compassion within it that belied the man who betrayed the supposed son of god."

"So why was it excluded from the bible?" asked Sam.

"Well, there is a lot of speculation, but nothing has ever been proven. However, when the codex of the Gospel was finally found in 1977, it quickly fell into the hands of private collectors and was handled very poorly. By the time it came into the public domain and was subsequently translated, so much of it was missing, thought to have disintegrated with the poor care it had been subjected to. But there were always rumours about pages being in the hands of collectors which will probably never see the light of day again. But if there are any then I believe I would have come across something before now. Trust me, I have been asked to authenticate so many pages claiming to be part of the original text but have yet to see an original document in all that time. Which makes boy wonder's find all the more remarkable." He smiled at Donovan as he said this to ensure that it wasn't misinterpreted as acrimonious.

"It was just pure luck," said Donovan, disarmingly.

"These things often are," replied Huxley. "That we've always known there are parts missing has never been in doubt. But what your finding has proved is that a section that was thought to be complete obviously isn't. And that means that there's more about the betrayal as that's the part where the anomaly appears. This opens up a world of possibilities and puts every crazy conspiracy theory back in play."

"Such as all the weird and wonderful notions spouted on these websites," Sam said, motioning towards the computer.

"But it also brings into play the more reasonable and potentially accurate interpretations that eminent scholars have put forth. Like the one you offer in your book, Professor."

Huxley sensed that this is where Donovan had been trying to lead him all evening and, now that they were finally here, Huxley had to admire the way the young man had played his hand.

Sam unwittingly assisted Alan as she asked, "What theory?"

"For that I think I might need more coffee," replied Huxley, heading to the kitchen again where he reached for the kettle. As he began filling it, a movement caught his eye. It was all he could do to stop himself from doing a double take and give himself away. Instead, he set the kettle boiling and left the room.

Once in the hallway he made for the room adjacent to the kitchen which overlooked the back of the house. Leaving it in darkness, he made his way to the window and peered out. He couldn't see anything at first but then caught the movement again. It looked like someone was crawling on the ground towards the house. His heart was racing and he was about to call out to the others when security lights on next door's house sprang into life and illuminated the whole of the back garden.

Huxley saw that it was a cat that he had been watching, the startled animal shooting off down the side of the house.

He hadn't realised that he had been so jumpy and made sure that he portrayed a calm demeanour when he returned to the study with fresh mugs of coffee.

"So go on then," prompted Sam, "tell me about your book as I seem to be the only one here who hasn't read it."

"Well, it's centred around Irenaeus and his commentary on the Judas Gospel and society in general at that time. There are some references to his work in other texts but they are quite limited so a lot of it is about filling in the blanks. And as the only original copy of the text is held by the Vatican and no-one is permitted to see it, then all we can do is allude to what he is trying to tell us from those bits and pieces available to us."

"The Vatican won't let anyone see the text?"

"Nope. And that's not for want of trying. I've submitted numerous requests. So, without seeing the original, I've speculated that Irenaeus shares with us a love story, two people united in a tenderness and fondness for one another that is apparent to all who spent time with them. A love story about Jesus and one of his disciples."

"Judas," whispered Sam transfixed.

"It's evident both from the Judas Gospel and from the writings of Irenaeus that there is a strong affection between the two. Some may say that it is the result of the close proximity that they had with one another and the work that they shared. But the same bond isn't evident with any of his other disciples. That is until John came along."

"You're saying that Jesus was involved in a relationship with Judas and then dumped him for a younger model?"

"Put crudely, yes. It is very clear from numerous texts that there was a very intimate relationship between Jesus and John and many have speculated over the years about the two being lovers. But what is less clear is the evidence that Jesus had a similar relationship with Judas before that."

"And that's why Judas betrayed him," concluded Sam.

"That's the theory."

"Wow," she responded, "that is heavy stuff. No wonder someone is willing to kill to protect a secret like that if there really is documentary evidence of that somewhere."

"Which brings us back to the missing parts of the Judas Gospel. The fact that we now know there is a good chance that the part of the gospel which discusses the betrayal is incomplete, begs the question who tampered with the document and what have they done with the missing pages."

"And you think this is what Stephen was looking at this afternoon?" asked Sam?

"I think it's a possibility. Alan, you said that he didn't bite when you suggested that the document wasn't complete."

"Not a flicker of interest. He dismissed it out of hand."

"And, Sam, you said that Simms was running around quite excited about something this afternoon?"

"He was. After his tutorial with Alan, Stephen came to see me and said that he felt that he had his work cut out redirecting Alan with his PhD. Then, later in the afternoon, he suddenly seemed to be questioning his initial appraisal and I think he might have contacted someone about it. I definitely heard him on the phone."

"But who would he have rung? And what would he have said to them that ended up getting him killed?"

"I don't know but I think it might be time to try and find out."

"How do you plan to do that?" asked Donovan.

"I'm going to call Sergeant Pepper," replied Huxley without a trace of humour.

CHAPTER 23

ROME – 1970

O'Connell stared at his host, still contemplating what he had been told. Spencer could see that the young priest was trying to reconcile what he had heard with his long-held beliefs. But there was still more to be said so Spencer pressed on.

Having convinced O'Connell that everything he had ever held to be true in his life was nonsense, the large man felt that he owed the dispirited priest a full explanation before asking him to embark on the next stage of the journey.

"There is no doubt in my mind that the scrolls were planted by the Church," he said gently. "I can show you maps and references and transcripts until I'm blue in the face but ultimately it comes down to trust. I think you know in your heart that I'm right but I don't want to push you beyond your limits."

"I'm fine, Spencer. Honestly, I am. It's just...." In his confusion, he found words difficult to form like there was a dam between his brain and his mouth.

Spencer feared that he had been too intense with his new charge and was about to suggest that they call it a night when the young priest continued.

"So why did they do it?" he murmured before finding his voice again and stating more boldly, "I accept that they probably did. The evidence you have shown me clearly points in that direction. And if anyone knows the abuse of power perpetrated by the Church throughout history, it is I. But I don't get what is in this for them."

Although he accepted the argument that Spencer was making, O'Connell thought that his host was missing something important. And even though he was excited to be in the presence of a man who he was completely in awe of and was anxious to prove his worth to, O'Connell pressed on.

"The Gnostics have all sorts of things in them that contradict Church doctrine. They aren't the sort of thing the Church would just give up to scrutiny without a fight. There's plenty in those documents that goes against what's in the bible."

"Exactly my point!" exclaimed Spencer. "So just think what they didn't release. How much more damning must it be? These slimy bastards, throwing morsels to the dogs while the meat of the goose stays with them. So what is so terrible that they can't possibly allow it to be seen by man?"

Spencer shifted his large frame uncomfortably in his seat as he once again moved into professorial mode. He explained that he had started to look at the documents that hadn't been found amongst the Dead Sea scrolls. Documents that were referenced at the same time as those which had surfaced. Documents that perhaps were more controversial in their teachings.

There were a number that he could have focused on but it was the glaring omission of the Judas Gospel that piqued his interest most. So he set about establishing a timeline for the codex. He uncovered evidence that it was held by a tribe based in Jerusalem that had fallen under the guidance of the Church around two hundred CE and he became convinced that the Church, once again, held the original text.

"If this was held back from the documents that they had seen fit to 'release'," he made the gesture to signify quote marks

The Judas Deception

as he said this, which O'Connell found quite comical from his new mentor but he suppressed a smile as Spencer continued, "then there must be something in it that would be devastating to the Church. We are talking fucking revelations here, sweet James. No doubt that there is something so extreme that the Church refuse to let it out of its sight. I mean, they were happy enough to let go of the Gospel of Thomas in which he reveals that he doesn't believe that Jesus died. Or that of Peter where he claims that Jesus wasn't flesh and blood but took the form of a fucking ghost to come amongst them. If that's what it is prepared to circulate then what is it actually hiding? That's the question, sweet James, that is the fucking question."

His face was puce with this last remark and he looked at the red-haired priest who was suppressing a smirk. Spencer broke into a broad grin and the pair began to laugh. O'Connell watched as his host replenished their drinks and knew that he wanted desperately to help this engaging man in his quest. And he was about to have that confidence tested.

"Got a plan, dear boy. Bit risky, precarious, seat of the pants, all that. Not going to lie, dangerous business to get mixed up in. Happy for your involvement to stop here if you like. No hard feelings. Part as friends. You go your way and I'll go mine."

The silence he received to this assured him that his charge was willing to hear him out so Spencer continued.

"Came across a chap a few years back. Nasty piece or work. Utter bastard, truth be told. But someone who knows more than he's telling about what the Church is hiding. Chief enforcer if you like. Tricky man to pin down. Not easily fooled. Based in Milan. Going to need some guts to trap him. Thought I might try. Write him a letter, pretend it's from the Vatican. Tell him to expect a visitor. Someone who is to be given access to secret documents. See how he reacts. Smoke him out if you like."

"That's why you wanted the seal," cried O'Connell who was so caught up in the rhetoric that he couldn't contain himself.

"Exactly, dear boy."

"But you'll need headed paper as well. I mean, the Vatican uses specially embossed paper with watermarks through it. Why didn't you tell me, I could have got some of that as well?" O'Connell was so enchanted with his host and immersed in the plan that he was gushing and he knew it. But he couldn't help himself.

"Relax, sweet James, relax. It's all in hand. Not without friends. In fact, bit of a crew, truth be told. Used their contacts at the printers. Already sorted. Seal's a bit more troublesome, hand crafted on the premises, unique, not so easy to get. Needed to be an inside job. Did it splendidly." In truth, Spencer was euphoric about his young charge's enthusiasm and thought that, with his help, the plan might just work.

So, he composed the letter that evening, stating that the Church would be sending a priest from their Archive Department and that he was to be given access to any and all documents relating to the Gospel of Judas. O'Connell, realising that it was Spencer's intention to use him as the patsy to lure the keeper of the prize out into the open, felt his first tinge of anxiety. However, he was as intrigued by the chase as the older man and so went along with the ruse.

"Not going to fall for it, of course. See straight through it. Be on the phone immediately to HQ. Red flag raised, all that. But with a bit of luck it might just provoke a reaction from him that will give us a clue."

"But don't we need to see how he reacts? Watch him or whatever?"

The Judas Deception

"Indeed we do, which is why I'm going to give this letter to my friend with strict instructions not to post it until tomorrow. That'll give us time to get to Milan and set up our surveillance. Are you in?"

O'Connell had returned to his hotel a confusion of emotions, the overwhelming one that of excitement as he thought about the adventure ahead. It was already late, but he was beyond tired and slept fitfully, finally rising and checking out of his room before joining Spencer at the train station where they climbed aboard a train for Milan.

They arrived late afternoon, the sky bright and showing off the piazza in front of the train station in all its ghoulish glory. Spencer immediately hailed a taxi that took them to an apartment in a stylish part of the city near the Cathedral.

O'Connell had expected a hotel but soon understood as Spencer entered the apartment and made straight for the large shuttered windows, opening them to reveal a balcony that overlooked the main road. He pointed to a building across the street and told the priest that it was where their prey lived.

He also said that he had arranged for a little bit of local help in the form of a telephone engineer who had disabled the phone line earlier in the day according to the note that awaited them on the dining table. This meant that their quarry wouldn't be able to ring the Vatican to confirm whether the letter was genuine or not. At least not from his apartment anyway.

"Can't stop him from going to the Post Office or wherever, picking up a phone. But reckon he'll leave it a day or two. Hope he does something to help us before then."

"Who is this man, Spencer?"

Harris had forbidden any talk on their train journey insisting the walls have ears so the two had spoken little about their mission. Now the Englishman looked at his companion with a malevolence that O'Connell would not have thought possible from his new friend.

"Evil incarnate, that's who he is."

His name was Antonio Grimani, a Swiss Italian one time cardinal who had gained quite a reputation as a problem solver. His methods were questionable but few ever did question them as the result was more important than the process and he found his talents called upon more and more. This much Spencer had found out anecdotally, as very little was ever written about the man who was known as the mysterious cardinal. But as his authority grew so too did the Holy See's reliance on him as an enforcer. Until he found himself with the keys to the kingdom. He knew where all the skeletons were and used them to his advantage. Now, Spencer was sure, there was nothing that he didn't know or have access to.

The pair watched as he sat at his desk in the room that he obviously used as his office. They had a perfect vantage point, Grimani's desk side on to them, the man himself facing away from their gaze. The evening slowly ebbed away, the two moving to the kitchen when Grimani retired to his living quarters. Spencer began preparing a meal, a fridge full of ingredients to choose from.

"What will happen tomorrow?" asked O'Connell.

"Hell if I know," responded his companion. Then, "Probably nothing. Letter arrives, he opens it, shrugs his shoulders, gets on with his day. Protocol hasn't been followed, code word not supplied, wrong signature on the letter, fuck knows. Waits us out, sees what we do."

"And what do we do?"

"Hope that he doesn't do any of the above. Hope he leads us to wherever the documents are hidden. Hope he opens a large safe behind one of his paintings and pulls out a treasure map with all the caches marked with an X."

O'Connell giggled before saying, "But seriously, Spencer, what's our next step if he doesn't do anything?"

It was the next step that Spencer fretted about as he knew that he would be exposing O'Connell to great danger. But he also knew that it might be their only choice.

"Let's worry about that tomorrow. For now, come, feast, indulge your senses with this wonderful food."

And it was indeed wonderful, O'Connell was greatly impressed by his friend's mastery in the kitchen, a room he himself would have been lost in if asked to prepare something. Afterwards they moved back to the lounge, Spencer taking up a position once more in front of the window to spy on their target.

After a while, he turned in his seat to see the young priest sitting on the sofa, legs wrapped beneath him as he read one of Spencer's own books. Over dinner, they had discussed their plan if Grimani did not react to the letter and Spencer knew that O'Connell was worried. O'Connell looked up, feeling the older man's eyes on him, and the two held each other's gaze in the warm light of the lamp between them. Spencer could sense the anxiety behind the eyes and moved his chair around so that he was sitting facing his charge.

"I know it's a big step, dear James, a step that I would only ask of you if I thought that it would actually prove successful to our goal. I wish, too, that I could tell you that there would be no risk but I would be lying if I did. Feel free to tell me to bugger off and I will understand perfectly, really I will. But it might be our best shot at finding out where anything is hidden."

"Do you think the documents are here in Milan?"

"I doubt that they are even in Italy but who knows. Grimani has spent his life as an enforcer for the Church and he moves around a lot but he has been based in Milan now for a while and I think he must be here for a reason. But this is a very dangerous man we are talking about, James, believe me, I know this from first-hand experience."

"What happened?"

"A few years ago I heard about a document that was held by a private collector. It was one that I had wanted to study for years so I made it known amongst my contemporaries that I would like to meet the man. Got completely blackballed, no dice. Cut-throat business, the whole thing. Sell your granny for a wotsit, all that.

"I'm sure it's not as bad as all that," countered O'Connell.

"Could take you to places where the mere mention of my name would have you thrown out, probably onto the nearest bed of nettles if they could. And I could find half a dozen names on every page of the London telephone directory who despise the ground I excavate. But those who trust me do so with their lives and I mine with them. Which is why I will never forgive myself for what happened."

O'Connell could see the pain in his friend's face and wanted to console but all he could do was ask, "What happened?"

"Well, when I got wind of another collector with something that was of interest to me, I tried a different tact. Approached an old friend, told him what it was about, asked him to do some digging on my behalf. Problem was it was a biblical text I was after. Should have known it would prick some ears up, put me in front of the beak if it came to light, explain how I found it, all that. But never thought, sent him on his merry way, doing my dirty work for me."

"You make it sound so ominous. So where does Grimani come into it?"

"Aha! Always so anxious to find out more. I love your inquisitive mind, dear boy, I really do. It fills me with such

The Judas Deception

drive and enthusiasm that I feel I can achieve anything with you by my side."

O'Connell looked both flustered and flattered by Spencer's comment and was speechless for a moment. But he already knew that he trusted this marvellous man in front of him. In the short space of time that they had been together, O'Connell had come to recognise what had been missing in his life and that he loved the passion so engraved within this great beast who talked and lived with such vigour.

He blushed with both pride and embarrassment as he said, "I will do whatever I can to help you, Spencer."

The larger man rose from his seat and gripped the young priest's hands with a tenderness that belied his mass. He held them gently, smiling benevolently upon the young man, and bowed his thanks.

At that moment, Spencer felt a bond with his charge which he relished and found himself reluctant to return to their conversation. But his need to emphasise the menace that Grimani presented was now all the more pressing as he looked upon the shock of red hair and the innocence which shone from those green eyes.

It was O'Connell who broke the silence.

"Tell me the rest of the story."

Spencer hesitated, unsure of how to respond, his instinct to protect. Sensing his reluctance, O'Connell pushed himself away, the better to look up into Spencer's eyes.

"Look, I know that you don't want to put me into any danger but I'm not some schoolboy who has just come out of short trousers. I'm capable of looking after myself if I have to. And I want to be involved in what you're doing. So I need you to trust me and I want you to involve me. That's why I'm here. Not just here in this apartment with you but here in this time because I want to find out the truth."

"Do you really, James? Do you? Think carefully about what you are saying. I'm talking about trying to find documents that I believe the Church have hidden away from public view. These manuscripts probably expose the bible as a fraud and Jesus as nothing more than a con man. Is that the sort of truth that you really want to find? Wouldn't it simply be easier to live in ignorance for the rest of your life?"

"There was a time that I would have said yes to that but since I have met you I have a newfound respect for life. And I can't live with a half measure of that life now. So I'm with you all the way, regardless of what we find."

"Okay, okay, you win, my boy." And so Spencer continued his story. "My friend was busy making enquiries when he got an invitation from a collector in Switzerland. He was keeping me posted with frequent letters and notes at my club. Went to join him, stayed nearby, incognito, all that. Waited to hear from him. Nothing. Then there was a flap at the big house where he was staying, police cars everywhere. What to do?"

"So what did you do?" asked a captivated O'Connell.

"Walked up to the house, bold as brass. Police everywhere. Said I was a police detective from London on holiday. Heard that there was a British subject staying here, wanted to check he was okay."

"They didn't buy it, did they?"

"I can be quite convincing. Took me inside. Showed me the dead body of my friend. All I could do to hold it together. Natural causes they said. Host found him lying on the floor. Doctor in the house examined him, said it was a heart attack."

"But you didn't believe it."

"Constitution of an ox, that man. No way he just keeled over after a fancy meal and a couple of glasses of vino. Poisoned, my guess. But couldn't let on. Had to run with it. Examined the room to show willing but just wanted to get out of there.

Then saw something, corner of my eye. Piece of paper in his shoe. Hadn't been noticed by anyone. Bent down, surreptitiously picked it up, slipped it in my pocket."

"Then what?"

"Got out of there like my pants were on fire. Except I was stopped before I made it."

"Grimani?"

"In all his glory. Course, didn't know who he was, simply another Swiss policeman. Just wanted out. Got hold of my arm, led me to a side room, asked who I was. Asked him who he was, what he was doing there, turned the tables. Wasn't having any of it. Here at the invitation of the owner, he said, looking after his interests. Who was I?"

"What did you say?"

"Bluffed like my life depended on it. Which it probably did. Sold him the same story. Told him, nothing I can do to help, natural causes, all that. Don't think he was convinced but house full of police, not a lot he could do."

"What did you do then?"

"Got the fuck out of Dodge, did not pass go, did not collect two hundred pounds. Practically ran back to the hotel. Cried my heart out. Only there that I remembered the note. Fished it out of my pocket."

"What did it say?" O'Connell was rapt.

"List of names, people at dinner, drawn a picture of the table. Little notes beside some names. Grimani's said KT."

"KT? That's it? Just KT? What does that even mean?"

"Knights' Templar. The Vatican enforcers. Deadliest police force ever."

O'Connell knew from texts he had read that the Templar were nasty but that had been centuries ago. "Maybe five hundred years ago, Spencer, but not now. They're more ceremonial."

"Oh, my sweet, naïve boy. If only. They are still as ruthless as ever, perhaps more so. Power of the Church behind them to sweep up the mess, cover it all up."

O'Connell was still unsure but murmured something appropriate and his companion continued.

"As soon as I knew he was Templar, there was no doubt in my mind that this was no accident. My friend had upset someone enough to attract the attention of the Templar. Once that happened it was never going to end well for him. Suspect he knew it himself."

"You really think so?"

"Trust me, dear boy, you do not want to get on the wrong side of the Templar. So perhaps now, you understand why I am reluctant to follow the second part of our plan. Because we're not just going after the Knights' Templar, we're taking on their head man."

O'Connell stood impassive, contemplating everything that he had been told and the fact that tomorrow he might just have to confront this cold-hearted killer.

CHAPTER 24

"Pepper," came the reply when it was answered.

"Hi George, it's Daniel."

"Have you any idea what fucking time it is, Dan?"

"Oh, come on now, George, you're not going to try and tell me that you're tucked up in bed beside the missus getting some much needed beauty sleep? Not with half the university on fire."

"Oh, you know about that, do you? Strange, because I've been trying to contact the Vice-Chancellor of said university to inform him but he's nowhere to be found. In spite of me ringing his mobile at least a hundred and fifty times!" There was a slight air of frustration in his voice but no animosity and Huxley knew that his friend was still very much on his side.

"Yes, sorry about that, George, but I thought it best to keep my phone off to stop any unwanted and unwelcome calls from Detective Inspectors who might have it in for me and are keen to pin a murder charge on my student."

"Oh, he's got more now, believe me. Not only did Alan Donovan murder Simms but you were in on it all along and the two of you then came along to the language department and set the place on fire to destroy evidence contained in Simms's office before we had a chance to look at it."

"So how does he explain the exits being blocked then?"

"How do you know about that, Dan?" then, after a pause, "There's a lot you're not telling me, isn't there?"

"Let's just say that we had the opportunity to check the burning building quite closely."

"You were in it when it was set on fire you mean?"

"George, we can discuss that at another time. For now I need a favour."

"Not another fucking one. Christ, Dan, my arse is already so far out the window on this one it's unreal. Blackburn practically has me working in cahoots with you. He's got me off doing some paperwork just to keep me out of the way I think."

"So are you at the station?"

"Yes."

"Good. Do you have the phone records for Simms's office?"

"Of course we do, what do you think we are, fucking incompetent or something?"

"Perish the thought, George."

"So, what about his phone records?"

"I need to find out who he called this afternoon."

"This afternoon? Why, what do you know? Come on, Dan, you've got to give me something here, I'm way out on a limb for you."

"Simms was checking something out this afternoon. We think he may have called someone about it and it alerted the wrong person to what he was looking into and they decided to stop him going any further."

Huxley filled him in briefly on what Simms had been working on, omitting Donovan's story about the additional piece of original parchment he claimed to have seen.

"Sounds complicated but you think he told the wrong person about his doubts? You believe it's as simple as that?"

"It's all we've got at the moment, George. I'm hoping that the phone records might help us out."

"Okay, hold on while I grab them." His Scottish accent always got thicker the more excited he got and Huxley noticed that there was definitely more Glaswegian in that sentence as he waited for Pepper to return. A moment later he was back on the phone. "You still there, Dan?"

"Of course I bloody am, where else am I going to be?"

"Well you never know with you, one minute you're right in front of me, the next you're half way down the street with our prime suspect in tow. Or maybe wherever you are has just been set on fire!"

"Yeah, yeah, you're a laugh a minute, George, I've got to say."

"While we're on the subject, by the way, just where exactly are you?"

"I didn't realise we were on the subject. Look, if I wanted the third degree from a copper I would have rung Blackburn. Can we just get on with the business in hand?"

"Aye, alright, keep your hair on," adding sotto voce, "what's left of it anyway."

"Look who's talking, smartarse, you still getting those invites from the Kojak convention?" joked Huxley.

"You can go off people very quickly, you know. Right, let's see what we have. Three calls this afternoon, all between two and three o'clock. Two international and one local. I suppose you want me to do my little super-duper thingy on our computer and find out who the numbers belong to, do you?"

"That would be great, George, if it's not too much trouble for you?"

"Nothing's too much trouble for you, Danny-boy."

Huxley knew that Pepper always referred to him as Danny-boy when he was at his most facetious and he was glad that his old friend had fallen into his natural manner when it would have been easy for him to take umbrage considering the bother that Huxley had caused him.

He listened to the sound of keys tapping on the computer keyboard at George's end of the phone and pictured the hulk of a man that he was leaning over the computer typing with two fingers and probably still hitting three keys at once with his giant hands.

"Just in your own time, George, I've got all night. It's not as though anybody's trying to kill me or anything."

"Aye, hold your horses, I've got to let the wee machine thingy do its business." Then, in a firmer tone, "In all seriousness, Dan, are you and the kid alright? I mean, forget about where you are exactly but, wherever it is, are you safe?"

"I hope so, George, I really hope to god."

"But you don't believe in god."

"That just shows you how bad things are."

"Aye, well you be careful and make sure you look after that wee laddie."

"I will, George. Don't worry about us. You just get on with the business of finding out who killed Simms and thereby kill two birds with one stone." Huxley deliberately hadn't mentioned Sam as he thought it best not to give away too much to Pepper as you never know when these things come back to bite you.

"You can rest easy in your bed, safe in the knowledge that Detective Inspector Michael Blackburn is on the case and will, no doubt, be making an arrest any moment now. Okay, I think the little machine thingy has done its work now as it seems to be giving me some names." Huxley smiled at Pepper's delivery knowing full well that the Sergeant was one of the most technically advanced and proficient people that he had ever met but he played dumb to everyone when he sat in front of a computer.

"What have you got?"

"The first call was made at six minutes past two and it was to National Geographic Headquarters in Washington. That's in America, Dan."

"Thanks for pointing that out to me, George."

"Well, you know what you academics are like, all brains but no actual useful information, so I just thought I'd keep you right. Okay, so that call lasted for five minutes and twenty three seconds, then, immediately afterwards, because it's registered as eleven minutes past two, he rang a place called The Maecenas Foundation for Ancient Art in Geneva, Switzerland. He was on that call for a little longer this time, seven minutes eleven seconds to be exact. Then his next call isn't registered until two fifty five when he rang someone at Trinity College. I don't know who, Dan, as I don't know who is registered to the extension but I can tell you the number. Maybe once you've got a name you can pass that on to me, sort of as a return of the favour, although that would be a first."

"Just give me the number you cantankerous old git." Pepper recited the number and Huxley grabbed a pencil and a scrap of paper from the desk in the library where he had been pacing while on the phone, Sam and Alan looking on and trying to pick up whatever they could from the one side of the conversation they heard. He looked at the number to see if he recognised the extension but he wasn't too familiar with the telephone numbers for each person at the college.

"It doesn't mean anything to me at first glance, George, but leave it with me and I'll let you know who it belongs to."

"Aye, just be sure you do. Remember, friendship is a two way street, Dan."

"Don't worry, as soon as I know, you will know."

"Do you think the calls have anything to do with his death?"

"I just find it strange that within a couple of hours of

accepting the possibility that his research had been taking him in the wrong direction and discussing it with some people in the field, he then is killed in broad daylight. I don't like coincidences, George, and this just seems like such a huge one to me. But was it the phone calls that sparked it or something else? I just don't know. How about his emails, have you checked them yet?"

"That, I'm afraid will take a little longer what with passwords and what have you. We'll get them but I can't say when unless you happen to know anyone who might have known his password and who could help us access his account?"

"No-one springs immediately to mind," Huxley lied, casting a glance in Sam's direction and wondering why he hadn't thought of the emails before.

"Yeah, well, if you do think of someone then let me know, won't you?"

"What's that, George? Yeah, just hold on a minute, I've left it in my jacket pocket. Let me go and get it." Huxley walked towards the door and left the study, walking towards the stairs.

"What are you on about, Dan? I only asked….ah, I see, you wanted an excuse to leave the room you were in as you didn't want the laddie to hear what you're about to say."

"There's no fooling you, Sergeant Pepper."

"So good they named a record after me."

"Just as well it wasn't a Police record."

"That joke wasn't funny the first dozen times either, Dan."

"Oh, where's your sense of humour," replied Huxley.

"Tucked up in bed fast asleep like I should be. Now, can you talk yet or do I still have to listen to your blarney while you get out of earshot of the boy?"

"No, we're fine now, George."

"So what is that you don't want the laddie to hear?"

"The laddie in question," started Huxley, "isn't telling me

everything that he knows but he's clever enough to act dumb when I confront him."

"You don't think he's involved in Simms's death, do you?

"I don't have him pegged as a killer but there's definitely more to it than he's saying. Something is working away in the back of my brain but it hasn't formulated itself into anything concrete yet. I'll get there but you could maybe help me."

"What do you need?"

"I need you to find out what you can about a Dr Max Redding. He works at National Geographic which is one of the places that Simms…"

He never got any further as Pepper interjected, "You mean the Dr Max Redding who's all over the news right now?"

"He's what? Why, what's he done?"

"He hasn't done anything, Dan. He's dead, Dan. Murdered. His body has been found in the boot of his car at Chicago airport. Been there a couple of days they reckon. Stabbed in the back."

CHAPTER 25

MILAN – 1970

By the afternoon of the next day, the pair knew their window of opportunity was running out and that they had no other option but to confront the man that Spencer believed to be the leader of the Knights' Templar. He was very reluctant to subject his newfound accomplice to the possible danger that a confrontation with Grimani entailed but could see little other choice.

They had watched him retrieve his post earlier and could clearly see him opening the letter they had sent. His immediate reaction had been to simply set it to one side. And, although he had picked it up a couple of times since, there had been nothing in his manner that had raised either hope or suspicion in the pair watching. Spencer wasn't entirely sure what he had been hoping for but knew that if they didn't act now it only increased the likelihood of Grimani verifying the authenticity of the request.

"Okay, you know what to say to him by way of introduction, don't you, James?"

"Spencer, will you stop fussing. We've been over this a dozen times already. I'll be fine. If he doesn't buy it I'll just get out of there as fast as I can. If he does and invites me in then I'll find out as much as I can. But we are either going to do this

The Judas Deception

or we aren't, we can't sit around here in the hope that he's going to come over and introduce himself to his new neighbours."

"By Christ, the reputation you red-heads have for being feisty is certainly well earned. Okay, my sweet James, you are right. But I just don't want to see a single one of those ginger locks of yours hurt in any way. I'll be right here watching you."

"I know you will."

"Be careful, dear boy."

The Irishman nodded his appreciation as he made his way out the door. They both knew that this was a risk and he was concerned himself about the reception that he might receive from Grimani. But he wanted to do whatever he could to help Spencer in his quest and to expose the hypocrisy of the Church that he had served all these years.

They had agreed that they had to make it seem as though O'Connell had just reached the city and so should arrive at the address by taxi direct from the train station in case anyone checked. So the young priest left the apartment building by the rear door, suitcase in hand and made his way to the station. Here he passed through to the concourse in front and stood in line as the queue for taxis slowly dwindled, eventually climbing into one himself. By this time he was sweating from both the walk and the wait in the afternoon sun and he felt that he looked like someone who had just undertaken a train journey from Rome to Milan.

The driver took him to the address given and, some two hours after he had left, a heavily disguised O'Connell arrived on the street he had departed from. This time, however, he got out in front of Grimani's house, making a big show of paying the driver and thanking him before looking around as though he had never been there before.

Spencer, watching from the building opposite, smiled at the performance and thought the young man a natural for the stage should he ever decide on a change of vocation. He saw his now bewigged and bearded friend walk to the door and examine the bells on offer before choosing one and pressing. From his vantage point Spencer could see Grimani rising from his desk and leaving the office as he went to answer the door.

Spencer was uncertain whether to be pleased or not as he saw the young priest being ushered in with a great flourish and no hesitation but consoled himself with the fact that their ruse had gotten them inside. He had, of course, had the apartment burgled on previous occasions, even going along himself once to check for possible hiding places, but had found nothing. Either the information was in Grimani's head or he had an ingenious hiding place which was beyond Spencer.

He watched as O'Connell was led into the study and invited to take a seat. Grimani himself walked back around the desk and retook his seat so he sat opposite his newly arrived guest. Spencer had a pang in the pit of his stomach borne from the normality of the whole situation. He had expected at least a confrontation of sorts with some proof of identity and assurances before any entry may have been proffered, so was uneasy at just how civilised the whole thing looked. O'Connell, for his part, seemed to be playing his role very effectively but that still didn't justify Grimani's lack of suspicion.

O'Connell, too, was surprised at the ease of entry and, now that he was in the presence of the man of whom Spencer was so wary, he could see from his physical appearance just what an intimidating figure he was. But upon answering the door and seeing a priest standing there he had said that he had been expecting the visit and invited O'Connell in without a second thought. Having been escorted up the stairs and into his very spacious apartment, O'Connell had followed his tall host into the very room that they had been watching for the

The Judas Deception

past couple of days and had to stop himself from casting a glance towards where he knew Spencer would be sitting.

Grimani, formalities out of the way by means of the young priest's refusal of coffee or aperitif, set about asking his guest about his journey from Rome and whether he had eaten. When the young man, whose Italian was excellent, advised that he had and that he didn't want to be a burden on his host for any longer than necessary, Grimani watched for any indication that he might be nervous or, even, frightened.

He had encountered a good many priests from the Vatican and he knew them all to have a similar vibe, ducks out of water when removed from their normal surroundings. He was getting that to a certain degree from the young man but there was something else there, an overcompensation perhaps of relaxation. He had no doubt that this was a genuine priest who had been institutionalised by a lifetime spent in the confines of the Vatican, making his visit here all the more interesting.

He hadn't been able to phone to confirm the authenticity of the would be visitor or his credentials but what he did know was that the letter he had received had not followed normal procedure for such a request and that the man sitting across from him now was not here in an official capacity. However, he was interested in finding out just why the young priest was here. And more importantly, how much he knew. One way or the other he was going to get some answers.

O'Connell anticipated having to prove his credentials to the man who now sat opposite him and, sure enough, as Grimani began to speak, he mentioned names and titles of certain members of the Vatican, deliberately getting positions wrong or speaking of priests who had died many years ago. O'Connell corrected him, knowing that he was supposed to but he guessed almost immediately that Grimani was simply toying with him as a cat does a mouse that it has in its clutches.

He played along for a few minutes before asking if he may use the bathroom to freshen up as he was feeling the effects of his journey. Lifting his suitcase, he rose and followed the directions given by Grimani to the nearest bathroom in the apartment and left his graceful host standing by his chair, his eyes following the priest as he left the room.

Returning a few minutes later he found the man relaxing in his chair, the letter that Spencer had devised now spread in front of him. O'Connell guessed that they were nearing the end game and hoped that he was able to make it through the next couple of minutes unscathed. By that time he could only pray that he and Spencer would know everything that they needed to.

"So just what did you hope to achieve by this?" asked Grimani, flicking the letter across the desk with disdain. He leaned back in his chair knowing that he had caught his prey off guard.

O'Connell stared back at him thinking that they had missed out a couple of steps and had progressed faster than he was expecting. He suddenly feared that his time was going to run out. He and Spencer had discussed what might happen if the meeting progressed this far and now Spencer's words came back to him, 'Bluff, bluff, bluff, dear boy, bluff like you have never bluffed before. Bluff like your life depends on it which it just might'.

"I don't quite understand, sir. I came here on the understanding..."

"You came here knowing very well that there are no such documents as those you are looking for and, what is more, the person who apparently signed this letter knows it too. So why then would he sign a letter telling me to arrange access for you to something that doesn't exist?"

"But I have come across references to the Judas Gospel

as recent as the sixteenth century and, when I asked about it, I was told that it had been in the Church's possession at that time. I was of the understanding that it still is."

"Well, I think that you are full of shit and I want to know who sent you. I can tell you that you won't be leaving here until you do." He reached for the drawer nearest to him on the right of his desk where O'Connell knew he had a handgun concealed, having been briefed by Spencer.

O'Connell sniffed the air and said, "Do you smell smoke?"

Grimani stiffened as he sniffed the smoke that was starting to seep under the door. "What the fuck…." He stood up suddenly but not before taking his gun from the drawer. He pointed it straight at O'Connell's chest and fired once. O'Connell keeled over, falling from his chair onto the floor just as shouts started from outside the apartment door. Grimani ran out of the room to find flames further down the hallway.

At the same time concerned neighbours were beginning to try to break through his door, obviously fearful that he was in danger. He knew what he must do and made straight for the safe hidden in his bedroom. He heard the door burst open behind him and the shouts of voices as people came into the apartment. He had to act quickly.

Spencer knew as soon as O'Connell had left the room that the young priest was in trouble. He raced down the stairs of his building and ran across the road to Grimani's apartment block. He knew the other occupants of the building were retired and were at home during the day so pressed the bells for both. It was the man from the ground floor who responded first with the others making their way down the stairs as he barged his way in.

"Fire! Fire!" he cried in Italian.

He started for the stairs, the others following in his wake apart from the man from the ground floor apartment who went to call the fire brigade. As they reached the middle landing, the smoke was billowing from under the door of Grimani's apartment. The Italians began shouting and banging on the door but Spencer knew that he had to get inside and try to help his friend.

He found a fire axe lying along the communal hall and grabbed it, swinging to hit the door as close to the lock as he could. It took him about thirty seconds but he managed to create a hole which he then reached through to undo the lock and open the door. He ran straight to the front room to find his charge, his friend, his accomplice lying on the floor face down, unmoving.

Spencer let out a cry and his heart sank as he realised that he had been directly responsible for sending the young man into this situation. He could only hope their plan had worked.

CHAPTER 26

Not for the first time that night, Huxley reeled at what he was being told.

"Christ on a bike, what the fuck is going on?" he murmured.

"You think there's a connection between that and Simms?"

"I can't say for sure, George, but it's too remarkable to be coincidence don't you think?"

"Well, now I know that Simms rang the institution that this guy Redding worked at, I think that it all sounds like it could be linked."

"And another knife wound?"

"Aye, indeed. Listen, what are you not telling me, Dan?"

"Nothing that I don't know, honestly George. It's just a… well, you know."

"A feeling? Aye, I know alright. I know all about you and your funny feelings. Strange the way they never turn out to be wrong. Christ, Dan, what have you got yourself into?"

"I'm not sure yet, George, but I think I'm starting to get there. Listen, I'm keeping my phone on from now so whenever you do get something let me know, won't you?"

"Aye, you'll be top of my list," Pepper mocked. "Seriously though, Dan, you need to be careful. Someone is out there gunning for you."

"Which is why it's good to know that I've got you ready to gun straight back at them."

"Aye, you can count on me to do that, don't you worry. One more thing, while you're there, seeing as how you would have been disturbing my sleep in the middle of the night if I wasn't already involved in a manhunt for you so haven't actually got to my bed. Does the name Father James O'Connell mean anything to you?"

Huxley began making his way back down the stairs as he responded.

"O'Connell? No, can't say that I've come across the name before. I don't usually hang out with priests and cardinals as a rule. I think it's the whole not believing in god thing. Although I think that's something I might actually have in common with most of them."

This produced a laugh from the other end of the phone before Pepper responded with, "Yeah, well I thought I'd try just in case."

"Why do you ask?" Huxley said as he joined the others back in the study.

"Oh, nothing really, it's just when Simms was killed he was holding a book open with a tab on the page. Written on the tab was the name 'Father James O'Connell'. Probably left there by a previous owner, you know what these second hand books are like, full of notes and scribbles and all sorts. I just wanted to eliminate it as a dead end. You know me, meticulous to the last."

"Very true, heaven forbid anyone should ever call into question your dedication to detail. But no, I haven't heard the name. What was the title of the book by the way?"

"Ammmm, hold on, I have it written down here somewhere. Ah, here it is. It was 'The Lost Gospel of Judas' by Spencer Harris."

The Judas Deception

Huxley's face betrayed little of what Pepper was telling him but Sam could see him drifting off into his own world again. She stood and went towards him to put a reassuring hand on his arm which seemed to jolt him from his thoughts. He nodded towards her to indicate that he was alright and made for the chair he had been sitting in earlier as he concluded his conversation with Pepper, assuring him that he would keep him advised of any developments at their end.

As he ended the call he reached for the book that he had been studying earlier, turning the pages as he searched for something he remembered seeing. He stopped as he came across the notation he was looking for. Sure enough it said 'Hidden Treasures Of The Vatican' by Father James O'Connell. He turned, holding the book in his hand and started to detail that part of his conversation with Pepper. He decided to keep the news about Dr Redding's murder to himself for now.

"And as you said on the phone, you don't believe in coincidences," responded Donovan.

"Not of that magnitude. I mean, here we are less than twelve hours since he was murdered and in that time we have come across reference after reference to the Judas Gospel. And now we find out that he was holding a copy of a book that might just help us unravel this whole affair. That's just a bit too much for me to swallow as being pure chance."

"What do you think Stephen's phone calls were all about then?" asked Sam, referencing the earlier part of the conversation that they had partly heard.

Alan stepped in at this point. "The National Geographic we know already have the document and are responsible for the translation so it would be only natural for Dr Simms to contact them if he had doubts about the validity of their work."

"And he knew people there as he had been himself before

on a number of occasions and he set up your visit there, didn't he?" asked Sam.

"Yeah, he used his contacts to get me access. So maybe he rang one of the people he knew there to ask them about the discrepancy."

"Yes, maybe," agreed Huxley, his mind elsewhere.

"And The Maecenas Foundation for Ancient Art in Switzerland," continued Alan. "They were the organisation responsible for finding the Codex in the first place. So, again, if he was tracing the origin of the discrepancy then it would make sense for him to contact them."

"Ah yes, the Maecenas Foundation, of course," added Sam. "He's been to visit them before as well, I remember the name now that I think about it. When he was researching bits of the document, he went to see them to get their take on some of the language used. He probably had a few contacts that he corresponded with regularly so he'll have tried one of them to talk about what he was thinking."

"That reminds me, do you know his email password?"

Sam thought about this for a moment and then nodded. "I think I might. Do you want me to give it a try?"

"Yes please. It would be useful to know if he sent any emails as well as the phone calls. It might tell us who he had been speaking to and, more importantly, if he had found anything else out that might have got him killed."

As Sam got to work on the emails, Huxley returned to the note that he had retrieved from Harris's book earlier. He managed to expose a corner and began to gently pull it back until the whole page opened up like a blooming flower, the aged paper and frayed edges the coloured petals. He laid it out on the floor in front of him and began to carefully smooth out the paper. There were drawings on the page, rough sketches made free-hand, some sort of code written alongside them.

Alan joined him. There was something familiar about the sketch but he couldn't quite put his finger on it so he set about trying to break the code to see if that would give him some guidance.

Meanwhile Sam had managed to open Simms's email. She began sifting through his Inbox but, finding nothing of interest, she turned to his Sent items

There were two from that afternoon. The first was to someone at the Maecenas Foundation for Ancient Art and Sam began reading through it. She started excitedly as she read and turned to the others.

"Listen to this, it's the email that Stephen sent to a Dr Robert Klaus following on from their phone call. It says:

'Hi Robert

Thank you for listening to the ramblings of a crazy academic and for agreeing to take the time to look into my suspicions.

As I said in my phone call, I am wondering if there is any way that the original papyrus might not have been complete when it was first discovered. I ask only because I have been alerted to a possible discrepancy in the translation that may point towards the pages not being in order. The only possible reason for this is that there is something missing and I'd be interested on your take on this. I know rumours have persisted ever since the discovery but these have all been shouted down with the subsequent release of the Codex and its translation but I might have some

> *new information which suggests that there could be some truth to these after all.*
>
> *Let me know what you can find and I will look forward to hearing from you soon.*
>
> *In the meantime, take care*
>
> *Stephen'*

"What do you make of that then?"

"Well, it confirms our suspicions that he was indeed running with the possibility that what Alan had told him was correct and that he was investigating further. Whether it was what got him killed is still undecided but it's a step in the right direction."

"There's another one to a Dodger101@hotmail. Anyone know a Dodger?"

"Nope, can't say I do. What does it say?"

Sam began to read it out.

> *'Hey my friend*
>
> *Thanks for the text earlier. I will definitely check out that reference later, I appreciate the tip. About the private collector, tell me more. Do you really think they've found some of the original?*
>
> *Hope to hear from you soon.*
>
> *Simmsy'*

The Judas Deception

"Interesting. The fact that he has used a nickname to sign off and it's sent to someone referred to as Dodger suggests that we are looking for an old school pal or friend from uni," said Huxley.

"It doesn't help that he's addressed it to 'my friend'. That tells us nothing," added Sam, rereading the message again to herself.

"Yes, one for the police to track down I think. They'll get an IP address off the email account and we'll see who it is then. In the meantime, Simms refers to a text. I hadn't thought about that but it'll hopefully be on his phone so Pepper might be able to give us more."

"It certainly sounds like it refers to what we are looking at. Private collector? Do you think that could be Alan's lead with the new fragment?"

"It's certainly a possibility." Huxley looked up to see what Alan had to offer but he had his head in his hands and appeared to be playing with his phone. Huxley wondered what was so interesting but decided to leave him to it.

"And what about checking out that reference? You don't think he means going to Prestige, do you?"

"That was my initial thought but without knowing the original text then it's maybe a bit of a leap. That said, it could mean our killer knew where he would be."

"That's just what I was thinking."

"I'll mention it to George when I speak to him next."

"What have you got there?" asked Sam, seeing the piece of paper in front of the boys.

"I'm not sure. It looks like some sort of drawing with writing by the side of it. When I say drawing I really mean rough sketches of geometric shapes of some sort. The writing by the side might be abbreviations linked with them but, to be honest, it looks more like code to me. It doesn't make a lot of sense, any of it."

"It is code," said Alan, suddenly jumping up, "and I think I've got it!"

"Really?" queried Huxley. "What is it?"

"It's actually a deviation of the ancient Greek alphabet and, if you apply a fairly simply mathematical formula then it forms the name of books. I haven't got them all but this one is definitely the *Principia Mathematica*," he said, lifting the sketch towards them and pointing to one of the codes by the side of a sketch of a rectangle with a corner missing.

"Do you think that's supposed to be a drawing of the book?" asked Sam, joining them.

Huxley looked at the drawing which could represent a very crude, childlike drawing of a book but it didn't make any sense to him. He thought about the book itself. *Principia Mathematica* was Sir Isaac Newton's most famous text but he couldn't see how it related to their current predicament.

"Why draw a sketch of the book if you are going to refer to it, albeit in coded notes alongside?" Huxley mused.

"To me, that would suggest the reference is to a specific copy of the book rather than the work in general."

"That's good thinking, Sam," agreed Huxley. "It would help to see what the other words are that are written in code."

While Sam and Daniel had been perusing the drawing, Alan had been working on one of the other coded words but had come unstuck.

"He's used a different code for this one. In fact, I've tried my formula on a couple of the others and it doesn't work. I think he may have used a different code for each of the clues."

Huxley looked more carefully at the sketches and, as he studied them, an idea began to develop in his mind.

"You know, I think this might be a map after all. In fact, I believe it might be a treasure map."

"Really?" question Sam. "What makes you think that?"

"The effort put into hiding it away, the coded message, the nature of the sketches. I think if we can crack the codes we might find something rather interesting."

CHAPTER 27

MILAN – 1970

Spencer turned O'Connell's body over, carefully holding the back of the young priest's head as he did so.

"Are you alright, my dear boy?"

"Yes, but you never told me it would hurt this much."

"Can't say I've ever been shot, even with a protective vest on? Can you move okay?"

"I think so," said O'Connell, sitting up gingerly.

"Come on then, we need to get out of here before Grimani realises what has happened."

He helped the younger man to his feet and supported him as they made their way from the room. The neighbours were standing in the hallway calling to Grimani who was still at the far end of the apartment. Spencer led O'Connell out of the building and down the steps outside. They could hear the approaching sirens, so quickly made their way across the road to where they had a waiting car. Spencer opened the passenger door and helped the young priest in before running around to the driver's side.

O'Connell reached under his tunic to undo the protective vest that Spencer had provided him with. The hope was that it wouldn't be needed, with the fire catching before Grimani had the chance to do anything, but Spencer insisted that

O'Connell wear it. They also hoped that Grimani wouldn't go for a head shot, playing the percentages.

"Few people do go for the head, no matter how good a shot they are. Slightest movement from their target can result in a miss. Much more likely he'll aim for the torso. Bigger target. Less chance of missing, all that. Christ, I can't believe we are talking about this. We must be crazy."

"We? I'm the one he is going to shoot!"

"Oh, sweet James, what are we thinking? Let's forget the whole thing. Fly away. Pack up and go. Just you and me. Timbuktu. Mongolia. Christ, the moon for all I care."

"And torture yourself with coming this far? So close to everything you have worked for? No, we are going to do this. Let's just hope you are right."

Truth be told, Spencer had his fears that Grimani may go for a head shot as well, the professional that he is, but he never voiced his concern to the young Irishman, instead torturing himself with the thought of his accomplice being killed all because of him. He knew that he would never forgive himself if that happened. Tried to convince himself that the percentages were on their side. Like a mantra, over and over again he kept telling himself that most people go for body shots. And luckily, in this case, Grimani had gone with the percentages.

Relief flooded him as he watched O'Connell undo the straps to allow the vest to come off. The young man winced in pain, feeling the bruise that was already beginning to flower on his chest.

"Are you sure you are alright, my dear?"

"I'll be fine. It only hurts when I breathe." He looked at Spencer and the two of them burst out laughing before O'Connell grimaced. "And laugh. Oh, that hurts. Stop it, Spencer."

But Spencer couldn't help himself. The release of tension

caused him to keep on laughing and O'Connell found himself joining his partner in spite of the pain it caused him.

"Did he try to salvage anything?" asked O'Connell, wincing.

"Well, he ran past the fire to his bedroom so it would appear that there was something worth saving but it could just be a picture of his mother, all we know."

"Do you think that it could have been the gospel?"

"I doubt it, I really can't see him having it personally, but it might be something that he needs to access it."

"Well, we'll find out soon enough if you're right about what he'll do next."

As he spoke, O'Connell saw Grimani running down the steps of the building, suitcase in hand, and towards his car just as the first fire engine arrived. He didn't even stop to acknowledge the presence of the fire brigade, bundling the suitcase into the back of his car before taking off quickly.

"Here we go," said Spencer as he made to follow.

The suitcase suggested travel which the pair had anticipated but whether by train, boat or plane was anyone's guess.

"Pack your passport, clothes, swimming trunks, all that. If the plan works, I expect he'll rabbit," then seeing the confusion on his partner's face, "do a runner, split, get out of town."

"Do you honestly think he'll go straight to the document?" asked O'Connell.

"Impossible to say one hundred percent but there's a chance. Bloody good chance, I'd say. Makes sense. Under threat, go to it, check security, beef it up if needed."

"And we just follow him wherever he goes?"

"Sounds silly when you say it but yes, that's the plan, dear boy."

The pair had prepared for every eventuality, suitcases packed and passports at the ready, as Spencer believed that

Grimani may well flee the country. He thought Switzerland, Grimani being a Swiss national. Perhaps Zurich, the city in which Grimani had grown up and home to the efficient Swiss banking system. Where better to hide such sensitive documents than securely locking them away in a Swiss safety deposit box? So, with Switzerland easily reachable by train and plane and even by road from Milan, the pair had tried to cover all possibilities.

"Which would you prefer?"

"Me? Couldn't care less, old boy. Each has its merits and each its problems. He gets on a plane then there is nowhere for us to hide and the potential for him to see us is huge. But then at least we know he won't be getting off until we reach our destination. With the train we would have to keep him under surveillance the whole way in case the bugger jumped off at Zermatt to ski down the Matterhorn. Less chance of being spotted perhaps but more chance of losing him. Car would work well for a while, but once we got onto lonely roads we would have to hang back a fair bit lest he spots us. Or maybe he would be able to outpace us, leave us for dust. Long shot at best. Just hope we actually get to that point."

Their plan had worked perfectly up until then, although he would have preferred it if his young companion wasn't now sporting a couple of cracked ribs. But, that apart, they had gained entry to Grimani's home, in the end much easier than they had imagined, and had been able to force a reaction out of him.

Once inside, O'Connell had played his part perfectly, leaving to use the bathroom at a point when it was unlikely to raise any suspicions in his host. That had been the signal for Spencer to make his dash across the road and alert the neighbours and gain entry into the building. O'Connell had taken his suitcase with him to the bathroom on the pretence that it was required then, once inside, had reached for the makeshift incendiary device and put it against the curtains before returning to the study.

He had anticipated Grimani toying with him for a few more minutes by which time the fire would have spread and he'd have more important things to concern himself with. But, unfortunately, his host had cut to the chase somewhat quicker than expected and the gun produced before the fire became obvious.

They had hoped that the fire would provoke a reaction from Grimani, causing him to retrieve anything important that was hidden in the apartment and to take flight with it. It seemed that they had got just what they wanted. The question now was where would be run to?

The answer was Milan airport. They had discussed this eventuality and now started to execute their plan. Anxious that Grimani didn't realise he was being followed, Spencer dropped his companion at the entrance. O'Connell, now dressed in civvies having disrobed, would wait in the hall and track Grimani's movements, taking great care to remain out of sight.

He saw the tall man stride purposefully into the terminal a few minutes later and go to a desk where he appeared to purchase a ticket. But O'Connell had no idea where to and didn't dare to move any closer for fear of being seen. Even if the disguise he had worn did prevent Grimani from recognising him now, he still didn't want to take the chance. Although he did wonder how the suave and controlled man who had shot him less than an hour ago would react to suddenly coming face to face with someone he thought he had killed. But O'Connell knew that now was not the time for such games.

He waited for Spencer to catch up, all the while tracking Grimani's movements from a distance. He watched as the Swiss checked in his suitcase, noting the desk number. Once

The Judas Deception

he was certain that Grimani had passed safely through to Departures, O'Connell made his way back to the check-in desk. It was a British Airways desk and the only flight that evening was to London leaving within the hour.

Time was of the essence and O'Connell quickly brought his companion up to speed before the pair hurriedly completed the formalities of ticket purchase and check-in and made their way to the gate. Now all they had to do was ensure that Grimani couldn't recognise either of them.

Having checked their suitcases, the pair were armed with only hand luggage. They headed to the toilets and took a cubicle each. Five minutes later they re-emerged, transformed in appearance.

O'Connell, no longer carrying the bulk of a protective vest, relied on the drastic change in physicality to throw Grimani off, a wig and moustache combo adding to the transformation so much so that even Spencer had to do a double take.

The large man was rather more difficult to remain inconspicuous so had decided to do exactly the opposite, hiding in plain sight. He was now garbed in an outfit that would have made even Liberace jealous, the sparkly silver sequined suit reflecting O'Connell's disguised face in a thousand distorted poses. A pink feather boa and peacock feathered hat further enhanced his appearance. As Spencer had explained when they were preparing their outfits, it was exactly the type of get up that if he saw someone wearing he would avoid them at all costs. They hoped Grimani might feel the same way.

The pair left the bathroom separately, Spencer leading in the hope that his distraction would allow O'Connell to slip out unnoticed. As well as the clothes, Spencer was also wearing blusher and heavy eye liner, making it all the more unlikely that Grimani would ever recognise him. That said, he didn't want to give the potential killer a close up view so, having made his flamboyant entrance into the lounge, he now made for a seat behind the Templar who was having a coffee and reading an Italian newspaper. Meanwhile, O'Connell had slipped quietly out amongst the other passengers.

The two accomplices, sitting at opposite sides of the concourse, watched as Grimani then left the café and browsed in the duty free shop before returning to the seating area. He took a seat rather closer to O'Connell than the young priest was comfortable with. But he supposed that this might be to try and stay away from the crazy man in the sparkly suit so he couldn't help but smile and sit tight until their flight was called.

Spencer had deliberately purchased seats that weren't together. While it increased the potential for one of them to be seated near to Grimani, it would at least mean that they could continue to avoid being seen together.

"Sitting across the aisle from you, close your eyes, feign sleep, snore, all that. Hell, fart in his direction, make his eyes water, can't see for tears!"

As it turned out, they needn't have worried as Grimani got up when they called for any first class passengers to make their way forward for boarding. Spencer had a momentary panic that they wouldn't be able to see him but then realised that they would all arrive at exactly the same time first class or not.

After an uneventful flight, they made to disembark, Spencer mincing his way along the plane to keep in character as he later explained. O'Connell, who had a perfect view of the performance, thought that there was an element of enjoyment about the big man's execution that suggested otherwise.

Grimani had checked in a suitcase and his pursuers had followed his lead so they joined him at the luggage carousel and waited. They stood behind him so they weren't directly in his line of sight but, with Spencer's rather noticeable attire,

The Judas Deception

Grimani couldn't help but observe his entrance albeit with visible disdain. But Spencer was careful not to get too close, leaving Grimani only with the impression of someone he would like to avoid if at all possible.

"If his case arrives first we abandon ours and follow. Bugger all worth a damn in either of them. Priest's garb and frilly knickers I shouldn't wonder in yours. Leave them to their fate. Other way round, just let it ride. Do the carousel dance. Grab it when he collects his."

As Grimani's stepped forward to retrieve his case, Spencer spotted his own coming towards him, O'Connell's already on its second lap. He thought it a somewhat drab and ordinary brown leather suitcase for such an audaciously dressed man and was glad that Grimani was already heading for the exit by the time he had retrieved it. It was just such incongruities that a man like Grimani may pick up on.

Once they had all passed through customs, the pair watched as their prey made his way towards a taxi. Hurrying, they clambered into the back of the next one on the rank.

"Follow that cab," shouted Spencer with a flourish of his arm as he pointed towards the now departing car that held Grimani.

The driver didn't bat an eyelid as he moved off in pursuit of the indicated taxi, later explaining that it happened more often than people think. Anyway he wasn't going to argue with some raging poofter with feathers in his hair, now, was he?

With a chase always likely, Spencer had thought of the need to get rid of his eye-catching attire and dress a little more normally. The driver had long ago set aside any misgivings he might have about his fare, thinking only of the money, so he acted almost oblivious as the large man in the back seat began to remove his trousers and sparkly jacket and replace them with a much more demure black jumper and slacks. It wasn't as though he hadn't seen it all before, as he told the other drivers later, I mean, he'd had Danny La Rue in the back of his cab only the other week.

The chase continued right into the heart of central London, the first taxi stopping outside Kings Cross train station and Grimani gracefully stepping out of the back and striding towards the entrance.

Spencer and O'Connell waited until he was inside before exiting their own taxi, the driver thanking them for the generous tip which Spencer had included for his 'discretion'.

"You never saw us, okay?"

"Never saw a bleedin' thing, mate, and no mistake."

O'Connell hadn't changed, his disguise not being so memorable and doing the job of hiding his face and rather obvious red hair. He was still wary, however, of bumping into Grimani so spent a minute perusing the concourse of the station before spotting the tall man in the queue for the ticket office. The pair waited and, once Grimani had his ticket, they followed his movements to the platform before dashing towards it in pursuit.

The train was preparing to leave, the guard watching the stragglers board, waiting to signal. Spencer rushed up to him, asking if tickets could be bought on board. The guard rolled his eyes but told him he could although they had to board now as the train was due to leave. They jumped on the carriage one down from that which Grimani had entered.

"It's all first class this end of the train, guv'ner," shouted the guard. "Second class is further along the platform."

"That's fine, thank you, just what we want," then, as an afterthought, "Amm, what train is this?"

The guard fixed him with a funny look before answering, "Cambridge express, innit" adding under his breath, "what do you think, you posh pratt!"

The Judas Deception

"Cambridge?" questioned O'Connell when they had settled in their carriage, Spencer having gone and looked through the dividing doors and spotted Grimani sitting with his back to them in the next carriage along.

"Yes, my dear James, it had struck me as rather odd as well. Why on earth would he be running to Cambridge?"

"Well, why would he?

"Buggered if I know. Only one way to find out."

"You don't think it could be a trap?" questioned the young priest.

"Could be any bloody thing. Could be on to us. Leading us a merry dance, run around, fuck knows."

The inspector came in and Spencer purchased two first class returns.

"Why returns?" asked O'Connell when the inspector had moved on.

"Just in case, my dear fellow."

"In case of what?"

"Look, I don't think we have been spotted, played our roles well, hidden in plain sight, all that. Man's a killer, no doubt. But even he must be bothered. Everything that happened in Milan. Perhaps he has seen us, perhaps not. Maybe just being very careful. And very clever."

"You think this is a bluff?"

"Can't be sure, old chap, but of all the places I thought he might run to, I certainly never expected my own, dear Cambridge. Could be wrong. Maybe Cambridge is all part of our journey. Maybe there is something there that he needs. Or maybe he is planning on sitting tight whenever we reach our destination before taking the exact same journey in reverse and heading back to London."

"Hence the return tickets in case we need to do the same."

"Exactly, sweet James."

As it happened, upon arriving at Cambridge, Grimani got off the train and immediately started walking towards town. O'Connell had never been to the city before and was unsure where they were in relation to anything, but Spencer had lived in the nearby village of Grantchester for years and was involved in university life as a casual lecturer so was perfectly at home.

He watched Grimani walk quickly down Station Road, his long legs swallowing up the ground as he headed purposefully towards the centre of town. Spencer thought it strange that the man hadn't taken one of the taxis waiting outside the station and realised that this obviously wasn't his first visit to Cambridge. This thought more than any other bothered him immensely.

He had kept a careful watch on Grimani ever since his friend's death, using his contacts both in law enforcement and institutions around the world to track the man's movements. But in all that time he had never known Grimani to be in Cambridge. So what had he missed?

"What are we going to do now?" O'Connell asked, shaking the big man from his reverie.

Spencer explained that the train station had been deliberately built on the outskirts of town to discourage students from yesteryear from taking the train into London on a whim and visiting family, friends and lovers instead of attending lectures.

"Of course, nowadays it's not as remote as it once was but it's still a good fifteen minute walk even at the pace he's going," nodding towards the tall figure striding away from them. The problem they had, explained Spencer, is that most people went everywhere in Cambridge on bike or, failing that, by taxi, So there weren't many people walking, not in that part of the city. "Makes us stand out, conspicuous, all that. Spot us a mile off. One backward glance, that's all it would take."

"But we've got to follow him. I mean, we've come this far."

"All in hand, my dear chap, all in hand." Spence reached into his pocket and, taking a set of keys, walked over to a bike secured against a lamppost across from the main entrance to the station. He used one of the keys to unlock it.

"Always leave it here when I go away. Never know when it will come in handy. Bit like now."

He suggested that they split up, O'Connell following on foot while he went on bike.

"I can keep ahead of him, track his movements, that sort of thing. Turn off down side streets, watch him pass, ride on ahead again. Keep him within sight, all that."

O'Connell could see the sense in this as Spencer knew the city and could anticipate Grimani's movements. For his part, O'Connell simply started walking, following some way behind because, as Spencer had already pointed out, he wasn't going to recognise anyone at that distance. He certainly wouldn't be looking for priests that he had recently shot and left for dead in a burning apartment.

"Plus, chap's so tall you can track him for miles. Easy to follow. Stands out from the crowd. Just keep your eyes on him."

Spencer gave his young companion a gentle pat on the shoulder before setting off on the bike, his large frame sitting rather more comfortably on the saddle than O'Connell would have expected.

The hasty plan the pair had cobbled together seemed to work well as they made it into town without either losing Grimani or, it seemed, attracting his attention.

He had walked in what, O'Connell was to learn later, was the most direct route into town, before heading along Trinity Street. The young Irishman was only half paying attention to his movements by this time so taken was he with the beautiful and historical buildings all around him. He wished that he was walking alongside Spencer who could, no doubt, illuminate him to the history of all the University and College buildings he saw rather than tediously watching the elegant figure ahead of him.

As he looked up to track his prey again, he realised that he couldn't see him anywhere and began scrabbling desperately around for some indication of where he had gone. He was in the midst of doing a full three hundred and sixty degree rotation when he felt a hand upon his shoulder and feared that he had, after all, been recognised.

"Lost him, did you, old boy?" cried Spencer, mirth written all over his face. "It's a good job one of us is bloody well paying attention. Come on."

"You scared the living daylights out of me, you buffoon."

Spencer immediately adopted a hunched pose, arms dangling by his side and started making monkey noises, much to O'Connell's amusement.

"So, where did he go?" he asked.

"He went, dear boy, into my very own College, right here," replied Spencer, pointing to the entrance of Trinity College.

CHAPTER 28

"What do you think we're going to find?" questioned Sam, worried that Huxley was losing his focus.

"I can't say for sure, but it appears that someone has gone to a bit of trouble to hide something. Don't you think it's worth a look?" he responded.

"I suppose it can't do any harm," said Sam.

"And it could be related to the Judas Gospel," added Donovan. "What do you reckon it's referring to?"

"I think that this could be a list of books," replied Huxley, pointing to the coded messages, "and each of the books listed perhaps represents a different section in a library. The drawings maybe refer the shape of the section." Huxley wasn't sure if he sounded convincing but he figured that anything that might distract them from what was happening around them could be worthwhile.

"Well, this house probably has more books than a lot of libraries so maybe it relates to where the books are in this house?" countered Sam.

"Yes, that would make much more sense," agreed Donovan. "So the sketches represent what, the shape of the rooms that they're in?"

"Not the shapes of the rooms," said Huxley, with a sudden flash of inspiration, "it's the shape of the window in the room.

I've always thought it bizarre that the windows in each room are different shapes. Just look at this one," he said pointing, "It has a fleur de lis at the top just like the bottom sketch."

"Yes and the bathroom has a round window just like the second one. I remember thinking it looked like a porthole when I took my shower earlier," added Donovan.

"Now all we have to do is break the codes for the other books. The chances are he's used pre-existing codes so maybe there's a code book somewhere in here that he used," offered Huxley.

"That's good thinking, Daniel, let's take a wall each," replied Sam as she made her way to the end wall of the room where there must have been hundreds of books lining the shelves that went from floor to ceiling.

Huxley couldn't help but smile as he noticed she had taken one of the two end walls which were smaller than the two longer walls that ran the length of the room. Huxley and Alan took a long wall each as the three of them searched for anything that might help them break the code.

As he searched, it occurred to Huxley that they didn't even know if this had anything to do with what they were actually looking for with regard to the Judas gospel but he felt that if it was important enough for Spencer to hide a coded note then it must be connected in some way. After a while, Huxley turned to see Sam reaching up for a book high on one of the shelves and found himself admiring the shape of her body as her top stretched up and revealed a little of her flat, toned stomach.

"You do know that there's a ladder," he said, indicating the device which was attached to the shelves on runners.

Sam ignored the offer, continuing to stretch and reach up towards the book that she had spotted. She managed to dislodge it and knock it from its place, making a grab for it as it fell. She turned and flashed Huxley a smile of triumph.

The Judas Deception

"I think I've found something," she said. "It's a book on famous ciphers. Perhaps he used some of them to code the letters he's written."

"It's worth a try. Alan, what was it that you used to break the code on the third clue?"

"That was fairly simple, I just applied an algorithm that I had learnt a few years back but it doesn't work with any of the rest."

"Hold on," cried Sam as she started to finger her way through the book, "some of the pages are marked. I wonder if he was leaving a clue on how to break the codes."

"Well, let's give it a try. Call out the details."

Sam started to recount the cipher and Huxley and Alan pored over the page to see if they could apply it to any of the coded words.

"I've got it," said Alan, pointing to the second line of writing. "It says *The Epistles of St Paul*."

"That's an interesting one and more in keeping, perhaps, with what we are looking for," said Huxley, "That would link up with the bathroom as it's the one with the round window. Great work. Are there any more pages marked in that book, Sam?"

"Yes, here's another." She showed the code to both Huxley and Donovan and the pair set about applying it to the remaining unbroken ciphers, Huxley starting at the top and Donovan going from the bottom up.

"This looks promising," muttered Huxley and then, "Yep, this is it. It's the top one. It reads *Milton's Short Poem*s. It is a rather eclectic mix of reading matter. I wonder what the connection is between them all?"

"Maybe they all have missing pieces of text from them or the originals were tampered with in some way? Or maybe he was just trying to put people off the scent."

"Yes, maybe. Still, it's all a bit strange and it doesn't tell us how it connects with the Judas Gospel."

"Perhaps if you get the last two pieces it will make more sense," suggested Sam. "I've found two more codes marked in the book if you want to try them against the book names?"

She brought the book across to them and put it on the table, her fingers marking the two relevant pages in the code book. Huxley and Donovan took one each and applied it to each of the words, both failing on their first attempt so swapping before they had success.

"*Oppenheimer's Bomb*," said Donovan, "Although I'm not sure how a book on the atomic testing in New Mexico has any relevance to the search for a missing gospel." He looked up to see an amused grin on Huxley's face.

Sam spotted it too. "What is it?" she asked.

"I've got *Winnie The Pooh*," Huxley answered, his smile spreading, "and I think I know what our connection is."

CHAPTER 29

CAMBRIDGE - 1970

"Bastard's using an alias. Fucking Giovanni Baresi. All the while I'm tracking Grimani and the bloody man is travelling under Christ knows how many different names. Turns out this Baresi has visited the college at least half a dozen times in the last few years."

"You never suspected he had different aliases?"

"Well, why would I? Not normal protocol, is it? Changing your name. New identity, all that." Inside Spencer Harris was kicking himself for missing something so obvious.

"What else did you find out?" The pair were in Spencer's house, a beautiful four bedroomed detached property in the sleepy commuter village of Grantchester just four miles from the centre of Cambridge.

O'Connell's face had lit up with delight as his newfound friend had ushered him inside for the first time with the well coined phrase of 'Ma Casa es Su Casa'. Although most of the rooms were uninhabitable simply due to the sheer number of books they held, O'Connell loved it, especially sitting in the study which was a room full of charm and elegance that looked out onto the most spectacular rose garden. It was here that the two now sat to discuss the findings of Spencer's reconnaissance visit to his College.

"Had to play it cool. Couldn't just waltz in with my size twelve's and demand information. Asked about subtly."

"Pah, that would be a first."

"Cheeky sod. I shall send you back to the Vatican whence I found you if you don't behave."

"I'm sorry, Spencer, I couldn't resist."

"Yes, well, put out the feelers as best I could without stirring things up too much. Attract attention to myself. That sort of thing. Asked around, different sources. Say he's a regular visitor, there most years. Friends with the old Master."

"The old Master? What was he like?"

"Couldn't stand the man. Kept out of his way. Differences, all that. Retired last year. Good riddance. New man came in. Young. Don't know much about him. Can't be any worse, my opinion."

"Did you find out why he's here?"

"No-one's certain. Researcher, best guess, uses the library, that sort of thing."

"So we can't say for sure that he came here because of us or whether he has a legitimate reason for being here then, can we?"

"Oh my sweet James, take that worried look off your brow, it really doesn't suit you. It makes your freckles look angry."

"I don't have freckles!"

"Yes you do," teased Spencer, a stupid grin on his face which grew even wider as his guest smiled back at the joke. "And very fetching they are to. Perhaps we should join them up. Might be a secret map, shows where the Gospel is!"

O'Connell feigned annoyance but, in truth, he loved how comfortable he felt around this man whom he admired so much.

"We're no further forward, are we?" he said later, the pair seated in wing-backed armchairs, O'Connell with his shoes off, feet buried in the deep-pile aubergine carpet that covered the floor from wall to wall.

Spencer looked up from the book he was reading, his face creased in bemusement. "What's that, old chap?"

"Grimani," replied O'Connell by way of explanation. "I mean, do you even know where he is staying?"

"Course I do. Do you think me an incompetent fool? Incapable? Useless? A buffoon?" He stood and once again mimicked an ape causing such forceful laughter from the young Irishman that he began to choke.

"Stop it," he wheezed, between coughs, "…please…. stop…I can't…breathe….it's too….funny."

"Glad I amuse you. Good for something then. Can't spy for toffee but I can make my friend laugh until he cries. Useful asset. Perhaps I can get Grimani or Baresi or whatever the fuck he's calling himself today to laugh so much he confesses where the Judas Gospel is!"

"So where is he staying?" asked O'Connell when he had recovered his composure.

"Taken a room in College. Arranged by one of the fellows. Don't know who. Couldn't find that out. Didn't want to press too much, give the game away. Played it casual, all that."

"So can we watch him from there? I mean stake out his room or whatever and follow him to see what he does?"

"Bit obvious, old chap. Be seen in no time. Wouldn't do at all."

"So what do we do? We can't just give up."

"Don't intend to. Have a plan. Know where he is going to be tonight, don't I?"

"You do? Where?"

"Fellows dinner at College. Booked it himself according to the porters. Never wrong those chaps. Know everything. Bagged us a couple of seats."

"Fellows dinner, what's that?" asked O,Connell.

"Ah, my dear chap, you will just have to wait and see."

The pair arrived late so that they could avoid sitting near Grimani, seating being on a first come, first served basis except for those on the top table. O'Connell was still in disguise but, for obvious reasons, Spencer knew he couldn't be.

"Hell can I explain I'm green with yellow spots and have a tail coming out of my arse!"

"It wouldn't have to be that extreme, just a few subtle changes."

"Listen, my sweet, I'm in my natural habitat. Bastard recognises me, can't really be surprised to find a Cambridge don in a Cambridge College, can he? Anyway, sneak in at the back, stay well away from him lest he should look into those beautiful green eyes of yours and recognise the sweet innocence that radiates from you. Realise he didn't kill you, try and finish the job. Where would I be without you, my sweet boy?"

So that's exactly what they did, taking two seats at the end table, well away from Grimani who was seated at the top table, Spencer having done a cursory check before they entered. The Swiss man had his back to the room, the table running the full width of the hall with seating on either side, the rest of the tables in the room running perpendicular.

"Means he can't look around the room, less chance of him spotting us," murmured Spencer as they took their seats, an enthusiastic waiter pouring their wine before they had even settled.

"This is amazing," commented O'Connell who was taken aback at the setting.

"Come now, nothing compared to what you boys have in the holy city, surely?"

"It's different. Yes, we have the finery on special occasions. But it's the atmosphere. The whole ensemble. Normally it's very austere. Meals taken in near silence. Not enforced, you understand, but more expected. They can be very sombre affairs. But here…" He gestured around the ambient room, full of men in suits and pressed shirts with the occasional pearl clad woman breeching the male dominant purview, the noise of busy chattering evident all around.

The hall was substantial with a high domed ceiling covered in gold gilt. Above, on three sides, ran a balcony, its horseshoe shape casting a shadow, giving a sense of intimacy only enhanced by the flickering candlelight that illuminated the tables. The fourth side finished in a slightly raised stage upon which sat the top table where Grimani was seated, O'Connell just able to distinguish him because of his height compared to those around him.

The young Irishman gave a start as Grimani suddenly rose to his feet before realising that everyone else was doing so. He questioned a look towards Spencer.

"Grace," murmured the large man as O'Connell stood to join him.

Someone at the top table mumbled some perfunctory prayer before the meal began in earnest.

"I can't believe you have grace in Latin," commented O'Connell when they were seated again.

"Seat of tradition, this, old boy."

"I'll bet there are quite a lot of similarities between the Vatican and this place," voiced O'Connell in all innocence.

"Wash your mouth out, that man! How dare you compare this high seat of learning with that corrupt and dysfunctional institution!"

Spencer delivered this in a tone of mock sombre but inwardly he was laughing at just how accurate an observation his new accomplice had made. "Out of the mouths of babes…," he purred to himself.

"What was that? Are you making fun of me you big ape?" then, as Spencer made to move to his monkey pose, "Oh, stop it. We're in company."

Their starters arrived and O'Connell became engaged in conversation with his neighbours, Spencer contributing with his usual bluster before retreating and allowing his charge to walk unaided. They had come up with a suitable back story for him, a visiting academic from Ireland, old friend of the family, staying for a while to do some research, first time in Cambridge.

As he watched his companion embellish the cover they had created, Spencer looked towards the top table, Grimani seemingly engrossed in the plate in front of him to the exclusion of those around.

Spencer tried to identify who he was sitting with but the fifteen candles, by O'Connell's count, in each solid silver candelabra failed to give off enough light to aid his efforts. They did, however, cause the cutlery to gleam in a most magnificent way according to his young companion, bringing a smirk to Spencer's face as he watched with fascination at O'Connell's pleasure. So he sat through the meal, biding his time before he could get a better look.

As dessert was being cleared away and coffee served, the Fellows started to move from their seats, some departing to the Fellows' Common Room for a glass of port whilst others filtered out of the door, home beckoning before a night of drunkenness overtook them.

Spencer could see that Grimani had remained sitting, three others with him, the group isolated by the departure of those around them. He stood and walked a little way into the hall, staying close to the edge of the room to remain as much in the shadow of the balcony above as he could. He went as close as he dared, using a pillar as cover, and was clearly able to see the trio with Grimani. They were the newly appointed Master, who Spencer had met only once since his recent arrival, as well as Charles Worth, the Junior Bursar and Dr Fredrick Hansel, himself a relatively new appointment.

He made his way back to the table and suggested to O'Connell that they go as there were now fewer bodies to provide cover for them and, in any case, they had found out as much as they were likely to.

"What do you mean?" asked O'Connell once they were outside in the mild spring evening.

"I mean that Grimani's choice of dining companions tells us quite a lot," responded Spencer as he led his accomplice towards Nevile's Court at the side of the dining hall they had just vacated.

"In what way?"

"All recent arrivals. Last year or so. Makes me wonder how they got here? What brought them? Who appointed them? Be interested to find out a bit more."

"You think they might be linked in some way."

"Damn suspicious that he should run to Cambridge at the first sign of trouble. What's here? Why? Then he cosies up with these Johnny-come-latelies right here in my own College. Don't like it. Up to something."

"You think he's maybe on to you? Tracked you down to here and is recruiting some friends to help him before…" He left the sentence unfinished as he wasn't really sure what Grimani would do but, having encountered the man's ruthlessness first hand, he shuddered at the possibilities.

"Don't see how. Done nothing to alert him since Switzerland. Kept off his radar. Stayed well away. Watched from afar."

"Maybe he saw you come into the apartment and rescue me?"

"Hmm, maybe," considered Spencer.

"You're not convinced, are you?"

They took a seat at the far side of the courtyard, benches conveniently set along the edge to allow those inclined to enjoy the tranquillity of the space. The bench afforded them a view of the exit of the dining hall whilst providing cover from an old oak tree in the middle of the courtyard. The pair thought it might worthwhile to see what Grimani and the others did upon leaving after the meal.

"I think there is more to it than that."

"Such as?"

"I mentioned that the new Master is young, right?"

O'Connell nodded in response.

"I mean very young. Ridiculous. Thirty something or other. A Master of a Cambridge College. And not just any College, Trinity at that. Head of the fellowship, in charge of the academic life of the place. Not something you give to a babe in arms."

"Aren't you just being a little prejudiced there?" countered O'Connell.

"Hell if I am. I'm right to be prejudiced. It's not right. Not at Trinity. Revered. Wizened. Experienced. Respected. That's a Master. Not some spotty teenager with snot running from his nose. Just doesn't happen."

"Well it obviously does because he's here."

"Yes, but how? That's my point. Don't you see, sweet James, he shouldn't be in post. Doesn't fit the job spec, all that. So how did he get it?"

"You think he was specifically selected in spite of his age?"

"Precisely! Now you're getting it. Go on."

O'Connell took the prompt, allowing his thoughts to flow freely.

The Judas Deception

"Ok, so the old Master, who you didn't like for your own good reasons no doubt…"

"Don't get smart."

"…so he is a friend of, let's call him Grimani for now because it's so much easier."

"Ok. And?"

"Well, we know that Grimani is a member of the Knights' Templar."

"Head, more like."

"Okay, the head. So he's in charge of the Knights' Templar and is a known associate of the retiring Master of Trinity College. So, what if this retiring Master is also Templar?"

"That's it, knew you'd get there. Every faith."

O'Connell beamed with delight before continuing. "So if he's Templar and he's retiring then perhaps they want to put someone else who is also Templar into that position."

"Excellent. My star pupil. Go to the top of the class."

"But how could they do that? Surely the appointment would be made by, I don't know, a board or a collective of some sort? It wouldn't just be the old Master naming a successor, would it?"

"You mean like selecting a pope?"

"Something like that, yes."

"Hell should I know. Just stating the facts. You're the one postulating."

As they talked, Grimani emerged with his compatriots. Rather than take the path back towards Great Court and the main body of the College, they instead started walking in the opposite direction, towards the river. The watchers sat on the bench opposite, thankful for the comprehensive cover offered from the tree. They observed the four men walk down the side of the dining hall, their body language furtive as they surveyed the grounds. As the four approached the wall of the College that overlooked the river, they stopped in a huddle.

The balmy May evening sky still had traces of sunlight sprinkled around it but a combination of the fading light and the cover provided by the tree was enough to keep the watching pair hidden, the quartet content they were alone. One of them took the lead, Spencer couldn't tell who from that distance, striding forward to the door of the building that lay to the side of the river. With a flourish he produced a key and ushered his cohorts in before joining them inside.

Spencer turned to O'Connell, his face a mask of surprise. "Well, I never," was all he could say.

CHAPTER 30

"You do?" Sam could not for the life of her imagine five more diverse and unrelated books and so couldn't possibly imagine how they were linked.

"I think so, yes."

"Would you like to share with the class?" she teased.

"Well, they are five famous works that are all housed here in Cambridge. In the Wren Library as it happens. Winnie the Pooh gave it away as A A Milne's original drawings and prose are famously held at the Wren."

"Alongside Oppenheimer's notes on the Manhattan Project," added Donovan. "Of course, it's so obvious now. But what do you think it means? Is that where the Judas Gospel is?" His voice rose in pitch with excitement.

"Let's not get ahead of ourselves," smiled Huxley. "First I think we should locate the five copies in question which are obviously in this house somewhere. I believe the bathroom might be a good place to start as we know it has a round window and hopefully has a copy of *The Epistles of Paul* somewhere therein."

They made their way upstairs and into the bathroom which was spacious enough to allow easy access for all of them. The three then started scanning the books contained along two of the walls.

"Here it is," cried Sam excitedly who, up to this point, only half believed that they had interpreted the drawings correctly. She made to pull it from the shelf but found that it wouldn't move. "I can't lift it."

"What do you mean you can't…..oh," said Huxley as he moved across to take hold of the book only to find that it was locked in place.

"Now that is strange," continued Sam. "We work out the codes only to find the first book we uncover is stuck."

"It's the first one we have found but it isn't the first one on the list." Huxley was looking at the five titles that they had written down on a scrap page. They were in the same order as on the original page from Spencer's book and he pointed to show that *The Epistles of Paul* was second on the list.

"So you think we have to find them in order?" asked Alan.

"I think it might be worth a try."

"So, what's first?" asked Sam.

"It's *Milton's Short Poems* and it should be in a room which has a square window with a V cut into the top which, I believe, is the front bedroom."

He led the way along the landing to the room in question. The walls, unsurprisingly, were lined with books and there were more piles of them on the floor reaching towards the ceiling.

"Ok, this should be the room," said Huxley. "Let's get searching."

They began to check the shelves, hundreds of books of all different shapes, sizes and age stacked side by side. It was Huxley who found it buried in the midst of one of the shelves on the wall facing the window. He called to the others, immediately reaching for it as he did. The book moved but not in the way he was expecting. He had put his index finger on top of the book to prise out the top corner and allow him to remove it from the shelf. The book had responded to his initial prompt

The Judas Deception

but, with the top corner now gripped between the fingers of his left hand, Huxley found that rather than slide off the shelf, the bottom corner of the book remained fixed to the shelf while the rest of it came towards him like a lever. He realised that this was exactly what it was.

"It's a hidden lever," he said.

"What, like in an old movie?" joked Sam.

"Yep, and if I'm right, it will work on a gradual release mechanism. In other words, the primary action must be engaged before the secondary motion can take place."

"So you think that the second book, *The Epistles Of Paul*, will now work in the same way as this has?" said Sam.

"That's the theory."

"To what end though?" asked Donovan.

"That, Alan, is what we will find out. Let's try number two again."

The trio made their way back to the bathroom. This time, when Sam pulled on the book in the bathroom, it moved, folding down just like the first one.

"Okay, what's next?" enthusiasm obvious in her voice.

"*Principia Mathematica* in a room with a large rectangle window with a missing corner. I'm pretty sure that will be the front room downstairs."

All three gathered in the spacious front room which overlooked the front garden and driveway. Here the furniture was limited to a settee and a couple of armchairs with the rest of the space, both floor and wall, taken over by books. Knowing what they were looking for now, however, they discounted the piles of books spread throughout the room and focused on the bookshelves.

It being the largest room they had been in so far, there were a lot of books to search through as they looked for a copy of Sir Isaac Newton's text. It took almost fifteen minutes before

Sam finally found it. Her testiness at the length of time it had taken was quickly replaced by excitement once again as the book folded itself down like the previous two.

"Three down, two to go."

"*Oppenheimer's Bomb* next in a room with a large rectangular window but this time it's vertical," called Alan.

"That can only be the landing, it's the only place that has a long window."

A quick search of the long landing uncovered *Oppenheimer's Bomb* which Alan pulled down and locked it in the release position.

"Right, that just leaves *Winnie The Pooh*."

The pair laughed as Huxley put on a high pitched voice before leading them back downstairs to the study where they had already spent most of their evening as the window matched the drawing.

They returned to the walls that they had already searched when looking for a book on codes and resumed their quest but this time for A A Milne's most famous creation. Ten minutes later, Huxley found it.

"What do you think will happen when you release it?" asked Sam.

"No idea but there's only one way to find out. Let's just hope the house doesn't fall down around us!" And with that he pulled on the book.

As it fell into place there was a loud click and a panel high in the wall above the top shelf of books opened. They looked up and saw the door of the panel open a couple of inches outwards and then stop.

"Well, well, well, a hidden panel. Now I know Spencer Harris really did watch too many old movies."

Huxley retrieved the ladder and manoeuvred it into place to allow him to climb up to the newly revealed panel. He drew open the door to show a hidden compartment. Reaching in, he pulled out a dusty, metal box which he then passed down to Sam before looking to see if there was anything else hidden inside. Seeing nothing he descended to where Sam and Alan were hunched over the now open box.

"Wow, it's a treasure trove, cried Donovan. "Old maps and notes and documents."

"There's even some old photos," added Sam who also sounded excited by the find.

Huxley looked down to see old black and white photos, maps with all sorts of markings on them and page after page of notes and scribbles, all seemingly in the same hand. There was also a book that lay at the bottom of the box and Huxley reached for it. He turned it over in his hands to read the spine. 'Hidden Treasures Of The Vatican' by Father James O'Connell.

"That's the name that was written on the tab in the book that Simms was holding when he got killed," he reacted. "And is also the book that Spencer has notated in his own work."

"What do you think it means?" asked Sam distractedly, as she stared in awe at the find they had made, the notes and pictures making the spectre of Spencer Harris seem real to her.

Donovan, too, was caught up in the spectacular haul and was busily searching through it in the hope that he may find something to support his own claim about the Judas Gospel. He was so engrossed that he wasn't even aware that Huxley was talking.

"I'm not sure," said Huxley, "but I think we may need to find this Father James O'Connell". As he said this he turned to the back inside page where there was sometimes a photograph of the author but found none.

He saw that he was talking to himself as the other two were enraptured in their own worlds. He was about to join them when he thought about the still open panel. This was something that Spencer had gone to great lengths to conceal and he felt they should return it to its former state now that the treasure had been uncovered.

He climbed the ladder again and was about to push the panel closed when he thought he caught something in the corner that he hadn't noticed before. He reached in and felt around, his hand alighting on an envelope. He pulled it towards him and looked at it. There was a photograph stuck to one side and a name written in Spencer's handwriting on the other. Huxley looked at the photograph and then at the name on the front before glancing down below. Both Sam and Alan were so engrossed in their findings that neither of them was paying the slightest bit of attention to him. Quickly and silently he slipped the envelope into the inside pocket of his jacket.

CHAPTER 31

CAMBRIDGE – 1970

Spencer and James watched as the four passed through the door of the building they had approached.

"What's the matter?" asked O'Connell, confused by his friend's consternation.

"Wonder what four respectable fellows are doing breaking into the Wren Library at this hour of the night?"

"That's the library?"

"One of them, dear boy. There are three in total within the grounds. The others are open twenty four hours but the Wren, well it's only open during the day. Except, it would seem, to some."

"What do you think they're doing?"

"Not looking for a fucking dictionary, tell you that much. No lights on, no reading lamp, prodding around in the dark. Need fucking x-ray vision to read anything. So why are they scurrying around in there of all places?" He pointed to the beautiful portico in front of him lined with arches and high windows which spanned the entire length of the building.

O'Connell followed his lead, noticing for the first time how breath-taking the structure was. Even in the fading light he could see there was a majesty to the edifice which belied its simplicity, the thirteen large windows giving a feel of somewhere tranquil and serene, a place where one could escape all troubles. Except it might be about to lead them into some instead.

"So what do we do now?" asked O'Connell.

"That, my boy, is a very good question. What is it? Late night expedition to check a hidden cache of documents? Secret orgy behind the Reference section? Pass the parcel in the dark? Or are they lying in wait for would-be pursuers?"

"Do you really think they might have spotted us?"

"Christ knows, my sweet."

The two spoke softly even though there was little chance of them being heard, even Spencer modifying his normal boom down to a low bellow. They sat contemplating whether to follow or sit tight and wait for their foe to re-emerge? After a while Spencer spoke.

"No reason for them to be there. Up to something. Skulduggery, you ask me. Lots of places to hide out. Why pick here? Too strange a place to choose. Think we should take a peek."

"So you think we should risk it?" whispered O'Connell, caught up in the subterfuge.

"I must admit, it's tempting. Poke around, see what's what. But part of me says that it's too dangerous. Should wait, all that."

"I can't believe that we have come so far and that I almost got killed at the hands of this man and now you have got cold feet."

"Precisely because you were almost killed that's stopping me, my dear. Saw you lying on the floor of his house, heart stopped, couldn't breathe, hoped earth swallowed me up, all that. Couldn't have lived with myself if you'd been killed. All thanks to my damned foolhardiness."

"But I wasn't killed because you knew what the man was capable off and we took the required precautions."

"Which is why we need to tread carefully now. Deploy caution. Fools rush in, all that."

"Well, it's been a few minutes and so far no sign of life. There are no lights on and I haven't seen any movement inside," offered O'Connell but it was hard to judge whether in support of caution or foolhardiness.

"Question is are they waiting to jump us? Enter stage left, senses attuned, sneak along the aisle, out pop the Templar brothers, bang bang, you're dead, hide the bodies behind the periodicals."

"But you said it yourself, why there? Aren't there much easier, more accessible places to lay a trap if that's what they wanted?"

"How right you are, dear fellow. Must be some significance, choice of venue, late at night. Has to mean something. Hell with it, let's do it."

With that Spencer jumped up, startling his companion before reaching down to take his hand and lead him towards the magnificent façade in front of them. They crouched low in the shadow of the doorway and Spencer checked the handle unsure if he was expecting it to be open or not. It was and he turned it quietly and pushed the door ajar while at the same time taking a step backwards for fear that someone would be waiting to pounce. When no attack came, he moved gingerly forward with such a lightness of foot that O'Connell found himself thinking how such a large man could be so dainty. Making their way through the door they stopped to let their eyes grow accustomed to the dark before moving slowly forward, all the while looking for signs of life. But there were none. The place was seemingly empty.

"Fuck are they?" whispered Spencer, his mouth close to O'Connell's ear so that his words didn't travel any further.

They listened carefully for any sound that might alert them to the whereabouts of the four but there was nothing and Spencer wondered where they could have gone.

Whilst the library was an immense amphitheatre to learning, it was predominately one single auditorium with no rooms to either side. The only exception to this was a small office at the rear and it was to here that he now guided his charge towards.

Designed with luminosity in mind, the building's classical proportions maximised both space and illumination with the high arched windows that ran the length of both sides of the building capturing any natural light and normally filling the long room with abundance. Even now, the light of the moon danced magically off the legion of books all around and the splendour of the building could still be appreciated. But there were strips of shadow along the far wall in which Spencer enfolded his large frame, O'Connell following in his footsteps.

When he reached the far end, Spencer peered through the lead panelled windows which decorated the internal doors of this grand palace but could see no sign of their prey. He was just reaching for the handle when he heard something from behind them.

He grabbed O'Connell and pulled him into an alcove that smothered the pair in darkness. They listened as the noise became clearer and the two could make out footsteps approaching from the main body of the room, footsteps that were heading towards them. The pair pushed themselves tight against the inner wall of the alcove and kept as still as possible. The footsteps came closer, their volume increasing as they got nearer and nearer. Then they stopped. Right beside where the pair were hiding.

Spencer pressed himself as flat against the wall as a man of his considerable bulk possibly could and vowed that he would go on that long overdue diet if he got out of this fix alive. His back was flat to the wall behind and he was looking out of the alcove at the figure of Charles Worth, the newly appointed Junior Bursar of the College and, thought Spencer, potential protector of the Vatican's dirty secrets.

Worth had stopped directly beside where both Spencer and O'Connell had hidden, the shadow the only thing protecting them from discovery. Spencer wondered if the man had been standing guard somewhere in the library and they had missed him when they had walked past, Worth hiding in the shadows himself. If that was the case then he couldn't have failed to see them, their only hope perhaps that Worth thought them already through the office door in front of which he now stood.

The moonlight that permeated the room was falling from the west of the building and therefore casting a fortuitous shadow that engulfed the pair whilst spotlighting the figure of Worth quite nicely. And the gun that he was holding. He turned now, gun in hand, and pointed it straight at them.

In the short time that they had spent together, Spencer had started to develop feelings for James O'Connell, and he felt perfectly awful for having exposed him to the danger of guns once already. Now, here they were trapped again due to his imprudence and his newfound companion was once more staring down the barrel of a gun. Or he would have been had he been looking but, in fact, O'Connell had pressed himself face first against the alcove wall and so remained oblivious to what was unfolding. Spencer was unaware of this, however, and his only thought was to save his companion, so he readied himself to charge Worth and accept his own fate in the hope that O'Connell could escape. But as he was about to sacrifice himself, Worth suddenly turned sharply to his side and held the gun in front of him in a two handed stance.

"The names Worth. Charles Worth," he declared to the auditorium before firing two imaginary shots into the main body of the library complete with sound effects. He then retraced his steps, Spencer and O'Connell listening to the fading footsteps until they were, once again, locked in silence. It was only then that Spencer dared breathe again, O'Connell realising that he too had been holding his breath the whole time and now sucking in a lungful of air. Both looked at each other, their fear evident but the urge to laugh also coursing through them which they were doing their utmost to supress.

"I think we can assume that the fool hasn't had his weapon for too long if he is going around pretending to shoot things," Spencer whispered in his accomplice's ear.

"But he is probably quite keen to use it on a real target given half the chance," countered O'Connell, reciprocating.

"Indeed. Time to get out of here, I think."

"Do you think it's safe?" asked O'Connell.

"Got to assume so. Didn't see us come in otherwise…" he let that go unfinished as he led the way back through the library paying special attention to the alcove where he thought the footsteps disappeared into. There was no-one there.

Once outside, Spencer quickly ushered them through the courtyards and out to the street before he felt able to relax and talk to his young charge.

"Are you alright, my sweet? No damage, mental or physical? Anything that needs to be kissed better?"

"I'm fine now that we're out of there. That was very frightening, Spence. I thought he was going to shoot us."

"Had me worried too for a moment. Relieved when he left."

The Judas Deception

"Where do you think he went?" O'Connell asked as the pair walked back towards Spencer's car.

"Best guess, some space/time portal," responded Spencer facetiously.

"Oh, stop it," said O'Connell.

"Or, my dear, a hidden room, somewhere in the building. Listened carefully to his footsteps, went off to the right, about halfway along. Checked out the alcove there, saw nothing. Closer examination needed."

"But, if you are saying that there is a hidden room in a building as well used as I imagine this one is, then how has it remained undiscovered all these years?"

"Good question, sweet James. Been churning that one over myself. Think it must be underground. Chamber of some sort. Accessed from above. Somewhere in the main body. Can't be anything else. Side panel or anteroom too easily found, building plans would show an inconsistency, dimensions all wrong. Famous building, studied architecturally. Both students and professionals alike. Anomaly like that, spotted years ago. Centuries even. So underneath, only thing that makes sense. And where better to hide ancient documents than in a place that no-one even knows exists."

Later, as they sat in the study of Spencer's house in Grantchester, the pair discussed further the potential of a hidden room beneath such a famous building as the Wren Library.

"Where better? Place is perfect. Look at the location. Right on a bend of the river, naturally protected on three sides. No-one going to dig there. How can they? Water and all that. So that just leaves Nevile's Court. Where we sat. Consecrated ground. Heart of the most traditional College in Cambridge. Place prides itself on its esoteric beauty. Sweet Fanny Adams chance of anyone digging it up. Not a hope. Not to mention, whole place is a protected heritage site. Wren alone has special status. Secure location. Safe as houses, so to speak. More to the point, no-one has ever had any reason to look for a hidden underground room."

"So you really think there is something hidden there?"

"The more I think, the more sense it makes. Land was once owned by Catholic Church. Henry Eighth comes along, tells them to hop it. Dissolved the lot. Set up his own church. Own religion. Gave the land to the College. All of it mind. Not just the land the College is on. Whole shebang. Very wealthy. Overnight it went from Church property to private property. Know yourself, my sweet, Church loves its underground rooms. Always been a habit of theirs. Underground rooms and passages in anything they built. Vatican has a labyrinth running underneath."

"So the rumours go. I believe it may be where Father Sanchez was taken when he was questioned by the Holy See. I've never found them myself."

"So, perfectly conceivable there's something under Trinity. A room used for hiding inflammatory material, stuff the Church don't want falling into the wrong hands."

"So you think that's where the Judas Gospel could be hidden?"

"Entirely possible, yes, my dear."

"So how do we get to it?"

"That is the big question."

The next morning saw the pair return to Trinity where Spencer learned from a colleague that Grimani/Baresi was due to leave later that day after lunch with the Master. They retired to a nearby tea room which afforded a view of the main entrance to the College and discussed what they should do.

"But what if he has the Judas Gospel? What if his whole reason for coming here was to retrieve the document because he didn't think that it was safe where it was? Now he has it on

The Judas Deception

his person and is going to take it elsewhere." O'Connell spoke urgently but kept his voice low.

"You could be right, my sweet James, but if there is a secret hiding place beneath the grounds of Trinity then it has remained undiscovered for hundreds of years. Concealed. Unseen. Buried. So why would they feel the need to now move it just because you came knocking on Grimani's door with some cock and bull story about having been sent by the Vatican. Already seen the man in action before. Similar circumstances. Response is to kill the threat. Not to move the manuscript. And he thinks he already killed you."

"What if he learns that he didn't? I mean, once he returns to Milan they will tell him that his apartment burnt down but they won't mention any dead bodies because there were none. Won't he wonder why?"

"I doubt that he will return to Milan. The man is a fixer, a god damned tool of the Church. He will go wherever they tell him to go and do whatever he has to do. Milan was just the latest in a series of short term stops for him. Never stays in one place for long. Believe me, I know. Tracked the blighter this last five years. Even if I didn't know his alias. Still knew where he was living. Moved around a lot. Different houses, different cities. Different countries, even. If he does go back he'll simply think the Church has cleaned up after him. Special cleaning service. Bloodstains and priests wiped away. Knockdown price. That way no-one mentions anything about it to him. But I think he will find a new place to stay for a while. Main problem is whether he reports back to the Vatican with a description of the priest who came to visit him. Whilst the description won't match you, the timing will. Just hope they don't put two and two together and realise that you have approached a Knights' Templar without permission. Or, indeed, good reason. Worse still, if he mentions that you forged a letter of introduction then they will want to know why."

"Well, it's not as though I ever intend to return there, Spencer. My life there is over. Perhaps I'll stay here with you."

Spencer looked at his friend with such a glow on his face that the sun could have gone into full eclipse and the room would still have been lit up such was the pleasure he took from those words.

"You mean, you're going to run away with the circus, dear boy?"

"Well someone's got to look after the monkeys," he laughed and Spencer joined him, the two lost in their own world for that moment.

"Then off to Mandalay we go and to hell with Grimani and all who sail in him!" cried Spencer, his normal boom rising and attracting looks from those sitting at the other tables. He stood and gazed around the room before continuing. "What need have we for such fools when we have all the bananas we need right here."

Eyes averted as he looked from table to table, the embarrassment of those seated apparent on their faces at this large man making such a spectacle.

O'Connell half smiled and half cringed as he grabbed at Spencer's arm and hissed affectionately, "Sit down, you're causing a scene."

"If a man can't have a bit of fun…." continued Spencer, still to the room, but halted by the force of O'Connell's tug on his arm. He sat again and winked at his young charge.

"You are such a buffoon but I do so enjoy being with you."

"And I you, my dear. Now, as we have complete privacy because these good people will be too afraid to even glance in our direction let alone try to listen to what we are saying, what is it that we have decided upon?"

"That we are just going to let Grimani go and follow the trail here in Cambridge."

"Quite right too, old chap. I say we try and find that hidden room and see what is down there. And, if need be, we can always watch the three stooges that Grimani has led us to and try to find out just what they know."

"You mean the secret of the Judas Gospel and the possible destruction of the Church."

"Indeed I do, my sweet, indeed I do. Not bad for a Tuesday morning." He raised his eyebrows as he lifted his cup to his lips and drank.

CHAPTER 32

Huxley closed the secret panel they had uncovered and climbed back down to join the others. Whilst the pair busied themselves on the floor with the discovered cache, he made towards the *Winnie The Pooh* book which had been the release for the panel. With the mechanism now reset he returned the book to an upright position and announced that he was going to do the same with the rest.

On his return the pair where now seated on the floor, pictures and maps and pages of notes spread out all around them.

"Find anything interesting?" he asked.

"It appears to be the notes relating to his search for the Judas Gospel from what I can gather," offered Sam. "I've only just started going through them but they appear to be in chronological order and they detail the trips he took and the findings he made. This one," holding up one of the pages, "tells a story about the death of a colleague in Switzerland which he insists was murder."

"Murder?" queried Huxley.

"That's what he's written. Says that he asked the wrong questions about a document linked to the Gospel and was killed by the Knights' Templar."

"The Knights' Templar? He really thinks that they were responsible for killing someone representing him?"

"Although the Swiss authorities deemed it natural causes."

"Do you think it could be the Templar who are after us?" questioned Alan.

"That very much depends on why they're after us. But they could certainly be connected with Simms's death, that's for sure. Maybe there's something in there," said Huxley, indicating the pile of documents they had uncovered, "that can help us point the police in that direction."

"Or tell us about the missing pages from the Gospel," added Alan excitedly.

"Maybe," conceded Huxley, his mind wandering. Then, "I think we need to go through everything here and see if there is anything that can help us before we face the police in," he checked his watch, "about seven hours from now."

"That's going to be a long job," said Alan. "Maybe we'd be better off taking it all to the Wren Library if you think that might be where Spencer was trying to point us towards?"

Huxley flashed him a look but the boy was too caught up with the document he was reading to notice.

"For the first time tonight, I actually feel like we're in a safe place. I think it would be a bit foolish to give that up to head back into the hands of the enemy."

Hearing the sharp tone in Huxley's voice, Donovan looked up.

"But if we're close to solving the mystery then isn't it worth it," he replied, matching Huxley's tone.

"I think solving the murder is much more important than solving the mystery. Perhaps you need to think about your priorities. We need to be able to go to the police in the morning with something substantial to clear your name. Isn't that what matters?"

Donovan looked like he wanted to argue but Sam stepped in.

"Dan's right. We need to focus on protecting you. And staying here and checking this treasure trove is exactly what we should be doing."

"I think this calls for more coffee," said Huxley, offering an olive branch.

"I'll get it," replied a surly Donovan, "I need to use the bathroom anyway so I can get the kettle boiling in the meantime."

He skulked out of the room leaving Daniel and Sam alone.

"Do you think he'll be okay?" Sam asked?

"I think he needs to face up to the reality of his situation. It's like he doesn't realise just how serious the situation he's in is," replied Huxley.

"It probably hasn't really hit him properly."

"Yeah, maybe," commented Huxley distractedly.

"What's on your mind, Daniel?"

"What?" he replied. "Sorry, nothing, ignore me. Just something nagging at the back of my mind. Or maybe it's just lack of sleep. A bit of rest would be nice. Probably wouldn't do him any harm either", gesturing towards the door as he heard Donovan descend the stairs.

"I don't think lack of sleep will be a problem for him. He's young. Don't you remember being his age and the all-nighters that you pulled? God, I used to be able to go on for days without sleep. Now if I miss a night's sleep I struggle for days to recover." She laughed as she delivered this last and Huxley smiled in sympathy with her.

"I know what you mean. I think a mixture of coffee and adrenaline is keeping me going for now but there will come a point when I just want to collapse in the corner."

They heard the kitchen door opening. Then came a cry of alarm.

"Guys, come and have a look at this."

They jumped up from the floor where they had been sitting and ran across the room into the hallway. Alan was standing in the doorway of the kitchen, pointing.

"What is it? What's the matter?" asked Huxley, a slight panic in his voice that he tried to keep under control.

"The security light, it's on," said Alan. "It wasn't when I put the kettle on a couple of minutes ago."

"Oh, yeah, that happened earlier when I was in here. It was just a cat. I saw it run down the side of the house. It's probably just come back again."

"Oh. Okay." He sounded almost disappointed but he felt more relief at Huxley's calm assurance so he set about making coffee while Sam and Huxley returned to the study and resumed their search through the cache.

"He was certainly determined to find the Judas Gospel, wasn't he?" voiced Sam, indicating the hoard of documents and photos.

"He was quite the adventurer," replied Huxley. "The sad thing is that he never got to see the Gospel after all the time he spent chasing it down. It was discovered just months after his death."

"That was very convenient," Sam said, sceptically.

"Yeah, you're right to be sceptical. Many believe it was thanks to Harris that the document was ever found."

"You mean that whoever had it left it somewhere to be found because people were getting too close to the truth?"

"That's the theory. I mean, we think of it as a document that has always been around but it's actually such a recent find. Can you imagine how protective the Church would have been at the time Harris was looking for it? It's little wonder he felt he had to go to so much trouble to hide everything in the way he did."

"Do you think that's to stop the wrong people from getting hold of his notes?"

"Possibly, but who are the wrong people? And why make the sketches and codes if you didn't want anyone to find them? He must have thought that someone he knew and trusted would be able to work out the code and find his hidden cache."

"Lots of questions but no answers."

Just then there was the sound of breaking glass. The two, once again, made for the hall, Huxley thinking that Donovan had dropped something. But Alan was already running towards them, alarm all over his face.

"Get out! Get out!" The vehemence in his voice brokered no argument and the two joined him in running for the front door.

As they reached it, Huxley grabbed the keys to the Landrover which was parked up outside before putting his hand out to block the now open front door as Alan was about to run through."

"What's happening?" he hissed.

"Someone's trying to break in through the back door. They smashed a panel," he responded in kind.

"So there could be others waiting out front for us. Perhaps the plan is to flush us out," suggested Huxley.

Just then there was the sound of splintering wood and a crash of what they assumed was the back door being forced open.

Sam said, "What choice do we have?"

With that, Huxley shrugged and made a run for the vehicle, all the while awaiting an attack from someone lurking in the shadows. But no such assault came and they all made it into the car unscathed.

It was only as he made to start the Landrover that Huxley

The Judas Deception

realised they had left the box with all the notes back in the house.

"We've left the cache inside. I'm going to go back and get it."

He made to get out of the car but Donovan beat him to it, rushing back to the door. Huxley made to follow, knowing that, if there were intruders in the house, that he couldn't let Alan confront them alone. He had barely reached the front door when there was the crack of a gunshot.

"Jesus Christ, Alan, are you okay?" He made to run into the hallway when Donovan came tumbling out, fear written across his face.

"It's too late, Professor, they're already in the house. If we go in now we'll be trapped and I don't fancy our chances of escaping for a third time. We've got to get out of here."

They jumped back in the car and Huxley threw it into reverse and backed them onto the garden before gunning the engine and shooting out of the driveway into the otherwise sleepy village.

"What the hell just happened?" shouted Sam, her mind spinning.

"I don't know but we can't stick around here to find out," responded Huxley. Then, "Alan, what exactly did you see?"

"Not much to be honest, it was more what I heard. There was a noise and when I turned to see what it was I saw someone swinging a stone at one of the glass panels in the back door."

"Did you get a look at them? Was it the same man from the Ball?" Sam asked.

"When I say I saw them, I only saw an arm as they smashed the glass and then reached through to the lock. After that instinct took over and I ran."

"So why did they smash the door down?" wondered Sam.

This time it was Huxley who answered her query.

"No key," he said. "In the back door I mean," he continued, seeing the puzzlement in her face. "They broke the panel to try and open the door but it's locked and I have the only key."

"Okay, so explain this to me then," there was a fury in her face that carried to her voice, the will to lash out just being kept in check, "what the hell was the point of it all? I mean, why break in the back if not to flush us out into waiting arms at the front of the house?"

"That's the one that's puzzling me too," confessed Huxley.

"Maybe there was only one guy," suggested Alan.

"It's possible. But then why attack from the rear? Why not come at us from the front, chase us into the back garden? We'd be pretty much cornered then. Unless we jumped over hedges and through other people's gardens."

"Maybe they were looking for signs of life so had gone round the back and when they saw me they made their move," offered Alan.

"That's a stretch, I think," replied Huxley. "It's almost like they wanted to drive us out the front. To force us to take flight. To leave them alone there."

"Yes, you're right," agreed Sam "like they wanted to make sure that we left that house. But why? It's not as though they could have known what we found there."

"Or that we'd leave it behind when we ran."

"Maybe they just thought that we'd lead them to whatever it is they're looking for. They could be following us," said Alan, looking over his shoulder.

Huxley had been thinking something similar and had been watching his mirrors for any sign of just that. There was nothing obvious but then he couldn't rule it out. But there was something else on his mind.

The Judas Deception

"And we haven't even addressed how they found us," he said.

"Well it had to have been the punters that we bumped into earlier. They must have mentioned it to the wrong person."

"Hmmm," was all that Huxley offered in response.

"Well, if they are following us," added Sam, "they're going to be severely disappointed as we haven't a bloody clue where we're going." Then, looking at Huxley, "Or do we?"

They were passing Wolfsan College on Barton Road heading towards Lammas Land, a favoured spot of students for sports practice but completely deserted at this time of night.

"I think we need to head back to Trinity College," said Huxley.

"What's there?" asked Sam, seeing Huxley was working something out in his head.

"Not what, who."

"Alright then, who's there?"

"We need to go and see the Dean," he replied.

"The Vicar of Dribbly?" queried Donovan, incredulous. "What the hell has he got to do with anything?"

"I think," said Huxley, "that he might be the key to this whole thing."

CHAPTER 33

CAMBRIDGE – 1970

The pair watched Grimani leave from the vantage of the tea room before making their way towards the Wren Library, both tentatively entering the vast amphitheatre that they had departed in such haste the previous evening.

"So, what are we looking for?" whispered O'Connell, conscious that the library was being utilised by a number of both students and dons as it was open for business.

"If I knew that then we wouldn't need to come in for a look," countered the large man, managing a lower tone than he had achieved at the tea house but still loud enough to receive admonishing glances from a number of directions.

Spencer led the way towards the area where he suspected Worth of having disappeared, looking around for any tell-tale signs that might alert them to a hidden panel somewhere in the wall or floor.

"Oh, this is ridiculous. Haven't a fucking clue what we're after. Waste of time, people around. Need solitude. A bloody big crowbar." His stage whisper fortunately didn't carry beyond O'Connell.

"Nothing like announcing that you know their secret," countered the younger man. "I mean, if you go in with the heavy artillery and start knocking down walls and digging up floors then I'm sure it won't take them long to find out. And then what? They have guns, Spencer. We can't afford to do that. We have to be clever. Figure out what the key is."

"Hmmm, perhaps your right. Hate it when you talk sense. No bloody good to anybody."

O'Connell smiled his amusement before suggesting "Perhaps it's a book that you have to press like in one of those old movies?"

"Fuck is this, Hitchcock Hour? Bloody library. Any book could be referenced at any time. Some student comes along, picks up Wuthering Heights, finds himself underground in a chamber full of forbidden fruits."

"Alright, it was only a suggestion."

Spencer could see the hurt on his accomplice's face and made to comfort him immediately. He took the Irishman by the hand. "I know, dear boy, I know. Only pulling your leg. Good idea. Thinking laterally, all that. What we have to do. Better than anything I've come up with. Which is nothing ad infinitum."

"So what do we do?"

"I think the best thing we can do is come back when things are a bit quieter and have a look around then."

"You mean when it's closed, don't you?"

"Got it in one, my sweet."

"But what if one of the three turn up while we're here?"

"You mean one of the holy trinity?"

"Oh very droll. Is that what you're calling them?"

"Indeed. That's exactly what we want them to do. I think we should stake out the place. Wait for one of them to come. Or maybe all of them, fuck do I care. We watch from the shadows. See what they do. Get our answer. Simple as that."

"Yeah providing they don't find us and then decide to shoot us."

"Ever the optimist, my sweet, that's what I love about you."

They returned later that night, Spencer revealing skills of lock-picking that O'Connell found frightening they were so good. But as night turned to day the two had gained nothing other than stiff necks from sitting on hard chairs all night, frequently moving to remain in shadow until dawns early rays began to pierce the sky. They repeated the pattern the following evening and the next three, the two becoming creatures of the dark, leaving just before daylight to retreat from the sun like vampires.

"How long are we going to keep this up for?" asked O'Connell as they sat tight against the wall of the library, hidden from any onlookers who should happen into the library at the witching hour.

"Long as it takes, dear chap."

"But it's been five nights now and no sign of anyone."

"I rather get the impression that they don't often disturb the chamber. Let sleeping dogs lie and all that."

"So we're just wasting our time here?"

"Quite the contrary. If we weren't here then we would be wondering if they were and then where would we be?"

They sat in silence for a long while, as had become their custom. Not uncomfortable silences, actually quite enjoyable as far as O'Connell was concerned. He loved every minute spent with this man and couldn't ever imagine growing bored in his presence, silent or otherwise.

"If we do manage to get…."

"When," interrupted Spencer.

"Okay, when we do managed to get into the chamber, what is it that you expect to find?"

Spencer looked at his friend, the dim outline visible only because he was so close. He wondered if he should dilute his answer, give the poor chap a weakened version but he knew that O'Connell was here because he too wanted to discover the truth. Mindful of their surroundings and the reason they were there, Spencer spoke softly.

"During all the years that I have been researching the Gnostics, I came across a number of references that suggested that there was something different about the Gospel of Judas. A little bit special. Stands out, all that. Problem was, damned thing wasn't anywhere to be seen. Couldn't follow the references. Nothing substantial, get my drift." He paused to take a sip of water from the flask they had brought with them before continuing. "Other Gnostics contradict the Jesus we see in the bible. Not a true picture. More to it than meets the eye. But none of them go off reservation. None of them suggest he's a psychopath with three bums or anything."

O'Connell laughed at the large man's delivery. He had come to regard these evenings alone with his companion as rather special, here in this beautiful structure, the two of them free to speak save only for the sound of a footfall or key turn.

"But some of them hint at the revelations made by Judas and support his claims. Trouble is they don't state what those claims are. Fall short of naming them. Nothing concrete. Like they're afraid. Embarrassed. That sort of thing."

"I can imagine that the Vatican would be very nervous about something like that," countered O'Connell.

"Hmmm, yes. Something you don't know, old boy. No reason. Never told you or anything. Was invited along to the Vatican library once."

"You came to the Vatican?" gasped O'Connell incredulously then, seeing the confirmation on Spencer's face even in the dim light on offer, he continued, almost in awe, "When was this?"

"Years ago. After the Dead Sea. Member of the UN team.

Normal protocol following our discovery. Reference material. Confirm providence, you know the sort of thing."

"I can't believe they let you of all people into the Vatican library."

"Just the normal library you understand. None of the dodgy stuff. Works available in other places but gathered under one roof. Convenience. Bloody fantastic collection. Magnificent. Complete awe. Anyway, wasn't the spiritual giant you see before you. Still forming ideas, learning my craft, all that."

O'Connell looked at the large man in disbelief still reeling from this revelation. The man he admired and who was hell bent on the destruction of the Church had come right into the heart of the citadel itself. If only they could see you now, he thought.

"Interesting system they had back then. Don't know if it's still the same, times move on, progress and all that. Everything labelled. Categorised."

"Yes, they're very big on that. Makes referencing a lot easier."

"Used sticky labels, different colours."

"That's it. It's still the same."

"Bit primitive. Surprised me. Security and all that."

"I've never really thought about it. Seems fine to me."

"Anyway, each of us were assigned an area. Specific project, check the texts from a certain region or time. Given something mundane. Boring. Simple. Brain like mine, needs a challenge. Started to wander. Have a look around. I was assigned orange."

"Orange? What do you mean?"

"That was my colour. My section. Books I was referencing. All in orange. Marked with a dot. Bottom of the spine."

"Oh, I see. Yes, little round stickers. I know what you mean now."

"Came across something. Tad strange. Looked out of place. But had to look closely. Wasn't obvious. Realised the dot was red. Bit faded. Looked orange from a distance. Only close up you could see. Piqued my interest. Started looking through it. Never seen it before."

"What was it?"

"It was a commentary by Titus Flavius."

"The one you asked your friend to find?"

"The very same."

"So you knew all along that it existed. You'd seen it already."

"Indeed I had," replied Spencer, a tinge of sadness in his voice. "I used him as a patsy to try and expose a lie. I knew that if he was told that the text didn't exist then they were hiding something. And if that then why not more? Alas, he died because of me."

"You mustn't think like that. He died because Grimani murdered him. You weren't to know that they would react like that."

"Perhaps I should have.

Spencer reverted into contemplative silence, his mind somewhere in the past. O'Connell looked at him, wanting to comfort him but knowing that they must remain alert, their vigil notwithstanding. Keen to learn more about his time in the Vatican library, O'Connell tried to nudge his friend out of his melancholy.

"So what was in this text by Flavius?"

"Ah, now that, dear boy is an interesting tale," Spencer responded distractedly, still lost in thought.

"Why don't you tell it to me?"

Looking up, Spencer smiled at his charge, the recuperative powers of his companion's fair face and fiery hair enough to bring him back to the present.

"Well, sweet James, there I was in the heart of the beast itself. All around me soldiers of fortune, prepared to lay down their lives for the Church. Me with only a shield of truth to protect me."

O'Connell laughed at the performance.

"I knew as soon as I began reading this ancient text," continued Spencer, "that I had in my hand a document that I was not meant to see. Obvious it had been misfiled. Whatever. There it was, in my section. Well, couldn't alert the powers that be to this, could I? Protocol was, all documents referenced must be signed for by the reader. Nothing to leave the building under any circumstances. Searches made every day. Knew I couldn't sneak it out, too big."

"So what did you do?" asked O'Connell, fascinated.

"Only thing I could. I ate it."

"You wha…" then, seeing the beam on Spencer's face, "oh, you clown. Really what did you do?"

"Put it back. Exact same place as I found it."

"You just left it there?"

"Came back the next day, it was still there. Took it down from the shelf. Read for a bit, put it back. Didn't want to draw attention to myself. Kept going back and forth. All day long. Signed out texts that were in other parts of the orange section, well away from it. Knew they'd check, see what I was referencing. Beady eyes on us all the time. Watched like hawks. Had to play it cool."

"And they never suspected."

"Took them four days. Came into the library. Went through my usual charade. Looked up documents, signed something out. Pulled texts from all around. Glanced at them. Maybe read for a few minutes. Put them back. Eventually went to where the Flavius text was and lo and behold it was gone. Acted casual. Nonchalant. Carried on with my work. Nothing said. End of the day, queued up, usual search. Nothing under the armpits, crack of my arse, that sort of thing."

O'Connell took a fit of the giggles at the imagery invoked by his friend only to be frozen by a raised hand from Spencer as he cocked his ear towards the door.

"What is it?" hissed O'Connell.

"Thought I heard something. Just the wind."

They sat in silence for a moment as O'Connell too tried to convince himself that it was nothing more than the sounds of the night that haunt old buildings. Relaxing as he heard the wind rattle against the windows he turned to Spencer once more.

"So no-one said anything to you? About the document?"

"So, there I was, standing in line, ready for my cavity search. All of a sudden, chap in a funny robe approaches. Cream with red and gold. Fancy."

"That's a Monsignor."

"That's the chap. Tells me he needs to talk to me. Urgent, confidential, all that. Takes me to one side. Begins asking me questions. Work related. What was I looking for? What texts did I reference? Did I notice anything out of place in my section? Anything unusual?"

"Really?"

"As I live and breathe."

"What did you say?"

"Told him nothing strange except a forbidden text of Titus Flavius that questions the whole foundation of your faith."

"You never?"

"Course I didn't, you sweet fool. Acted like I didn't have a clue what he was talking about. Told him about my work, great detail. Bored him into submission. Left it. Nothing more said. Text gone forever. Didn't matter. Read most of it anyway."

"So what did it say?" O'Connell had almost forgotten

about the document's controversial contents such was his interest in Spencer's story.

"The book was an early commentary of the region around the time of Jesus. It suggested that he was a figure of interest to the Roman authorities and that they were watching him closely. In the text, Flavius mentions some of the speeches made by Jesus, speeches not recorded elsewhere, speeches which showed Jesus as a political activist, stirring up the downtrodden against the Roman Republic. There were references to his childhood when he had been disrespectful to both his parents and the leaders of the Temple. Emphasis placed on his close relationship with prostitutes and miscreants and suggestions that his life wasn't as pure as people would like to believe."

"Nothing new in any of that," replied O'Connell, "just the sort of thing that appears in any number of commentaries. All without foundation I might add."

"Ah, ever the believer, sweet James. Such an honourable and yet sad characteristic. Granted, there have been others who have made wild claims and failed to substantiate them but Flavius actually backed his up. Text from speeches. Testimonies from spectators. He was the original investigative journalist. Dug around. Found the story. Chased it down. But it was his claims about the relationship between Jesus with Judas that got the most attention. Stated that Judas was approached by the authorities. Inside man, that sort of thing. Said they had a bind over him, knew him for what he truly was. Use it against him unless he cooperated, all that. Suggested Judas was an easy target, ready to turn. Fallen out with Jesus. Big row."

"What about? Did it say?"

"Fell short of that. I'm afraid. Just said that he was a willing spy. Spilled his guts about Jesus. And the rest of them apparently."

"All for thirty pieces of silver," commented O'Connell.

The Judas Deception

"I think there was a lot more to it than that and I honestly believe the truth lies in the Judas Gospel. That's what I expect to find down there, my dear. The truth."

Spencer looked at his watch before declaring that it was time for them to be going, daybreak just around the corner. They sneaked out of the library, checking the coast was clear. Once in the privacy of Spencer's College room, a small but comfortable study within the grounds, O'Connell turned to his companion.

"Do you think there is any significance in the fact that no-one has been near that place since Grimani left? I mean, maybe there's some special ritual that they have to do that requires all four of them or something?"

Spencer looked as though he had been punched such was the shock on his face. He raised his hand and smacked his forehead in admonishment.

"By Christ, why didn't I see it before? Sweet Jesus, it's so obvious. Fuck was I thinking. Not thinking more like."

Anxious to stop the large man from going off on a ramble, O'Connell asked, "What? What is it that you missed?"

"Of course it requires all of them. That's all part of the security. None of them can go alone. No single one of them can be overpowered and forced to give entry. It requires them all to be together. Each of them to turn their key. Good Christ, it was there right in front of me all the time. Oh my dear, sweet, innocent James, always coming up with the right answer. Oh, how I could kiss you."

"Key? What key? What are you talking about?"

"The key, my friend, of Arragones."

"What is the key of Arragones?" O'Connell asked when he had managed to calm Spencer down, such was the excitement generated by this realisation.

"It's so obvious. Right in front of me all this time. Too

distracted by chambers and documents. Couldn't see the wood for the trees."

"You still haven't told me what it is."

"The key of Arragones is a Templar tradition. A key divided into four parts. Each part must be inserted in sequence and turned simultaneously in order to open the lock. They used it to open chests they carried with them. Torture devices, who knows what inside. Haven't seen it in use for years but, of course, this chamber would be centuries old so it makes sense. Perfect sense." Spencer slapped his forehead again to indicate just how foolish he felt at not having thought of this before.

"So the only way into the chamber is if all four men are present with their part of the key."

"Well, it doesn't necessarily have to be those same four but yes the principle is the same."

"Therefore we need all four parts to the key before we can even attempt to get in. And that means getting each part from the four men who have a piece."

A sparkle came into Spencer's eye as he listened to O'Connell voice his thoughts.

"Ah, not necessarily, my boy."

"What do you mean?" Then, seeing the excitement in his friend's face, O'Connell asked, "What is it?"

Spencer jumped up from the sofa and began to pace the small room, his elation growing. He stopped and looked directly at the young priest then, almost in a whisper, he said, "There is one man who has all four parts. A replica which he wears around his neck. Ornamental if you like."

"What?" stammered O'Connell, partly in confusion, partly just to play for time as he tried to absorb what he was being told.

"Exact copy of the key," continued Spencer. "All the parts with one person."

"And just who would that be?" asked O'Connell, still trying to come to terms with this fresh revelation.

Spencer looked intensely at his young companion, a smile spreading across his face as he announced, "The Chaplain of his Holiness himself, Monsignor Domineco Di Natele."

CHAPTER 34

Cambridge is a compact city where space comes at a premium. With its narrow streets and historical buildings the centre is predominately pedestrianised, vehicles requiring a permit to get beyond the bollards restricting access. Huxley had no such pass so rather than make for the front entrance of Trinity, he drove along the Backs, parking on the far side of the river at the back of the College.

Trinity had a gated driveway which led to a private bridge over the river and a back entrance into the grounds. Huxley reached for his key and, as he did so, checked his surroundings. All appeared quiet apart from some stragglers returning from the nearby Balls, bow-ties long ago discarded and heels being carried, not worn.

Huxley recalled that it was only a few hours ago that he had entered the College via this gate for dinner. It seemed like a lifetime ago now, like he had passed into another world, a parallel universe of sorts where madness and mayhem ruled and somewhere in real time he had left the meal and gone home where he was now fast asleep in bed.

But the time for sleep had long gone. They were close to uncovering the truth, he could feel it. A truth that someone was desperate to stop them from finding and he knew that the only way to make sure they were safe was to get to it before it

The Judas Deception

was too late. Huxley was starting to put everything together and he believed they would find the answers they needed with Dr John Connelly, the Dean of Trinity. The other two weren't so convinced.

"But what makes you think that the Vicar of Dribbly has anything to do with this?"

"That's Dr Connelly to you, Alan."

"Yeah, whatever. I don't see how this helps us. We should be trying to find out where the missing parchment is, show the police that I have nothing to do with all this."

"First of all, where has this sudden urgency to find the missing parchment sprung from? I thought we were interested in finding the people responsible for killing Simms and trying to kill us?"

"It's the same people!" shouted Alan.

"We don't know that for sure. And second," Huxley held up a hand to indicate to Alan that he should let him finish, "if I'm right, Dr Connelly may be able to point us towards both."

Alan was about to raise an objection when he registered what Huxley had just said. It was Sam who asked the question on both their minds.

"How do you think he's involved?"

"I'm not entirely sure but his presence at the counsel of war tonight intrigues me."

"But he didn't say a word while I was there, I told you that. It was the other three that subjected me to what was, to all intents and purpose, an interrogation."

"Precisely. He didn't say anything. So why was he there?"

"And based on that you've come to the conclusion that he's behind everything that's happened to us?" Sam was incredulous and didn't mind showing it.

"I didn't say that," countered Huxley as the three neared the private bridge that would take them into the back of the

College, "I said that he may be the key. You'll just have to go with me on this one, it's a bit of a gut feeling."

"Well what if your gut is leading us right into the hands of the people who want us dead?" Alan asked in a stage whisper, conscious that they were nearing the grounds.

Huxley was about to answer when his phone started to vibrate and he reached into his pocket to retrieve it. He saw that it was Pepper.

"What news, George?"

"None fit for printing, Dan. Are you okay?"

"Fine thanks, why do you ask?" Then, "Hold on George, you're breaking up."

He wanted to have a private conversation with Pepper so pretended that the signal wasn't good, indicating to Sam and Alan that they should wait by the gate for him as he moved back down the pathway.

"You trying to get away from the laddie again, Dan?" asked Pepper, wise to the move.

"There are just a couple of things I would rather not have anyone else hear for the moment, George."

"Oh aye, like what?"

"You first. You must have something important as you've never been concerned enough about my welfare to call me in the middle of the night before."

"And here I was trying to help." He gave a mock sigh. "Aye, alright then," before changing to a more sombre tone. "I'm worried about what you've got yourself mixed up in, Dan. This murder in America, it's serious. Looks like he was tortured before finally being killed. I won't bore you with the details but trust me when I say it's bad."

He left that to hang, knowing Huxley would fill in the blanks himself and then continued, "I know I'm just a simple

The Judas Deception

bobby, Dan, and not up there with you when it comes to all the intellectual stuff…"

"Here we go," said Huxley rolling his eyes. He waited for his friend to carry on.

"Well, you'll be pleased to know that I managed to put two and two together and I think I might have come up with the right answer. Turns out this dead bloke was the head of something important at the National Geographic. You'll have heard of them you being an intellectual and all, Dan. That's the sort of thing you academics read, isn't it? Yeah, well, anyways, there I was wondering why you might think this is linked to Simms in some way when lo and behold there on my wee computer screen is the list of telephone calls he made this afternoon. One of which was to the National Geographic Headquarters in Washington D C. Now, I gets to thinking could this be what my good friend Dan was trying to point me towards and if so then why the bloody hell didn't he just say so in the first place!" This last was shouted in mock admonishment.

"What and steal your glory?"

"Aye, well, it's all very well joking around but even I've managed to work out that you're in a lot of trouble."

"You don't know the half of it, George."

"Well, whatever it is you're up to, I honestly think that you'd be better off coming into the station and letting me look after you both. These are very dangerous people we're talking about."

"You're right, I know that, George, but I think I might be on to something and I want to see how it plays out. If I'm right then it will point us to the culprits. All of them."

"What do you mean by that?"

"I get the feeling that I'm being manipulated."

"Aye, you're not the only one," countered Pepper.

"I'm serious, George."

"Oh aye? Something not quite right in the world of Professor Huxley."

"More a feeling than anything."

"Back to those feelings, eh? Dangerous territory, Dan."

"Don't I know it. It's like there is someone sitting in the background working me like a puppet and all I can do is go along with what they want me to do."

"I'll look forward to being there when you figure it all out, Dan. Because if there's one thing I'm sure off, you'll get there before anybody else does. Although it would be nice if, for once, I wasn't too far behind. So maybe if you can give me any more pointers now that I'm looking in the same direction as you?"

"I was just about to, my friend, because I'm going to need your help."

Huxley spoke quietly into his phone for a couple more minutes, outlining his suspicions to Pepper and asking him to follow some leads, deliberately walking back towards his party a couple of times to give the impression that his call was coming to an end and that there was no importance in anything being said only to stop and turn away again as if the caller had just raised another point.

Alan Donovan watched his face with interest, looking for any indication that Huxley may be finding out some vital information, clues that might help lead them to their goal but there was nothing in Huxley's expression to suggest that this was anything other than the police trying to find out where they were. He pulled his own phone from his pocket, still carefully wrapped in its protective waterproof cover, to check for any messages. Seeing none he began to compose one of his own while he waited for Huxley to finish.

The Judas Deception

Sam Davison wondered what could be so important at this time of the night, when they were in fear of their very lives, that Huxley had to go off for a chat. She tried to think about what had just happened in the house and why there hadn't been anybody out front waiting for them. Whatever way she looked at what had happened, it didn't make any sense and she couldn't help but think that there was more to it. She and Huxley had been in the study when they had first heard breaking glass. That bit she remembered clearly. Her immediate thought had been that Alan had knocked something over in the kitchen but when she heard his cry of alarm she had become very anxious. What on earth could be happening? Then it was all a bit of a blur. She had jumped up and raced towards the kitchen only to be pushed in the opposite direction by Huxley and the fleeing Donovan who was shouting about being attacked. Then there had been the gunshot. But no-one had been hit. Even though there was a clear line of sight from the back door all the way down the hallway. So was the gunman not a very good shot? Or had it been just to scare them? Did someone, perhaps, simply want them out of the house? So they could look at the cache that had been uncovered? But how had they known? So much didn't make any sense. Maybe she should raise it with Alan as they waited for Huxley to finish his call? She looked across at the young student, his head bowed in concentration as he played with his phone.

"Alan?"

Donovan looked up at the sound of his name but just then Huxley returned.

"Sorry about that. It was Pepper just updating me. Nothing much to tell other than to say that they managed to get into Simms's emails and wondering if I would like to tell them our current whereabouts. I declined. Shall we?" He motioned towards the locked door at the rear of the College, producing his key as he approached it.

Once in the grounds, the three crossed the courtyard, the night as dark as it had been at any point in the evening, and made their way to the Dean's lodgings.

Huxley said, "Let me do the talking, will you? I can't be certain about his involvement and I don't want to spook him."

The others nodded their ascent and Huxley knocked on the front door. He noted that the place was in darkness and took that as a good sign. Not sure what sort of reception they would receive, Huxley realised that he was anxious about seeing whether someone he had considered a friend might actually be mixed up in everything that had happened that night.

A light came on upstairs, its glare penetrating the curtains and casting a dim halo around the trio. A pair of feet appeared at the top of the stairs and then the Dean of Trinity College began to descend them.

He was in the process of pulling on a jumper over a t-shirt that was already in place and fastening the belt on a pair of trousers that looked as though they had just been hastily put on. It was obvious from his features that this was a man who had just been awoken from sleep. Huxley took that as a good sign.

Finally the hall light was switched on and the Dean looked out the door, trying to focus through still half shut eyes on Daniel and his other visitors. The door opened and he said, "Daniel, how nice, how nice. What can I do for you at this ungodly hour of the night?"

"I'm sorry to disturb you, sir, and I appreciate that it is a ridiculous time to be calling upon anyone, but we felt that we really must talk to you as soon as we could. It's about Simms."

"Ah, yes, poor Stephen. Well then, you had better come in, all of you," nodding a greeting to Sam and Alan as they

The Judas Deception

moved forward, "and perhaps some tea to aid my rejuvenating powers. Somehow, I think I might need my wits about me, am I right, Daniel?"

As he spoke he reached for a pair of loafers which he pulled on over his bare feet before turning towards Huxley as if in anticipation of an answer.

"That depends on just how much you can help us, Dean."

"I think it might be a case of us helping each other, dear boy. Now, let's go through into the kitchen."

They followed him through the cosy house, the Deanery not as impressive as the lodgings set aside for the Master, and into a small kitchen which had a sturdy wooden table at its centre. Connelly invited them to take a seat at the table while he busied himself making tea. Once done he joined the others at the table with a tray laden with a teapot, cups and milk.

"Shall I be mother?" he said, before filling the cups. "Now, what is it that you think I can help with?" addressing his question to Huxley.

Huxley noticed that, even in his haste to dress and answer their call in the middle of the night, Connelly had still managed to put his hairpiece into place, although it seemed slightly askew. He smiled to himself as he realised now, after all these years, why it was that Connelly wore it.

Huxley thought himself a considered individual but not so much that he didn't have a reckless streak in him. There was a time for caution and a time for abandon and a wise man knew when the right time for each was. Huxley hoped he was wise enough as he took a gamble.

"I know who you are, Dean." He looked across the table at the man who had worn the title of Dean of Trinity College for a number of years now, looking for some indication that he had guessed right and, seeing none, continued anyway. "Or should I say Father James O'Connell."

CHAPTER 35

Rome – 1970

As soon as he said it, Spencer knew he'd made a mistake. He had tried to backtrack, pretend that he wasn't sure of his facts, that it might be a different key that the Chaplain wore, but O'Connell knew he was lying. Lying to try and protect him. Because Spencer could see it in O'Connell's face, here, at last, was something he could do to prove his worth.

"It's madness, utter madness, sweet James. You can't go."

"Can't you see, it's perfect? I have the ideal cover, heck, you can't even call it cover. I live there. I'm simply going home."

"But that's not your home anymore. Said so yourself."

"Yes, but no-one else knows that. I can go back anytime I want."

"Told them that you'd be gone for a year. More even. Damn strange you're back within the month."

"Not really. It happens all the time. Priests are creatures of habit, especially in the Vatican. Everything is set out for you. Plenty of them go travelling and come back very quickly because they can't get used to the freedom. The lack of routine, having to think for yourself, arrange for laundry and food and mass, it all takes its toll. And they get lonely. So they go back. I'll just be another priest who couldn't cope with the world."

"But Milan? Grimani? You can't go back. Know all about

The Judas Deception

you. What you did. Arrest on sight. Straight to jail. Do not pass go."

"You said yourself that there is no way that he could know it was me. The disguise means that, even if he did report back to his masters, the description that he'll give won't be anything like me. Plus, you said that he wouldn't say anything. Wouldn't want to rock the boat."

"Just said that. Put you at ease. Didn't want you worrying. Course he'll have gone running to headmaster. Killed a man, far as he was concerned. House burnt down. Police involved. Had to account for his actions."

"Well, whatever he has done, it hasn't been traced back to me. Father Sanchez said that he had heard nothing."

"Sanchez. Damn fool. Never trusted the man."

"You trusted him enough when he chose me."

O'Connell let that hang in the air for a moment, knowing that Spencer was simply voicing his fears. When he continued it was in a much more conciliatory tone.

"Besides, I don't intend to be around for long. I go back, wait until dark, break into the Chaplain's rooms and steal the key of Arragones. I'll be gone before they even know I'm there."

"I just can't let you do it. I can't, my boy. It's too much."

"I'm not doing it because you asked me. Quite the opposite. I'm doing it because I want to, Spencer. Because I know how much it means to you. And even, in spite of that, you would never ask me to. I'm doing to further our cause. I'm doing it for truth. I'm doing it because I've lived a lie for too long.."

They had spent the last week discussing it, Spencer always reluctant, O'Connell the enthusiast, countering his companion's objections. During that time they had come up with a plan. Not the most elaborate, thought O'Connell, but then most of it would be down to chance and how he coped with the obstacles he knew would be faced. Spencer had fed scenarios to him and each time he had come up with a resolution, not all of them fool-proof by any means. Most of it he would be flying by the seat of his pants and he knew it. But they were too close now to give up.

"I wish I could be there with you."

"I think you might stand out in the Vatican, Spence, my friend."

Spencer smiled at the familiar use of his name, a trait exclusively reserved for this red-haired angel who understood him so completely.

"Anyway, you will be with me in spirit. And every time I come across a difficult situation I will simply think 'What would Spencer do?'."

"And then do exactly the opposite. Yes, yes," finished Spencer, the riposte having been one of O'Connell's favourites over the past few days. "Cheeky sod. Maybe I should let you stay there. Hell with it."

O'Connell pretended to pout, giving Spencer sad eyes. "Awww, you know you don't mean that," he said in his best baby voice.

"Cut that out. Ring the Vatican myself, tell them your plan. Throw you in their dungeons, let you rot. See if I care."

But he did care, all too much. That was the problem. His bluster masked the fear he felt inside. They had debated this long and hard, Spencer insisting that he would rather have the young Irishman alive and well than any stupid, bloody gospel from yesteryear. But O'Connell knew that he was developing feelings for this great man, feelings that he couldn't quite comprehend but was keen to explore further. And, if they didn't complete their quest, it would always be there, nagging in the background. He didn't want resentment to flourish somewhere

The Judas Deception

down the path because Spencer had given up his dream, his lifetime ambition, his years of work just for him. So the plan was hatched and provision made for O'Connell to fly back to the Vatican and return to the bosom of Mother Rome.

O'Connell chose not to inform his masters of the planned return in the hope it would catch them off guard and buy him some time before his motives were examined. He knew that there would be questions to answer but he didn't plan to be around for long enough.

"Just to be clear. Arrive late, night shift just starting, tell them it's all been cleared. That'll work, yes?"

"Stop worrying, I know what I have to do. The guards might wonder why they haven't been informed but I can blame the day shift for the mix up. And there won't be anyone around for them to check with. Evening meal, prayers, mass, they won't want to disturb any of that. So they'll let me in with the intention of checking in the morning. It's not as though I don't have the right papers or credentials. They're all in order. They might shout about it for a bit but they'll let me in with instructions to report back before breakfast."

"But you won't be there. Flown the nest by then. Gone. Done a runner. No hanging around. In. Out. Bam. Yes?"

"After they've escorted me to my room I will wait for them to leave me alone and then execute our plan."

"If you can call it that," said Spencer, pouting. "Farce. Travesty. Charade. Definitely not plan."

O'Connell had been nervous walking to the citadel, his legs wobbling as he approached the gate. Then downright petrified when he was ushered in, his calm exterior masking the fear churning his stomach as he explained the situation to the Swiss Guards on duty. But no alarms had been set off, no uniformed officers came to drag him away. Instead there were frowns and furrowed brows and plenty of cursing in Italian before they handed the red-haired priest his papers and welcomed him back to the Vatican.

He was, as predicted, escorted to his quarters, the guards insisting on carrying his bags. He thought that he had convinced them of the legitimacy of his claim but then one of them spoke.

"We will, of course, need to see you tomorrow morning, Father. Check with your Cardinal why we weren't informed. Formalities, you know how it is."

"I understand," he replied, "but perhaps a little later," he finished, yawning.

"Of course. You must be tired. Please, don't let us keep you. Good night, Father."

O'Connell retreated to his room, his knees buckling once he was alone. Then he waited. Sitting on his bed, he was aware of the fear that gripped him every time he heard someone in the corridor, expecting a knock on the door, for them to unmask him as an imposter, for the spy that he was. But, of course, he was the perfect spy in that respect because, as a Vatican priest, he was hidden in plain sight.

Gradually the footfall eased as evening became night and people began to settle in their quarters.

"Soon as it's quiet, make your move. None of this four in the morning bollocks. Hear me. Seen out of bed at that time, questions asked. Go before midnight, still okay to be walking around. Right?"

"I can find a reason."

"Like what?"

Spencer's question still loomed large in his mind as he crept out of his room into the quiet corridor. The truth was he wasn't sure what he would say if he encountered someone.

As he inched his way along the corridor, he went over the

The Judas Deception

first part of the plan in his head. Everything else would be directed by whatever happened from there.

The Vatican was not a prison camp, although sometimes it was hard to distinguish a difference. Rules and directions were there for the most part as guidelines to promote harmonious living. There were a few notable exceptions but, as O'Connell wasn't planning on having any women in his room, he didn't have to worry about the swift retribution such a violation would bring.

'No, what I'm doing they haven't legislated for because no-one would ever be stupid or foolhardy enough to try!' he thought.

Being found wandering the labyrinth of corridors within the city after lights out wasn't exactly a punishable action, more frowned upon. So he was anxious to avoid bumping into anyone.

Reaching the end of a corridor there was a door in front of him that would lead him into an area where his presence would be questioned. Cracking the door open an inch to check the corridor beyond he could see that there was no-one lurking on the other side. He eased the door open a little more in order to peer down the hallway both ways. All clear. Left took him towards the main body of the Vatican with its kitchens, dining halls and other facilities for the general populace. But O'Connell turned right and the passage that led towards the heavily guarded Papal apartments.

In the five years he had lived within the city walls, he had been afforded the same rooms. A modest bedroom, small bathroom and an area given to prayer and meditation, replicated throughout the living quarters. There had, however, been a brief sojourn when had he been asked to vacate his rooms to allow exterminators access following an infestation of vermin. During this time, he had been housed in a guest room within the papal apartments. It was this first-hand knowledge of the layout that allowed him to formulate his, rather sketchy, strategy.

This had come in useful as Spencer's attempts to obtain plans of the Vatican buildings had proved troublesome and the design sketches he had ended up with lacked any sort of detail.

"Thing shows the bloody drains. Fuck use is that to anyone!"

"It's fine. I know the layout. I can find it without a map."

"Good thing too. Bloody useless," Spencer had mumbled, slightly shamefaced that it was the best he could come up with.

Regardless of how detailed a map they used, the one thing it would not have shown was where the guards were situated. For this the pair had no choice but to rely on O'Connell's memory

"Guards here and here, you say," chimed Spencer in his best Sergeant Major voice, slapping a pointer onto the sketch they were working off.

He had indicated either end of a walkway that joined the common area of the city with the papal apartments. The guest room that had been O'Connell's makeshift home lay to one side of this, the main apartments housing the Pope and his senior staff on the other. Of this fact O'Connell was certain. What lay beyond the walkway he could only guess.

"Two either end, that's what I remember."

"Nobody patrolling the walkway itself?"

"No need, no-one can gain entry onto it without passing the guards outside first. And a priest who acts as a gatekeeper. In my experience it is he who is more officious than his armed counterparts," responded O'Connell. "He will see it as a slight if anyone unauthorised gets past his mark and is likely to be more vigilant as a result."

"Plan's over before it's even begun then," sighed Spencer.

"Oh stop being so melodramatic. Where there's a will, there's a way."

And there was, or at least, O'Connell hoped there was as he neared the door that would lead him directly to this same custodian.

"But what will you say, dear boy, to convince this guardian of righteousness. Shoot you down immediately, Have you arrested. Thrown in chains."

"There is a specialist library beyond the walkway. I have used it on occasions before. I'm sure I can convince him that I can't sleep and thought I would do some work on something that is stuck in my head."

"And he'll by that?"

"One can only hope."

Except, now that he was here, O'Connell could see just how flimsy it all was. A glass panel in the door afforded a view of the walkway and its protectors, a Monsignor whose red-lined robe declared a man of efficiency and precision. Bluffing a way past such a man was not going to be easy but he couldn't see any other way of getting onto the walkway. Alongside him stood two guards, their attention trained on the passageway directly in front of them which served as the main approach to the walkway. O'Connell had come from the side and now ducked back out of sight as he steeled himself. Playing the scenario out in his head, O'Connell made to rise but, as he did so, a movement beyond the glass caught his eye. Cautiously he peered through the panel and saw something that caused his blood to freeze.

CHAPTER 36

The others turned to look at Huxley, the surprise evident in Sam's face and a tinge of fury mixed in with it for good measure.

"What are you talking about?" It was a barbed question hurled at Huxley, half in query at his claim and half in anger as to why he hadn't shared his suspicions with them earlier. Huxley smiled calmly, knowing that he owed an explanation. But it would have to wait as there were more important matters to deal with now.

"It has been a long time since anyone has called me that, Daniel," responded the Dean. There was nothing in his voice to tell Huxley whether he was alarmed by the confrontation. "Can I ask how you found out?"

"There were a few things that pointed the way but I suppose I was intrigued by the fact that Simms phoned you earlier this afternoon, just hours before he was killed."

Sam flashed him a look, remembering that he had denied knowing who the call to the College had been to. But she saw something in Huxley's face that told her he was on to something so she held back her frustration. She could see that Donovan was struggling to put all the pieces together and wasn't so sure that he would keep himself in check for much

The Judas Deception

longer. The Dean replied before he had a chance to raise his objection.

"Yes, most unfortunate business. Poor, poor Stephen. I told him to be careful but he didn't see the danger. But I can't really see how a phone call could help you make such a leap as you have, Daniel. I mean, I know that you have a brilliant mind and that many would call you a genius, a word I don't use lightly but I think in your case it is entirely justified. But that doesn't explain how you have uncovered a secret that I have spent the last forty years carefully concealing."

"As I say, Dean, the call was what set me thinking but it was only when I saw an old photograph that we found earlier in a house in Grantchester that I finally put all the pieces into place."

"Ah, that would be a picture of dear Spencer and me. Have you got it with you, Daniel?"

Huxley reached into his inside jacket pocket and removed the photograph and handed it to the Dean. The others moved around him to study the picture as well. It showed the two men together standing arm in arm, a beaming smile filling the plump features of Spencer's face while that of his young companion showed contentment. The photo showed the vibrant red of James's flame hair, in stark contrast to the black wig that sat atop the Dean's head now, but as they looked beyond that the beginnings of recognition began in both Sam and Alan as they examined the picture. The eyes looking out from the photo were so full of life and vitality that they made the picture feel alive. And it was here that they could see the ancient remnants of the wizened man who sat before them now. A wall of books dominated the background behind them and as Sam looked closely at the picture she recognised the room.

"That's the study in the Grantchester house, isn't it?"

"Oh, that it is, my dear. How I loved that house. Spencer

and I spent many happy days there and I only wish there could have been many more but, alas, the man you see in that photo died the same day I heard about his death. It was the saddest day of my life."

"You loved him very much, didn't you?" asked Sam, recognising the deep affection in the man's voice and eyes as he spoke.

"He was the most wonderful person that I have ever met. He lit up a room just by walking into it. He taught me how to live and I glory in every moment that I got to spend with him."

Sam made her way back to her seat at the table taking the opportunity to wipe her eyes when her back was to everyone because the Dean's words had moved her. Alan, too, returned his eyes clouded with suspicion rather than sentiment.

"But tell me, Daniel, how on earth did you recognise me from such an old photograph?" asked the Dean.

"The photo was hidden in a secret compartment in the house, Dean, with quite an elaborate set of clues that needed to be solved in order to find it. It was obvious that the clues had been left behind by Spencer in the hope that they would be found by someone he expected to look for them. It all started with a coded message inside a book and he knew that this book would hold special significance for someone who knew him well. Someone who helped him in his quest. Someone who knew the house intimately and who he expected to understand what was hidden there. The fact that Simms had contacted you at a time when he was seeking information on the Judas Gospel made me think that perhaps he had received some guidance from you previously. This made me think that you could possibly be the someone Spencer expected to follow the clues. The question then was why you hadn't."

"I couldn't go back there, not at first. Then, when I did pluck up the courage, I would break down after what happened."

"What do you mean? What happened?" asked Sam, her voice rising in pitch as she spoke.

"You mean you don't know? But then why are you here?"

"We're here, Dean, because we believe that you might be able to help us find some answers. Because people have died and we need to find out why. And because we are lucky to still be alive ourselves and until we find out who is trying to kill us and what it is they are trying to protect then we won't be safe. And I think you know a lot more than the bumbling persona that you hide behind pretends to let on."

"You are right, of course, Daniel, this is all just a façade that I have adopted over the years to try and remain out of sight from anyone who might still be interested in finding Father James O'Connell. Even this," he reached up and removed the wig from his head to reveal an almost bald scalp with just a hint of ginger stubble protruding from the back, "was used as both a prop to disguise my real identity and to add to the idiocy that people associated with the Vicar of Dribbly."

"So what happened?" asked Sam again.

"Spencer and I upset the wrong people. People who are very dangerous. Ruthless people who aren't above killing. Evil men who hide behind ordinary masks. Men right here in Trinity College."

"The same men that you had dinner with tonight, Dean?" asked Huxley.

"The very same, Daniel."

"What the hell!" exclaimed Donovan, growing frustrated. "Does somebody want to explain just what the fuck is going on around here?"

"That might be a good idea. There's a lot has happened tonight, Dean, and I think there is a lot that you can tell us about it. Perhaps it would be best if you start at the beginning."

So he did.

CHAPTER 37

ROME – 1970

O'Connell watched in horror at the guards patrolling the walkway. The walkway that he needed to access in order to execute the next part of his plan.

Spencer's words came back to him.

"Nobody patrolling the walkway itself?"

"No need, no-one can gain entry onto it without passing the guards outside first," had been his confident response. Except now there were.

The roof of the walkway was flat and the plan had been for O'Connell to climb onto this once he had gained entry..

"Get onto that walkway, then straight out the window. No glancing backwards, swift movements, no time for thought. Instinct from here, dear boy. Window open, stand on the frame, reach up, grab the roof, haul yourself up."

It had sounded so simple, the pair even practising on Spencer's study window. Only now there were guards patrolling it.

He looked around desperately for an alternative route. The hallway was made up of individual staff quarters, each door leading to a set of rooms similar in layout to his own. Except the final door nearest the walkway. Here, he knew, was a storage room used to house cleaning products and surplus furniture, a graveyard for unwanted mattresses. He made for it, reaching for the handle and grateful to find it unlocked. He realised that the movement of the door opening could be seen by those in the corridor beyond so, keeping low, he pushed it slightly open, just enough to squeeze his crouching body through before gently closing it.

He paused a few seconds, unconsciously holding his breath as he waited for the door to be flung open and his treachery exposed. But nothing happened. His eyes adjusted to the darkness around and he walked towards the window on the far wall of the room, careful not to bump into anything and alert someone to his presence.

He looked out of the window to the courtyard three stories below, his mind spinning as a possible solution came to mind. The thought of it filled him with dread but he knew that if he was going to complete his mission that danger lay whichever way he chose. This seemed as crazy an idea as any.

He reached for the latch and firmly pushed open the window, the muggy heat of a July night in Rome hitting him. He leaned out, arching his head around as he did so to allow him to look up. The room was on the top floor, a pitched roof above. Guttering ran along the edge of the roof and a drainpipe dropped down from this beside the window. If he could climb up onto the roof above, this would allow him to drop directly on top of the walkway.

Without giving himself time to think, he eased himself out onto the window ledge, keeping a firm grip on the frame of the window. Instinct made him look down and he swayed at the drop below him, sweat overwhelming his body. Realising that this was a foolish idea, he was about to abandon his plan when his clammy hands slipped from the window frame. With his hold now gone, he teetered precariously on the ledge, momentum toppling him towards the abyss below. He made a desperate scramble for purchase but his balance was gone and he began to fall.

Instinctively O'Connell's hands flailed, striking the ledge, and he managed to grasp the edge with one hand, stopping his fall. Dangling by one arm, the pressure was too great and his body screamed with pain, seeking the relief that letting go would bring. Only his fear of death willed him to hold on.

With all the strength his feeble body could muster, O'Connell reached up with his other arm and grabbed the ledge above. He knew that, even with two arms, he would only be able to hang on for a short time. His only option was to try and haul himself up to the window and crawl through to safety. He tried to slowly haul himself up but his strength was drained and he could find no purchase for his feet as he hung helplessly.

The limited options available to him flashed through his mind. He looked at the drainpipe to his left and considered that this was his best option, perhaps his only option other than plunging to his death. He stretched out his left hand towards it and was just able to touch it. As the pressure on his other arm reached breaking point, he threw himself towards the drainpipe, an all or nothing gamble. He made a grab for the black metal tube and managed to wrap both hands around it before bringing his feet to bear on either side and give him a firmer hold. The respite he felt was short lived as the realisation that he was still three stories above ground hit home. But it sure beat the alternative. He looked up.

The pitched roof above was very acute and would be difficult to negotiate but he figured that it was a damn sight safer than staying where he was so began to climb towards it. Curling his legs upwards, he then stretched his arms above to grip the pipe before pushing with his legs to propel him

The Judas Deception

upwards. It took him five minutes and he was breathing heavily from the effort but he made it onto the roof.

Pausing to gather his breath, je huggedthe tiles around him as though they might reciprocate. Adrenaline still coursed through him and he knew that he couldn't wait for long lest it ceased and he became paralysed with fear. He inched his way along the roof precariously until he reached the corner. From here he could see the walkway that he had planned to climb out of to access the roof. Except it hadn't quite worked out that way. But his alternative route had worked, albeit nearly costing him his life. And it now allowed him to execute the next part of the plan.

"Across the roof, over the ledge, drop to the balcony, easy as pie. Except if you pick the wrong balcony. Or break your ankle dropping. Or someone sees you. Or you fall off the fucking roof. Madness, dear boy! Sheer folly. You're not doing it. Final, no argument, all that."

This was an hourly occurrence, O'Connell having to assuage Spencer's objections. He wondered what Spencer was up to at that moment and whether he would ever get to see the big man again. But this was a fleeting thought, adrenaline carrying him forward.

Crawling to the pitch of the roof, out of sight of the guards, he gingerly lowered himself over the side, dangling just above the flat roof of the walkway. There was nothing else for it but to drop the last bit. He could only hope that any noise he made in landing didn't alert those below to his presence.

He let go and hit the roof below with a thud that sounded like a gunshot in his own head, twisting his ankle as he landed awkwardly. He crouched in the shadow of the building and waited for the inevitable shouts from the guards below. But nothing happened.

He cautiously peered over the side of the walkway, lying

flat on the roof to afford him a view through a window but he saw only the same scene as earlier, the monsignor busying himself with paperwork as the guards patrolled up and down. He couldn't believe that they hadn't heard his landing. Or maybe they had put it down to something mundane. After all, who would be expecting a rogue priest to be vaulting the roof of the Vatican in the middle of the night?

He was grateful for the warm, clear night. High above the ground, exposed to the elements the last thing he needed was to be fighting wind and rain, although it meant that sound travelled further across the still night air. He moved as lightly as he could across the flat roof, staying as close to the edge as he dared as it would be less likely to betray his movements. He doubted that anyone more than a few feet away from him would be able to see him even with the moon intermittently breaking through the clouds, but he hoped that none of his fellow priests were looking out of their windows in case they chanced upon him.

He was still on a high from his brush with death and almost sprang onto the building at the far side of the walkway, a mirror image of the one he had almost fallen from minutes before. His tired arms cried out in protest as he hauled himself up onto the roof but O'Connell ignored the pain, dragging himself onto the slates and flattening himself against the slope of the roof.

He knew that the front of the papal apartments lay on the far side of this roof. All he had to do was sidle up the tiles and over the apex to the other side. From there he would be able to hang down from the roof and drop onto the balcony belonging to the Chaplain of his Holiness.

As the Pope's right hand man, the Chaplain was obliged to travel with the Pope and was often out of the country, such was the itinerary of the Head of the Church. But Spencer and O'Connell had checked his schedule and knew that both would be in residence for the next three weeks, so Monsignor Domineco Di Natele should be in his apartment. At least, O'Connell hoped he was or all his efforts would have been in vain.

He began to creep up the slope of the roof, reaching the top just as the moon made an appearance. In the light he could see the grounds of the city far below and he shuddered at the sudden realisation of just how high up he was. The thought was enough to make him flinch, causing him to slide back down the roof slightly. As he did so he caught a movement out of the corner of his eye somewhere to his right.

Peering cautiously over the top, he surveyed the tiles as they fell away from him, slowly taking in the whole façade. Seeing nothing he made to climb over when he caught the movement again. This time he was able to pinpoint the origin. He saw the outline of a man leaning against one of the chimney pots, dressed in the full regalia of a Swiss guard complete with gun.

O'Connell almost lost his footing and slid down the slope a little such was his hurry to duck out of sight. Grabbing hold of the slates around him, he held himself in place, lying flat as he considered what to do.

This was turning into a nightmare, so many things they hadn't allowed for.

"Bound to be some sort of surveillance up there. Guards stationed, trip wires primed, alarms set, fucking pigeons with machine guns, all I know."

"Not on the apartments. They have some sentry posts to the side of the Basilica. There was quite a fuss about that as they wanted them on the church itself but there was no way that was happening."

But Spencer had been right, as ever. Of course, now that

he was here and could see what a great vantage point it was, he understood the wisdom of placing a guard here. He could practically see the whole of St Peter's Square along with the majority of the Basilica itself, the dome stretching into the night sky.

Any attempt to scale the pinnacle and move down the far side of the roof would be futile as the guard would clearly see him. Suddenly the absurdity of what he was doing hit him and he almost laughed out loud. He took a moment to gather himself knowing that it was as dangerous now to go back as it was to continue.

Reaching into the pocket of his robe, he took out a small torch which he had brought with him. Although it may prove useful in the latter part of his plan, he felt that it could be better employed now as a diversion. Leaving the light switched off, he threw the torch as hard and as far as he could to his right before pressing himself flat against the slope of the roof again. He heard the noise of the torch as it landed on his side of the roof and slid down the pitch towards the guttering. Within seconds the guard appeared at the top of the roof, carefully negotiating the climb as he came to investigate the source of the noise.

O'Connell moved quickly mimicking the guard's movements in reverse. The young priest scrambled down the far side of the roof, all thoughts of safety gone as he concentrated on getting to the edge before the guard had a chance to return.

Reaching the guttering, he peered over to get his bearings. The balconies of the apartments below were visible and he counted along from the far end until he reached the third one. This was the balcony that would lead directly into the apartment of the Chaplain of his Holiness and O'Connell scurried along the roof until he was in line.

Knowing that the guard was likely to return to his post

anytime soon, O'Connell dropped to his knees before gripping the edge of the guttering and lowering his frame into mid-air once again. At least the drop he was now faced with was somewhat more manageable but he had already hurt his ankle and didn't fancy having to put all his weight on it again. However, he knew that hesitating wasn't going to help him so he prepared to let go. Then he heard a noise from above.

He held on with all his strength as the urge to let go almost overwhelmed him. A light shine on the roof almost directly over where he hung as the beam of a torch passed over the tiles. O'Connell guessed the guard was back and still searching for the source of the noise, his investigation having expanded to this side of the building. He held his breath knowing that the slightest sound may give him away. The beam passed right overhead and he knew that if the guard looked over the edge of the roof he would be caught red-handed. A mixture of exertion and fear brought O'Connell out in a sweat and within a matter of seconds his whole body was soaked, his hands becoming wet and slippery and his tenuous grip on the guttering ever more fragile.

He could hear the guard's footfalls overhead and the light from the torch rested on the spot just beside O'Connell's hands and the priest knew that he would be discovered any moment. Then the beam swung violently towards the far end of the roof and the guard began moving quickly away from him, seemingly drawn to another spot.

O'Connell could wait no longer and let go, his arms burning with the strain. He fell more than dropped but landed softly on a prayer cushion that the Chaplain had left on his balcony, his ankle welcoming the protection offered.

He stood slowly, shaken and winded but otherwise unscathed. The soft landing deadened the sound of his fall and he was thankful to see the beam of the guard's torch continue away from him. He was also glad to see the apartment that he had finally arrived at was in darkness, no lights suddenly blazing at the sound of his clumsy approach.

"Important thing about picking locks, got to listen carefully. All about the tumblers, the way they rise and fall, form a pattern, all that. Oh, do pay attention. This is important. Arsing around at a time like this."

"Sorry, Spence, I really am listening. It's just…."

"What? It's just what?"

"You look so handsome when you're being serious."

"Oh, stop it. Damn tomfoolery. Important stuff here. Life may depend on it."

"I'm listening. Honest."

"Well take that stupid smirk off your face."

It had taken O'Connell some time to master the art but with such a patient teacher and lots of practice he had become quite proficient in opening locks.

He reached into his pocket once again, this time in search of the lock picks that Spencer had presented him with upon graduation. Walking over to the balcony door, O'Connell bent down to get a good look at the lock. It appeared to be straightforward enough and O'Connell made to open the pouch with his picks when, on a whim, he tried the handle of the door. It turned easily in his hand and the door opened with a click.

Once more, the young priest stood holding his breathe, waiting to see if the noise would attract any attention. After what seemed to be minutes but was, in truth, only a few seconds, he let out a long, slow, sigh of relief. He pulled the door towards him, waiting for a squeak from the weathered hinges but getting none.

Heavy velvet drapes hung menacingly over the doorway, the thick, rich material seemingly acting as a force-field, preventing him from entering the room. O'Connell reached

The Judas Deception

forward, prodding at the curtains as he tried to find the parting, all the while hoping that no-one stood on the other side watching as he comically stabbed at the material to form a shrouded apparition of himself.

The drapes parted to reveal the room beyond in darkness and O'Connell stepped into the stifled air, tension fighting adrenaline for control over his body. As the curtains fell back into place, the room was lost in total darkness. O'Connell stood to allow his eyes to become accustomed to the blackness but it was impossible for him to see anything. He rued the loss of his flashlight, thinking of other less valuable items he might have discarded but knowing that none of them would have sufficed.

He heard snoring from somewhere to his right so if, as he hoped, he was in the right room then the Chaplain of his Holiness was sleeping soundly and covering any noise he might make as he shuffled along in the darkness. But he knew that one wrong move could result in him knocking something over. He needed light of some sort otherwise he wouldn't be able to see what it was he was looking for.

He reached behind him, feeling the luxurious warmth of the rich velvet and slowly began to part them, allowing a chink of moonlight to fall into the room.

Now the room had sufficient light to allow him to see the layout. It was vast, a huge auditorium of sleep, a fitting place for a prince to lay down his head at night. Which is exactly what the Chaplin was, a prince to the Pope's king.

Able to see enough to navigate his way around the room, O'Connell began to make his way towards the bed.

"Can't sleep with the damn thing on, can he? Choke himself. Dead. Gone. Kaput, all that. Death by stupidity. Has to take it off. Put it somewhere safe. Handy. Wouldn't want to go searching for it next morning. Wants it near. Beside table.

Chest of drawers. Cabinet of some sort. Fuck do I know. It'll be there somewhere. Mark my words."

And sure enough, Spencer was right again, O'Connell allowing a smile to play on his lips for just a moment as the glint of metal and jewels came from a cabinet next to the bed.

"Look at his neck," Spencer had ordered, holding up a picture, "I mean around it, not the neck itself. Know what you're like. Too literal. See? The chains. Chains of office. Wears them all the time. Jewels galore. Ever fall on hard times all the Vatican has to do is sell these. Worth a fortune."

"Won't he keep them locked away?"

"Why should he? Who's going to steal it? Fucking Vatican. No-one's going to break into the Vatican. Struck down with lightening, all that. Hogwash, but that's what makes them complacent. Don't worry, they'll be there. Now, see this, the silver chain? Four keys at the bottom? That's the one. It'll be with wherever he keeps the rest of the stuff."

O'Connell edged alongside the bed, heading towards the cabinet on which he could now make out those same chains of office. They had been tossed carelessly on top of the cabinet, no concern for their upkeep, just a priceless tangled mess that someone else would have to tidy up. O'Connell knew that the Pope had dressers who helped ready him each day and suspected that the Chaplain had a similar entourage who would attend to such duties.

Not that they were much use to him now as he realised that he'd have to lift the bundle in order to try and identify the chain he wanted. It was either that or abscond with the whole lot. But hoped the theft might go unnoticed, especially if the Chaplain gave such little thought to the precious jewels he wore. Perhaps it may be days, weeks even before he realised that something was missing.

He saw the four small keys hanging from a chain and

began to trace backwards from them, freeing the silver from the gold that entwined it. Carefully he released it link by precious link from its priceless incarceration, quietly undoing a particularly difficult knot where the chains had become entangled.

Suddenly there was a grunt from beside him. He turned to see the prone figure stir slightly, the steady snores interrupted. O'Connell froze, watching the Chaplain's face as he rolled off his back and onto his side, moving closer to the intruder as he did. O'Connell held his breath as he waited to see if the Chaplain would wake up but the sleeping figure seemed to have settled back into sleep. Then, suddenly, his eyes popped open.

O'Connell almost screamed in panic. He stepped back in fright as the Chaplain's eyes looked straight at him. Or rather they looked straight through him as he then mumbled something incoherent before closing them again and resuming his previous breathing pattern as sleep consumed him once more.

O'Connell stood mesmerised. He couldn't quite believe what had just happened and also that he hadn't soiled himself. He vowed that he would never do anything brave or foolish again if he could only get out of this one alive.

Taking hold of the silver chain he had come to steal, he yanked it clear of the others before setting the rest back on the cabinet and backing away from the bed, all the while watching for any signs that the Chaplain's subconscious was processing what he had seen and would alert him to it at any moment. But nothing happened. The man continued to sleep and O'Connell turned to make his way back towards the balcony. It was only then that he saw the outline of someone else standing in the room watching him.

CHAPTER 38

Rome – 1970

The woman was silhouetted in a doorway that O'Connell hadn't noticed before, the moonlight reflecting off the tiled surface of a bathroom beyond.

O'Connell barely had time to register his thoughts of why someone was in the bathroom of the Chaplain of his Holiness in the middle of the night before there was an ear piercing scream that seemed to fill the whole apartment.

The prone figure in the bed woke with a start, his native Italian curses not lost on O'Connell as he fumbled to make sense of what was going on. His concern at drawing attention from the guards outside quickly dissipated as he realised that there was an intruder in the room.

O'Connell's plan had been to sneak back out onto the balcony and over the roof again.

"In, out, poof, gone just like that." Spencer had blown on his hand to indicate something vanishing.

"But how do I get back onto the roof?"

"Fuck do I know? Use a chair, table, whatever, climb on top, haul yourself up. Your bloody stupid idea. Suicide. Lunacy. Stay here. We'll elope. South Pacific. Hula skirts, all that."

"What if he wakes up and sees me?"

"Then run like hell!"

The Judas Deception

Which is precisely what O'Connell now did. In the dim moonlight he could make out two doors further along the corridor. Guessing that one of them led to the Chaplain's living accommodation, O'Connell opted for the other which he hoped would lead him onto the private corridor of the papal apartments. He reached for the handle but the door was locked.

The room filled with light as the Chaplain switched on a lamp and O'Connell turned to see him climbing out of bed. He realised that the two figures were both naked and guessed the reluctance of the Chaplain's companion to react earlier to O'Connell's presence might have something to do with this.

There were more shouts and curses from the Chaplain aimed at O'Connell who was desperate to escape the room. With the light now on, he was able to see that there was a key in the door so made to turn it before either figure had a chance to stop him leaving. He flung the door open and ran out into the corridor beyond. A quick scan showed a guard to his right, stationed outside the Pope's accommodation, so O'Connell went left.

The guard was caught in two minds as to whether to apprehend the priest who had just exited the Chaplain's quarters or whether to hold his post. It wasn't the first time he had seen a visitor sneaking out of the Chaplain's rooms but normally it was done more subtly, a parody of implausibility played out for his benefit. All stupid grins and too much volume as they played to the gallery but the guard played along, nodding his greetings when eye contact was inevitably made to see if he was buying it. There were even times when the visitors, women for the most part, would dress in priests' garb and pretend they had been there officially.

He was paid for his discretion as much as anything and had no intention of giving up such a privileged position just because the Chaplain of his Holiness couldn't keep it in his pants.

But this departure was different, too hurried, an urgency about it that suggested that the priest scurrying away had been there under duress. All the more reason for him to ignore it. He jumped to full alert, however, when the semi-clad figure of the Chaplain appeared in the doorway, in the process of tying his dressing gown, a look on his face that told the guard that something was seriously amiss. The shouted order to pursue left him in no doubt that this was an intruder. Reaching for his two-way radio, the guard contacted his colleague who was stationed around the corner at the far end of the corridor. The end that O'Connell was now running towards.

He was running blind, unsure of where this would lead him or where there might be other guards. But standing still wasn't an option. When the shouts came they were from both ahead and behind and he knew that he was in trouble.

He looked about him furiously but his only options were forward or back and both led him straight into the path of an armed guard. The one running towards him drew his pistol. He shouted an order in Italian, a slight quiver in his voice as if uncertain that he should be pointing a weapon at a priest, especially here of all places.

O'Connell used the hesitation to consider his options. Perhaps he could talk his way past the guard, point the finger at those behind as the trouble-makers. But he knew that the Chaplain would hold sway around here. No, he was going to have to find something else. He spotted a lift door to his left. It had a notice saying it was for the private use of the Pope and O'Connell feared that it might need a key to operate it. But in the absence of anything else, it was worth a try.

He pushed the call button and the door pinged open immediately. The young priest jumped in, grateful for the

The Judas Deception

sanctuary. But with the door wide open he was still exposed so he searched for some way to close it. An illuminated button indicated that the lift could only go one way, up to the cupola at the top of the Basilica. O'Connell reached out and pressed it hurriedly as he turned to see the guard now running towards him. The door began to creep closed, O'Connell watching as the guard raised his weapon to fire. He hit the button again in the hope of speeding up the process as he knew that if the bullet entered the lift then it would be sure to hit him either directly or by ricochet. He closed his eyes. The gun-shot never came. When he opened them again he could see that the door was closed and the lift was slowly making its way upwards. Up to the cupola on top of the dome of St Peter's Basilica.

Being more used to the chambers under the city, it had never been O'Connell's practice to regularly taste the rarefied air from the roof of the Basilica. But he had ventured up occasionally to marvel at the view of the city that one could enjoy from the vantage point so he knew that he was climbing even higher than he had already been this evening. And, more importantly, he had absolutely no idea of how he was going to get down.

Also, he couldn't be sure that he wasn't about to be met by an armed guard up there. Once the lift door opened onto the cupola, would he be surrounded by a whole raft of guards? Did they patrol the roof of the cathedral in the same way they did the apartments? Would they, perhaps, shoot first and ask questions later? He braced as the lift came to a stop. The door opened.

CHAPTER 39

Rome – 1970

There was no-one there. O'Connell nervously poked his head out of the door but he the cupola was completely empty. Just the warm night air to greet him.

He knew it was only a matter of time before armed guards came crashing through the door from the stairwell so he rushed out of the lift, frantically looking around him for a means of escape. Hearing a noise behind him he turned to find the lift door was jammed against something and, as he looked down, he realised that the set of lock picks that Spencer had given him must have fallen out of his pocket and landed in the door's sliding mechanism. That meant that the lift couldn't go back down. It would seem his luck was finally turning.

Inspired by this, he looked around him to see if there was something that he could use to jam the stairwell door closed with. A flag bearing the pope's crescent flew from one side of the cupola, its pole seemingly long enough, O'Connell reckoned. He went across and grabbed hold of it and tugged hard to free it from its base. It came away much easier than he had expected and he nearly toppled over the parapet of the cupola. After all he had been through, he thought, that would be a very indignant end.

Taking hold of the pole and flag, O'Connell ran across to

The Judas Deception

the door leading to the stairwell and jammed it through the handle, effectively blocking any attempt to push the door open from the other side. He knew it was only a delaying tactic and that the guards would break through the barrier with little effort but at least it bought him some time.

He looked at the scene below, St Peter's Square awash with light as the moon broke through the cloud cover. It looked beautiful, the symmetry perfect, the obelisk precisely in the middle of the square and in line with the doors of the cathedral.

He was shaken from his reverie by the sight of a van driving quickly down the Via della Conciliazione heading straight towards the Square. He guessed that the alarm had been raised and that this was reinforcements being called in to help with his capture. He knew he had to find some way down before it was too late.

There was now a commotion from the doorway of the stairwell and he turned to see a number of guards through the window inset into the door. He looked over the edge of the cupola and could see the huge façade of the church far below, statues of Christ adorning the top. It was a huge drop to this and the only way down was over the vast dome which he now sat atop. But with no other options and the guards now breaking down the blocked door, O'Connell reluctantly edged over the parapet and lowered himself onto the dome.

Having only ever viewed it from below, it looked like a gentle spheroid, the elegant curve of the roof like a teat being offered to God in supplication but now that he was actually standing on it the drop seemed almost sheer.

He grabbed hold of a stone carving at the base of the parapet and slowly lay down, searching for hand or foot holds that would give him some support. There were windows cut into the dome at various places and the decorative stonework around these would offer some support if he could just angle himself towards one.

Shuffling across so that one such window lay directly below him, he let go of his anchor on the parapet and slid towards it. He dropped much quicker than anticipated and his already damaged ankle bore the full brunt of his weight as he hit the carving below him, causing him to shudder with pain. But he had no time to stop and dwell on his discomfort as he could hear voices above and guessed that the guards were close to breaching his makeshift defences. Unless he could get to the foot of the dome before they did, he knew he was a sitting duck.

Using the stonework around the window, O'Connell looked down to see where the next foothold lay. It was the same distance again so he set himself to repeat his aerobic act, lining himself with the next window below. This time he was able to brace himself better for the impact, causing only minimal discomfort. He looked above him and could see movement on the parapet as the guards began to circulate around it in search of him.

With no time to think, he made to line himself up with the final window in the sequence and allowed himself to drop towards it, hitting it with greater force as the drop became steeper the further down the dome he got. With no more windows below him, he had no choice but to dangle himself from the carvings and prepare to drop the final few feet to the base of the dome. From there he saw that he could climb down onto the facade. Providing, of course, he landed on the base. If he missed it then he would plunge to his death.

Fear got the better of him at this point and he hung for a few seconds desperately trying to think of a better escape route. A bullet pinged of the stonework beside him and it was only then that he heard the report of the gun fired by a guard above. Another quickly followed, ricocheting on the bricks of the dome itself. O'Connell let go not caring how or where he landed as he recognised it was his only chance of survival. He fell through the air before hitting something hard with first his feet and then his knees as they scraped the edge of the base. As he landed. O'Connell reached out with his arms and made a grab for the surround which decorated the bottom of the base. His hands grasped thin air for a moment before latching onto the stonework. His whole body screamed with pain from the battering it had taken but somehow he managed to hold on, his legs flailing as they tried to find some purchase. Bullets still rang out from above him but he was now out of their line of sight, the base of the dome covering him.

He afforded himself a short breather and looked down at the Square in time to see the approaching van screeching towards the security gatehouse on the far side of the vast arena. It wasn't showing any sign of slowing down as it reached the barrier and O'Connell was surprised that the guards hadn't raised it before now to let their colleagues through.

As he watched, the van barrelled straight through the barrier and accelerated across the square towards the front of the cathedral. The guards in the gatehouse ran out and began firing at the moving vehicle. O'Connell was completely bemused by what was unfolding but welcomed the distraction as he began to make his way down the wall, using the decorative ornamentation that Michelangelo had so thoughtfully designed.

Once on the façade, he glanced up to see the guards above trying to gain a vantage point that would give them a clear shot of their target. O'Connell used the cover of the dome and the shadow cast by the parabola to make his way across the façade. He had the outline of a plan in his head but it was still very sketchy. If he could get to the front of the façade then he might be able to jump down onto the enormous colonnades which ran along both sides of the Square in a crescent shape, a walkway linking each of them for the entire length. Perhaps if he could make his way onto these he could run to the far end of the Square and…well, that's where it all got a bit hazy. First he had to get there and in order to do that he would have to run the gauntlet of gunfire from above as he entered open territory.

It was then that the guards above began to fire at the van below, word having reached them from their colleagues that this was another breach in security and that the van and its occupants should be considered targets. Using the diversion, O'Connell made a quick run for it, his damaged ankle and broken body notwithstanding.

As he reached the front of the façade, some of the guards evidently began directing their fire towards him as bullets hit the ground around him. Running on pure instinct now, O'Connell didn't even hesitate as he made the leap from the façade onto the colonnades. In his former life as a regular priest of the Vatican he would never have dreamed of being able to soar across the ten foot gap that separated the two but this new action version of himself managed it with room to spare and he fell into a roll as he landed, almost as though meant although in truth it was simply dumb luck.

Having rolled, he crashed against the first statue adorning that side of the colonnade, a life size image of St Peter himself, thus providing him with cover from the shots raining his way. Not taking any time to dwell on matters, he picked himself up and began to hobble as quickly as he could along the top of the vast colonnade, going from statue to statue and using them as cover.

He stopped to rest about halfway along, the depth of the crescent at this point putting more distance between him and the guards still positioned on the cupola.

He looked down into the Square to see more guards

emerge to his left, all of them armed. They immediately began to concentrate their fire at the van which was now seemingly tracking his movements.

The van stopped just below him and he saw two figures emerge from the covered canopy at the back. They began to return fire at the guards, one focussing on those in the Square whilst the other fired into the shadows of the dome of the basilica. The guards ran for cover and the hail of bullets that had been raining down on both the van and O'Connell ceased for a moment.

It was then that O'Connell heard the most magnificent sound that he could ever imagine. Choirs of angels playing a trumpet chorus could not match the melodic sound of Spencer's voice shouting to him from the Square below. O'Connell looked over the edge of the colonnade not daring to believe that the voice was real, that his sub-conscious was playing tricks with him after all he had been through. But, sure enough, the broad unmistakeable stature of Spencer Harris stood some forty feet below, three other figures around him.

They began to unfurl something and O'Connell realised it was a blanket being used as an emergency crash mat for him to jump into. Relief flooded his body as, at last, he saw a way out of this nightmare. But as quickly as it came it disappeared as he was overwhelmed with fear at the thought of jumping from the relative safety of the colonnade into this small target below. He didn't think he could do it.

There were shouts from below and the two men who had been returning fire at the guards ducked behind the side of the vehicle as more gunfire was aimed in their direction. The bullets, too, began to once again ping around O'Connell and he ducked back behind the statue of whichever saint was now affording him protection, possibly St Michael given the sword that was sheathed by his side.

He knew that he wouldn't be safe here for long and by waiting he was exposing his rescuers to greater danger. He determined to jump and stood to prepare himself, using the sword to haul himself to his feet. As he did so, he slipped and lost his footing, falling flat on his back just as a bullet whistled past him and struck St Michael's sword exactly where he had been standing moments before.

Without a further thought, O'Connell reached up and again used the sword as leverage, this time holding it to maintain his balance before launching himself from the colonnade into the waiting blanket below. The group holding the makeshift crash mat were taken slightly unawares such was the haste with which O'Connell jumped but recovered to brace themselves just as he hit it, providing him with the softest landing he had had all night. Lowering him to the ground, Spencer moved towards him for a quick embrace.

"No time to explain. Got to get moving. Chaps risking their lives, all that. Follow me."

He led O'Connell to the back of the van where, once again, the pair with guns were providing some cover fire whilst the rest of the group, O'Connell now amongst them, jumped into the van. The vehicle started moving off and the two gunmen turned and chased after it, grabbing the back of the canopy and vaulting in almost in unison, their movements so fluent. The van accelerated and there was a shout from the cab up front to brace themselves as it battered its way through a concrete bollards, its speed and reinforced front ensuring their escape. Gunshots continued to ring out but they were more distant now as the van sped away from the mayhem.

"How….I mean, what….how…?" stammered O'Connell.

"All in good time, old chap, all in good time."

CHAPTER 40

ROME – 1970

They drove through the deserted streets of Rome, the lateness of the hour making progress easy. The driver, Sergio, kept to the back streets and alleys as much as possible knowing that the lack of traffic also made tracking their movements so much easier for the authorities. Soon the streets became roads and the buildings became fewer as they headed towards the foothills of the city.

A few minutes had passed and the natural high of what had just happened began to wear off. O'Connell looked around at the faces in the back of the truck with him, elation of a job well done written across them. He turned towards Spencer, keen to fill in the blanks that were running around his head.

His friend was sitting with his head back, arms wrapped around himself as if trying to keep warm. It was then that O'Connell noticed the stain on the side of Spencer's clothes. A dark stain that hadn't been there before and now seemed to be growing. A stain that could only be blood.

"Oh my god, Spencer, you're hurt," he cried, rushing towards his friend's side.

The others looked around and then, noticing the blood, ran to assist. The flurry of activity that followed left O'Connell feeling even more of an outsider as he could only look on in horror as Spencer's shirt was ripped open to reveal a hole in his side. All this because of me thought the young priest and the guilt overwhelmed him.

Spencer drifted in and out of consciousness as they made their way towards their final destination, an old farmhouse on the outskirts of the city where medical help awaited him. He could see faces in front of him, concern or concentration written across them as they tried to stabilise him or attend to the wound. And through it all he could make out the red hair of his accomplice and companion and he wanted to reach out towards him and tell him that everything would be okay, that even if he died right here, right now, it had all been worth it if it meant his friend was safe.

But he didn't seem to be able to form the words, the incoherent spluttering that projected from his mouth causing alarm and confusion amongst those around him as they told him to rest and not to try and speak. But he needed to tell James, his dear sweet James, needed to tell him….needed to tell him something. What was it he needed to say? He knew it was important. Knew that the young man needed to hear it. He couldn't quite remember what it was now, couldn't seem to focus on….

The truck passed through a large gate and continued to the end of a long, dusty driveway which led to the back of a large sandstone house with outbuildings that looked as though they may have been damaged in the war and never repaired. What war, O'Connell couldn't be sure but it was into one of these buildings that the truck was taken, the crew dismounting as soon as they came to a stop.

A stretcher was fetched and Spencer rolled onto it gently, his large bulk notwithstanding. Then, with military precision, O'Connell noted, he was carried into the large house and the young priest couldn't help but think that they had done all this before. There was a certain efficiency that suggested that Spencer wasn't the first gunshot victim that had been brought into this place and he hoped that this meant that they had the resources required to help him. Not only hoped but, unable to break the habit of a lifetime, O'Connell prayed.

For the next four hours the young priest felt like an anxious relative pacing a hospital waiting room waiting for news from the operating theatre. Only his waiting room was a desolate barn, the operating theatre a kitchen in an aging farm house and the chances of survival greatly reduced by lack of facilities, tools or practising surgeon. Instead, the crew who had so heroically rescued him as he ran across the rooftop of St Peter's Basilica, now formed the surgical team in whose hands hung the life of his friend. Although it was obvious that this wasn't the first time that they had found themselves in this situation, he knew that their efforts were limited and would soon reach a point where they could do nothing further except hope.

Eventually O'Connell was ushered into a garish, split level room, the summer sunshine streaming through the open curtains and bouncing off the orange walls and producing a sheen off the varnished floor that made it look slippery in patches. There was a step that led up to the raised area of the room where a king-size, rickety brass bed dominated the space, the frame seemingly straining under the weight of the patient as he lay deadweight, a makeshift saline drip hanging to the side. O'Connell got the impression that the team felt a priest was of more use to Spencer now than anyone else, even one whose faith had lapsed as demonstrated by his recent act of larceny against the Church.

In spite of his U-turn on all things religious, O'Connell found it hard to leave a lifetime of ritual behind completely and fell into prayer frequently as he sat holding his companion's hand, waiting for some indication of life.

It was unusual to see Spencer's large frame so still and inert, this great lump of a man so normally full of life and vitality, his drive and passion all embracing, his energy knowing no limit. O'Connell loved being caught in the whirlwind of life with him and couldn't reconcile this motionless mass with what the man he knew and loved. This fervent zealot, this adoring fanatic, this life-embracing enthusiast reduced to a faint pulse and shallow breathing all because of him.

Guilt and grief waged an on-going battle in O'Connell's heart for the next three days, the young priest barely able to eat or speak and with sleep coming to him in fitful bursts as he refused to leave his friend's side. And then the most wonderful thing imaginable happened. Spencer's eyes flicked open. Just for a moment, the briefest of blinks, a barely perceptible movement that O'Connell almost missed. Afterwards he wondered if there had been other such flickers that he had missed during a period of slumber or while he visited the bathroom or some other arbitrary function that could have waited while his companion fought with all that determination and zest that he had in abundance to hold onto this world.

But for now he simply rejoiced that the eye had moved and that there was a sign of life, albeit a weak one.

His shouts could be heard all over the house and brought a pounding of feet as the others made for the room which served as the intensive care unit in this makeshift field hospital. His excitement was somewhat tempered by the less than enthusiastic response from the rest of the team but O'Connell knew that it showed the fight that his friend was putting up and recognised in such a battle that there was only ever going to be one winner.

More flashes followed, a blink, a mumble, even, for one fleeting moment, a squeeze of O'Connell's hand and the young man delighted in what he appreciated to be unquestionable signs of recovery no matter what the others may believe. A recovery that became ever more apparent as the days passed and flickers developed into moments, movements into gestures, mumbles into words.

It took several weeks and a lot of effort and determination both on the part of the patient and of those helping him but the mass of energy and fervour that was Spencer Harris was soon in evidence once again as he ordered about all those around him.

A return to full health was painfully slow for someone used to doing what he wanted whenever it best suited him and his bluster and pomp deserted him at times as he struggled with his lack of movement and energy. The frustration was all the greater for the knowledge that they now had the Key of Arrogenes and, with it, the power to gain entry to whatever secret chamber lay beneath the Wren Library. A chamber full of hidden documents and treasures.

"All in good time, my friend," said Sergio, the voice of reason and self-appointed leader of the motley crew who had become O'Connell's band of brothers over the passing weeks.

"Hell with that. Go now. Fit as a fiddle. Ready for anything," blustered Spencer who still had trouble standing unaided.

But reason had prevailed and, instead, Spencer contented himself with work on a plan of action.

"I still don't know the full story of....," O'Connell found it difficult to reference the night that he had almost lost his own life and that of his friend. In the end he simply settled for "...that night."

They had spoken about the crazy events from O'Connell's perspective many times, sometimes just the two of them, Spencer weak and wane but delighting in the recounting by his accomplice. Other times it was the whole crew gathered, spellbound by O'Connell's tale, each asking for their favourite bit to be recited in more detail. But when O'Connell asked about their involvement they simply deferred to Spencer who, citing fatigue, promised to fill the young man in at a later date.

"Fairly simple, really. Knew it could all go tits up for you, wanted to help somehow, be on hand, all that. Chaps have helped me out before, few occasions actually, good bunch, efficient, resourceful, bloody brilliant, truth be told. Seem to like me, some reason, get on well. Told them the problem, came up with a plan. Got hold of some walkie-talkies, same as the guards, parked close enough to get in range, listened in, heard when all hell broke loose. Couldn't just sit by, do nothing. Told them to hit the Square, worry about details afterwards. Turns out we could see you. Radios going crazy, intruder on the dome, shoot on sight, all that. Tracked your progress, saw you jumping onto the colonnades, brilliant by the way, inspired. Followed you round, know the rest."

Even that short explanation had left Spencer exhausted and it would take weeks of prompting from O'Connell before the details of the exercise were drip-fed to him. He marvelled at the willingness of these men to put their lives on the line to help him and was humbled by their heroism. But regardless of his admiration, he was determined to do whatever he could to talk Spencer out of going any further with this ludicrous ordeal.

"You almost died, Spencer. I almost died! Surely, between the two of us, we have used up all our lives and we should settle for what we have."

"Perhaps you're right, my dear. Pack it all in. Leave them to their mysteries, their subterfuge, pull the wool over eyes, all that."

That had been the starting point but as the weeks passed

and his strength returned, Spencer was soon plotting their next move.

"Sergio to sort out passports, identities, all that. Yes, Serge? No problem, man of your means? Good, leave that with you. Change appearance, disguise, new clothes, the lot."

"But we're wanted men. We've stolen from the Vatican. My picture is up in train stations and airports. We'll never make it out of Italy."

Sergio and his men had been keeping a keen eye on reports and, sure enough, the press did run with a story about thieves breaking into the Basilica and stealing priceless works of art. O'Connell's picture was printed in all the papers alongside descriptions of the others which were so vague as to be useless.

"Well, you're certainly a liability, give you that, my sweet," replied Spencer, mockingly. "Think we'll have to cut you loose, go your own way, all that." He winked at the others but his plan wasn't too far off doing just that. However, he could never abandon his fair James and so he came up with a plan that he thought would work best for them all. Now all they had to do was execute it.

CHAPTER 41

ENGLAND – 1970

"Would you stop fussing so!" The exasperation in Spencer's voice was superficial as he allowed James O'Connell to take his arm to climb the steps of the house that they had called home for the past three months. Convalescing wasn't something that the large man did well and it had taken a great deal of persuasion from both O'Connell and the rest of the crew to stop him from rushing immediately back to Cambridge.

True to his word, Sergio had come up with documents for both Spencer and the young priest, even going so far as to maintain the Irishman's natural cover and keeping him as a member of the church, albeit an Anglicised version. A haircut, a wig, some subtle blemishes about his face and Dr John Connelly had been born. The wig had been Spencer's idea.

"Hide in plain sight, old boy. Who's going to challenge you? Too embarrassed to say anything. Everyone will shy away from it. Elephant in the room and all that."

"But it looks ridiculous," cried O'Connell.

"Exactly my point, sweet James. The more ridiculous the better. Anything that distracts from those beautiful red locks of yours."

"But why can't I just dye it? It would be a lot easier."

"Ah, but not as effective. People trained to look beyond the colour. Match it with the complexion, all that. Much better to have a syrup on your head that will distract them. Why would anyone trying to disguise themselves wear something so obvious? Answer, they wouldn't so move along."

"Well, it feels ludicrous."

Spencer looked with amusement at his friend and smiled. "It's only for other people's benefit. I still get to see the wonderful, sweet boy that has captured my heart. Those lovely red locks albeit shorn to the bone but still distinctive and endearing."

O'Connell blushed as he so often did at the big man's gushing. "I suppose you're right."

"No suppose about it, dear boy. Spencer always knows best. No, the wig is for public consumption only. No matter how ridiculous it makes you look!" He darted through the doorway in which he had been standing and into the next room followed closely by a book which had been the closest thing to hand to O'Connell as he looked to throw something at his friend's teasing remark.

He had grown quite accustomed to it over the months since he had first began wearing the hairpiece. That had been back in Italy when Sergio needed photographs for the new IDs. O'Connell's hair had been shaved off, his eyebrows dyed, make up lightly applied to cover freckles and give his complexion a little more colour and a pair of spectacles added just to complete the makeover. It was subtle but the change was efficient. The wig just a neat distraction.

For Spencer, the initial weeks following his injury had seen him lose a considerable amount of weight which acted as a natural disguise for him and changed the shape of his face drastically. Add to that the beard that he had grown and he was almost unrecognisable unless one looked closely.

The passports that Sergio had acquired for both men were Canadian, an effect on the accent which was easy for Spencer to mimic but which took some practise for his companion.

"Stop laughing at me," groaned O'Connell, turning to look at his cohort. "It's alright for you, Mr Harris, you can fall into different languages and accents at the drop of a hat."

"That's Mr Wilson now," replied Spencer, holding up his new passport.

They had reverted to the original plan once Spencer had recovered sufficiently to move without the need to stop every few steps to gather breath. The walking cane he relied on became part of his cover, Spencer insisting that Sergio acquire him a fine oak stick with polished silver handle which fitted his North American longing to be of more English persona. As his fitness improved so the dependence on the cane diminished and it converted to an accessory used to great affect when in public places.

The two, accompanied by Sergio and the rest of the crew, made their way the short distance to the Italian coast. From here a boat took them all to Corsica, landing on a private jetty in the dead of night. The villa to which the jetty belonged was the summer residence of an old friend of Spencer and he was happy to allow his former drinking partner the use of the place for a few days whilst he was off in the casinos of Monte Carlo.

They played the enchanted tourists for three days before boarding a ferry that took them to mainland France. It was the first test of their passports but, despite O'Connell's fears, they received nothing more than a cursory glance from the bored immigration officer in Marseille as they passed through.

A series of train journeys then brought them all separately to Paris where they reunited briefly before heading to various ports in France, Belgium and Holland in order to catch their respective ferries to England, their ultimate destination.

The Judas Deception

Although long and drawn out and perhaps more cloak and dagger than was ever required, O'Connell, or John Connelly as he was now beginning to think of himself, enjoyed the protracted journey as he got to spend all his time in the company of the man he most wanted to be with. The pair made for Calais to avoid any unnecessary border crossing and the preventable examination of their new papers.

"Ah, England, England, my fair England," Spencer said soto voce as the white cliffs of Dover came into view.

"Who said that?" asked O'Connell.

"I did, just now," responded Spencer, laughing. "Were you not listening?"

"You big buffoon."

"Accent, my boy, accent. Don't let it drop. Always stay in character, you know that." And with that he flourished his walking stick and pointed in the direction of the approaching cliffs and bellowed in his foghorn Canadian accent "My god, it's the white cliffs of Dover. Aren't they fabulous!"

O'Connell cringed at the pronouncement of Dover as it rhymed with mover but typically the big man, for regardless of weight loss he was still a large man in both stature and character, could get away with just such incredulities.

For the newly born John Connelly, this was always going to be the acid test. Getting into France via Corsica was one thing, the bored civil servant caring little about anyone entering French soil from an outlying island. But entering the UK was, in his mind, going to be a much tougher affair and he wondered at the wisdom of his newly procured hairpiece which sat rather obviously atop his head. He realised that he was sweating and Spencer threw him a look that said relax. They had been through this already.

"Got to stay calm. Relaxed. That's the key. Don't give them any reason to look twice at you, all that."

"But this bloody thing on my head is going to make them look twice."

"Trust me, natural embarrassment will stop them. They'll want to but then won't dare. But if you sweat or scratch or look like your bloody constipated then they will be all over you. Like a rash. Like a…well, I don't know like a what but just don't do it."

Those words echoed in the young priest's ears and he relaxed his breathing as he fell into step with the other passengers around him beginning to disembark from the ship. Spencer was somewhere ahead of him, the straw boater he wore making him distinctive as he moved along.

They had agreed that they should approach separately and that Spencer would go first to test the waters, his acting skills so much more honed than those of the now John Connelly. Like a mantra he went over it in his head. My name is John Connelly and I'm a minister from British Columbia here to write a book about the rural churches of England. The paperwork he had contained a letter from a publisher confirming just such a deal together with various notes of locations and lodgings.

As he made his way within the snake of bodies shuffling along the arrivals hall, he became aware of the stares he was attracting. He had grown somewhat accustomed to them over the previous weeks but this was the first time he had been in a queue with the same people surrounding him for any length of time. He could feel their eyes on him. But as soon as he looked in any particular direction the gazes dropped and people became very interested in their newspapers or the shoes they were wearing that day. Spencer was right, he thought, they want to look but they don't dare in case I catch them. However, the general populous was one thing but a trained government employee whose job was to look beyond the superficial was another matter altogether.

He edged closer to the booth where two uniformed men, one either side, sat checking passports and entry documents. There was no sign of Spencer so he had to assume that Mr Calvin Wilson was now among the official residents of the United Kingdom of Great Britain and Northern Ireland. Either that or in some side room being questioned about a dodgy passport. But he couldn't afford to think like that as a wave of panic washed over him. Calm thoughts, think only calm thoughts.

He heard a muffled shout in front of him and felt a hand on his shoulder as the person behind gently brought his attention to the fact that he was being called forward to the control booth. Without any time to think about what was happening, John Connelly stepped towards the free officer who was beckoning him, papers held loosely in his palm. Upon reaching the booth he handed everything he had over to the immigration officer.

"Blind them with science, my sweet. Give them the lot. Boat tickets, train tickets, receipts from the buffet car, fucking sweetie papers from your pockets. Give them everything you've got, let them sort out what they need. And remember, not too tight. Tight grip suggests something to hide. Hold them loose."

The officer raised his gaze up at him, taking a good, hard look at the face before alighting on the obvious wig. Immediately his eyes dropped and O'Connell saw the man fight the urge to look up again as the reflex to do a double take consumed him. He did well, instead focusing his attention on the paperwork that O'Connell had handed him and suppressing the grin which O'Connell saw beginning to form on his lips.

Still averting his gaze the officer said, "Is this your first visit to the UK, Mr..ah..Connelly?"

"Reverend Connelly," O'Connell corrected remembering to adopt his phoney accent, "and yes, it is."

"I see. And what is the purpose of your visit, Reverend?"

"I'm here to research some material for a book I'm writing on the rural churc…"

"That's fine, sir," interrupted the officer, "I can see it all in the paperwork you've given me. Sorry to have kept you waiting. Thank you for your patience." With that he stamped the Canadian passport and handed everything back to the young man, already looking beyond him to the next person waiting in line.

O'Connell couldn't believe it. It really had been quite straightforward after all. He began walking towards the exit of the building, shaking his head as he went. All that worry, all the fears he had dreamed up in his head, for nothing. Just then, someone placed a hand on his shoulder.

"Excuse me, sir."

O'Connell turned, a smile already on his face as he expected to see the hulking figure of Spencer behind him putting on a funny voice and trying to scare him. But it wasn't Spencer he saw when he turned and for a moment his heart stopped.

"I'm sorry," he stammered, forgetting for a second his accent before recovering and managing "is there a problem with something?" in his new dialect.

A customs guard stood in formal attire complete with pips on the shoulder, his gaze fixed on the suitcase O'Connell carried by his side.

"Would you mind if I had a look in your luggage, sir?"

O'Connell hadn't been prepared for this, his efforts so focused on getting through passport control he hadn't even given a second thought to the possibility of being stopped at customs.

"Ammm, I..." he began, panic starting to grip him.

"If you could just open your case for me, sir." The nasal tone had no inflexion in it whatsoever, a monotone of nothingness, just recited lines from a set script that didn't allow for any deviation. Appealing to a better nature was pointless as he quite clearly didn't have one. O'Connell could see that here was a jobsworth who robotically followed the instructions set down in a manual and for whom emotions were something checked in at the door as he entered the workplace. Reluctantly he manoeuvred the case onto a platform at the side of the room and began to unfasten the buckles. As soon as they were loose, the customs man stepped in and opened the lid of the case to reveal the contents. He began to rifle through them.

"Isn't there some way of making a false bottom in the suitcase?"

"Fuck do you think this is, James Bond or something?" That had been Spencer's response to him when he suggested hiding the Key of Arrogones in his luggage. "No, it's too dangerous. Get stopped and they're bound to look at the case and they will check it thoroughly. Empty it, tap it, check for false bottoms, that sort of thing." He smiled as he said this last but O'Connell knew that he was being serious.

"Okay, so what do we do with it? They are bound to be looking for it. News of the theft has been all over the papers."

"Many weeks ago, my dear. People become less vigilant over time."

"Even so, they are still going to be keeping an eye out and they will know it when they see it. I mean, I can't just walk through with it hanging around my neck, can I?"

The look in Spencer's eyes told him that that was exactly what he was supposed to do.

"You can't be serious? You just want me to walk into the UK past everyone wearing the Key of Arrogonnes for all to see?"

"Not quite. Put it under your collar. No-one's going to look under a vicar's collar, are they? Sacrilegious, all that."

"Surely there are better ways to smuggle the damn thing in," countered O'Connell as they sat in a Paris hotel room, the rest of the crew listening on.

"Well, can you think of any?" questioned Spencer.

"Did you pack the case yourself, sir?"

O'Connell was shaken from his reverie by the question from the customs official. Composing himself he turned and smiled at the uniformed man.

"I did."

"Would you mind stepping to the side for a moment, please sir?"

"What on earth for?" Get uppity but not arrogant, Spencer had coached him.

"It's just routine."

O'Connell moved to the side as guided by the official's outstretched arm.

"What seems to be the problem?" Go on the offensive. Put them on the spot. Ask them to justify their actions.

"I can assure you, sir, it's all just routine," came the monotonous reply.

"You keep saying that but I don't understand what it is you expect to find."

"Would you mind putting your arms straight out to your side please, sir?"

"Put my arms out to my side! What on earth for?"

"Purely rou…"

"Routine," interrupted O'Connell, "yes, I know, so you

keep telling me but you won't explain what it is you are actually doing."

"If I could just ask you to hold your arms out, sir, then I'm going to pat you down. It's standard procedure. Nothing to worry about at all, sir."

"Well, if it's so standard why aren't you doing it to everybody?" countered O'Connell but he had already adopted the pose requested and the uniformed official began to conduct a body search. Be stroppy but not obstreperous. In the end they will search you if they want, making it difficult will only add suspicion. As the official's hands passed under O'Connell's arms and down his torso, the young priest come minister tried to stay relaxed but couldn't help but flinch as the exploring hands made their way up towards his chest.

CHAPTER 42

ENGLAND – 1970

"Are you wearing something around your neck, sir?" asked the official as his hands came to rest on the shape of the adornment which hugged O'Connell's chest.

"Ah, yes, that's my crucifix. A present from my late aunt." The young priest hoped that he sounded much more confident than he actually felt. The ordeal of getting past the immigration official at border control had been quite enough for him and, despite the ease with which he had been ushered through in the end, he felt drained with the anxiety of it all. Now he was trying desperately to remember what they had decided was the best tact to take in this eventuality.

"Do you mind if I see it, please, sir?"

The lack of any inflexion in the voice was really beginning to grate on O'Connell's nerves and he felt like screaming at the man to leave him alone and go and harass someone else with his nasal tones and bad breath. But he didn't. Instead he replied calmly, "Is that really necessary?" He almost added officer to the end but Spencer had warned against this.

"Don't have any powers of arrest. Don't be reminding him of what he isn't. Make him uppity, determined to be difficult. Best to avoid calling him anything."

The Judas Deception

"I'm afraid it is, sir. If you wouldn't mind taking it out from under your shirt just so I can see it, please?"

"Ah, there you are, Reverend. Been looking all over for you, thought you must have got lost somewhere. Fallen down the loo as they call them over here, eh." Spencer walked brashly towards the pair, cane raised in greeting.

"Excuse me, sir, but I'm afraid I will have to ask you to wait over there until we are finished." The customs officer pointed towards the far side of the room where other arrivals from the ferry were making their way through the terminal towards the exit.

"Of course, my good man, just wanted to make sure that the good vicar here hadn't strayed too far from his flock. No problem, I trust. Man of the cloth and all that. Above reproach. Pillar of our society. I'm the cad. I'm the one you ought to be searching, isn't that right, Reverend?"

"Really, I'm fine, Mr Wilson, you should go on ahead without me, I'll catch up shortly."

"Well, if you're sure." The big man lingered for a further moment before turning sharply and striding towards the exit, his cane leading the way.

O'Connell turned towards the fussy little man beside him and said, "I'm sorry, was there anything else? I really should be meeting up with the rest of my party before they disappear without me."

"If I could just check your crucifix, Reverend."

O'Connell could see that the officious man wasn't going to give up and so he reached beneath his garments and pulled out the chain that hung around his neck. Suspended from the end was an ornate wooden cross encrusted with emeralds and rubies. O'Connell lifted it towards the officials face but the man gestured that he had seen enough.

"I'm sorry to have detained you, Reverend. Purely routine, you do understand."

"Of course," replied O'Connell, relief almost making him forget the accent but he caught himself just in time. Efficiently, he began to repack his belongings into the suitcase.

"Don't rush. Don't want to give the impression that he might have missed something. Make him think twice. Search you again." Spencer's voice loomed large inside his head as he did up the buckle on the green leather case.

He turned to check that he was free to go but the official had already returned to checking the passengers before him, eyeing his next victim. This was simply a job to him, one that he was extremely good at, O'Connell had to acknowledge, so it was without apology that he watched as O'Connell made his way towards the exit.

Spencer was waiting outside, the picture of serenity.

"You great buffoon, what on earth were you playing at!" O'Connell admonished in a harsh whisper as he approached.

"Thought I was bloody brilliant," responded the big man in his usual foghorn.

"He could have searched you. And then what would you have done?"

"He only had eyes for you, my dear. And who could blame him. Knew once he clocked the syrup that he would drag you in. Never any danger of him searching anyone else whilst you were around."

The argument raged for days, O'Connell chiding his friend for taking such a foolish risk, Spencer countering by saying that anyone travelling with the wigged wonder, as he referred to his companion, would be innocent by association. And, besides, they had gotten through unscathed, hadn't they?

They had chosen the Norfolk coast which had plenty of

old churches to fit O'Connell's cover and was close enough to Cambridge, their ultimate destination.

Their seaside hideaway had become a home from home as the two settled into a familiar pattern of strolls along the promenade and afternoon tea at their favourite haunts. O'Connell found it idyllic and was in no hurry for it to end but he could see how restless his partner was becoming.

"I've spent years hunting this down, my sweet. Years! Sanctimonious bastards trying to tell me that it didn't exist. But I knew. Oh yes, I knew they had hidden it somewhere. And in my own beloved Cambridge of all places! You can't expect me to wait forever now that we are so close."

"No-one is asking you to, Spence. We just have to be very careful."

"Fuck do you think I am? Of course we have to be careful. We've been fucking careful all the way. Everything thought out to the nth degree. We're here, aren't we? In England. Fifty miles away from the place. We would never have got this far unless we were being careful. Now it's time to be bold. Find that hidden chamber and see what treasure is hidden below."

Whilst the pair had settled into their comfortable lifestyle by the sea, the rest of the crew had taken up residence in and around the area, allowing them to make frequent reconnaissance visits to Cambridge to test the lie of the land.

"But we don't want to alert anyone to our presence," O'Connell had protested when initial plans were being made.

"Trust me, sweet James, these guys could break into Fort Knox and no-one would know they were there. Luca, the damn fool, got involved with a woman one time in Columbia. Began seeing a lot of her. Regular thing, all that. Fell into a routine, predictable. They came for him in the dead of night. Even with all his skills and training he could do nothing against a dozen of them. Took him hostage. Deep in the jungle. Guards, lookout towers, booby-traps, the works. Fifty men, armed to the teeth, vigilant, vicious. Nigh on impossible to attack. These boys broke in, rescued Luca along with three other hostages and made their escape without a single Columbian knowing they had been there. And they did it all in daylight. Christ alone knows what those poor bastards thought when they went to check on their prisoners later that day. So if they want to sneak into a Cambridge College and keep a watch on movements within the library then you can rest assured that they will do it quietly, efficiently and with the minimum of fuss."

Initially Sergio and his crew reported on nightly checks being made on the library by at least one of the three men responsible for the protection of the chamber. Normally four or five times during the night, staying for anywhere up to an hour a time.

"That's good," beamed Spencer, "means they haven't moved the loot. Still there. Nowhere else for it to go. Trying to keep it safe, stop anyone accessing the chamber itself. Only a matter of time before complacency sets in."

And sure enough, the nightly vigils became shorter and less frequent until a pattern of sorts began to emerge. That's when Spencer started to get fidgety.

"Oh, do sit still, Spence."

"Wasn't aware I was doing anything, my boy."

"You're drumming your fingertips on the arm of the sofa. And if you're not doing that then you're tapping your feet, or humming or clicking your fingers."

"Very musical family I come from is all. Don't know what all the fuss is about. Chap can't play a tune when he wants. Bad form."

"Now, stop it. You know very well that you're only doing it because your mind is elsewhere. Somewhere in the bowels of the Wren Library no doubt."

The Judas Deception

"Well, it's almost time to make a move."

"I'm scared, Spence. What if they catch us? I mean, look at what happened at the Vatican. You were almost killed."

"Never mind me, my sweet, what about you! Crawling across rooftops, climbing down domes, jumping off monuments, all the while being shot at. Just because you wanted to help me. Should we let all that go to waste? I think not. We're so close now and the Church can only sit and hope we don't act. They're exposed, vulnerable. If they could they would simply move everything hidden under there but they haven't. Still keeping watch. It's all still there. Just waiting to be uncovered."

"You don't know that for sure. They could have moved whatever's there when we were still in Italy."

"Always possible. But something tells me not. It's the way they're watching. Not a constant guard like they don't want to draw attention to it. Just enough to satisfy themselves that no-one has been there. My guess, they've been told to act natural. Nothing amiss, that sort of thing. But they can't help themselves. In and out because they know that whatever's down there is damning."

"So how do we ensure that we're not caught?"

"That, my dear, is all in the planning."

The planning, inevitably, was Spencer's remit. He had already recognised the need for four of them to be present in order to use the key, the separate components having to be turned simultaneously. This meant the remainder of the crew keeping watch, some inside, some outside the building, communication being made via hand-held radio.

"Why don't we just eliminate the watchers?" asked Sergio. "We could tie them up and stand guard over them until you're finished in the chamber."

"Be better if we didn't alert them. In and out before they even realise. Keep them in the dark. That way, if we need to return, we can. Take them hostage and they'll go running to their masters as soon as we let them go. Lost the element of surprise then. Also, no way of knowing if they have some secret code of communication which, if not followe,d brings the cavalry calling."

What was evident from the checks being undertaken was that no-one was actually entering the chamber, merely checking to see if it was open.

"Needs four of them to open. Only three keeping watch, sometimes alone, sometimes together. Which means that they can tell just by looking at the entrance whether it's been breached or not. Reckon the entrance can't be closed without reversing the process for the keys. Simple logic, really."

"So how does that help us?"

"Well, my sweet James, it means that we can't stay down there for too long. Not without increasing the possibility of being caught. Ideal scenario for us is if they don't even realise we've been there. In and out. Quick and easy. Only need to establish what's down there. Then we can decide how to proceed."

They agreed that any raid should be carried out during the night, the team of watchers having noted that the latest check by any of the Knights was at three am and these only infrequently.

A trial run was arranged for the following evening with the strict instruction that they would proceed no further than finding the location for the keys. O'Connell pressed Spencer for a promise that this was as far as they would go and found himself supported by Sergio who was keen on tying his leader down to specifics in order to better co-ordinate the team. Reluctantly, the big man acquiesced and Sergio began to outline the plan for entry.

They approached from the rear of the College, the River

The Judas Deception

Cam separating them from their goal. With the bridges guarded by gates and manned around the clock, Sergio had moored two dinghies along the bank, well camouflaged from view, to navigate the short crossing to the opposite side and the main College grounds. Well practiced, having gained entry to the grounds this way on numerous occasions during their watching brief, the team were soon huddled in the vast shadow of the magnificent library. From here the men, each well-versed with the plan, took up their respective positions, their look-out points covering all approaches. They waited until half past the hour and, when no-one came, Spencer and O'Connell together with two of the Italians made their way quietly inside the Wren Library.

The solemnity that an empty library inspires provoked a quiet awe from the group rather than any great need for caution. They had sentries posted and back-up in place if required, whatever the threat. So it was with a somewhat graceful air that they made their way towards the area Spencer had identified as being the entrance. They used the natural light of the night together with directed torch beams to guide them to the wall in one corner, stopping before it.

"Shine the torch here," Spencer directed softly, his hand pointing towards an inscription carved into the stone.

"Herein lies the answer to all mans' secrets"

Spencer pointed to the dot on the first 'i' in the inscription. "Notice the way in which the edging has been eroded? Suggesting that it has been rubbed at over the years. I think, gentlemen, that we have our first keyhole."

The others looked closer and could see what Spencer was referring to. They began to look for similar erosion on the other letters. O'Connell found one at the bottom of a 't', with Luca quickly following up with one in the midst of the 'w'. It took some minutes, however, before Spencer finally spotted something in the apostrophe, his fingers finding it first quite by accident. It looked darker than the others, hence more camouflaged, and Spencer thought that it had been deliberately blackened to disguise it. But he had no doubt that they had found all four keyholes and his excitement grew as he realised that they were about to see if all their efforts to obtain the Key of Arrogones had been worth it.

"Ah, the moment of truth," he said as he opened the silver tip of his cane to reveal the hiding place of the artefact. They each took one of the keys that comprised the whole piece before taking up a position in front of the holes they had uncovered.

"Do you think it matters which key goes in which hole?" enquired O'Connell, his hand shaking slightly from excitement as he prepared to insert his key.

"Only one way to find out," responded Spencer, putting his key in the hole they had eventually identified in the apostrophe. He waited for the others to do likewise and then said, "On my count. One, two, three, turn."

They turned in unison. Nothing happened. They tried again. Still nothing.

"It would appear, my sweet, that it does matter which key in which hole. There are twenty four possible combinations. This is number one. Sergio, you keep your key where it is, the rest of us will try moving ours first."

"How will we even know if it's worked?" wondered O'Connell.

"Don't worry, we'll know," Spencer said decidedly.

And they did. It was on their thirteenth attempt and O'Connell couldn't help but think what that said about superstitions. There was a click and a stone tile to their left lifted out of the floor. The four looked at each other but contained their joy to smiles, although O'Connell really wanted to whoop with delight.

The Judas Deception

Spencer was the first to get to the raised slab and, as he bent to lift it, Sergio and Luca were immediately by his side conscious of the large man's recent wounds. But as they pressed their fingers beneath the slab they found that it slid back quite easily.

"Ah, castors," commented Spencer. "How clever." The others followed to where he was pointing and they could see that the heavy tile had little circular stone rods beneath which acted like ball bearings and made the slate easy to slide into and out of place once the mechanism had been realised.

"Ingenious," said O'Connell.

"Indeed, my dear. Wren, you see. Knew what he was doing. Brilliant."

"You really think that Sir Christopher Wren was responsible for this?"

"Course he was. Had to have known. Couldn't have designed all this otherwise." Spencer pointed all around him.

"Wow, it's amazing to think that it still works so effectively after all these years."

"Man was a genius. Right, shall we see what he was trying to keep hidden?" Spencer made for the entrance to the underground chamber that now stood revealed.

"But you promised, Spence, that this was only a trial run and we would stop once we found the entrance."

"One little peek won't do us any harm. Serge, you stay here with Luca while James and I have a little explore."

"No," replied Sergio firmly.

"What?" said Spencer, somewhat taken aback.

O'Connell looked relieved to have an ally but then Sergio continued, "Luca can stay here but I'm going with you. What if there is someone waiting down there? You need protection and that is what I am here for."

"Actually, good thinking, Sergio. So glad you're here.

Okay then, let's see what we have." Spencer shone his torch down into the chamber, illuminating a stone staircase which led into the darkness below. He began to descend, Sergio following closely behind. They had only gone a few steps when Spencer let out a small cry.

"What is it?" O'Connell asked in a half shout.

"I do believe that the good folk of the Catholic Church have installed electricity," came the reply. "I think I've found a switch." He threw the lever which he had found and, sure enough, the whole chamber burst into light. The men gasped at what they saw below them.

CHAPTER 43

"What?" asked Huxley, captivated by the narrative that Connelly had shared.

The others looked on in anticipation as they waited for Connelly's answer.

"Nothing," came the reply.

"What!" It was more of an incredulous shout from Donovan than a question but it still drew an answer from the older man.

"Nothing," he repeated. "Absolutely nothing. Just a vast, empty chamber."

The trio stared at him, each expecting him to add more to the story but he just sat in contemplative silence looking down at his empty tea cup.

"And that's it?" cried Donovan, the frustration written all over his face.

"That's it, yes," mumbled Connelly, weary now. "I managed to persuade Spence to leave it that night, although with some difficulty I can tell you. But we returned the very next night and the one after that and so on for weeks. We searched every inch of the place, looking for any evidence of what may have been there or trying to find hidden compartments in the walls. But there was nothing. Eventually the Italians had to return home and without them to keep watch it was too dangerous to go although Spencer was all for continuing the search. Even though we had looked everywhere he was determined to keep going until he found something but I managed to persuade him to leave it."

"That must have been very difficult."

"Indeed it was. He refused to accept that there was no trace. Kept telling me that there had to be something." He dropped his voice down a few octaves and continued, "Has to be, dear boy, simply has to be. Impossible otherwise."

"So what did you do?"

"What could we do? Short of confronting our adversaries and demanding they tell us what they knew. Which would have only alerted them to our involvement and so bring the might of the Church down on us. So we retired to our house by the sea and I tried my best to distract Spencer with other things."

He drifted off again and Sam smiled wryly at him. She caught his eye and he looked enquiringly at her and then laughed.

"Oh, Dr Davison, I didn't realise what I said. You have such a wicked sense of humour, just like Spence. I didn't mean…well, I just meant that I tried to interest him in other projects, searches, requests from other academics who wanted to reference his work. Eventually we felt it was safe enough to go back to his house in Grantchester. We would sometimes stay there and he returned to work at the University so there was always something to keep us busy. But I knew that he would never really be able to let it go and I suppose he was always thinking about his next move. That brilliant mind of his whirring away, looking for a solution. And then I think he found one and they killed him."

"They being the Templar?" asked Huxley.

"In one guise or another, Daniel, yes."

"But you suspect our friends from earlier this evening?"

The Judas Deception

"I believe they were involved. Whether directly or indirectly is immaterial."

"What did the police say?" queried Sam.

"Oh, they dressed it up to look like an accident, car running off the road and into a tree, enough of an impact for the petrol tank to explode and incinerate the body, burning any evidence. The police put it down to just another tragic accident."

"But you don't buy it?"

"Not for a minute, Daniel. You see, after he was shot, Spencer never drove. He couldn't. It caused him too much discomfort. I had to drive him everywhere. So, whatever happened to him, I know that he certainly wasn't driving that car when it crashed."

"And where were you whenever he died?" Donovan said, accusingly.

"That, Master Donovan, is the one thing that still bothers me to this day. Could I have prevented his death if I'd been with him? I knew that he had come up with something in his mind, something he thought would solve the puzzle that had been perplexing him for so long. It was there in his eyes."

"What was it?" asked Donovan.

"That I don't know. He was forever the dramatist, he loved the big reveal. Packed me off to our house by the sea to collect some things while he took the train the Cambridge. He said he was going to arrange for Sergio and his crew to come and visit. I was due to meet him two days later when he promised to tell me everything." Again he dropped his tone to mimic his lover. "Got to dwell on it, dear boy. Mull it over, all that. Not quite finalised it. Let the old grey cells work on it. Two days, give me two days. Meet you at Grantchester. Tell you all."

"But he never did," said Huxley.

"No. That was the last time I ever saw him. If only I'd insisted on going with him he might still be alive."

"So you don't know what the big revelation was?" Donovan again anxious to focus on the search.

"Alas, no."

"But after the risk you took getting the Key of Arrogones. Weren't you curious to find out? I mean, didn't you try and work it out yourself? Go down into the chamber and try and see what it was that he had come up with?"

"That, I'm afraid, young Alan, was the last thing on my mind. As soon as I heard what had happened I'm ashamed to say that I went into hiding. I fell back into character and adopted the role of the Reverend John Connelly like my life depended on it, which I truly believe it did. I began writing the book that was all part of my cover, immersing myself in the work to distract me from the grief that I felt. But all the while I kept track of what the bastards who were responsible for killing my sweet prince were up to."

There was a sudden venom in his voice. "Do you know what they had the cheek to do? About a year later they actually released the Gospel of Judas or at least a sanitised version of it. Did the same with it as they did with the Dead Sea Scrolls, put it and a couple of other documents in a place where they knew they would be found. They knew that more people would come looking for the document so they decided to distract them with a safe version."

He looked up, fire brimming in his eyes. "These are cunning, devious people that we are talking about. I was determined that I wasn't going to let them get away with it. So when the job as Dean of Trinity College came up I applied and for the last thirty years I've been sitting side by side with the men who ruined my life."

Tears started to flow freely down O'Connell's face and he buried his head in his chest as the emotion of reliving the events of his past overwhelmed him. He looked up after a short while, a sad smile spreading over his tired face. "You must think me a very foolish old man," he commented.

"Not at all, Dean," responded Huxley. "I think it is an amazing tale that you have told us tonight and I can understand just how special Spencer Harris was to you. I know him only by reputation and, believe me, I wish that I could have spent just five minutes in his company. I can't begin to imagine how devastated you were by his death. But I am glad that we have been able to conclude our investigation."

"What do you mean?" shouted Donovan. "We haven't concluded anything."

"I think we have taken it as far as we can, Alan. Thanks to Dr Connelly, or should that be O'Connell," he paused to look at the Dean who merely waved his hand in a gesture that suggested it mattered little to him, "we have been able to identify those who are most likely responsible for killing Simms and, probably trying to kill us as well. So now we can take what we know to the police and let them use their full resources to prove what we suspect."

"But we can't just leave it there. What about the secret chamber? What about the Judas Gospel?"

"I think Professor Huxley is right," countered Sam. Huxley knew that the use of his title was to highlight to Donovan that he was amongst wise counsel and that what had been decided was for the best. But Donovan was having none of it.

"We can't just give up. What about the stuff that Harris was working on when he was killed? The fact that he was killed, according to the Dean here, proves that he must have been close to discovering the truth. We owe it to him to find out what that is."

It was a passionate outpouring but Huxley was in no doubt now that it was purely self-serving. He noted the use of Spencer's surname along with the veiled accusation aimed at Connelly and wondered if Donovan realised that his mask was slipping, the subservient victim just wanting to clear his name no longer in evidence as the quest for buried treasure got within reach. Huxley decided to play along knowing that it was the best way to bring everything out in the open. He just hoped that Pepper was keeping his side of the plan.

"Maybe you're right, Alan. Perhaps we do need to dig a little deeper. After all, the police might just think we are trying to deflect attention away from you without giving them anything concrete other than fantastical tales of daring do and adventure." He smiled at O'Connell to show that he meant no offence and the Dean could have sworn he caught the merest of winks from the Vice-Chancellor.

Sam looked up sharply, surprised at Huxley's statement. She was about to say something but the Dean lightly touched her arm as he turned to Huxley and said "What is it you need us to do, Daniel?"

"Well, the photo wasn't the only thing I found at the house tonight. There was also this." Huxley handed O'Connell an envelope.

Sam now recognised that Huxley was up to something so rather than react with frustration at once again being kept in the dark, she instead watched as O'Connell opened the envelope and removed a letter from inside. He began to read it silently.

> *"My dearest James*
>
> *I'm sorry that I have been so distracted lately. I know that you have guessed that my mind is occupied more and more with this whole business. I can't leave it alone, I'm afraid, my love. I believe the truth is still to be found in that*

chamber and I am going to do everything I can to uncover it. And if that means risking my life then so be it.

Wren knew about the chamber when he was planning the library. Had to. No other way he could have built it. I've spent the last while chasing down everything I could find on him and I think I might have the answer. But if I'm right then I'm probably putting myself into harm's way. So if you are reading this then it's because I haven't returned. If that's the case then I want you to do something for me, my sweet. Run! Run as far and as fast away from this place. Don't try and follow in my footsteps. You have already done too much for me. The thought of you dying over my obsession would be too much to bear so promise me you will go. Get away from this place. Leave it all behind. Start a new life.

I'm sorry, my sweet James. You are the purest, dearest thing that has ever happened to me and finding you has made me appreciate life in a new way. I wish it was enough but it never can be until I find the answer. So I must go on, my dear. Please forgive me. I will love you always.

S

PS There will always be a heart in my place for you.

O'Connell let the tears roll freely down his face and drip on to the table as he held the letter and read the words of his lover. He passed the letter to Huxley who read it aloud to the others. Sam immediately put her arm around the Dean and he looked up at her with a half-smile on his face.

"All these years I've felt guilty about running away and hiding behind a false persona. Such a cowardly thing to do. In my heart I've always known that Spence would have wanted me to do exactly that but I've always felt that I was letting him down. It's just nice to hear him say it. It gives me a certain sense of release. I know it sounds strange but it feels good."

"I think I understand, Dean," responded Sam.

"But it doesn't tell us anything," cried Donovan, his frustration boiling over.

"Oh, but I think it does," replied Huxley. "It tells us that he believed Wren was the key and that by looking at Wren's life and work he discovered something that led to his death."

"But how does that help us?" whined Donovan.

"Well, I guess we have to find what he found. Dean, can you tell us what it was he was investigating on Wren?"

Connelly looked at the three people seated around his table as if assessing what he should tell them before beginning.

"It had all started some time before when he began investigating the life and works of Wren. Oh, he tried to hide it from me but he was never the tidiest of men and I kept finding books on architecture and biographies of the man. Then plans of buildings started sprouting up all over the house and I knew it had to be linked with this whole business. We would do everything together normally but he started going off by himself claiming meetings with other colleagues, university business or whatever excuse he could come up with."

"And you didn't ask him what he was doing?" questioned Huxley.

"Oh, I did, Daniel. I knew that he was up to something but when I asked he just smiled that smile of his and told me not to worry my silly little head. That when he knew for certain he would let me know and not a moment before."

"But you had your suspicions?"

"Indeed. So when he casually suggested a visit to St Paul's Cathedral one day I knew that it was more than just a sightseeing tour. He was looking for something, I was sure of it. And I think he found it."

"What happened?" asked Donovan, perched on the edge of his seat.

"We were standing in the Whispering Gallery and he was acting the buffoon. Rather than whisper he was shouting so that his words were echoing off the walls. Then he just stopped in mid-sentence and I could see by his countenance that something had clicked in that brain of his. But by the time we had walked outside, he had calmed down, chewing on his lip. That was always a sign that he was in deep thought. Then he packed me off to Norfolk while he came here." He waved his hand in the vague direction of the College grounds.

"So all we have to do is figure out what it was that he saw," cried Donovan.

"I'm not sure it's as simple as that, Alan, but it might be worth a go," said Huxley.

"Isn't that a little dangerous?" quizzed Sam. "Wouldn't we be better doing what you suggested before and going to the police with what we have? I mean, say we do uncover something that tells us just what it was that Spencer did to get himself killed. Surely, then, by following him we would be putting ourselves in grave danger?"

"But we've come this far," said Donovan. "We can't give up now. Besides, the police still have me in the frame for murder and there's not enough here to prove otherwise. We need to find the Gospel before anyone is going to believe me."

Huxley could see that Sam was going to counter this so quickly interjected, "Alan's right, Sam, we have to go on. It would be best for everyone, I think."

He had walked behind Alan whilst saying this and now gave Sam a look that the boy couldn't see. She read it and knew that Huxley had something up his sleeve and, from what she had seen already, they were pretty big sleeves full of all sorts of tricks.

"I remember Spencer getting very excited when we went to visit the Greenwich Observatory. He kept talking about Wren's fascination with domes."

"Domes? How does that help us?" cried Donovan.

Huxley shot the young lad a look of admonishment, anxious that the Dean's thought process not be interrupted. "Go on, Dean," he prompted.

"Well, as I said, he began to talk about all of Wren's buildings that featured domes. I remember going to visit some of them and I always got the impression that Spencer was looking for something specific. He kept saying that Wren was a stickler for detail, the sort of man who dotted every 'I' and crossed every 't'."

"Perhaps if we have a search for Wren's domes on the internet that might tell us something?" offered Donovan.

"It's as good a place as any to look."

Donovan took out his phone, which was still encased in its protective plastic bag, and began to search. He found a timeline detailing Wren's work. Huxley, looking over his shoulder, pointed to the entry for the Wren Library at the College.

"So the thinking is that whatever he found in the chamber under the library influenced his later works. So we have to look at anything that comes after that." He began to list the buildings which Wren designed after 1667.

"But the Dean said that they were in St Paul's when he had his eureka moment," challenged Donovan, pointing to the entry which showed that the design for the cathedral was done before the Wren Library.

"If I'm not mistaken, I think you'll find that the original design was later modified by Wren," Connelly replied.

Huxley took the phone and began to check the web again for more information on what most consider to be Wren's masterpiece. He had dismissed it initially as he knew that Wren had submitted his plans for the cathedral following the great fire which devastated London in 1666, a year before he started work on the Library at Trinity.

"Ah, here it is. You're absolutely right, Dean. Wren altered the initial plans for St Paul's in 1678 adding, would you believe it, the dome for which it is now famed."

"So the dome was only added after he had started work on the library?" asked Sam.

"It would appear that way."

"What does that mean? Like, does it help us in any way? Does it tell us where the Judas Gospel is hidden?" Donovan fidgeted with his hands as he asked.

"I'm not really sure, Alan, but I've got a feeling that we're on the right track. There is no doubt that Wren's architecture was inspired by those buildings he saw all around Europe at the time but I find it interesting that his fascination with domes comes later in his life. Even to the extent that his most famous dome, that at St Paul's, was almost an afterthought. So what prompted it? What made him change his plans and go in that direction? Could it have something to do with his involvement with the library here and the chamber which he would have discovered underneath?"

"What are we doing sitting around here?" chimed Donovan. "Why aren't we in the chamber itself seeing what he saw. Maybe then we'll figure out what Harris discovered. After all, there are four of us. All we need is the Key of Arrogenes." He looked hopefully towards the Dean.

"I'm afraid that I don't have the Key anymore, my young friend. It disappeared the night that Spencer died. He kept it hidden in the lid of his cane of which no trace was ever found, either burned up in the fire or taken by however killed him."

"And even if we did," countered Huxley, "we don't know if we would be walking right into an ambush. There are people trying to stop us from checking on what Simms may have discovered and that, ultimately, is the underground chamber. I'm pretty sure that if they have gone to the lengths of trapping us in burning buildings and trying to abduct us at gunpoint and Christ knows what else, then it doesn't take a genius to realise that they will more than likely be guarding their prize as well. If we walk down there, from what Dr Connelly has told us we would be exposed targets as soon as we started down the steps. Easy pickings for them."

Donovan looked crestfallen. They were so close but without the Key of Arrogenes they would never be able to gain entry into the chamber. His face lit up with an idea.

"Maybe there was something else stashed away in the hidden panel. You know, as well as the letter and the photograph. Maybe the Key was in there too. Or a clue to where the old man might have put it."

"There wasn't anything else behind that panel, Alan, I can assure you of that. And, anyway, unless you've forgotten, someone tried to shoot you when we were in that house so I don't think going back there would be very wise at the moment."

"It's probably all clear by now. Whoever it was wouldn't have hung around."

"You seem very sure about that," queried Huxley.

"Yeah, well, you know, with the gunshot and shit he probably got scared and ran off himself."

"He? I thought that there was more than one of them?"

"He. They. What difference does it make? I'm just saying, whoever it was probably isn't there now and maybe we should go back and have another look around. Maybe there's something else hidden away. Something about whatever Har... Spencer, found out about Wren and the library."

"I don't think that would be very wise."

"So, what, we're just going to sit around here and wait for the answer to present itself!" complained Donovan.

"Without the Key we can't even access the chamber, even if it was safe," Sam responded.

"Did Spencer have it with him the night he died?"

The Dean looked at Huxley, surprised at his question. "He took it everywhere with him. That cane never left his side. Sergio used his contacts to check with the police to see what possessions were recovered with the body and there was no sign of the cane at all."

"Seems strange that there was no trace whatsoever either of the cane or the Key."

"I've often thought so and just assumed that it was taken by whoever killed him and staged the accident."

"Unless Spencer put it in a safe place." Huxley raised a suggestive eyebrow towards Connelly.

"What makes you say that, Daniel?"

"Well, he took the trouble to write the letter to you as though he suspected that his life might be in danger. I just wonder what other precautions he may have taken."

"I can't think where else he would have hidden anything. I mean, why not just put it with the letter?"

"Perhaps he wanted to give you a better chance of finding it. Put it somewhere that only you and he would know."

"I can't think where that might be, to be honest, Daniel."

A silence fell over them. Sam Davison was sitting at the table, Spencer's letter in her hand, reading through the sad yet loving words to the man that he so obviously loved. She smiled as she read the post script.

"It's funny that he's written 'heart in my place for you' instead of 'place in my heart for you'," she commented, a wry smile across her face.

"Actually, no, he meant what he wrote. It was his funny little saying. There's a tree in the College grounds in which he carved a heart with our initials in like we were teenagers. Silly really. He called it his place for me." Connelly looked up, a light in his eyes as a thought dawned upon him and, as his gaze met Huxley's, he could see that the Vice-Chancellor had exactly the same idea as him.

"Shall we go and take a look?" asked Huxley.

CHAPTER 44

The darkest hour held Cambridge in its grasp, enveloping the city like a blanket, holding the heat of the previous day as the four left the Dean's cottage.

"There's no way that there could be anything there after all this time," Connelly said, but there was an excitement in his quivering voice and a spring in his step as he led them across the courtyard towards the ancient oak tree that had sheltered him and Spencer that first night he had set foot in Trinity College.

As they approached the tree, he looked carefully at the gnarled trunk, before reaching out and touching it gingerly as if afraid that his touch would cause the eight hundred year old oak to crumble into dust.

"Spence did this one night when we sat here watching the library. He was such a big buffoon."

Huxley looked to where the Dean was touching. He could just make out the shape of a carving but it was only when he shone a torch onto the tree that he could see that it was their initials separated by a heart, the sort of thing teenagers would do as an act of love. Connelly saw the embarrassment on Huxley's face as if he had just disturbed some intimacy between the lovers.

"I know, it was so silly, but that was Spence. He said that

some of the students would get the blame for it. He had such a wicked sense of humour."

"That's it? You brought us here to show us a stupid carving?"

"Patience, my dear Alan. It's not just a carving." He pushed on the heart and it moved, making a half turn and exposing a hole in the tree trunk about the size of a tennis ball. Sam gasped.

"Clever, don't you think?" Connelly said. "It was our own private post-box. Spencer would often leave little notes for me to find in here."

"He really was so very sweet," said Sam.

"And you never checked it after he died?" asked Huxley, surprised that the Dean hadn't thought to come to here before now.

"Of course I checked it, Daniel. Not for many years now but there was a time when I checked it every day even though I knew he was dead. I honestly thought he would have left me a note to tell me what he was up to. Indeed, I even hoped that he might have sent me something from beyond the grave. Silly, isn't it? But I just wanted to keep his memory alive, to have one last conversation with him, to hear his laugh again. Sitting here by our tree and checking the hidey hole were just ways of doing that. So, yes, Daniel, I've checked it. I've checked it over and over in the vain hope that there might be something hidden away that I missed."

"So why are we here? If you've already checked it then it's obviously a waste of time." Donovan's impatient was palpable.

"Well, Alan, in the same way as I checked here, I also checked his house thoroughly and found nothing. The fact that you clever things came along and found something that has been hidden away for years tells me that there is always a chance that I missed something here too. So I thought I would

The Judas Deception

show this to you and see if you can find anything that I might have missed all those years ago."

Huxley shone his torch into the hole. It wasn't much bigger than the opening that gave access to it, just a small hollow in an otherwise solid trunk of wood just below head height, or, at least, just below Huxley's head height. There really wasn't much to miss in it but he felt obliged to search it given that Connelly had brought them there. He tried to put his hand into the opening but couldn't get it all in so had to make do with his three middle fingers scrambling around the hole.

Connelly was more effete in build with dainty fingers and could probably do a far better job of examining the hiding place than Huxley could but when he suggested that the Dean take over, Connelly was reluctant.

"Even my slender hand is too broad for the hole, I'm afraid. It was just a dropping place for notes and letters so I really only ever had to reach in with a couple of fingers and pull it out. I doubt that I could do any more than you are doing now."

"Perhaps I could try," commented Sam. She held up her hands to show thin, elegant wrists with long, willowy fingers.

Huxley indicated for her to have a try and she carefully inserted her hand into the hole and began to feel around. After a few moments of patting dry, cold wood her face lit up.

"What is it?" asked Huxley.

"I think there's something at the back of the hole, some kind of fishing line maybe. It's held in place by a tack of some sort by the feel of it. I could be wrong but I think there might be something attached to it."

"But how? The hole isn't big enough to hide anything more than a few sheets of paper," ventured Connelly.

"There's a gap at the back of the hole that seems to lead to a drop." She fumbled with her delicate, manicured fingers again before saying, "Yep, I've got it. There's definitely something attached. I'm pulling on it now."

The three men waited anxiously as Sam Davison slowly worked at the line before finally declaring that she had found something. She withdrew her hand and opened it for the three to see.

"It's the Key of Arrogones," whispered Connelly excitedly.

Alan's face lit up, the delight of this discovery written there for all to see.

"It really is the Key, isn't it?" he said eagerly. "That means that we can enter the chamber and look for ourselves." He turned expectantly to Huxley.

"Let's not get too far ahead of ourselves. Remember, there are dangerous people who are out to stop us investigating and the one place that they know they can trap us in is the chamber."

"But we're so close to uncovering the truth and that is, after all, what we want to do in order to clear my name."

"You heard what the Dean said when they entered the chamber before. There's nothing down there."

"There must be, otherwise why would they be trying to stop us so desperately? And besides, we found the hidden compartment in the Grantchester house which no-one else has before. And we've just found a set of keys hidden in a tree trunk for over thirty years. Who's to say that we won't find something down in the chamber that has eluded those before us?"

"The young man does make a very good point, Daniel. Perhaps we should go and take another look."

Huxley looked reluctantly towards the shrouded building across the courtyard, so daunting yet with an air of grandeur even now. There could be anyone lurking beneath the pillars that raised the library off the ground, an army of protectors with weapons ready to defend with their lives. But then why

The Judas Deception

hadn't they attacked already? It wasn't as if they had held back before, at the Ball, on the river, in the house at Grantchester. All the while they hadn't hesitated to confront the would-be trackers and had openly shot at them when they had escaped their clutches. Yet here they were right beside the entrance to the very thing they seemed to be protecting and there was no-one to stop them from going inside. Either they were convinced that they had scared off Huxley and his cohorts or they were confident that no-one would find anything in the chamber even if they did manage to get inside. Or perhaps they were simply waiting down below, guns at the ready if anyone should dare breach the sanctuary.

Huxley gave an involuntary shiver but turned towards the library and said, "Okay, let's go."

"Yes!" cried Alan, giving a fist-pump.

"Perhaps we should see what's waiting for us down there before we start celebrating," ventured Huxley.

"Or who," added Sam.

One of the benefits of his position was that Huxley had keys to a lot of buildings including the Wren Library. So, upon reaching the door, he dug into his pocket and pulled out a master key which opened most of the locks around the university buildings. Sam shone a torch over the lock as Huxley eased the key in and turned. A sharp, repetitive beep started to sound as Huxley pushed open the door, indicating that an alarm would go off shortly unless the appropriate code was entered into the panel lit up in front of him. He stepped forward and quickly punched in a five digit code and the noise stopped.

"How on earth do you remember all the different codes throughout the university, Daniel? It really is amaz...ah, of course, your eidetic memory, I forgot. Unlike you who never forgets anything."

"Believe me, Dean, it's as much a curse as a blessing."

With the four of them inside, they began to make their way towards the centre of the large room that was the Wren Library, Sam and Alan acting as ushers with their torches whilst Huxley led the group, all the while carefully scanning the darkened corners for any sign of movement. But there were none. It appeared that they were alone.

"Okay, Dean, perhaps you could show us where it is we need to be heading," said Huxley in a stage whisper, the reverence of the building seemingly making ordinary speech seem sacrilegious.

"It's been a while since I attempted this, Daniel," replied Connelly, mimicking the Vice-Chancellor's whisper.

Moving gingerly towards the far wall, Connelly instructed Sam to shine her torch against one of the central pillars before discounting it and moving towards the next one along. On the third he stopped, reaching to touch the wall with his fingers. When they alighted on a small hole in the inscription, he stopped.

"This is it."

"You're sure?"

"As I can be, Daniel. It has been a while and my eyesight is a lot worse than it was forty years ago but I think this is the one."

"So how does it work? With the keys, I mean?" asked Alan.

"Hold on," countered Huxley, "before we do anything we need to try and establish if anyone has been here before us and if they could be down there waiting to ambush us as soon as we set foot inside."

"No need to worry on that score, Daniel. The keys must remain in place in order to open the chamber. They can't be removed. So there can't be anyone lying in wait for us."

"So how do we get in?" persisted Donovan.

"Well, that's slightly more difficult, I'm afraid. There's a specific combination that must be followed, right key in right hole, if you get my drift, otherwise it doesn't work."

"Any chance you remember the combination?" asked Huxley.

"Alas, my memory is not like yours, Daniel. Would that it were. But I do remember that this," he held up one of the keys which appeared to be thicker than the others, "goes into the second hole. It was the only constant in our attempts as it's too big for any of the other holes."

"Well, that's a big help," moaned Donovan.

"Sorry to disappoint you, young Alan, but it has been a long time since I had the courage to stand here."

"It's fine, Dean," replied Huxley, "we'll just have to wing it.

It took them twenty minutes during which time Donovan's frustration grew ever more palpable and the sun's rays began to filter through the dark curtain holding it back from the world. It provided them with a little natural light through the magnificent arched windows that set the library apart from the numerous others in the city. Then there was a click. All four stood frozen until Connelly reached down to the floor and slid back a slab that had popped up on their latest turn of the keys. Beneath the large stone slab lay a staircase which was hidden in one of the giant pillars that supported the building, raising it off the ground to protect it from potential river floods. Or, perhaps, to hide a secret chamber below.

Connelly looked up at the rest of them. "Shall we?" he said.

CHAPTER 45

As the only member of the team who had been down there before, Connelly accepted Huxley's invite to lead them down, conscious of the fact that, even though he had convincingly said there wasn't, if someone was waiting for them down below that he would be directly in the firing line. He felt that it was fitting and it would give the others a chance to flee so was happy to undertake the role.

His hands traced the stone wall to his left as he began his descent until he found the switch he knew was there. Flicking it, he illuminated the vast chamber below and, even before they had reached halfway down the staircase, it was obvious that nothing had changed since he had last visited there. The chamber was completely empty.

They descended the long staircase which took them deep into the bowels of the earth, directly below the library, and Huxley marvelled at the feat of engineering involved in both the making of the chamber and the construction of such a large and prominent building above. Once beyond the constraints of the pillar which hid the beginnings of the staircase, it lay open on the right-hand side as they descended, allowing a view of the vast cavern below and causing each of them to hug the wall to their left as they made their way down.

The room reached up to around two thirds of the height

The Judas Deception

of the staircase, Huxley guessed and seemed to have been chiselled from a huge rock-face. It stretched out in a large rectangle below them, about the size of a football pitch if perhaps slightly irregular in places and curved up into a dome at the top. The echo of their footfalls began to resonate around the cavern and Huxley realised that the acoustics must be amazing and that this was probably used as a place of worship during times of persecution. Although bare of any ornamentation, there was a certain austerity about the place and Huxley found himself marvelling at the achievement of those responsible for the making of it all those centuries ago. But there was no escaping the sheer nothingness that lay down here.

"I don't believe it. There's nothing. Nothing at all," wailed Donovan as they reached the bottom of the stairway.

"I did warn you," chided Connelly.

"I know but I just assumed that you had missed something, a carving or air vent that would lead to a hidden passage if the right lever was pulled or button pressed." His despair was palpable.

"It really is a magnificent space," commented Huxley, listening as his words bounced back on themselves.

"Fuck magnificent," cried Donovan, "it's fucking empty!"

The profanity reverberated around the auditorium like a chastisement and Huxley actually winced such was the noise.

"I think we all get your frustration and disappointment, Alan," responded Sam, "but shouting about it in a place where even the merest whisper can be heard across the room is overdoing it a bit and can only draw unnecessary attention to us."

"I said almost exactly that to Spencer when he was bellowing in the Whispering Gallery in St Paul's," said Connelly. "In fact, that's when he went a bit funny."

"By Christ, of course," cried Huxley, the excitement evident in his voice. "That must be it!"

"What must be what, Daniel? You're not making any sense."

Huxley walked across to the long wall that ran down the left side of the chamber. He gently placed his hand against it and began to run it along the stone.

"Notice that this wall isn't straight."

The others looked towards the wall, their eyes following Huxley's hand as he slowly moved along it.

"By God, he's right. It's curved. I never noticed that before," murmured Connelly.

"Just like the Whispering Gallery," continued Sam.

"Yeah, yeah, big whoop. So what? What's that got to do with the price of eggs?"

Huxley stopped, his hand still resting on the wall in front of him. Then he pressed his mouth up against the stone and began to whisper on the spot where his hand had been. As he did so, something amazing happened.

CHAPTER 46

As Huxley whispered, the wall around began to move, slowly sliding back upon itself, the stone moving to reveal a passageway.

"Oh my god," gasped Sam.

"Holy fuck," cried Donovan, "I knew it! I fucking knew it! There had to be something down here. You've found it, Prof."

"Oh my, that's astounding," murmured Connelly, moving towards the wall.

"It's all to do with vibration," commented Huxley as he took a peek around the corner of the passageway. It took the form of a long corridor that looked to Huxley like it would comfortably take his height and still have room for more and, like the main auditorium, there was electric lighting along it. This allowed him to see all the way along it until it stretched around a corner and out of sight.

"How on earth did you work that out?" asked Connelly, moving to join Huxley at the entrance to the newly revealed opening, peering cautiously around as though fearful of what he might find.

"I've been mulling it over ever since you mentioned Spencer's reaction when you visited St Paul's. The whole thing with domes got me thinking about their significance. Then we came down here and the echoing of our voices made me realise that the acoustics are quite something and that perhaps it was relevant in some way. When you mentioned that he had paid particular attention to the Whispering Gallery in the Cathedral, I guessed that he had seen that this auditorium was similar in its make-up. Indeed, I'll be very surprised if Wren didn't use this as his inspiration for the design of St Paul's.

"But how did you know to do it on that particular piece of wall?" asked Davison.

"Well, I figured that if precious documents were kept down here, then conditions would have to be conducive to their maintenance. That means there can't be too much moisture in the air. This room is quite cold and that would be too brittle for delicate ancient parchments. They would need something a little warmer but not with too much humidity. So I just ran my hand along the wall until I found a warm spot. I guessed that if there was something hidden behind the wall then it would be there.

"Never mind all that," said Donovan, who was now standing at the head of the passage "how about we go and see what's down here?"

"Careful, Alan," responded Huxley, "what if the reason that no-one was lying in wait here to ambush us was because they are hiding down there?" He nodded in the direction of the end of the passage.

"But the Dean has already said that no-one can be down here. The keys weren't in the holes upstairs."

"That doesn't mean that they couldn't have locked someone in here."

"We have to look. We've come this far."

"Okay, but let's not go rushing along somewhere only to find that it's a rat trap."

"What do you suggest, Daniel?"

"I'm thinking that maybe we should go back and get some help."

"No way, man," the American more prominent in Donovan's accent as he used the slang. "We're here now, we've gotta move forward."

"I can see the sense in going for help, Dan, but who can we really trust?" questioned Sam. "We're here because the police want Alan for questioning and there are people out there trying to kill us. Right now, here feels just about the safest place we've been all night."

"So you think we should explore what's down this passage?" Huxley responded, pointing towards the opening.

"Why not?"

"Why are we even debating it? We should be down there by now discovering the truth about the Gospel of Judas and whatever else might be hidden there," chimed Donovan.

"Alright, but we need to be on our guard. We don't know where this is going to lead to. We go down in single file and make sure our backs are covered. Dean, can you go point and watch behind us?"

"I think I can manage that, Daniel."

"The Dean's had a very emotional couple of hours, perhaps I should go at the back," offered Donovan.

"Really? I thought you would want to be up front in amongst the action," commented Huxley.

"I just thought that you might want someone a bit more alert back there. No offence, Dean."

"That's quite alright, young Alan. I think the boy may have a point, Daniel."

"Fair enough, if that's what you want then let's do it."

They formed a line, Sam falling in behind Huxley with the Dean ahead of Donovan. Cautiously, they began to make their way along the passage towards the curve where they lost the line of sight. Huxley edged forward slowly, listening carefully for any sign of life ahead of them. The bend seemed to continue as they edged around it and Huxley felt like they were coming back on themselves. There didn't appear to be anyone waiting to pounce but he knew the importance of remaining vigilant so he signalled for them all to stop for a moment.

"What's the problem?" whispered Donovan from behind.

"No problem, I just wanted the chance to listen without the sound of our shuffling." Huxley kept his voice low but stopped short of whispering.

They stood in silence, straining their ears for any sound.

"Anything?" asked Sam.

"It's very eerily quiet," responded Huxley. "Okay, let's carry on."

Twice more they stopped, Huxley convinced that he could hear something but he was alone in this so they continued until an opening appeared ahead of them. Guardedly, he led them towards it. As they neared he could see that it opened up into a large room that, again, appeared to be empty. The lack of any greeting party, whilst welcome, unnerved him and he couldn't help but think that perhaps something lay further ahead, lurking somewhere in the wings.

Once convinced that the room was clear, he stepped inside, the others following. The roof was much higher here than in the passageway and the stones on the walls were huge solid blocks that had been purposely put in place to create the feeling of a fortified room, almost like a huge prison cell. A large wooden table with eight chairs around it sat in the middle of the room and, at the front of the room, beside the entrance, there was a huge wooden door with no markings or locks on it. The only other interesting feature apart from the door was a carving on the wall opposite.

Huxley went over to it to take a closer look. It showed

the image of two knights riding on horseback, each holding a shield with a cross on the front of it. The image was encircled by writing. Huxley tried to decipher what it said. He started at the top of the circle and worked his way around to come up with

SIGILLVM MILITVM XPISTI

"That's the seal of the Knights' Templar," said the Dean who had followed Huxley across the room. "It means 'The Chosen Soldiers of Christ'. I recognise it from the countless Templar references that Spencer used to peruse."

"Well, at least we know that we are in the right place." Huxley checked the rest of the room for any other symbols or markings but, finding none, he returned to the door. He guessed that it led to a similar passage as the one that they had just come through and wondered how many more such passages existed. Perhaps there was a whole warren of corridors lying hidden beneath Cambridge, known only to a few and giving them access to an entire network of secrets.

He moved closer to the door to examine it for clues as to how it opened and was joined by Alan who was growing in excitement and anticipation with every step they had taken since finding the hidden panel in the Wren.

"Do you think you can open it, Professor?"

"I doubt it, Alan. Lock picking isn't really my speciality and, even if it was, there isn't even a lock to pick on this. Anyway, I'm tired and I think we have enough now to convince the police that there is more to Stephen's murder than at first meets the eye. I'm sure that, if we show them this place, they will find a way through the door and see where it leads to. Whatever they find, by that time your father will be here and I'm sure he will be able to tidy up whatever mess you're in."

"Why wait, Danny, when we can finish it now?"

They all spun together at the sound of the voice which

came from the entrance. Turning they saw a handsome, rugged man in his early forties, guessed Sam, with eyes more penetrating than inviting and a smile that was bordering on cocky. Although she did think that the gun that he was pointing at them might be tainting her judgement a little.

"Hello Paul," said Huxley.

"You don't seem surprised to see me, Danny-boy."

"I had a feeling that you might be somewhere near by."

"That's always been your trouble, too clever by half."

"I'm sorry but what am I missing here?" asked Sam who was watching the exchange between the two men while trying hard to keep an eye on the gun that was being held steadily in the large hand pointed in her general direction.

"This is Paul Donovan, Sam, my old room-mate from my days as an undergrad. And, of course, Alan's father."

"Please excuse both my ignorance and my language but would someone like to explain to me just what the fuck is going on?"

Sam was getting a little tired of people pointing guns at her and was equally frustrated by the fact that everyone else seemed to know what was happening but not telling her. The frustration was evident in her voice as she continued.

"Why is he standing pointing a gun at us? And isn't he supposed to be in America? What was all that business about him trying to get the first flight to England to help his son out?"

Huxley looked a question towards his old cohort. Paul Donovan made a sweeping gesture with his free hand and said, "Be my guest, Danny, you seem to have all the answers so go ahead. The floor is all yours. In fact, why don't you all sit down where I can enjoy your presentation all the more, Danny-boy."

The Dean moved gratefully towards the nearest chair, his legs not as young as they once were and feeling the effects of standing around for too long, not to mention his heart pounding at the sight of a gun. Huxley and Sam followed, taking seats at the far end of the table, as if putting that little extra distance between themselves and the gun might help them in some small measure. Lastly, Alan sat at the opposite end taking the seat next to where his father was standing.

Huxley made sure that Donovan senior was content for him to begin before addressing his answer to the group rather than just directly to Sam.

"I suspected something strange was happening quite early on. When I got a phone call from Paul earlier, I accepted it at face value, a cry for help from an old friend. But knowing you as well as I do, Paul, I knew that there would be an ulterior motive. After all, why me? Just because of the advantages my position gives me, I could think of any number of people better placed to help out your son. There are a dozen lawyers who we both know well who would have had Alan out of police custody within two minutes and had the authorities so tied up with red tape that it would have been Thanksgiving before they were even allowed to mention the words 'American citizen'. So it had to be something else. Then there was the unrecognisable number that you used to call me. You said that the call was being re-routed via your London office but that didn't ring true, if you'll pardon the pun."

"You're basing all that on a phone number that you didn't recognise. Christ almighty, Danny-boy, you really do over-think things, don't you?"

"It's always been one of my big problems, Paul. But I was right, wasn't I? The reason I didn't recognise the number is because you were here in England and using a different mobile."

"You mean to say that all this time you knew that Alan's father was here and yet you still led us on this merry charade?" Sam's exasperation was beginning to bubble over.

"I couldn't be sure, Sam. As I say, I only suspected that

there was something more to his phone call than met the eye. That's why I wanted to get Alan away from the police to see if I could figure out what. When Alan told me about the discovery in Washington, I figured that he would have shared that with his dad. The fact that Paul never mentioned anything of that to me in his call suggested that he wanted me involved before I found that out."

"But why?" asked Sam.

"Because he knew that once I was put onto the trail of something that I would continue to dig until I found out as much as I could."

Huxley looked up towards the man with whom he had shared so much of his youthful energy. Paul Donovan stood watching over them all, a smirk spread across his face, the gun still held firmly in his left hand, pointing towards them.

"Very good, Danny. I knew you wouldn't be able to resist the pull of the challenge. I also knew that if anyone was going to find out what we needed to know it would be you."

"You mean that you are responsible for everything that has happened to us tonight?" Sam was incredulous as she thought about how close to death they had come at the hands of this man in front of them. "But I don't understand, you were trying to kill your own son."

"No, I had nothing to do with those attempts on your lives. Quite the opposite in fact, I was most keen to keep you alive."

"But the fire? That wasn't you?"

"Yes, what about the fire, Danny-boy? Why don't you tell us what you make of that then?"

"Well, I think it was an attack by what we now know as the Knights' Templar according to what Dr Connelly has told us. It was a genuine attempt and Alan would have died along with us had we not managed to escape. I think that they

The Judas Deception

followed us from the Master's Lodge earlier this evening and, when they saw us going into the faculty building, guessed that we were investigating what Simms had been doing that got him killed. I figure that they saw it as a perfect opportunity to stop us meddling and also destroy any evidence left by Simms. I don't think they cared whether we lived or died, just so long as we stopped looking into Stephen's affairs. I think most people probably would have after something like that."

"But what about the abduction at the Ball and shooting at us? Was that the Knights' Templar too? Or was it all just staged by Mr Donovan here to bring us closer to our goal?"

"Oh, I have no doubt that it was the Templar again at the Ball and they nearly scuppered Paul's plans. You see, he's been tracking our progress ever since we made our escape from the faculty building. Am I right, Paul?

"Actually, I've been tracking you ever since you entered the bookshop this evening. Who do you think rammed the police car that allowed you to escape?"

"That was you?"

"Ah, so I do still have the capacity to surprise you. Well, that is good to know. Yes, I've been watching carefully since then. The fire was unfortunate. I never saw them start it but I did try and help by clearing one of the fire exits. By the time I did, though, you had already made your escape. It was quite by chance that I saw the three of you jump from the roof onto the fire escape. Lucky for me I did so that I was able to track you into the Ball."

"So why didn't you stop those men from trying to abduct us?" asked Sam, the anger visible in her face.

"I was waiting for them to take you across the bridge and away from the party before I was going to intervene."

"And just what do you mean by intervene?" asked Huxley.

"I'd planned to create some sort of diversion that would distract your abductors and allow you to escape."

"So even then you wouldn't have given up the charade of hiding in the shadows. You were quite content to watch your son being held at gun point." There was incredulity in Huxley's voice.

"You seemed to be more than capable of dealing with whatever was thrown at you, Danny-boy. Kudos on the punt escape by the way." Huxley nodded an acknowledgement but didn't say anything. "Anyway, once you were on the river I did what I could to help."

"And what exactly was that?" asked Sam.

"I think that he gave us a helping hand by firing on our attackers when we were on the bridge and that's why the young lad propelling the punt fell off causing our attacker to miss with his own gunshot. I'm pretty sure that there was a bang just before our attacker's gun went off."

"Is that true? Were you there? You could have stepped in and stopped the whole sorry business at any point instead of letting us almost get killed?"

"Let's just say I was happy watching from the wings and it wasn't always possible for me to jump in. There were certainlu some hairy moments from my perspective."

"Yeah, well it was no pleasure cruise for us either, I can tell you," replied Huxley.

"I hadn't anticipated that they would make such a direct play for you as they did at Queens'. I saw you going into the Ball, of course, and knew that it would be difficult for me to follow as I wasn't exactly dressed for the occasion." He indicated the jeans, shirt and jacket combo that he had on, along with his Timberland boots. "And as I don't carry the same authority as you around here, Danny, then it was always going to be difficult to blag my way in. From my vantage point though I was able to see you emerging from the first aid room with an additional member who seemed to be paying very close attention to the Vice-Chancellor. So then I ran around to the far side of the river and tracked your movements from there. It wasn't ideal and I lost you a couple of times but managed to get there in time to put your attacker off his game just when he was about to kill you, Danny-boy."

"What do you want, Paul? Do you expect me to be grateful? We wouldn't have faced any of this if it hadn't been for you playing sick little games and endangering your own son, for Christ's sake!"

"You didn't have to do any of it, Danny. You could have simply remained with the police and held Alan's hand while they questioned him. Sooner or later they would have had to let him go because he didn't do anything wrong. But you had to get involved, just like I knew you would. So don't try and put this on me. You could have stopped anytime you liked and gone to the police who would have laughed at your ridiculous story but at least you would have been safe. But, oh no, not the great Professor Daniel Huxley. He has to show everyone how clever he is and solve the puzzle, doesn't he? Well, tell me, Danny, what else have you figured out?"

"I knew that Alan was keeping in touch with someone. It took me a while to be sure but then there was the attack on the house at Grantchester. At that point I knew it was you."

"Are you saying that he was responsible for attacking us at Spencer's house?" Sam pointed an accusatory finger in Paul Donovan's direction as she spoke.

"Yes, that's exactly what I'm saying. When we discovered the notes at Spencer's house and the clue to the Wren Library, he and Alan needed to move us on. I think they faked the attack on the house by breaking a window and firing a shot. I'm guessing if you ever get a chance to check you'll find a hole in the ceiling or somewhere safe like that, just enough to scare us into action but with no danger of actually harming anyone otherwise that would have ruined their plan. I think that once we had found what it was he needed then he was anxious to get us back into the city so that we could begin the search for this." He indicated the cavern that they were now in.

"It also gave me a chance to read what Spencer had left and get up to speed on the search. I must say that you panicked us a little, Danny, with your heroic attempt at going back into the house to retrieve the documents. That nearly put paid to our plan. Luckily Alan was quick witted enough to run in ahead of you before emerging and convincing you that it was too dangerous."

"So you are both in this together then? You set this whole thing up," demanded Sam perhaps feeling that now the Templar had been removed as the primary threat that maybe everything was going to be okay.

"Oh yes, my dear, it was a combined effort in the hope that Danny could lead us to this point. And I must say, you have done a splendid job, my old friend."

"But I don't understand," said Sam, "why the need for a gun? We are all on the same side."

"Not quite," said Huxley. He looked into Paul Donovan's eyes. "It was you in the bookshop, wasn't it?" It was more statement than question but Huxley was desperately hoping that he was wrong.

"That snivelling little twerp, Simms. Alan brings him everything he needs, presents it to him on a plate and asks for his help in uncovering the conspiracy. All he had to do was contact you, Danny-boy, that's all we needed. I knew if we could get you digging then we'd have a chance of uncovering something. But oh no, he refused to believe that the translation was wrong, that he could have possibly missed something when he had examined the manuscript. So he throws Alan out on his ear. For Christ sake, my son was presenting him with probably the most sensational find ever in the history of the bible and he couldn't see it. I didn't realise it then, but he had obviously made calls to certain people who alerted the Templar to the possibility that people were asking the wrong kind of questions. So I thought the only way of making sure that we got what we wanted was by eliminating him. After all, he was just a means to an end and we couldn't have him stealing all the glory."

"And the body in the car at the airport? Was that your handiwork too?"

"Redding was on to us. He knew that Alan had breached the confidentiality agreement. He was threatening to have Alan arrested. I couldn't allow that, it would have alerted the wrong people. So I did what I had to do."

"You are mad, Paul. You can't possibly think that you can get away with this?"

"I thought I just had, Danny. I mean, here we are in a chamber which has lain undiscovered for centuries. Thanks to you guys doing most of the leg work we have found our way in to the holy of holies and can now expose the truth of what the Church has been hiding for years. The fact that there may have been a few sacrifices made along the way is neither here nor there. Let's face it, the Church have killed thousands in the name of god over the years, all in an effort to force feed a load of religious shit to the masses and keep the truth from them. The beauty of this is that we can take them to here. Experts will examine whatever documents we find and declare them genuine and we can bask in the glory of being the men that brought down the Church."

"So this is all just for a bit of glory?"

"Glory, fame, money. You know, the usual reasons that

people do crazy things. The same reasons that have had you running all around Cambridge tonight."

"I've been running around all night trying to help your son gather evidence that he had nothing to do with a murder only to find that he was in it up to his neck all along."

"That has always been your problem, Danny-boy, you are just so trusting. Give you the puppy dog eyes and cry injustice and Professor Daniel Huxley will ride to your rescue. As soon as these bastards tried to cremate you earlier you had all the evidence you needed to go to the police and cry foul. But, oh no, you got the scent of something big and juicy and there was no way you were going to give up on it. You wanted to find this place as much as I did, you're only disappointed that I've come along to spoil the party."

"I don't understand, Paul, surely if you wanted this so badly there were easier ways, better ways even to go about it. Why didn't you just approach me in the first place and we could have examined the facts together and solved the puzzle without anyone getting hurt?"

"Don't you get it yet, Danny-boy? Don't you understand that the whole force of the Catholic Church will stop at nothing to prevent people from finding these documents. The only reason that they have never been destroyed is that they thought, in here, they had the perfect hiding place. Even when it had been breached before by Harris and his cohorts, they never got beyond the outer chamber. They thought they had somewhere that no-one would ever get to. We are talking about documents that expose the corruption that the Church has undertaken or been party to for centuries. Manuscripts that demonstrate the vagaries of those held to be holy and righteous to the world. Papyrus that tell the real story of Jesus Christ. Through there," he shouted as he pointed towards the locked door, "lies a document that declares that Judas betrayed

Jesus to the authorities because Jesus spurned his advances in favour of having a relationship with his disciple John. Judas betrayed the supposed son of god because Jesus traded him in for a younger model. It was a simple act of jealousy, a classic love triangle and it resulted in Jesus being condemned to death by the government of the day and portrayed as the saviour of mankind because of his sacrifice. He was killed for being a homosexual. And the evidence is right down there."

"You don't think that they are just going to let you take it?"

"Of course not, Danny-boy, but that's where you come in. The Templars know that you are running around trying to find the secret hideaway so all their focus is on you. I saw them running about all over the city desperately looking for you. They didn't realise the connection with Spencer and so never thought about Grantchester as a hiding place and refuge. In fact, you probably would have been safe there for as long as you needed."

He raised his eyebrows sheepishly before continuing.

"But I had to get you moving again as, unlike you, I don't have all the time in the world. I intend to be out of here long before anyone thinks about looking for me. And you're just the distraction that I need. I sent the Master a text message a little earlier to tell them about the house in Grantchester and that you were there. I knew that they would rush straight to it in the hope of eliminating you and whoever else was helping you. Oh, don't worry, I left all the paperwork from Spencer's little hoard lying on the floor for them to find. Once they read through it and realise that you know the whole story, they'll come right back to here to try and protect their secret artefacts. And then they will find you in here and figure that they have arrived just in time to stop you from finding the documents. But, of course, it will be too late by then as I will have already taken what I need and be well clear of here before they even realise what has happened."

"You got all that from a text message that you sent the Master? Why on earth would he believe anything that he received in a text message from you?"

"Two reasons, my dear Danny. One, he is desperate and will take any help he can get at the moment. And two, he doesn't know that it has come from me. He believes that it comes from a trusted source. A good friend. Another Templar."

"The number you phoned me from, it belongs to somebody else, doesn't it?"

"Well done, Danny-boy. Exactly right."

"And what happened to him?"

"Suffice to say that he won't be running to help out in their attempts to stop you. But the Master believes that he has used his sources to find out Spencer and has passed that information along to help his colleagues."

"You really are a sick bastard, Paul."

"Perhaps, but I'm the one with the gun and that's all that matters. Now, time is pressing on and I'm conscious of the fact that the Knights' Templar are going to come a-calling shortly so, any ideas on how we get this door open?"

"None. I think this is as far as you go. How does that fit in with your plan?"

"I'm afraid it doesn't Danny-boy. I think you need to put that big brain of yours into action and come up with a solution. We all know that there has to be a way through it."

"Short of burning it down or blowing it open, I can't think of a way through it."

"I don't think we have time for all that now. Besides, it would be much more symmetrical for you to solve this one last puzzle."

"Look Paul, I'm tired, I've been up all night trying to help your son and I have no motivation whatsoever to help you find a way through to the inner sanctum and whatever waits beyond."

"Well let's see if we can't give you some motivation."

Paul Donovan moved his arm slightly to the left and fired his gun.

CHAPTER 47

The sound of the gunshot was muted by the silencer that was on the pistol so rather than an explosion of sound there was just a soft expulsion of air as the single bullet flew out of the gun. The noise came from the Dean as he screamed in agony as his right shoulder shattered from the impact of the shot.

"What the fuck?" shouted Huxley.

"You've got two minutes to come up with something or the girl gets it next. Come on, Danny-boy, tick tock."

"You're completely insane."

"Hey, less talking, more action. It's your time that you're wasting."

"Okay, okay. Right, let's see. Ammm, well there's no lock or handle on the door so there is no obvious release there unless there's a hidden panel on it somewhere but it's a solid block of oak so I don't see how."

Huxley rose and went to the door where he ran his hands once again over the smooth service looking for any tell-tale ridges that would point towards a release button within it. Finding nothing he started to look around the rest of the room but, again, saw only the Knights' Templar crest that was imprinted on the wall.

The Judas Deception

"That's a minute gone. Do you want me to put another bullet in the Dean just to encourage your thought process?"

The groan from Connelly told Huxley that he was already in great pain and the thought of that intensifying certainly did nothing for his resolve as he tried to cope with his shattered shoulder.

"No, no, it's fine," shouted Huxley. "Right, nothing on the door. So there has to be something on the walls somewhere."

He started to run his hands along the wall around the door to see if there was a nub or ridge that might trigger its release. Finding nothing he began to move around the wall towards the front of the room where Paul Donavan was positioned.

"Don't be thinking of trying anything funny now, Dannyboy. I'll shoot you as quickly as any of the rest of them."

"And then we'll all be trapped. Great idea, Einstein."

"What, you think you're the only one that can figure out how to open the damn thing. You only scored two points more than me on your finals, don't forget, Professor. And my son is a freaking certified genius more than capable of matching your brain power."

"So why am I the one lumbered with the task of finding the release? And with the added threat that you might shoot an innocent person at any time."

"That's what makes it so exciting, Danny. Anyway, you're the man, aren't you? You're the one who found the door in the auditorium."

"That was down to Spencer and his pointing us towards Wren. He was right when he said that Wren dotted his 'i's and…" Huxley stopped.

"What?" asked Donovan senior.

"I wonder," muttered Huxley who was again on the scent of something and seemed oblivious to the danger that he faced.

He walked right past Paul Donovan who stepped back, keeping the gun trained on Huxley the whole time.

"What are you thinking, Dan?" asked Sam who was getting used to people threatening her life and appeared relatively calm as she tried to minister to Connelly's wound.

"It's something that the Dean said earlier about Spencer's take on Wren. He said Wren was all about the details, he dotted the 'i's and crossed the 't's."

"So fucking what? Is that the best you can do?" said Alan Donovan. "Fucking shoot one of them, Dad."

"Hold on," said Huxley, "we dotted the 'i' upstairs so I wonder if we have to cross the 't' down here?" He was now standing in front of the crest directly opposite the door on the other side of the room. He moved his hand upwards and ran it along the letters that encircled the two men on a horse.

SIGILLVM MILITVM XPISTI

"It's Latin except for the XP in Christ which is Greek. The XP symbol's origin lies in the early roots of Christianity but came into popular use after the Emperor Constantine had a vision of it and, according to legend, converted to Christianity in the early fourth century. So I wonder what will come to pass when we press the 'T' in Christ?" He did so but nothing happened.

"Maybe it's the other 'T' in the motto?" cried Alan. He stood now and rushed towards the crest but his father shouted for him to move away.

"I don't want to give any of them the chance of pulling anything. You come over here beside me, son. We'll let the hired help do the work. Go on then, Danny, press the other 'T'."

Huxley moved his hand round to the second 'T' and pressed. Again, nothing happened.

The Judas Deception

"So much for that bright idea. Right, Danny, I think you need another incentive."

Donovan senior lined the gun up on Sam but Huxley didn't seem to be paying any attention to what was going on around him.

"Cross the 't's," he murmured.

"What?" said Paul.

"Dot the 'i's and cross the 't's, " said Huxley again, almost to himself."

"Yes, so the fuck what? What are you mumbling about?"

"Cross them," answered Huxley, turning towards his captor. "Make them into crosses."

He reached for the '*T*' in *XPISTI* again but this time, rather than press it, he pushed at the bottom of the leg of the 'T' and forced it upwards. It moved and as it did so there was a click and the wooden door sprung open a couple of inches inwards.

"You did it, Danny-boy, you fucking did it. I knew you would. You fucking genius. Come on, Alan, through you go."

Donovan pushed his son towards the door, keeping the gun trained on the other three as he followed.

"I think it would be rather fitting for you to wait quietly here until your friends from the Templar arrive. I mean, it's only fair, seeing as how they have been desperate to catch up with you all night. And just to make sure you don't try and follow us…"

He reached into the bag hanging by his side and pulled out a can of lighter fluid which he began to liberally douse all over the wood of the freshly opened door. He then took a match and, as he stepped through the door to follow his son, he struck it and set the door on fire, pulling it shut as he did so. The flames took hold immediately forcing the others back to the far side of the room and blocking their access to the archway they had entered from. Huxley immediately grabbed at the table and began to haul it out of the path of the flames before it, too, caught fire. Sam followed his lead and pulled the chairs away too but it only served to highlight the futility of their plight as the flames got drawn towards the open doorway and their only escape route.

As the fire grew in intensity, the trio huddled against the far wall, the table overturned on its side to provide some protection from the heat.

"Shit, what are we going to do now?" asked Sam.

"He's been very clever," said Huxley, calmly assessing the situation.

"What do you mean, clever?"

It was Connelly who answered, the initial pain of his wound having subsided.

"Daniel means that by closing the door he has made it look like we don't know how to open it and have resorted to burning it down ourselves. A door that size will take a long time to burn so the Knights' Templar will arrive long before it does and, when they do, they'll think we have made it this far but got stuck and set fire to the door to try and get through. Once they take care of us they'll have little reason to think that somebody already got through and breached their sanctuary. And even if they do decide to check their cache, I'm sure Mr Donovan will not hesitate to introduce them to his own brand of American justice."

"Quite right, Dean. How are you holding up?"

"Oh, I'll survive I dare say, Daniel. It hurts like hell, pardon my language, but it's not going to kill me. Just a pity the Knights' Templar will."

"I think we have more immediate problems," responded Huxley as the flames from the door increased in intensity, "like finding another way out of here."

The heat was beginning to increase in the confined room and he looked around for any sign of another exit or a possible weakness in the stonework which may offer them some respite. Sam was focusing on the crest.

"Why did you press that particular '*T*'?" she asked Huxley?

"What?" replied Huxley, confused.

"There are two '*T*'s in the crest, how did you know to pick that one?"

Huxley flashed her a look of puzzlement, his mind focused on his second fire of the night, a trend he could live without. Then, "Oh yeah, I see what you're saying. To be honest, I just pressed the first *T* I saw."

He looked across at the others.

Connelly added, "Spencer always said that Wren dotted all the '*i*'s and crossed all the '*t*'s."

"I wonder what would happen if I pressed the other '*T*'?"

He hurried back to the crest and reached for the second '*T*'. Again he put his fingers on the base of the carved letter and pushed upwards. It, too, began to move and, once the leg had moved upwards far enough to change the 'T' into a cross, they heard another click, this one to Huxley's left, on the far wall from where they had entered the room. Huxley turned to look and was amazed to see that the stonework was hiding another doorway. Part of the wall had popped out and Sam was already beside it, pulling it open.

"It's another passageway," she cried.

Connelly started laughing. "I think our friends may have gone the wrong way."

CHAPTER 48

Huxley walked over to the opening that was now fully exposed thanks to Sam's endeavours. He looked down a short corridor with a wall directly ahead. Huxley assumed there was a turning in the passage there, the path continuing at right angles to where they stood.

Turning, Huxley found his two companions already standing behind him ready to enter the passageway if only to escape the growing heat of the room. He led them both inside, pulling the stone doorway to but stopping short of shutting it. He looked with concern at the Dean's shoulder injury. "I think we need to get you to a hospital, Dean. This," he gestured at the passage, "can wait for another time."

"In order to get to a hospital we have to get out of here first and we can't go back the way we came. And once the Donovans find out that there's nothing in their passage, they're going to come back this way and find the real hiding place," commented Sam.

"Not to mention the Templar on their way here to tidy up whatever mess they find. Even if we did survive the flames we'll just be presenting ourselves to those same people who have already tried to kill you tonight."

"Firstly, if the Templar are any good at their job, and I like to think that they are, I imagine that there's enough

The Judas Deception

documents hidden at the end of the false trail to keep any would-be trespassers occupied for hours before they realise that it's all very tame in comparison to what they are expecting. As for them coming to get us, let's just say that I've got an insurance policy that will protect us."

"And what exactly do you mean by that?" asked Sam, with more amusement than annoyance at what seemed like yet more subterfuge on Huxley's part.

"Well, my good friend George Pepper has been closely following events through the microphone that I have hidden in my lapel. If he's doing his job properly," this last with a hint of mocking to the hidden device, "then there will be a fleet of police vehicles heading for the College grounds to apprehend any assailants along with both Donovan senior and junior. As such, we can wait here for our rescuers and get the Dean to hospital to get patched up."

"Sod that, Daniel, we could be waiting here for ages. I say we head down this passage and see what lies ahead. For all we know there may be another way out and we'll be standing around waiting for nothing." Connelly sounded keen in spite of his injury.

Huxley looked with admiration at his friend. "Are you up to a bit of exploring then, Dean?"

"Try and stop me, Daniel."

"Sam?"

With the imminent threat of both fire and execution seemingly eliminated and with a certain gratitude that she was with a man as forward thinking as Professor Daniel Huxley, Dr Sam Davison was filled with a courage and sense of adventure that surprised her.

"Why the hell not," she replied.

Turning, Huxley looked towards the wall at the end. Now

that he was inside the passage, he couldn't see any evidence of the expected turn at the end of the corridor.

"It looks like there might be another obstacle to overcome," commented Connelly, reading the younger man's mind.

"Oh yeah," continued Sam, "it looks like a dead end ahead. You might need to summon that big brain of yours into action one last time yet, Professor."

"Well, only one way to find out."

With that Huxley began to move towards the wall ahead, the others following. As they approached, Huxley carefully examined the stonework around them. It had been carved out of solid rock and there were no features to suggest hidden passages beyond.

The light was dimmer here and Huxley looked around to see that even the electrics that had been installed only extended halfway along the passage, throwing just enough light to dimly illuminate the furthest wall. It looked exactly like the dead end it was.

Huxley began to rub has hands gently along the walls and asked Sam to shine the torch she was still carrying to give him some more light. She moved closer as she did and Huxley got a brief trace of something floral, momentarily distracting him. They moved along the remainder of the corridor like this, Sam staying close to shine the torch at Huxley's prompts, Connelly shuffling behind them, his shoulder numb but his mind still sharp.

When they reached the end, Huxley and Davison shared a look that suggested that they both felt this was nothing more than a red herring and perhaps the Donovans had gone the right way after all.

"But why have this passage at all?" asked Sam, still standing just behind Huxley, her torch moving in line with his hands as he continued to caress the wall around.

"I don't know," responded Huxley. "It strikes me as very odd that they would make the door so obvious and this passage much more difficult to find and yet this seemingly leads to nowhere."

"The whole business seems odd to me," commented Connelly, "but I'm just thankful that it gives us somewhere to hide until the cavalry get here."

"Yes, I suppose you're right, Dean, we should be thankful for that. I guess we just have to wait for Pepper and his cohorts to come and find us."

"Are you sure that thing is even working?" asked Sam, nodding towards Huxley's lapel.

"Well, I hope so," replied Huxley, as Sam turned to make her way back along the corridor towards where the Dean was standing, "but even if it isn't then he knows exactly where we were hea…"

Huxley's words were lost as the ground beneath him began to shake when Sam moved away from him and then he was suddenly falling. The others looked in amazement at him plunging through the floor.

"Where did he go?" cried Sam.

"I…don't…I…" blustered Connelly.

The pair were looking at the floor where Huxley had been standing. The ground was intact and there was no evidence of a hole through which anyone could have fallen. Had the two not seen it with their own eyes they would never have believed that Huxley had gone through the solid base that lay in front of them.

It was Connelly who recovered first. "I think it must be a hinged stone."

"A what?"

"It's a stone that has a hinge in the middle and is set

balanced until weight is put on one end then it tips up. I remember Spencer telling me about them in the Pyramids."

"But I was standing where Dan was. Why didn't it tip then?"

"You must have been balancing each other at either end of the stone. It was only when you moved that the weight at one end was greater and so the stone moved."

"So, should we follow?"

"I don't see any other way out."

"But what if it's a huge drop. He could be lying badly injured right now and we'd only be adding to the problem by following."

"You might be right, Sam. I would offer to hold onto your feet while you tip the stone and see if you can see what is below but…" Connelly indicated his shoulder.

"But I could hold onto yours, Dean. That is, if you are up to it?"

Connelly looked at her, determination in his eyes and gave a nod. They walked to the end of the passage stopping short of where Huxley had fallen through. Connelly lay on the ground and, once Davison had a firm grip of his ankles, he inched forward using his strong arm.

When he felt the stone begin to move beneath him, he braced himself fearing that gravity might be stronger than Sam Davison but he needn't have worried. As the stone swung, Connelly began to drop but this was countered by Sam's weight, so he found himself hanging upside down and looking down onto a platform below, the drop a manageable eight feet by his approximation. Huxley was standing looking up at him.

"Hey, I thought you guys were never coming," said Huxley.

"Oh, Daniel, it's good to see that you're okay." Then, to Davison, "It's alright, Sam, Daniel is fine."

"Can I let go?"

The Judas Deception

"No!" cried Connelly.

"It's alright, Dean, if Sam can lower you a little more I can grab your good shoulder and take your weight. You'll be fine."

There were a few protests from Connelly but he eventually allowed Sam to hang him by his ankles until Huxley grabbed hold of the older man and swung him around the right way, setting him down on his feet. By that time, Sam knew what awaited her so she, too, stepped on the stone and seconds later, it swung open again and she came through feet first.

She was prepared for what awaited her so was ready for the hard landing, crouching as she hit the ground and going into a roll. Huxley didn't have any such luxury, having plunged through suddenly, and he admitted to the others that he had been fearful as he started to fall. But it hadn't been that much of a drop and he was able to absorb the impact as his feet hit the platform that presently held them. It was only now that Connelly and Davison looked around them. Sam let out a gasp of astonishment.

"Impressive, isn't it?" commented Huxley.

Below them lay a semi-circular room about twenty feet deep, Sam guessed, with polished wooden shelves lining the walls all the way around. The shelves were full of documents and manuscripts which were perfectly preserved in the temperate climate of the room.

"Wow, it's magnificent."

"Their own private library hidden away. It really is amazing."

"Breathtaking," whispered Connelly.

"Shall we go and explore?" asked Huxley, pointing towards the staircase at the end of the platform where they stood.

CHAPTER 49

The Donovans ran along the corridor lit up in front of them, excitement driving them forward. Paul Donovan had known that Huxley would be the man to solve a puzzle which had stumped everyone else over the centuries. The man always had been too clever by half. But not clever enough this time. His face when I shot the Dean, he thought, chuckling to himself as he led his son around a long bend, the passage meandering now, the walls narrowing all the while. He sensed they were getting closer, adrenaline coursing through his veins at the thought of what lay ahead.

Forced to slow as the tunnel became increasingly restrictive, Alan had a chance to catch his breath and finally voice his thoughts.

"But, Dad, how are we going to get out again?" he asked. "I mean, why light the fire? Surely the threat of the gun would have been enough?"

Donovan senior stopped to turn and look at his son, an act which was considerably more difficult than it would have been just a few dozen paces back as the corridor narrowed claustrophobically. His dilated pupils looked monstrous in the harsh light of the naked bulbs that illuminated the cramped space, shadows looming large and spectral. Alan actually took a step back as he looked up at his father.

"I couldn't risk them going back to the top and trapping us inside or, worse yet, calling for reinforcements. I deliberately made sure they were trapped on the wrong side of the chamber so that they would be stuck there for as long as the blaze rages. Or, better still, burnt to a crisp!" He laughed throatily.

"But how do we get out?"

"Out? Good god, son, we're not even in the chamber yet. We haven't reached our goal, nay, our destiny. And you want to leave!"

"I didn't mean that I wanted to leave," whined Alan as he began to follow his again mobile father around another turn, "I just meant that we're going to have to either tackle the fire ourselves or, if it's gone out, find ourselves trapped inside as the others will seal the entrance."

"Don't worry about that, boy, I've got it all sorted." Paul was now hunched over to negotiate the tight space that stood between him and the untold riches ahead. As he turned yet another tight corner, however, he let out a cry of delight that caused his son to bump his head on the top of the passage as he looked up.

His pain was quickly forgotten as he followed his father's footsteps and found a winding staircase just in front leading downwards into a vast chamber below.

"Wow, do you really think this is it, Dad?"

"Has to be, doesn't it? Stands to reason, all the obstacles that have been put in the way to stop people from getting to this point." He stood at the head of the staircase, allowing the sense of anticipation to overwhelm him. Then, like a schoolboy fleeing his environs on the last day of term, he ran down the stone stairs, Alan on his heels, his yelp sound-tracking their descent.

At the bottom Donovan senior stopped suddenly causing his son to crash into the back of him.

"What's up, Dad?"

His father pointed to the arched entrance that stood before them.

"In there, son, is the greatest historical finding known to man, the truth about everything the Church has ever tried to hide. And here we are on the threshold of being the ones to discover it. I just want to savour the moment so that I can tell all those who interview me in the coming weeks and months how it felt. That instant before tearing a fissure in the fabric of history."

"I like it."

"Right, let's go and see what these charlatans have been hiding from us all these years."

The two stepped through the archway.

CHAPTER 50

Pepper had lost radio contact with his friend but not before hearing Paul Donovan firing a gun. By then he had already taken the ragtag team of officers he was able to muster and put them into position around the entrance to the Wren Library.

His gut instinct had been to rush inside when he first heard the conversation between Paul Donovan and his captors but Huxley had already told him what to expect and that he should wait until Donovan had said enough to incriminate himself before making their presence known. Now he was cursing himself for leaving it so late.

The crack of the gun had come through loud and clear on the earpiece he was wearing that was linked to Huxley's wireless mic. In fact, he had been amazed at just how clear it all was given that his friend had told him that they would be quite a long way underground. The pair had used the equipment before but never in these environs and so it had been more by luck than design that it had actually worked. But, since the clear ring of the gunshot, Pepper hadn't heard so much as a crackle of static and he now feared the worst.

Leaving half a dozen men to surround the entrance to the library, he had led the four remaining constables inside to try and find the secret entrance that Huxley had said would lead to the chamber below. The porters on duty had been keen to help when the police showed up and offered to accompany them and switch the lights and heating on in the building but Pepper had assured them that it was better that they keep their distance. That meant that the library was still shrouded in darkness save for the faint rays of a rising sun that were beginning to penetrate the horizon.

Having briefed his team, they entered stealthily, their eyes peeled for movement. Sure enough, just as Huxley had advised, there were two men adopting the pose of sentries in the far corner of the building, their outlines just visible.

"He'll have back up with him, George, so be careful when you come into the library. It's the only way that he can guarantee his escape so I imagine he'll have got a couple of ex-military types to protect him. I doubt he'll have given them the full story and I can't imagine them wanting to get into a shooting match with the police but you never know."

This had been during the phone conversation they'd had shortly before entering the grounds of the College and Pepper had urged his friend to wait for his arrival with back up before proceeding. Although Huxley had agreed, he advised his friend to stay out of sight and follow everything on the mic. They had arranged the frequency and Pepper was only to break cover if the equipment failed to work.

"You're my back up, George. I need to know that you're not going to let him escape. As soon as he is back in the Wren, you have to be there to stop him."

"But we could come down and arrest him in the chamber rather than you taking the risk that he might decide to kill you all."

"I'm afraid that's a chance that we will have to take. I don't know how easy it is to navigate down there and we could end up having a rather awkward hostage situation. Anyway, I've got a strange feeling that Donovan senior will want to keep me around just in case there's a snag. He's relying on me to figure out the puzzles and I think he realises that you never know when the sneaky bastards are going to come up with another fiendish way to stop people getting their hands on what's down there."

That had been two hours and one gunshot ago. One gunshot that he had heard. Perhaps there had been more and they were all now dead. He knew that he had no choice but to follow his best friend down into the depths of the underground world that existed beneath this city.

Having given clear instructions to his team, they shuffled forward, keeping low and using the rows of books to cover their approach before ensuring that the trained marksmen accompanying him had the two sentries in their sights. Once he got the thumbs up from their leader he shouted clearly whilst remaining in his crouched position.

"Armed police, put your weapons down on the ground and your hands behind your head where they can be clearly seen."

The two men looked startled and Pepper thought that they couldn't have been from any branch of the military worth their salt. He had trained with the army in his days as a police cadet and knew that it was as much about mental agility as it was physical ability. His guess was the pair were simply hired muscle, two gorillas there to intimidate and scare rather than to protect and assist. No matter how stealth their approach had been, had the two been properly trained then the change in atmosphere and temperature alone should have alerted them to the presence of others in the building. Now they seemed confused, unsure how they should react to a situation that they obviously hadn't prepared for.

Their hesitation was all that Pepper needed. Giving the order to rush them, the firearms officers moved in front of the two bodyguards, their weapons trained on the centre of their torsos. Whether because of their size or simply through lack of forethought, the two gorillas appeared to be unarmed, used to overpowering any attackers by their sheer size and brute force. Confronted with guns they were sensible enough to realise their limitations and put their hands in the air.

"Hands behind your heads," came the call. The men obeyed.

Whilst gorilla one was ordered to his knees, Pepper made his way behind to snap on handcuffs. It had been a while since he had been so hands on and secretly he was thrilling in it but, as he watched another of the team cuff primate number two, his thoughts quickly returned to the danger that his friend was undoubtedly in.

Radioing for backup to come and escort the goons out of the building, he turned his attention to the wall in front. Having been linked to Huxley by mic since arriving in the grounds, he had been privy to everything that had happened so knew what to look for in terms of entering the underground world. But seeing the keys inset into the wall before him and the entrance to the staircase uncovered in the pillar, he was astounded by the ingenuity that had gone into the design and marvelled that this had possibly been the work of one of the greatest architects who had ever lived.

He looked into the entrance at his feet, peering as far as he could before the steps spiralled out of view. What lay below he couldn't begin to imagine but he only hoped that he wasn't too late to save his friend.

Once the musclemen had been escorted away, Pepper summoned his team together. Leaving two standing guard with instructions to challenge anyone coming up through the hole in the floor, he led the others down into the depths of the city.

CHAPTER 51

"It's magnificent," cried Sam as she explored the contents of the room, running from papyrus to papyrus like a debutant admiring dresses for the ball, her eye constantly drawn to the next one along.

"Amazing," echoed Connelly who seemed to have forgotten about his injury and was marvelling in the cache they had uncovered.

Huxley, excited by what was truly an astonishing collection, was more circumspect in his examination. He wanted to find the Judas Gospel, the very document which had caused all the alarm of this evening. The choice of manuscripts was overwhelming and Huxley wondered how he was going to identify the prize. He wasn't sure what he had expected but now realised that he had thought the Gospel of a disciple would be prominently displayed in some way, standing out above anything else held. Now he wondered how he would identify it. They all looked the same to him.

"I've found it!"

What Huxley had mistaken as professional excitement, jumping from text to text, had actually been Sam Davison cursorily checking each document to see if it matched the Coptic script of that of the Judas Gospel. She was standing over a very unremarkable manuscript half hidden by those either side which, Huxley now understood, had probably been a deliberate part of its disguise.

"Are you sure?" he questioned as he walked towards her.

"Fairly," she responded with a smile. "I mean, I can't say for certain, but it's the right language and style and there is a reference to the disciples of Jesus on the opening page so I'm going to stick my neck out and say this is it."

"Well, that's good enough for me. How about we take it and get ourselves out of here."

Connelly, who had been watching the exchange distractedly, turned to the pair now and queried, "And just how exactly do we do that?"

"Hmmm, good question, Dean, how indeed?"

Huxley surveyed the room. It was a large cavern that would have made a decent wine cellar in a Bavarian palace with room to spare. The staircase they had descended led to a stone floor which formed the straight edge of a semi-circle, the room unfolding in front of this. Polished wooden shelves ran from one side of the semi-circle to the other following the curve of the wall and rising three high, the highest readily accessible to all but the vertically challenged. Above this, the solid stone wall rose intimidatingly before doming back on itself, encompassing both the room and the platform above which had broken their fall upon entry. This platform acted as a balcony to the room below and the stone which they had fallen through was at least eight feet above this and there didn't appear to be any means to climb back up to it. There were no doors at either end of the balcony and nothing but solid stone floor and walls in the room itself. To all intent and purpose, it appeared the three were trapped.

"I know it's an obvious thing to say but there must be a way out," offered Sam, "otherwise how did the Templar or whoever guards the place get out when they came down here?"

"Unless they didn't come down here," Connelly remarked. "Perhaps they only came down so far to make sure that nothing had been breached but they never actually came down as far as this."

"It's possible, Dean, but someone came here to deposit the documents at some point. There had to be a way out for them. I mean there are no skeletons lying around of dead underlings who were forced down here with the manuscripts in the first place and left to die." Huxley jiggled his eyebrows in comic effect as he said this producing a laugh from his companions.

"Okay, Einstein, point made," retorted Sam, "so tell us how we get out of here."

"I don't suppose either of you brought a ten foot ladder with you?"

"Ha ha. Funny man. I can see why the women love you so. Do you have any ideas?"

"Well, I'm guessing that there is another mechanism which will open a hidden door somewhere which we could spend time looking for."

"I sense an 'or'," said Sam.

"Or I could lift you onto my shoulders and you could climb up through the hole we came in by and go and get help from Pepper and his band of merry men who I assume are, by now, swarming all over this place."

"Ok, that works for me."

"Then let's do it."

The three climbed back up the staircase onto the platform, Huxley holding the Judas Gospel under his arm. Reaching the top, they stood below the stone through which they had entered and Huxley cradled his hands to provide a foothold for Sam to climb onto. Bracing her hands onto his shoulders, Davison put her weight onto her left foot which she placed in Huxley's hands. As she was about to launch herself, there was a tremendous eruption below and the platform that they stood on began to tremble. Then the walls all around exploded.

CHAPTER 52

"There's nothing here. It's all just shit," cried Donovan junior.

"You're sure, son?"

"Dad, I know a real codex when I see one. These are just fragments of manuscripts which could be found in any half decent library. There's nothing here that even comes close to being like the Judas Gospel. It isn't here."

"But it has to be." Paul Donovan looked around the room the two had ended up in.

It was a high ceilinged rectangular shaped space which, like the room they had abandoned the others in, was constructed from stone blocks rather than carved out of the rock like the passageways that had led them to it. Even the ceiling some twelve feet above was set with large stones giving the sense of a reinforced bank vault and enhancing the impression that it was a place to store valuables.

The two side walls were devoid of any ornamentation whilst the wall which they had entered was also bare apart from the unguarded archway to the left hand side of it. Focus was, therefore, directed to the long wall at the back of the room which held a number of alcoves each with documents and artefacts contained within. The lights, seemingly attached to a central junction box that activated all points throughout the whole underground chamber once switched on, also hung from this wall, the metal casing protecting the bright bulbs stark against the backdrop of ancient documents. Everything suggested that this was where the Judas Gospel would be hidden away from the world and Donovan senior felt that there must be something they were missing.

"I'll bet those crafty bastards have put another hidden panel somewhere in here and that's where the Gospel is."

"But where?" asked Alan, the frustration evident in his voice.

The pair looked around them, searching furiously for some indication of a secret hideaway within the room.

"We need Huxley here to find it," Alan bemoaned.

"Fuck him. We don't need his help. I have everything we need right here." Donovan senior patted the bag that hung around his shoulders.

"What is it, Dad?" Alan looked at his father, fingers fidgeting up and down his leg.

"I'm fed up with vibrating walls and hidden fucking triggers. It's time to use the old fashioned method." Senior reached into his bag and produced two long, thin sticks topped with a stretch of wire.

"What the fuck is that? Is that dynamite?" Receiving nothing but a grin in response from his father, Alan continued, "Are you serious? Do you even know what the fuck you're doing with that stuff?"

"Of course I do," countered Donovan senior, "I'm not a fucking idiot, Al. There's enough here to blast through the wall without bringing the whole place down on top of us. If Huxley hadn't gotten us this far, I would have used it sooner. But Professor fucking Perfect always has to have the answer, doesn't he? So it saved me some hassle. But now…" He indicated the wall in front of him. "There's no way the Templar would go to all this trouble to protect such a secret place unless there was something worth having down here. And we both know that the one thing they fear being found more than any other is the Judas Gospel. It has to be here somewhere. And if it's not here," he picked up a pile of manuscripts held in one alcove before dropping them back into place, "then it has to be hidden away behind this wall. And I'm going to find it."

Taking a stick in each hand, he placed first one then the other at opposite ends of the wall holding the manuscripts, before unravelling the electrical wire attached to the top of each. He called for his son to follow him back into the passage, the two taking shelter against the side of the tunnel.

"So how exactly does this work?" croaked Alan, his mouth dry.

"Don't panic, son, I've done this before." Reaching into his bag he pulled out an electrical connector, placing the end of one the wires in the left side before repeating this with the other on the right. "Once I press the clip on here," holding up the connector, "the pulse will cause an electrical charge which will surge through the wires and set off the explosives. The amount of dynamite should bring down that wall and, possibly, cause a bit of structural damage to the room but nothing more than that. We'll then see just exactly what is hidden behind there."

"I just hope to Christ that you know what you're doing, Dad."

"You worry too much, son. I told you before when we had to kill Simms that you can't make an omelette without breaking a few skulls. Now crouch down and cover your ears. This could be noisy!"

He pressed the clip.

CHAPTER 53

Huxley fell backwards as the platform started to shake from the blast causing Sam to overbalance and land on top of him. The pillars holding the platform collapsed and the whole structure began to fall. As it did so, Huxley twisted his body to try and protect Sam from the fall, the manuscript he held falling from under his arm onto the ground below. The section that had been holding them fell straight down before hitting debris from the collapsing pillars, causing it to angle at forty five degrees and become a slide down which the pair skidded unto the chamber floor.

"Are you okay?" checked Huxley, helping Sam up from the stone floor.

"What the fuck just happened?" cried Davison.

Huxley was as shocked by this outburst from Miss Prim and Proper as he was by the explosion itself and he turned his face from her to hide both his surprise and amusement.

There was dust everywhere and he was trying to peer through the grey smog that encircled them to see if he could make sense of what had happened. He could make out a dark space to the side of the room which began to mould into something clearer. It was a large hole in the wall at the side of the chamber which had sent rock flying across the room and documents scattering all around the chamber. Then, looking around the room he asked, "Dean? Dean, are you okay?"

There was a low moan from the top of the staircase which remained intact before Connelly heaved himself up from his prone position and looked down at the devastation below.

"What the fuck just happened?" he voiced, mimicking Davison.

Huxley grinned but was concerned that his friend was masking his pain but Connelly indicated that he was fine and jst needed to time catch his breath.

Content that everyone was as well as they could be given the circumstances, Huxley turned his attention back to the hole as his mind began to piece together how this could have happened. Both the rumble which had preceded it and the explosion itself told him that this was something deliberate rather than natural and he wondered if they had triggered a booby-trap or if there was something else behind it. His answer came in the shape of Paul Donovan.

"Well, well, well, what do we have here?" said Donovan as he stepped through the hole that he had made with the dynamite. Once his ears had stopped ringing from the explosion, he had heard voices coming from the chamber that lay beyond the room that he and Alan were in so had taken out his gun again. He stood now with gun in hand surveying the scene in front of him.

He hadn't known what to expect as he neared the chamber, the voices too indistinct to make out clearly. Perhaps the Templar had more guards posted down here, lying in wait. But what he definitely hadn't expected to find was Huxley and his cohorts in a domed room full of manuscripts.

"You're just the fucking proverbial bad penny, Danny, aren't you? How did you get in here? No, don't bother, I don't need to know how, I just need to make sure that you don't get out."

Alan appeared at his father's side and looked around the room. As perplexed as he was to see the three, he was much more interested in the bounty that now lay before him. The blast had, undoubtedly, caused quite a number of the documents to fly across the room but there were still plenty in place on gleaming shelves. Mesmerised, he walked towards them, reaching out with reverence as he took hold of one and began to read.

"Is it there?" asked his father.

"I don't know yet. There's lots to check."

"How about it, Danny-boy, did you find it?"

"We only just got in when you blew the place apart," lied Huxley, "so I've no idea what's hidden here."

He resisted a backwards glance towards the fallen platform beneath which the dropped manuscript had fallen. His main concern was to get out alive, everything else could wait. But he could maybe use this knowledge to their advantage.

"Why don't we all look for it?" he offered.

"I don't think so, smart guy. You just want to try and get close to Alan, make a grab for him and try and bargain your way out of this."

"There's no fooling you, Paul."

"Actually, I really don't see how you can help me anymore. I think it's time to end this party." Donovan pointed his gun at the centre of Huxley's chest, his hand steady, his smile sadistic.

"But what if there's another puzzle? Don't tell me that you're actually going to do some of the work yourself, Paul? Are you sure you can manage."

"You arrogant bastard, Huxley. You just think that you're fucking god's gift, don't you?" Donovan's face was full of

The Judas Deception

hatred and he started towards Huxley, the gun now held as a club.

"Dad, no! Can't you see that's what he wants? He's trying to goad you."

Donovan senior stopped in his tracks, his son's words bringing him to his senses. He looked at Huxley and shook his head.

"You nearly had me, Danny-boy. Very clever. But I'm afraid your time is up."

He took aim with his gun again and Huxley could do nothing except stare down the barrel. Then he felt the ground begin to shake beneath him. For a moment he wondered if it was just his knees quaking before he realised that something else was happening. There was an oppressive pressure encompassing the room, a pressure which seem to overwhelm him. Donovan obviously felt it too as he looked around in confusion.

"Wha…what's going on?" he stammered.

Huxley used the distraction to dive for cover towards the fallen masonry from the platform, getting behind the stones, Sam following.

"Prepare yourself," said Huxley.

"For what?" queried Sam.

At that moment the front wall of the chamber burst open and water began to rush in. The beautiful polished shelves, which had gleamed like new cars in a showroom, were suddenly splintered and sprayed across the room as the boundary wall of the chamber gave way to the increasing pressure of the river behind. The force of the blast sent Alan spiralling into his father, the pair landing on the floor, enveloped by the onslaught of water as the river found a new tributary.

As they fell Donovan senior lost hold of his gun and it fell into the deluge that now surrounded them. The water covered the surface of the room, sweeping over Huxley and Davison as they sheltered behind the broken stonework, rising to just above their knees, sodden manuscripts floating around them. Huxley chanced a look towards the balcony where Connelly was watching on in disbelief as the water level began to rise. Sam started to panic as she felt the freezing liquid creep higher and higher up her legs but Huxley calmed her with a look as he nodded towards the hole in the wall created by Donovan's explosion. Once it reached the level of the hole, the water began to flow in a new direction, a myriad of passages to explore and permeate.

The Donovans struggled to their feet, father helping son to stand, two obstacles for the flow of water to navigate around. Senior looked at the devastation around him and let out a Neanderthalic bellow. The irony that it was his detonation which had sufficiently weakened the boundary wall was not lost on him. Anger seeped through his being and he stared at the main object of his ire.

"You! This is all down to you!"

"How do you figure that, Einstein? It was your explosion that caused all this." Huxley held his arms out to either side. He felt a lot safer now that Donovan had lost his gun.

"Don't try and get funny with me, smart guy. You couldn't just leave it alone. You had to prove yourself smarter than everyone again and find your way into this place. It should have been me. It was my place to find. I've been searching for it for years. You've been involved for less than twelve hours."

"Doesn't really say much for your skills then, does it, Paul?"

"I'm going to gut you like a friggin' fish," screamed Donovan as he reached into his pocket and produced a six inch knife with a menacing serrated blade.

Huxley looked at the blade and wondered if it was the

same one that had killed Simms, his mind once again focused on his mortality.

"Give it up, Paul. You've lost. There's no way out of this."

"Yeah, for you and me both, old friend." He began to wade towards Huxley, knife raised, the murderous hatred in his eyes clear for all to see.

CHAPTER 54

Pepper was in awe of what he found as he descended the stairs. It was like a cathedral had been carved directly from the rock, the size of the amphitheatre that he found himself in simply breath-taking. But he didn't have time to stand and stare. His thoughts were still focused on finding his friend and making sure that he was alright.

Leading his troops, he made his way towards the opening in the far wall which was the only obvious exit from the room and through which, Pepper imagined, Huxley had passed, followed closely by his crazed assailant.

As he meandered his way along the passage, he kept his gun drawn, conscious that around every bend trouble could be lying in wait. It was as he and his men approached the room with the still burning door that he first felt and then heard an explosion trembling throughout the cavern.

"What was that?" asked one of the troops.

"I don't know but I don't like the sound of it. Come on," commanded Pepper.

Reaching the room, Pepper motioned the men behind him to stop. The whole room appeared to be on fire, a feat which puzzled Pepper given that it was made up almost entirely of stone. A quick survey allowed him to see the burning door on one side and the table and chairs which were also ablaze on the

The Judas Deception

other filling the room with viscous, orange flames. He ducked back around the corner to shelter from the heat, giving a brief summary to his men.

"What are we going to do, Sarge?"

"Fucked if I know, laddie. We can't go any further without putting the fire out but that could take forever."

Just then there was another blast and bits of rock from the roof of the passage fell onto the men standing there.

"Fuck, the whole thing's going to collapse, Sarge, we have to get out of here."

"Nobody goes anywhere," shouted Pepper, although he too was worried that the structure was going to give way. But his friend needed help of that he was sure.

"Well we can't just stand here, Sarge, we either have to go on or go back."

Pepper knew that his men were right. Reluctantly he decided that they had to go and find something to put the fire out with, thinking that there must be extinguishers back in the library. Just as he was about to give the command, there was a crash behind him and water rushed into the passage they were in, covering their feet as it flowed past. Pepper looked around the corner at the room and saw the door had been forced off its hinges and was now propped against the far wall, held in place by the flow of water that was now dowsing the flames that had raged just moments before. Seizing his chance, Pepper rushed towards the open doorway, his men splashing behind him.

CHAPTER 55

Huxley watched the blade of the knife inch ever closer to him, the water restricting Donovan's movements to slow motion, thereby increasing the torture. That same water made it impossible for Huxley to make a dash for the opening and possible escape. But, even if he could have done so, he knew that he couldn't leave Sam and the Dean behind with this madman. The water also meant that he couldn't use his legs to kick out and defend himself, it all had to be upper body and, with a knife, Huxley knew, that speed and fluidity of movement were key. He watched Donovan's advance, junior standing with an agitated smile on his face behind but not making any move to involve himself in this dog fight.

Donovan was coming straight at Huxley, his body turned at ninety degrees, leading with the arm holding the knife. Huxley checked his progress, watching the line. As he did so, his brain was calculating all sorts of permutations and the beginnings of a plan began to form in his mind.

He reached behind him and took hold of Sam's hand, squeezing it as he gripped and hoping she would understand that he wanted her to follow his lead. She squeezed back sensing that Huxley was about to try something. Anything was better than just waiting for this lunatic to advance on them with a knife. Huxley stayed still, waiting for the most opportune

The Judas Deception

time before making his move. As Donovan got to within six feet of him, Huxley lunged to his right, Davison following in his wake as she realised that Huxley was making for the steps leading to the platform above, or, at least, what remained of it.

Half swimming, half wading, Huxley got to the side of the steps before Donovan had time to react, the move taking him by surprise as he thought he had his prey trapped. Using the steps as a support, Huxley propelled himself onto them above the waterline, thus freeing his legs. He turned and reached down to help Sam up onto the steps too but, as he did so, Donovan lunged towards her, grabbing hold of her left arm and hauling her backwards. She reached up in desperation, her right arm extended towards Huxley but Donovan continued to drag her towards him until she lost her footing and sunk into the water. Donovan tightened his grip on her arm and dragged her upright, the knife edge placed against her throat before Huxley had the chance to react.

He was just about to leap towards the pair when Donovan said "Stay where you are or I swear to god I will slice her open, Huxley."

"Now, take it easy, Paul. You know that it's me you want. Why don't you let Sam go and I'll come to you. There's no reason why anyone else has to get hurt."

"You don't get it, do you, smart guy? I'm going to kill you all and then blame it on the Templar. That way I can still be the hero who rushed to your rescue but was too late. Still, on the bright side, look at all these documents that I discovered."

"You truly are deluded. Who's going to believe any of that?"

"Look around you, Danny-boy. There's no-one else here. No-one knows what happened. I can tell them anything I like."

"You really think you can get away with everything you

have done, don't you? Well, I don't know if you've noticed but all your precious manuscripts are dissolving before your eyes including the Judas Gospel. It's all been for nothing, Paul."

"We'll see about that." Donovan transferred his grip from Sam's arm to her hair, pulling it hard to force her head back and expose her neck.

Seeing what he was about to do, Huxley made to leap towards them but, before he could jump, a figure fell from the broken platform above landing on top of the pair. Donovan fell backwards in surprise, releasing his grip on Sam and landing on his backside in the water.

"What the fuck…?" He looked up at the balcony above and then at the fallen figure trying to make sense of what had just happened.

Huxley dived across to where the figure of Dr Connolly lay face down in the water, the shock of the impact knocking the breath from him and leaving him limp and prostrate. He turned him over and began to drag him back towards the steps, reaching for a still shocked Sam Davison as he did so.

"Not so fast. I've had just about enough of all three of you. Now it's time for all of you to die."

"I don't think so," said a voice with a thick Scottish accent from behind him.

Donovan turned to see three armed men in police uniform standing in the hole that he had blown in the wall, their guns pointed towards him. His son stood with his mouth open, shoulders slumped, staring at the policemen.

"Jesus fucking Christ, what the fuck is going on around here! I just don't get it," screamed Donovan senior.

"That's always been your problem, Paul," responded Huxley, "forever two steps behind everyone else." Then, to Pepper, "Nice of you to join the party."

Pepper smiled, pleased to see his old friend in good spirits.

The Judas Deception

"Sorry but the plagues of fire and water kind of held us up, you know. Are you sure there's no god?"

Huxley gave a sheepish grin to the policeman. Then, "Word to the wise, George, don't be afraid to put a bullet in this one." Huxley pointed towards Donovan.

"What, be careful, he bites, you mean?"

"Look at you with your Dickens quotes."

"Aye, it must be your influence on me, eh?"

He winked before issuing commands to the Donovans to drop their weapons and get down on their knees. The pair obliged, senior still trying to figure out where it had all gone so wrong and wondering how he could talk his way out of it. With guns trained on both, Pepper moved behind the pair and cuffed them before ordering his men to take them back up to the library. Then he turned his attention back to Huxley and his cohorts.

"Seriously, Dan, are you all okay? I heard gunshots."

Huxley had made it back to the steps and eased Connelly's body down onto them. He was checking for any sign of life.

"The Dean took one to the shoulder but he also jumped from the balcony to save our lives."

"Is he...dead?" Sam stumbled over the word, half from the shock and cold that she was experiencing and half from fear of it being true.

Connelly's head began to move and his eyes fluttered open. He coughed before opening his eyes wider, trying to focus and reaching out with his good arm. Huxley took hold of his hand and squeezed. Connelly looked up at him.

"Did I get him?" he asked.

Huxley started laughing. "You were brilliant, Dean."

Pepper went to Sam and put a protective arm around her. "It's okay, everything's going to be just fine. Let's get you out of here, alright?"

She nodded and smiled her thanks to him before reaching over to Connelly and kissing his cheek.

"Thank you, Dean. Thank you."

CHAPTER 56

Huxley let his head fall forward in exhaustion. The pale glow of the morning sun was enhanced by the flashing blue lights of response vehicles as the entrance to Trinity College played host to members of all three emergency services. Wrapped in a blanket in a bid to combat the cold that threatened to permeate his bones, he hoped it wouldn't be long before he could go home and change out of his wet clothes.

He looked across the quad to where Sam Davison was being helped into an ambulance, the shock of her near death experience at the hands of the Donovans hitting her as soon as Pepper put his arm around her. She had begun shaking violently as he led her through the underground maze and back to the sanctuary of the library which served as both makeshift hospital and jail until Pepper managed to summon back-up.

Huxley had sat with her for a while, holding her hand and reassuring her that everything was alright now but he knew that it was a chemical reaction that had taken hold of her and that nothing he said was going to really make much difference. Still, he was happy to hold her, this beautiful, intelligent, brave and daring woman who he had shared such an experience with. She had amazed and delighted him in equal measure throughout the evening and he hoped he would be seeing a lot more of Dr Sam Davison in the future.

When a paramedic had come to take her to a newly arrived ambulance, Huxley had walked out with her just in time to see the first ambulance departing with the Dean on his way to Addenbrookes Hospital to undergo surgery for his shattered shoulder.

He made his way across to the wall at the perimeter of the College and sat down, the adrenaline that had been coursing through his body for most of the night now beginning to fade and leaving him feeling spent. Pepper was supervising the transport arrangements for the prisoners, anxious to ensure that nothing was going to go wrong at this late stage. He looked across to his fatigued friend and smiled, a look of triumph and relief on his face. Even the arrival of one DI Blackburn into the midst couldn't dampen his spirits, the Inspector in tow with the Assistant Chief Constable. But by then Pepper had decided that he'd had enough and so left others to fill in the blanks, instead ambling over to where Huxley sat.

"Fuck me, Dan, you don't half get yourself in some scrapes."

"Maybe it's the knowledge that I have Cambridge's finest to bail me out if I ever bite off more than I can chew."

"Aye, well I think you almost choked on what you bit off tonight. Christ, you had me worried."

"You were worried! I was the one being shot at, set alight and generally threatened all bloody night!"

"And you still walk away without a scratch on you. Honestly, I don't know how you do it."

"A heady mixture of luck, good fortune and blind ignorance."

"Aye, you could be right, my friend. And the laddie was in on it all along?"

"Right up to his neck and then some."

"When did you know?"

"I suspected something was up right back when the car taking us to the station was hit. It was the way he reacted, like the most obvious thing was to run away from the police rather than seek your protection. I knew then that he had deliberately involved me, I just didn't know why."

"You mean the whole thing was staged?"

"In all its glory. And that got me wondering what had happened to Simms in the bookshop."

"You thought the laddie had done it?"

"No, I was certain that there was no way he could fake the reaction he had when he saw the body. His pallor was ashen when I arrived. That was genuine. But I guessed that he knew more than he was saying."

"Aye, I didn't like him for the murder myself. It just didn't ring true. Although no doubt old big nose over there will make sure that everyone knows that he wanted to arrest the boy."

"That's a fun conversation for another time and place. The last thing I need at the moment is Detective Inspector bloody Blackburn telling me how he was right all along, even if it was mistakenly."

"Well, prepare yourself, cos he's not going to let this one go for a while. He was livid when he learned about your 'escape' as he called it," Pepper mimicked his boss making the quote sign, "threatening all sorts against you. If it wasn't for the fact that the ACC is here he would be all over you like a rash right now. But there's brown-nosing to be done so you might be alright for a while.

"Thank Christ for that."

"So, is that when you guessed that the dad was involved? You know, when you went running off with a fugitive."

Huxley saw the smirk on Pepper's face as he delivered his line.

"Fuck off, George."

"Ah, come on now, Dan, you're not going to deprive me of the odd dig here and there, are you?" He smiled before repeating his question.

"Not quite. I thought Alan might know who had killed Simms but was too afraid to say. Maybe hoping that if he kept quiet for long enough it might all go away. In fact, I thought that was the case for quite a while and that his reluctance to end up in police custody was his vain attempt to bury his head in the sand and hope that it would all go away."

"The shit storm resulting from that murder, there was no way that was ever going to happen."

"I just hoped that if I could get him to calm down he might see sense and I'd be able to convince him to turn himself in and tell you everything he knew. That's why I took him to Grantchester. The thought of a bit of respite and some sleep would help. In the morning he'd see things differently."

"And then the house was attacked and that's when you realised there was more to his story."

"You catch on quick, old man."

"Hey, less of the old. Just cos I can give you ten years. Anyway, you told me what you suspected when we spoke earlier. As you say, the whole thing felt contrived."

"Without a doubt. There's no way anyone could have guessed where we were. They either had to be tracking us or they were told. I have no doubt that there are agencies in this world that can track mobile signals and all sorts of shit, George. Christ, for all I know, you lot even do it. But, if that was the case, then wouldn't they arrive mob-handed? Not a solitary gunman who misses a sitting target from six feet. It all just felt a bit, I don't know…"

"Theatrical?"

"As good a term as any. Yeah, like I was part of a production but someone had forgotten to give me a script. Of course, I

The Judas Deception

didn't really have much time to think about any of that as Alan came bursting out of the kitchen and practically bundled us out the front door. But I thought it very strange that someone as panicked as he was, ran back into the house ahead of me when I went to retrieve the documents that we'd uncovered."

"But once you had time to think it all through you knew that some things weren't adding up."

"The picture was starting to become a lot clearer, let's put it that way. On the drive back to Cambridge I could tell that his furtive looks behind us held no conviction like he knew that there would be no-one following us. Just like he knew that there wouldn't be an accomplice waiting for us out the front when we fled. Once you start looking at things from a slightly different perspective then it becomes a lot more distinct."

"And the thing in America that you had me look into?"

"Yep, once I realised that there were more bodies lying in the wake of this whole bloody mess and that the trail led back to America, I knew that Alan was involved in the thing more than just as incidental bystander."

"The dad."

"Had to be, didn't it?"

"It makes more sense now than it did when you rang me earlier. To be honest, if it had been anyone else I would have been thinking that they were crazy."

"And yet you gave me the benefit of the doubt, how nice." Huxley gave the policeman a playful punch on the arm.

"Fuck that, Dan, you live on your own planet most of the time. Everything you say sounds crazy to me so I just figured that I'd better play along to humour you. I mean you were jabbering on about secret societies and conspiracies and multiple murders by a crazed man and his possessed son…"

"I think you'll find that I said obsessed son."

"Whatever, to*mate*o, to*mat*o. And corrupt officials, including your own Master I might add."

"Did you find them?"

"As you said, all at the Grantchester house. How did you know?"

"To be honest, it was a lucky guess. I knew that Donovan would want them out of his way when it came to the end game."

"They just looked so shocked when we arrived to take them into custody. I almost felt sorry for them."

"I wouldn't waste your sympathy over them, George. After all, they are the ones responsible for trying to kill us in the fire at the Sedgewick site as well as abducting us at gunpoint in Queens' Ball. God knows what they would have done with us had they succeeded in getting us away from the crowd."

"You really think it was them?"

"Without a doubt. Them and whatever local support they had immediately handy from the Templars. And let me tell you, there will be more of them on the way. The Vatican aren't just going to sit back and watch their kingdom crumble around them. Expect reinforcements and a whole lot of trouble.

"Above my pay grade, Dan. I just have to deal with the eccentrics like you and your lunatic ramblings. And I haven't even got to the underground chambers and hidden ancient manuscripts. I mean, even your dear old mum would have been hard pressed to believe a bloody word you were saying, the way you were jabbering on."

"Firstly, I think you will find that I was giving very clear and concise instructions and information, I was not jabbering."

"You should have been at my end of the phone."

"And secondly, I was right about it all, wasn't I?"

"Aye, well I'll give you that. And by the way, your instructions sounded a lot more like orders to me."

The Judas Deception

"Well, I am in charge of all investigations within a four and a half mile radius of Great St Marys."

"Oh Christ, here we go again. You know what, Blackburn's right, you are off your rocker."

"Seriously, though, George, thanks for coming through for me."

Pepper looked at his old friend, the toll of the past twelve hours evident on his face. "You know that I'll always be there for you, Dan."

"I know. And I appreciate it."

"You bloody better cos I am going to be in a heap load of shit on this one."

"Don't worry, I'll make sure that everyone knows that you were acting on my ord...I mean instructions." He winked at Pepper. "So, what did you find out?"

"Well, you were right...look who I'm telling, of course you were bloody right. Donovan senior did arrive in the country a few days ago. Tuesday to be exact."

"And when was the car with the body left in the boot parked at the airport?"

"Surprise, surprise, Tuesday."

"Well there's a coincidence."

"Indeed."

"How was it found?"

"Sheer bloody luck by the sound of things. Some honest citizen owned up to hitting the wing mirror when he was parking up. Left his insurance details and asked the airport authorities to pass them on to the owner. They contacted the police who ran a check only to find that it was registered to...?" He shrugged a question.

"National Geographic by any chance?"

"Bingo. A few phone calls later and they've established that it was used by one of the directors. When no-one could contact him, the police went to have a look at the vehicle themselves. One of the officers tried to call him while they were beside the car, heard his phone ringing from inside and decided to investigate. Opened the boot and hey presto."

"One dead director and a whole can of worms."

"You got it."

"Christ on a bike."

"And all for a piece of parchment that may or may not prove that the aforementioned messiah was having it away with his disciples."

"Beautifully paraphrased, George. Be sure to use that line when you're talking to the press later."

"But honestly, is that what it was all about?"

"In a nutshell, yes."

"And?"

"And what?"

"Did you find it?"

"Didn't you hear?"

Pepper realised that in the midst of everything he hadn't had the chance to tell his friend that communication had been lost. He recounted what he'd heard.

"To be honest, I was amazed they worked at all given how far underground you were."

"It shouldn't matter. It's not like a mobile where you need to have access to the network signal for it to work. These are linked to each other," he removed the transmitter from his pocket and pointed to the earpiece that Pepper was still wearing, "so, as long as they are in range of each other, then they should be fine."

"Yeah, well, they didn't. I heard a gunshot and it went dead which is pretty much what I thought you were too!"

"Well it bloody well took you long enough to come and check!"

"You told me not to spook Donovan when he arrived, to stay well back and let him think that there was no-one watching him. 'Don't follow him, George.' 'Sit tight and wait, George.' 'Let him come down and shoot us, George.'" These latter were delivered in a mock Irish accent.

"Ha ha, very funny. I only told you to let him come down and find us as I knew that was the best time to get him to confess. He would want to show off how clever he had been."

"Aye, and it nearly cost you your life. And that of that bonnie lassie. Not to mention what happened to the Dean."

"I know. That was a mistake. That was me trying to show off a bit too much. I should have let you come down and arrest him as soon as he entered. I feel awful about both Sam and the Dean."

"Come on now, Dan, it's all thanks to you that they're both still alive."

"Yeah, but I should never have involved them in the way that I did."

"It was their own choice as far as I can make out. No-one forced them to come along with you. I mean, as far as I can make out, the Dean was only there to show you where the keys were hidden. Just where does he fit into all this?"

Huxley realised that Pepper and his team hadn't made it into position until after the Dean had recounted his adventure and so had missed it all as he was out of range of the transmitter. He spent the next ten minutes summarising Connelly's story about Spencer and the Judas Gospel before filling his friend in on the events that he had missed in the underground chamber. For a man brought up on the streets of Glasgow and no stranger to the weird and wonderful things that people sometimes do, Sergeant George Pepper sat with mouth agape as he listened.

"Fuck me, that's some story, Dan. There's a book in there somewhere. The media will eat it up."

"Yeah, well they can hear it from someone else. Right now I just want to go home, go to bed and forget about everything that's happened since dinner last night."

"So, what happened to the manuscript then?"

"Probably lying in ruins with all the rest of the documents down there. Once the river burst its banks and came rushing in then they all got swept up. I doubt there'll be much to salvage once everything has been cleared."

"But you got a look at it though, didn't you?"

"What do you mean?"

"I know you, Dan. You said that you found it and took a hold of it. There's no way that you didn't have a wee peek. And with that memory of yours, you'll remember every word."

"George, I don't know how you think an eidetic memory works but I can't just glance at something and have an image stored in my head. I have to read it or hear it to remember something. Even if I did have a glance, it's not as though I had a chance to read the bloody thing. Not with a maniac trying to shoot me or stab me or generally kill me."

"Aye, well, I just thought that maybe…"

"Maybe what?"

"You know, that you had read something that would give us the answer."

"I didn't think you'd be that interested?"

"In knowing if the supposed son of god was really just some chancer who liked to hang around with his bunch of merry men and get it on with them when the sun went down? Who wouldn't want to know that?"

"Sorry to disappoint you."

"It was just a thought."

Huxley looked into his friend's face, a smirk creeping onto his lips.

"Anyway, it was all in Coptic script and you know what I'm like with funny languages." He winked at Pepper as he rose from the wall and started to head back towards the College entrance.

"I bloody knew it," said Pepper almost to himself, then louder, "I bloody knew it, Huxley. You know, don't you? You bloody well know. Come on then, tell me."

Huxley kept on walking.

THE END

ACKNOWLEDGEMENTS

This novel started as an idea in my head some years ago when I was first introduced to the Cambridge Constables by Carl Hodson. The thought of academics and college porters having full police powers got me thinking about how that could be used in a story. Carl may have introduced me to the organisation and the concept but he is in no way responsible for any inaccuracies within my portrayal of them.

A huge thank you to my friends and family who have helped, supported, encouraged and guided me over the years that it took to complete this project. And special mention to Shreeya Nanda and Darren Coxon for their willingness to act as proof-readers and editors extraordinaire and for their comments which helped develop and shape the final product.

Saving the best for last, my eternal gratitude and humble thanks to my wife, Katharine, for her constant encouragement and help throughout and for the dedication which she showed in reading draft after draft of the story. It is because of her love and support that I was able to complete this book.